The Last Wolves Of Mars

The Last Wolves of Mars

Clark Carr

Illustrations by Richard Royce

Published in the United Kingdom in 2010 by
Bank House Books, PO Box 3, New Romney, Kent, TN29 9WJ

www.bankhousebooks.com

Acknowledgement
The Illustrator wishes to acknowledge and thank the photographers at the website www.firstpeople.us for the wonderful photos of wolves that inspired the illustrations.

British Library Cataloguing in Publication Data
A catalogue record for this book is available from the British Library

ISBN 978-1-9044087-1-0

Typesetting and origination by Chandler Book Design
Printed by Lightning Source

Contents

Prologue
THE OPERA

How did I allow myself to get dragged into this? He knew the answer, as everyone else at the entrance to the Great Cave knew, and he knew they knew. It made him nauseous. He couldn't believe he had agreed to come.

Oh, he knew *why* he had agreed. His son had asked him. He was just ashamed of himself for having given in so easily.

How had he ever let his son talk him into coming? Robes were habitual formal wear to song festivals or other entertainments, but he hated them. That's why he never attended this kind of event. Old and decrepit as he was, it had taken him an hour at his eyrie den to get over his disgust at the reflected image of himself, an old wolf in robes, and just come down to the event. He resolved to get through the night without biting someone . . . or someone's wife.

"Ambassador," intoned an Elder's wife as the old dog and her consort trotted by.

Ambassador, indeed. He hadn't asked to be made extraplanetary representative. Under the circumstances the concept was absurd. Anyone could have the post who wanted it. But not before he had given it his best, ice damn it. An impossible task, he grumbled. He stood outside the entrance to the Great Cave Hall and fidgeted with his clothing. He looked up through the ocher sky towards the moon. How is she? he thought. Has she succeeded? He should be at the General's quarters, waiting to hear back from her. But the General had said, "No, go. Nothing will happen before morning. Go."

"Dad, if you come, come dressed, or don't come at all," his son, Apollo, had warned.

"But . . . what am I to do . . . strut and preen? I mean . . . honestly!" he had sputtered, hoping to talk the young wolf artist out of this nonsense.

"Strut all you want. Preen or don't preen. But art is not just on the stage, Dad. It's before you even arrive. It's how you dress. It's how people will look at one another. I *want* you all to be uncomfortable! Look at our situation. The status quo is gone forever. Let's dump it over the cliff with ceremony!" Apollo had laughed.

"Why an *opera* anyway!?" Loos had barked to his son. "Couldn't a storytelling have done as well?"

"I'm just calling it an opera. Everyone will expect one thing and . . . get something else."

"Like what? What are you luring me into?"

"Not telling. That would be no fun. Come . . . or don't come, Ambassador Father," Apollo had snapped, and loped away.

How could I refuse that dare? Loos thought.

"Good evening, Justice," he said as old One Ear walked up to him. "Do you feel as—"

"As stupid as you look? Yes, I do, but Wife threatened divorce if I didn't comply. 'The social event of Third Spring!' she said, 'We won't miss it.'"

"Dear heart, I'll pretend I didn't hear you say that," said One Ear's wife, appearing miraculously out of the milling pack, as wives do when expected to be out of earshot. "We'll discuss it later, dear."

"I wouldn't have thought you would come," said Loos to One Ear.

"I could have said the same about you. We'll hear from those above as soon as anything happens. Anyway, enough of war and misery. Let's have one night of art and song."

"You look enchanting, Ambassador," One Ear's wife murmured with a distressing lack of candor, and then with her teeth pulled One Ear back into the circling social pack.

Loos tried to think of something acceptable to reply, but was stymied. There are advantages and disadvantages to wives, he thought. His own wife would have cut Apollo's head off, he was certain, and wired him for "adjustment" if Apollo had suggested *she* wear robes to a Spring Ball. That's why we're divorced, he thought. Worse than divorced. She is beyond robes forever. Crash and burn, she won't even wear a *body*, much less a costume! He made a last failed effort to adjust his wrap, shoulder pads and all, into some kind of less miserable discomfort, and then turned to trot out to the edge of the public landing circles to have a last smoke before he had to sit through the evening's performance.

The afternoon light was fading from the immense canyon walls opposite where he stood, their shadows darkening through gradations of grey, ochre, olive, umber. Other folk were flying down to the Cave and landing around him. Others sailed the internal canyon airs, in and out of the knife edge of shadow cut through the dust by the upper far canyon wall. Catching the still warm upcurrents and cooling downcurrents was a favorite pastime. He never tired of it. Who could? Inhaling the nasty, bitter draft of his pipe, to the frowns of those landing nearby, he had to restrain himself from stepping off the cliff edge for a quick piptail dive and swoop as he used to do as a pup before going in to school. The child never dies, he thought. This made him feel better. He turned round to walk back.

And his breath was taken from him.

Apollo was right! Garlanded couples were sailing down, landing, and walking towards the great arch of the Opera doors. The late sunlight smote with red heat the carved stone of the cliff above the Cave. With that and the shadows of the descending couples, the grand whole was a play of light and motion. Like dust motes whirling in a sunbeam. *Your show had better be something to match this,* he telepathed to his son, as he put out his pipe and stuck it in a hidden pocket.

Oh, it will be. It will, pathed his son back, *and I love you, too.*

The Ambassador sauntered into the Grand Den of the Opera, assuming as much dignity, or at least invisibility, as he could manage.

* * *

The performance took long enough to begin. Of course, Apollo had patiently explained to his father's non-comprehending ears that the "performance" was the "wholeness," not just what happened on the stage, but the before and after and sometimes what happened despite the stage or in contrast to it. The performance will be between their ears, Apollo had said.

That didn't sound good, Loos thought. Yes, he could remember having felt the urgent importance of such artistic distinctions with his own creative efforts as a young Storyteller, only a hundred years back. We all swore we would suicide before we hit eighty, he remembered. Apollo was barely older than a pup and still spoke and thought like a whelp, despite everything that had happened to him. To all of us, he thought.

For the first time in a long while, Loos had that wonderful *outside* feeling. It was normally much older, at two hundred years or so, that one started spending more time outside than in one's body. The consequences of knock knock, hard-body society, the stresses imposed by the *physical* world, the apparency of tick-tock time, altered vastly in proportion once one had something to compare them to – *the Outside.* To outside the body. To *after* the body. Freedom is pleasant, he thought as he perceived the broader space, pleasant even if for a moment only.

Inside the Opera Cave the costumed audience took on a dreamlike, nightmarish aspect. Loos was amused. Although the exact point still eluded him, there was certainly a "ceremony" going on even before the evening's performance started. The males who out on the landing had been exchanging estimates of cost of costume during a war economy were now anything but comfortable, staring at the stage curtain, hoping the piece would begin. The wives were still admiring one another. Loos scratched until One Ear, sitting next him, nipped and muttered, "Stop it, you old fool."

Finally, the tall curtain parted. The great stage was bare except for three unique stringed instruments. Apollo had invented a variation on the harp, it seemed. A trio of elegant, great semicircular metal forms were positioned like horizontal bows supported well off the floor. Or they may have been metallic *arms*. That made him shiver, and he noticed others shuddering at the same thought. Strings passed from a performer's chair up over the metal frames, hanging various distances down the other side. Figured weights of precious metal hung at the end of each string like jewelry.

Three performers padded out in synchrony. Their torsos were shaved naked. The audience gave a gasp. Wolves *never* shaved their skin. Loos looked more closely. Something was tattooed on them. Machinery? He didn't want to go there. Only a century ago this would have been considered obscene, but since the Promethean exodus tattoos were the least of anyone's problems. Is Apollo trying to suggest some kind of choice, Loos wondered? If we don't jump off the planet, maybe we can just jump out of our skins? In order to manifest what? Maybe just to act up in some outlandish way.

The performers strode around the stage and then jumped up to sit solemnly at their horizontal harps. They began to pluck at the instruments with front claws extended. It was lovely in its simplicity. Through a clever telepathic trick the weights at the bottoms of the strings came to life. They became creatures sitting in swings at the end of each string, imaginary *two-legged* pixies kicking their legs. Where had Apollo come up with two legs? What did it mean? Loos thought. As the harpists continued to play, the strings began to swing up and back to varying heights. The song of the harp trio thus took on a sliding rise and fall in tone as the strings were variously stretched by the animated swinging weights, each note rising and then falling in an oxymoronic chaotic harmony. Electronic pickup and orchestration of harmonics swelled in volume to fill the hall. The mythical swinging miniature figures now stood on their swings and really put themselves into it. Up and down. Discordance melded into concordance into discordance, a drunken choir.

The musicians lifted their muzzles and began to howl softly along with the harps, their three voices nearly but never quite synchronizing in classic wolf style.

The audience could not resist. They began one by one to raise their snouts to ululate in choral unison.

The light shining down on the performers began to flicker, and their skin stories seemed to animate, bodies becoming screens for a pantomimed tale. With the wildly swinging harp strings, ever more strongly amplified, and the lurid colors on the skin, it was hard for Loos to see the details of the tattooed stories. They seemed to have something to do with removing your head and pouring out your brains, then putting on wings, and . . . Loos couldn't follow. A bird-like spirit flying from body to body. Legs and heads falling off. Bodies becoming machines.

Suddenly the performers stopped plucking their harps and ceased howl-singing. The music, however, continued as the harps' hundreds of strings dipped and swung, slowing as the animated figures returned to being just metallic weight, and entropy took over. The volume decreased, the droning melodies reduced to echoes, then . . . silence. The stage lighting faded, replaced by one brilliant spot in front of the harps' semicircle.

After a suitably uncomfortable pause the audience heard a flapping from up and behind them. Out of the darkness above soared a great fish hawk down towards the stage and into the circle of light. It landed behind in the stage shadows and, walked, perfectly erect, back to down stage center. Oh no, thought Loos. He recognized this bird. It spread its beautiful wings, revealing brilliantly colored under-feathering. The creature surveyed the room with a penetrating bird-eye, presenting first one side of its face and then the other. It spoke.

"I am Chronos. Am I not sentient?"

The audience, already hushed, went dead still.

That's one dead bird, thought Loos. And it's the cliff for my son, too.

"Shall I demonstrate my qualities of selfhood? Of wolfdom?" the bird asked, in elegant, high-clan voice tones.

The audience began to shift uncomfortably on their floor

cushions. One or two darted hostile looks at the Ambassador, who all knew to be Apollo's father.

Chronos began to sing. Without accompaniment – just his own voice. A sad but lovely aria of vowels. And the vowels became words. And the words became some kind of poetry. ". . . What is a wolf but another kind of dog? What is a dog but not a cat? Dogs, cats, birds, bodies. Am I this body? What am I but a vessel for spirit? The artist is not . . . his artifact . . ." and so on into other abstract Apollo noodlings, which left behind Loos and the rest of the audience.

They had little attention for what was being said anyway, when confronted with the fact of an *animal* – talking and singing. Not an animal with a voice telepathed from another. This was an animal, singing intelligibly on its own.

Many in the audience pathed now to the Ambassador, *Your son has created a non-wolf intellect! Apollo has broken the Law of Wolves!* And worse comments. Males and females were getting up and pulling off their finery, clearly feeling they had been made fools of. Mutterings of *Sacrilege . . . and at this time.*

The boy's in for big trouble, thought Loos, turning to look behind him at Justice One Ear, knowing he would soon need to face the Justice in Council. One Ear smiled wickedly back. Surely charges would be brought for Apollo's sorcery. That's what other wolves would call this conjuring of intelligence in an animal body. No one had dared for millennia to use the term "artificial" in relationship to intelligence. He wished Apollo had clued him in to what he had been planning. Chronos was *their* secret and should have stayed so.

The audience continued to get up and leave, grumbling disparaging remarks, snapping teeth. Chronos left off singing to openly harangue the audience. If a bird could shout, that was what he began to do. "What makes you so smart? Do you know who I *really* am?" and other similarly adroit wisecracks. On its clawed feet it flapped about the polished stone floor. Apollo trotted out from backstage and glared at Chronos. Apparently this had not been part of the script.

Loos had failed to notice that an aide of General Scar Shank had entered the Opera Cave and was signaling to him from the end of the aisle. The aide gave up and barked, "Ambassador!" Loos looked to the side. The aide body signed that he needed to speak. *Now?* Loos signed back. *Here?*

Yes, the aide signaled, grey lipped and serious, pointing outside with his muzzle and then padding out. Loos followed him, ignoring pathed queries from friends and non-friends. *Couldn't you cage in your son? . . . Wild, irresponsible . . . Illegal flights of fancy . . . At this time?* He closed his mind and pushed through.

"What is it?" he asked the aide outside, irritated but also afraid to hear what was urgent enough to interrupt the evening's ribald and bizarre entertainment.

The aide said, "Prometheus has attacked."

He looked blankly back. The message was incomplete.

"Sir, there was a nuclear explosion. Some kind of strike at our Space Capsule."

"Some kind of strike? Prometheus has used nuclear weapons? *Nuclear?*"

"Yes, sir." The aide looked down.

"What else?" asked Loos. "Did anyone survive? Has . . ."

"I am terribly sorry, Ambassador. We believe the occupants of the Nose Cone have been killed. And the moon itself seems to have broken up."

"The *moon*? Broken up? What are you *talking* about?"

"We don't know for sure what's happened, sir."

Loos curled his tail under. His neck dropped. He looked round. Evidently news of this catastrophic turn had reached other government figures. He saw One Ear with several Elders. One Ear signed to him. *We'll talk elsewhere.*

"Ambassador, we must leave," urged the aide, pointing to a government speed flyer on the Opera's landing pad, waiting.

"No, I don't need a tandem. I'll fly to Scar Shank's office personally."

"What happened at the Opera, sir?" asked the aide. "The audience seemed to have been stirred up already."

"Oh, Apollo just chose the worst conceivable moment to make a public demonstration in favor of non-wolf intelligence.

Something about spirits and bodies. I don't know."

"You're joking."

"Do you know Apollo?"

"Yes, sir. He and I are friends. Well, as much friends as anyone can be to Apollo these days." Loos snapped a look at him. "Excuse me, sir, but you know him. I guess you're not joking."

Loos handed his opera cape to the aide, who helped him into his flight pack. Before tilting off the cliff edge into flight, Loos looked up at the sky, purpling now into night. He was at the still hub of a circling chaos, Apollo and Chronos here, the Prometheans somewhere out on a destroyed moon, his daughter possibly dead. War, art, death – revolving round him. The vertigo was merited. I predicted this, he thought.

Apollo, he telepathed privately as family could to family. *Thank you for your strange entertainment, but . . . I have to go. Have you heard?*

Yes. Damn, ice damn, Prometheus has stolen my thunder again.

Yes. But have you heard about Athena?

No. What? Has something happened to sis?

I don't know. Possibly.

As Loos dropped off the cliff and soared into a long curve, he heard Apollo's howl telepath into space, reaching out to his sister. *Are you alive?*

Not for the first time Loos asked himself how they had come to this pass.

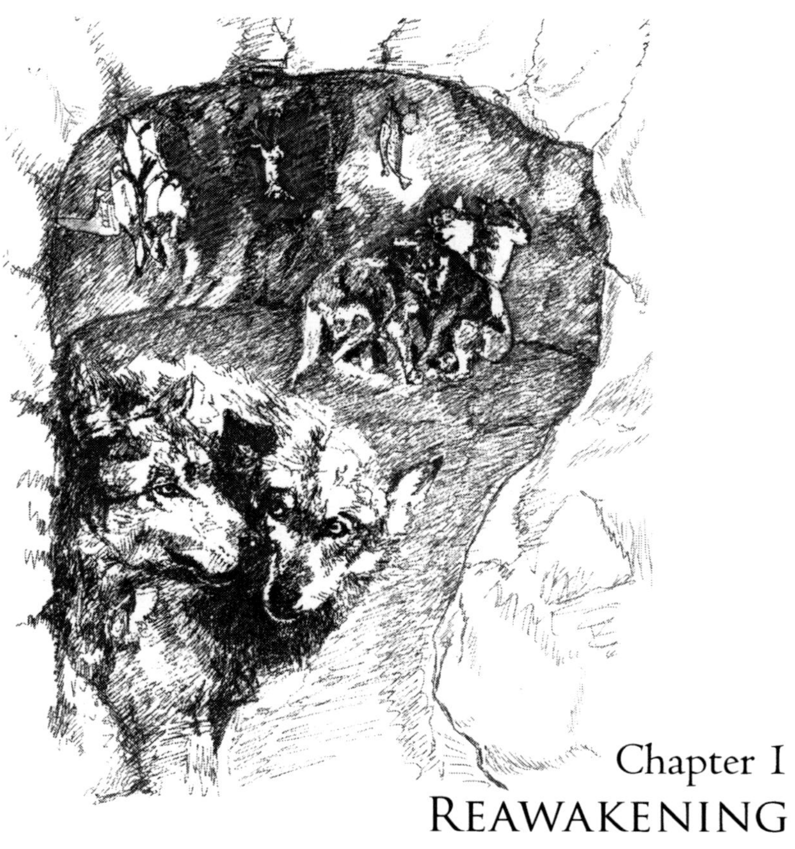

Chapter I
Reawakening

Again they came out of hibernation. Again, as in countless earlier times that the race had awakened, this was as if for the first time. Crawling up out of the dark and through evolution, not just with the body, but through the construct and time sense of the mind. Just so, each creature emerging from the deep winter cave into the warmth of Second Spring would spend his first day, perhaps much longer, reinventing what and who he was.

It was easiest for the newborn, as life was truly new for that body. First came the joy of recognition in being, then the suffering and grueling regeneration of mindfulness. The reborn would have centuries to play again the scenes of the already written play before they contributed new scenes, maybe new acts.

For others, waking was agony. It did not feel new at all, but old, terribly old. First there was the factor of starvation. Based on Mars's distance from the sun, its real summer was very short, the three springs and two falls longer, but winter longest. The species had forgotten how it had survived winter before the solution of hibernation, before the first clever aborigine dug deep enough not to freeze solid after he fell asleep (also having had the good fortune to eat well before he lapsed into unconsciousness). Hibernation was the logical answer to lack of food across the six-month winter. If you couldn't eat, sleep. Digest your own body. And sometimes, in those brutal years when winter lasted *all year* long, while you slept – eat whatever was next you. But we will speak no further of that. That was long ago.

The problem with digesting the fat and tissue of one's own body as fuel over the months of winter was that one woke, when food was not immediately at hand (nowadays it was carefully provided) to a craving which drove one mad. Before recorded times Martians who survived the spring weeks of hungerlust and murder learned in autumn to set aside nutritious food at the hibernation cave mouths, and also plenty of water, stored so that the same spring sun that woke the sleepers would melt water for drinking. After drinking there was swimming, which washed grimy bodies. In turn came play and frolic to further rouse the beslept mind from its dreamscapes.

The next problem was amnesia. Until one had taken in enough calories and drunk enough life-saving water, the body engine simply couldn't spark self-consciousness. Post-hibernees, or cavedogs as they called themselves, stared moronically at one another, wondering *Who is that?* and *Where am I?* Slowly arose a kind of froggy self-awareness, including of the fact that one was filthy with slime and strange excretions. Then the marvel of wolfkind organization appeared, and the communal pack and family hierarchy took over. By this time intellect had become wolfish again.

After waking, drinking, and washing, the wolf clans struck out for their remembered homes on the surface. But first they displayed a lot of animalistic behavior, amusing and much written about. Some persons "froze" in this pre-conscious state or descended into it when they experienced a shock in life. The treatment for animal dementia was plenty of heat, light, and water. The same thing that drew a wolf from his cave of hibernation drew the insane from an internal retreat into the mind cave. Any other mental treatment had long since been found to be toxic, more destructive than helpful, and was not only avoided but strictly illegal.

The third complication of hibernation was sexuality and reproduction. Many Mathematicians theorized that this was the crux of hibernation and why Wolves had descended back into the caves. The personal and painful crisis of procreation, consuming the sex of another, taking it into oneself and producing from that a body for a new person. It was as painful or more for the person whose sex was consumed, of course. Some hypothesized that procreation had in the distant past occurred during waking and on the surface. Most rejected the notion. Streets and homes would have been filled with blood. It would have been too painful. How would someone consciously ever let someone else *do* that?

In any case, millennia earlier, the race had evolved that the creative/destructive act of procreation occurred during cave sleep. At the beginning of winter clans feasted beyond bellies' content and then crawled down into deep, natural steam-warmed caves. Lying close to one another, family by family, they sang and hummed themselves to sleep or noodled with Math. When months later they awoke, they were of course nowhere near where they had fallen asleep. All was a knot of bodies, and there were recent, bloody newborns suckling at sleeping mothers' tits.

Not long before the close of hibernation season the pups were born. They wriggled sightlessly to the nearest tit of the bitchmother. All bitches of a cave where pups were born during hibernation called one another Sister, and helped to raise one another's pups. Males who had contributed flesh to start a new baby awoke hungrier, starving, but knowing they were now fathers.

The number of procreations per wolf was normally two or three over a lifetime. The reason was obvious. The planet could not support too sizable a population of large land creatures (that is, larger than a mouse or rabbit). Thus pups were rare and beloved. The genders and overall population achieved an approximate balance. Planetwide, the number of pups born was proportionate to the total number of deaths by accident, disease, or war the year before, including death during hibernation. Although there were always just a *few* more, a few additional beings coming to Mars or arising from the Outside or wherever they came from. Sex on the surface, "light sex" as the wolves called it, as opposed to "dark sex," was non-reproductive, hence just another form of affinity, or lack of it, as sex has been throughout Creation.

There were unaccountable consequences from this seasonally nocturnal dark sex and procreativity. Waking was far more confusing than just being hungry, thirsty, and stupidly wondering where was food and drink. The question "Who am I?" became "Am I a mother?" or "Am I a father?" Hypothetically, discovery of one's motherhood or fatherhood should have made no difference, as it was all a matter of chance, but so is drowning in spring floods or being eaten by a swordfish. In reality the literature and songs of Mars revolved around this complex issue. Dark sex might seem "a simple matter" to persons several centuries after they had last procreated, but rarely even then. As one progressively woke up in the warm spring sun, couples who had been living together before hibernation would seek one another out. Sometimes there was a new pup. In their initial exhaustion it made no difference. Later it made for lots of difference. A male and female going back to live together as parents had at least one hundred years of raising a whelp to confront. With wolfkind there was not really a choice – couples were matched for life. Literature and song never ceased to chew on this. Was it a good thing or a bad thing? The totem that the same two individuals who went into the cave together should continue to cherish and support one another after hibernation proved over millennia to be an unbreakable instinct, no matter the cerebral rationalization of the individuals. In other words, once joined in a life-coupling, or marriage, there was never a real divorce. Ever. If two individuals chose consciously not to go back into the same cave together they might live separately, but both would remain barren unto death. And usually one or the other, or both, would develop some kind of dementia. They could take up with other partners, but these relationships were generally snubbed as "sterilities." Even science never solved this problem – artificial insemination was fruitless, and drugs were out of the question. Of course there could be adoption. Infrequently a young wolf in his or her first few dozen years might choose another parent couple, or parents would adopt a whelp or young wolf. For some reason, however, this produced a century or so of sterility in the young person, so it was not an inconsequential choice.

The Martian phrase was "Sex is not Math," meaning that in the life of real wolf beings two plus two never equaled four. It might equal anything, but the *logical* was the least likely outcome. Of course this was Martian think. Martian wolves love their Math.

* * *

This particular morning, the wife of our future ambassador was again coming out of hibernation. Isle was her name. Although she couldn't remember this at the moment, she had an awareness that the heaviness at her chest meant she had given birth during the winter. Having crawled from the cave she lay near its mouth, enjoying the sun. She became aware of others' movement and crawled with them to the shallow pool. She drank and rested, and drank and rested, and then slipped naturally into the pool. Someone behind her said her name, "Isle," nibbling and scratching her back, helping to clean her. She turned and looked at him. It was her sparsely furred husband. "Loos," she said, and started licking him clean, too, with pool water.

"Wife."

"Husband."

They quietly embraced, nipping awkwardly because of the child which was happily hanging on for life and suckling at the tit, utterly as content to be below the surface of the water as above (typically Martian).

Then out of their post-sleep stupor they realized their gift and doom, the intersection of which with their lives could not be said to add or subtract, but rather wreaked their Mathematics into a whole new dimension, actually that of all Mars, even the solar system. The gift was that they had had not one pup, but *twins*.

"No wonder I'm so exhausted," said Isle.

Loos grasped one pup in his teeth and Isle the other, and they raised them up into the air to have a look. "Male pups. Our first wolf children." The boys squalled with desperation at this first separation from milk. Utter despair, hopelessness.

"As spirited as you," said Isle, smiling just a little as she took back the boys, who each clawed their sightless way to sustenance.

"Food," mumbled Loos. He swam through the mingling winter-pale, otter-like bodies of his clan to the pool's edge. Exhausted even by this slight effort, he rested there until he had energy to crawl on paws and knees to the food bins. Simple feeders designed for the low intelligence of wakers, these disbursed nutritious multi-grain and fish jerky nuggets, sweetened with high-energy sugars, vitamins, and other nutrients. He stuck in his muzzle, got a mouthful, and sprawled on his stomach, chewing the miraculous wonder of it for a delicious eternity before he had to snatch another mouthful and move on, compelled by others clambering over his body like carpet to get to the bins. Back at the pool he tongued food into Isle's mouth. She licked his snout clean, chewed the food, and kissed him, thus giving him a few grains back, which their tongues fought over, but he won. This gave them their first little laugh.

Life was returning.

By now group splashing had started, and ribald jokes about who must have had sex and who was the father. Theirs and other pups were held up to show off. Beautiful, all legs and fingers, toeclaws and dewclaws (grown long and opposable in Martian wolves), their fur a tinge of green, turning from reddish to grey green, as they all responded to the life-giving nutrition of sunlight, the food of all foods.

Gradually the Pack's intelligence rose. They began to think of where they should be, what they should be doing. Couple by couple, or individually, or in clans, they left the water and gathered around the cave mouth, dripping in the sun. A few males ventured back into the cave and returned carrying two lifeless bodies. It was not unusual that some could not survive the winter hibernation. This time it was two, Alfredus and Lilliana, a couple as it almost always was. They were old, old, old, and death and passage were appropriate.

"Praise them," said one of the survivors. "Praise Alfredus. Praise Lilliana." Their bodies, shrunken and dirty with cave slime, were still smiling. The group telepathed *Alfredus? Lilliana?* There was no answer from the Outside. "So they have been reborn," one said, "taken on new bodies." The new whelps were held up for all to see. "Hail, new Alfredus" was called out, although to whom none would know for a long time, until "Alfredus" would come in his new life to remember whom he had been in his last. "Hail, Lilliana."

Then, as they sang and hummed the Song of Rebirth, they carried the bodies to the pool where they carefully washed them, all partaking to touch them for the last time. When they were clean, everyone in the clan nuzzled and licked them once more, and they were carried to the edge of the cliff, where the gathered could hear and see far below the wall-to-wall Great Canyon rush of First Spring's palest bluegreen icemelt surging downstream. At this phase of the year the Great River was hundreds of feet deep, chunky and clanking with glacier ice, churning a wider passage for itself. The clan stood, silent and in awe of the beauty and force of the river. Then they let drop the former bodies of Alfredus and Lilliana, which bumped Cliffside only once and then disappeared into the clashing waves. Up and down the Canyon ridge they could see the same ceremony being performed for other winter-departed bodies. So habitual had become the yearly Reawakening that even without speaking to one another, miles and hundreds of miles apart, the many different clans, after climbing out of hibernation, were returning their dead to the river within seconds of one another. Waiting for this treasure, silvery sleek thirty- to forty-foot swordfish with iridescent dorsal fins proudly erect leapt to catch the cast off bodies midair, or to pluck them from the water. Soon the beautiful fish leapt no more, and their fins disappeared beneath the waves.

"Praise them," the clan said.

Then, as ten thousand times before, they turned and wandered back to denhomes, stepping tenderly on bare paws, again sensitive to stone.

Chapter 2
TWINS

As twins, the wolf pups at first looked very similar, but physically identical or not, there was never any doubt that they were to carve out different chunks of the universe as their own distinct zone.

The first remembered self-determined action of one, when his younger brother by minutes seemed to divide his parents' attention, was to whack him in the eye. The injured party sang out his protest and dismay at this re-introduction to life's innate unfairness with such loud and musical eloquence that it revealed art. Thus the whacker was named Prometheus, the whackee Apollo. (Or the Martian throaty wolf equivalent in sound. One could also translate the names as Tool User and Spirit of Art.)

And Apollo did sing. His infant yodeling and howling was taken mostly to be noisome disapproval – "I want food and I want it now." But when Isle and Loos matched his warbles with sounds of their own he would follow them as best he could. Lullabies he loved even more, always trying to sing along, though not well. The will was there. The vocal capacity was not. Perhaps he was just too young. But as he developed other means of expression or bodily control he used them to imprint art on his world. Marking up walls. Carving on his dad's writing pad. Dressing up in parental clothing, cutting the pieces down to his size to their displeasure. They also figured out, only after someone else suggested it, that Apollo's frenetic jerks, twitches, and wriggles might be some form of dance. They had worried that he might be spastic, but never let the concept fully imprint itself. Epileptic might not have been far off, given his later life experiences with trance. Apollo displayed no precocious talent such as reborn artists had. He simply had an inexhaustible appetite for doing the stuff of art. His parents hoped he would grow out of it.

Prometheus was worse. The same energy, but directed more towards limits or targets, discovering the projectile range of missiles, everything being either missile or target. Food, utensils, bowls, eventually his body, and then his brother's. How far could he throw it, push it, drop it? What would happen to it? As do all children, he knew he was immortal and would survive any jump, fall, leap. He assumed his brother would, too, when launched without prior consent on an experimental journey over some edge. Loos and Isle at first thought he had evil intentions toward his brother, as in straight-on murder. However, Prom's putting his own body through the same tortures as he would his brother refined their analysis to murder/suicide. Before long they saw that it was simply . . . sport. Prom wanted to run, jump, swim, fly, preferably into, over, or through something else. It would have had a military, destructive aura to it except that he laughed so much in the doing of it. Delighted, joyful laughter. Which is how Prom would con Apollo into imitating whatever impossible maneuver Prom had just failed at. In a bleeding, skinned, bashed wolf cub body at the bottom of a cliff, he would roll over, chortle and say, "Come on, Pollo, it's FUN!"

"They're a pair," friends of their parents said. It was more like binary planets orbiting an invisible center of gravity created by their own energies. Big trouble, mumbled the Elders, and they were right.

Wolf cubs have it in their nature to be playful, as do all creature cubs, and Martians were no exception. Their bodies were excellently adapted to the environment. Although they hibernated through long and savage winters, they needed fur and photosynthetic help from the meager sun during the almost equally frigid summers, even then when Mars was closer to the sun, having greater mass.

Snow and ice make for slipping and sliding, so wolf children as well as adults made sport of it. But not just following gravity with belly and back-sliding on slick fur down precipitous, miles and miles long slopes. Their lithe canine bodies had powerful hind and forequarter muscles and claws which grew to nasty lengths and could be sharpened to cut through anything — all the better to use to revel in going up mountains and cliffs as much as down. Climbing developed an entire language of its own, which along with fishing and flying became the dominant metaphors for the species in its waking phase.

Awake, however, one had to move to stay warm. Varieties of climbing sports evolved. Hauling huge masses up inclines was a popular masculine team sport. Upracing was masculine, downsliding for both sexes, though dominated by bitch wolves' extra slippery fur. Springtime upracing partook of sexual and mating games, where adolescent males chased females. Off season, like as not, females chased the males.

Their extended lives graced Martian wolves with vigor and elasticity of body for centuries longer than humans. One could, therefore, excel at one sport to perfection and public acclaim, and then try another and another. It was a life made for Prometheus. He grew himself to a body-stretch length of nine feet, not bad for an athlete. He could tear up cliffs or mountain slopes, ice or rock, at world-record speeds with a matching endurance. "Promethean" came to mean unmatchably swift or unrelenting, enduring power. Later, of course, the meanings darkened. Prom surpassed his brother in such sports and enjoyed lording it over him in the adulation of females, at least those attuned to sporting prowess. Apollo pretended to ignore this aspect of his brother's physicality, being quite content himself to lure females in with the wilier web of song and dance.

Like brothers of any planet or species, they wrestled. This too was a Martian sport as well as a martial and survival skill. In grappling, brawn isn't everything. Suppleness beneath slippery fur and skin counts for much, unless one is fighting for blood with claws extended and teeth bared. The brothers regularly tussled. As they grew into adolescence they used this close contact martial art more than any other to compete physically. And why not? There is pleasure to be found in leaving a brother behind in a race, but it doesn't heat the blood like tying him in a knot, near-throttling him, and now and then throwing him off a precipice – despite parents interfering to protect life and limb. Prom had the power, but Pollo had the con or craftiness. For each time that Prom got his brother in a death grip and twisted his back to the breaking point, there was another when Apollo tricked Prometheus into a fall and pounced to grab his jaw from behind and bent his head as far back as he could force it. But until adulthood there was something in the brothers that avoided the finality of murder. The intent was there, no doubt of that, but after a few rips of the skin, some healthy bloodletting, and a bone-crunching bite or two, they would inevitably let up at the last moment, panting and red of eye. After the requisite grumbling, glaring, and furlicking, they would then critique one another's form and newfound tricks. Soon they would be off to attack hapless friends.

Almost always they would remember to relent at the last. There was the time Prom had Pollo raised yards above the ground, threatening to hurl him out the cliff cave's entrance if his brother didn't promise to give over his wolfbitch of the moment. Apollo duly considered this, but was interested in this girl cub's voice for his band (as well as for sex), so he spat back a juicy morsel about something he knew of Prom's sexual diversity. On impulse Prom tossed him out into space. It was a killing drop indeed, more than a thousand feet straight, but through a fluke of a strong gust (or Apollo's expert airsailing technique), he got his claws into stone, and after ripping out a few, halted his fall and climbed back. Prom watched him crawling back and slithered down to help him up, apologizing, saying he'd lost his temper (thinking mostly, of course, of what his parents would do once they found out). Poll took advantage of his brother's momentary introversion to push *him* into freefall. Even is even.

Prom could have died, too. But didn't. Nor did the parents learn about it, of course. The brothers had to make serious amends for the broken furniture and blood on the walls and ceiling, but the long-suffering mother and father knew better than to ask for too many details of exactly what had occurred. They knew the boys' love/hate relationship. They understood that the brothers wouldn't kill each other from deep malice aforethought. If it were to happen it would be a sudden act and swiftly done. All Martian life followed such a rhythm.

Endurance through chance was wolflike and Martian. It was unremarkable to die from the elements or wild life. Life was not cheap, however. Martians were constructed to survive and live long – or die young. What followed, sometimes, was that if one sibling died one or all of the others suicided to join him. Hate is hate, but love is love. That was the parents' worry, that one brother would dispatch the other in a feat of derring-do and then feel obliged to off himself to join his sibling Tweenlives. Loos told Prometheus that if he killed his brother it wouldn't do him any good to follow him into the Light because Dad would not be far behind, and Prom had *no idea* what death was like until he'd been killed *after* he was dead. That put the fear in Prom, for a time.

Apollo scored points, but in his own manner. During his earliest study of chemistry he regularly used his brother as unwitting poison tester. The idea was to find out what *could* kill or transform another into something reptilian or fishlike, but not to actually *do* the deed. This is the heart of science in a boy or girl's mind. There were a few times when their stomachs had to be pumped, Pollo doing in both his brother and himself. Or their eyes and fur had to be washed of some awful smelling or near permanently fur-dying concoction. Once Prom made his brother lose great chunks of fur, and Apollo never forgot the impression that furless, bare, naked skin made on him.

The greatest sport or physical art was flying. How could it not be?

Most clans and den families lived near rivers for fishing and the other uses of water. The yearly cycle of freezing and melting cut deep ravines and canyons, so Martians made their homes in found or created caves up in canyon walls. They also had to be secure from the cold of the seasonal Killing Wind. Although the wolves were superb climbers, this form of locomotion limited cargo transport and also precluded easily visiting others in the thousands of cave dwellings, offices, and other businesses dotted up and down for thousands of feet along endless miles of canyons or mountains. Therefore it was natural to experiment with flight. Wolves watched Martian gulls, eagles, and vultures. Mimicry led to kiting, then body-lifting kites. Through accident, someone discovered parachuting. Parasailing started up virtually the next day. Experimentation with variations of airfoils led to true airsailing. Via many crashes and dead dogs, they learned to navigate the complex up, down, and sideslip drafts of canyons, and even the great winds.

But this wasn't real flying. Within a few generations of sail flight the Martian wolves bred and sculpted their bodies to be thinner and lighter. Although terribly strong, they'd never been bulky. Soon some became near sailplanes themselves. They discovered they could maneuver in the air with less and less artificial canopy. Clothing style rapidly shifted for cliff dwellers, to incorporate pockets where light sailcloth could be packed away. At first as a lark, then sport, then everyday travel, one walked to an edge and simply tilted into a fall, ripped out sailclothing, and floated the air waves. A number of young people who first tried this plummeted to the rocky gorge below, but when has that stopped youth or experiment?

With powerful shoulder and leg musculature, they added "flapping" to "sailing." A myriad of winged mechanisms were tried and many adopted for differing purposes. The all-round favorite, along with ubiquitous sailclothing, was the most simple and efficient — a combination of a ribbed coat or cape which automatically spread to wing-shape, assisted by a set of ingenious pulleys and springcords to add distance, power, and spread to the wing stroke. Given their knowledge of how to use sailing to ride air currents, rear leg extension as the prime motive force for win-stroke, self-powered flight kept one aloft as long as one was awake, it seemed.

Versatility followed. And then daredevilry. Where there is flying there is swooping. And diving. And landing on a point. Or on a vertical wall. One wouldn't think it with canine bodies, but if you haven't seen dogs fly you haven't seen flight.

Aside from military and police uses for flight, it became the sport of sports, spawning whole new kinds of art and entertainment. Flockdancing was a group activity to mirror the swooping swirling majesty of migrating birds. Accompanied by airborne musical instruments it became airorchestra or airband. What rock and roller would want to be pegged to the ground if he or she could be doing loop the loops? Diving and swirling with lights or smoke canisters produced many styles of airpainting, beautified by shifting air currents. For sure there was contest. Who could fly the highest? Won by wolves who asphyxiated themselves at unbelievable altitudes. Who could dive the fastest and farthest? Many disasters there, but soon forgotten after a new daredevil's exploit. Who could fly with the least artificial support? Won by idiots jumping off cliffs holding what seemed to be handkerchiefs.

And dozens of air games. Ball games chasing balloonballs or throwing rocks. Targeting games of avoiding been shot from the ground or the air. Hunting or chasing one another. The uttermost glory of clouddiving. Gritty sandstorm flying. Air races. Up and down mountains, to the poles and back, and always and forever dashing *through* canyons, usually just a hair's breadth above the river surface.

Non-flying civilizations lack words for this, that is for non-self-powered flight. Water sailing terms capture some of the concepts – stealing another's wind, leeward, windward, windjamming, jibbing, surfing. Just a few Martian air terms that also applied as metaphors to life were "heatseeking" (searching for an updraft), "coldseeking" (dropping into a downdraft), "currenting" (being carried by an airstream with no effort of one's own), doing a "nailgrabber" (landing on an inhospitable vertical surface). And obvious terms – drafting, bombing, rocketing. Martian metaphors multiplied, became obsolete or archaic, then were reborn with each new flying discovery, escapade, or learned skill. Athletes and artists ceaselessly expanded the horizon of possibilities.

Aloft, Apollo and Prometheus became more than twins. Airflung, they were soulmates. The term was "airmates," pairs who flew together so often they knew exactly what the other would do. To watch these two fly was achingly beautiful but terrifying. You could not discern where the thrill of impossible maneuvers ended and the artistic joy of freeform acrobatics began. Their familiarity with each other's bodies, muscles, gestures, facial expressions, and that enigmatic spiritual extra that twins possess, allowed Pollo and Prom to fly in perfect formation, no matter the invention of the moment. Or for one to break from that in perfect, though unpredicted, counterpoint or mirror image. Your heart soared as soon as you saw them. Even if they were just a double speck high, high up, you could tell it was the Twins. A favorite of theirs was to fold their wings flat and, inches from each other, plummet thousands of feet like spears, straight, utterly straight down. Then far past the point of safety, impossibly late, they unfurled their wings and together sailed up in a great life-affirming curve. The Twins' Arc it will always be called. In public. In private it was known as the Death Wish.

They never fought aloft. Ever. Certainly they would play in targetball games and throw vicious volleys of granite balls at the other, but this was game. They might fight it out later, landed, whether a particular strike was within the rules or unnecessarily rough. Never in the air. The air was for art, for song. It was the perfect embodiment of freedom – sacrosanct, at least for the brothers.

Not infrequently one saved the other from a nasty, potentially fatal, fall. They learned as young cubs, just starting out, to keep an eye out for each other. This is how they discovered the Death Wish Dive. Apollo had snapped a springcord or forgotten to properly attach one and lost use of one wing. As he fell he had the instinctive foresight to keep the other wing rigidly extended. This slowed his descent, turning it into a spiral, but still he had far enough to fall to die. "Prom!" he screamed, just once. Prometheus, who had been practicing above, saw, and folded himself into a lance and dropped to his brother, gravity accelerating to speedcatch him. Clutching each other, they limped to a safe landing. "Let's do that again!" said Poll. After they had repaired Apollo's wing up they flew, and dropped like stones again, screaming like eagles. Others tried to duplicate their move. How hard can it be to fall like a dead weight? But no one could ever capture the breathstopping quality of the paused moment high above, holding, holding, then the sound of wings slamming shut, the plummet, and the impossibly late gorgeous arc away from certain serious punishment. When Isle first saw it she turned to Loos, like any mother, to say, *Shouldn't we… ?* But Loos shook his head. *The air is their element,* he thought to her, *To try to instruct them or discipline… to restrain anything about them up there? No. They will look after one another.*

Which is what they did except for once, when there was nothing either could have done.

Chapter 3
THE WILDING

The wolf twins stood nervously in front of their father and mother. They shifted from leg to leg, scratching up the floor unconsciously with claws extended. Not that they could have cared. They had been waiting years for this moment . . . or what they hoped this moment would prove to be. Loos had called them back from school with no explanation given. That alone made it as obvious as sending up a flare. They looked from Father's to Mother's face, decoding every clue they could glean. Both Loos and Isle were doing their best to maintain a fishface (blank eyes, meaningless grin), but not succeeding too well. Father had this nasty glint in his eye. Mother smelled just a bit of fear, the odor of concern for another, not for self. They had sniffed this often enough when she had dragged them back from one of their misadventures, afraid for their damnable trust in twins' luck.

(This was really just a matter of actuarial percentages. On cold and dangerous Mars two people who hung together had considerably more chance of surviving, one often able to rescue the other, whereas one foolish person would be over the cliff without claws.)

"I expect you know why you're here," Dad said.

"We sure hope we know," said Apollo.

"We better know," said Prometheus, "or . . ."

"Or what?" snapped Loos.

"Or . . . I don't know. Something . . . nasty. Come on, Dad. Tell us."

Loos smiled, turning to Isle. "Should we tell," he said, "or drag it out unbearably?"

"You better tell them, or we'll have to sand a new floor," she said, looking down at the grooves being carved by the boys' claws.

"All right. All right. Yes, it's true. The clan finally has Four Hands together. You'll soon be able to leave on Wilding."

The boys whooped and slapped paws, bumped rumps, nipped snouts, and did spontaneous little dog dances, shouting "I knew it! I knew it!"

They had been waiting years. They were now nineteen. A person could go on his or her first Wilding after eighteen years of age. But it was not a solitary adventure. Unless there had been some natural catastrophe decimating the clans, a clan waited until there were ninety-six or more young males and females of age before they were sent out. Clans resorted to banding together to get Four Hands, if they had to, but only when the quorum could not be gathered within twelve years of one clan's births. A Hand was four times six, of course, the six digits on a foot or hand (the "hand" being the front foot). Four times that was ninety-six, only one of many obvious formulations stemming from their duodecimal counting system. Ideally it was forty-eight males and forty-eight females, but it had been ages since the exact quorum could be matched within one clan.

The Wilding was the first and certainly most major rite of passage for a young Martian wolf. There was much tradition to it. Groups of ninety-six young wolves were escorted by family and friends either north or south towards the nearest planetary polar arctic until they were at the last major organized community. There was feasting, singing, and dancing for three days and nights. Then at dawn on the fourth day each young Wilder shed all his or her clothes or coverings, down to fur. Taking only a backpack with three days' food, they set out, naked, away from civilization to spend a minimum of a Martian year . . . Wilding.

For their first twelve day dog trot away from powered civilization, they were constrained to help one another and take no independent action. After that there were no rules. There were no Laws of the Wild. Based on what each individual experienced, what he or she had to do to survive, one's first Wilding molded one's personality, often for life. What was remarkable, or perhaps not, was how varied the experience could be, and how differently individuals within a wolf pack responded to the same Wilding.

It was voluntary. It had not always been so, but a few thousand years before, after one Wilding killed off all the wilding-age youth of an entire clan, some mothers and fathers sued for justice. After years of acrimonious debate it was agreed that a wild-age youth did not *have* to go on a Wilding. But nervous parents could not intercede. The choice was for each youth to make. In the ages since not one youth had ever chosen to stay behind. Thus young hormones have and always will trample over cautionary fences, despite the best intentions of older hormones.

What else the moderation of justice forswore was that anything that a Wilder did should have official consequences in civilized society, after his or her return a year or more later. There were *no* rules for the duration of a Wilding. Some conceived that in some distant future eon, when all of Mars was covered with the scars and tattoos of civilization, there would not be a need for each generation to go to the School of Tooth and Claw. Others argued to the contrary, that until parents stopped sending their children to the university of the wild, Martian wolf civilization would stay brutish, wanton, not fully civilized.

The majority ruled, however, and their rule was that "staying wild" was much, much preferable to succumbing to the sickening niceties of a too protective civilization. Ancient memory told of a time when this *had* occurred, when the predecessor Felines had been the intelligent, dominant race, but "cat claws lost their sharpness" – and the wolves' did not . . . hence now there was no cat civilization, only a few feral tigers or mountain lions. The bears had been before that, and birds before them, all the way back to fish, it was thought. No, better to test each generation against the ferocity of nature, both the nature of the elements, and the worse, far more dangerous, nature of what becomes of a male or female between the left and right ear, or deep in the bowels, when he or she has reached the personal limit of cold and hunger. Then one is confronted with both the demon and the angel spirit of self. One learnt much by observing during a Wilding the play between the dark and light forces of life in one's companions. And in oneself.

One survived. Or did not. Survivors returned. By tradition returnees did not speak of what had transpired, nor write or sing of the bone marrow specifics. But Martians were telepathic, at least within families. So they knew. Obscured by dark mental curtains or locked away in vaults of 'Don't Look Here' were the untold histories. Besides, in Martian society you were either waiting for your first Wilding, had already lived through it, or were waiting for your next one. The Martians did not rest on remembrance of things past. Every ninety-six years one could go on another Wilding, with those of one's surviving generation. Later Wildings were of shorter durations and with much less of a quorum than Four Hands. After the sixth (at 576 years of age), it was for only a month – unless an ageing Martian simply walked himself out onto glacier ice and rock until spirit departed body.

* * *

It was the dawning of the fourth day. The feasting and partying were over. That it was Third Spring this far north did not mean much. It was cold. Each family gathered around its loved one or ones to wait for the glinty morning sun to rise a hand's breadth above the horizon. It was time for parents to waste the moisture of breath and attempt advice. The youth were tired from days of dancing, excited, charged with the juices of adventure, and too plain dumb to listen. Loos and Isle said nothing to their boys, but they did try to sneak a little extra food into their packs. The Wilding Gatekeeper would remove it before they left, but every parent still tried. Wilders were allowed one civilized article besides the pack itself, as long as it was not a weapon or tool or overt clothing. It could be jewelry, or a small musical instrument, a keepsake . . . something to remind the lonesome soul of home. Parents talked for weeks after their teenagers left about what the totem they had taken meant. But all those who saw that both Pollo and Prom had put a *book* in their backpacks could not believe it. Pollo put in a thick tome with classic plays and epics, which he swore he would memorize before he returned. Prom had a thick table of mathematics and physics formulae, which he too intended to commit to memory. Loos just shook his head, and Isle bit her lip.

The parents looked at each other, remembering their own first Wildings. Reaching to touch, they exchanged lightning flashes of each other's memory. Loos, killing a great bear with a Hand of other wolves hanging on the rampaging beast, several packfriends torn to shreds. Isle, standing on a cliff that gave way and falling into a raging river – watching all her mates *not* jump in after her until her girlfriend came and, seeing Isle being swept away, leaping into the foaming waters to join her friend no matter where the waters should take them. Loos fighting off invading wilder wolves, come in the night to steal his food, with a club. Isle, exhausted, late in the Wilding, tagging along behind a near feral wolf, willing to do anything for the scraps of food he threw her. Loos alone, in a deep blizzard, curled up in a snowhole, telling himself a story about summer back in the canyon and feeling a strange spirit warmth pervade his bones. Yes, they had been formed by their experiences, although each of them would have thought, perhaps rightly, that it was the other way around: they had formed the experience which they then underwent.

It came time for the Four wolfling Hands to depart. All were holding their snouts to the horizon. Yes, the sun was up a nose. Time to go. There were neck hugs, nips, and murmurings. By tradition those staying behind hummed a deep-throated rhythmic "Urh! Urh! Urh!"

while making a standstill stomping thump, which the departing youth used to time their pacing, until they could no longer hear it but only felt it through their feet.

* * *

Once on the march the ninety-six formed up into Hands of two dozen each. They had twelve days' march to do, and the nights were cold. All slept in a huddling mound, the outer ring periodically climbing over the others to snuggle into the central warmth. On the fourth or fifth day, as their stolen-away backpacked food was running out, there was still no wildlife to be found. They began to eat scraps of vegetation. On the seventh day they saw a herd of antelope off in the distance, but when they tried to creep up to them their number was too large to hide. The herd ran off. So they agreed among themselves that they had better split. They did, each Hand heading off in a different direction.

Pollo and Prom's Hand were poor hunters. Luckily they came across a small lake populated with fish, and all got happily soaked catching a bellyful. They could have stayed there, but knowing they had a year to spend, further adventure beckoned, so they moved away from sure food to the more interesting unknown. Days later the group was starving again, until it came upon another Hand of wolflings which had killed deer. They stood, turning in sad forlorn circles, and were thrown begrudged bones and scraps, gifting which they knew would be rarer in future, and in fact was, when weeks later another hungry group came upon *them* in their own better fortune. Some of them did not want to give those beggars anything.

What they all shared was the ambient beauty of the far north, of great distances, the sky and stars, the blue greys and umber reds, the pleasure of open space rolling out before them with each next spacious day. And also what was under their feet. As they trotted along the edge of a great glacier ice sheet, looking down at the arctic sea far below on one side and the expanse of white ice on the other, they could feel the world move beneath them. The glacier was alive, creeping ever downward. As it scraped the earth and stone far,

far below, shivering waves were sent up to the surface. They felt they were walking on the skin of a great, sleeping beast. The groans of the ice confirmed this. It was not magical. It was more *real* than anything ever had been.

However, reality soon spoiled this immanence of life and universe with certain mundane facts, missing facts – such as, that if one had cloth in one's backpack one could have unraveled it to make string with which to fish. That twenty-four was still too many to find food for, that perhaps even twelve were. They kept splitting up into more feedable packs. First Autumn was coming soon enough, and they feared the descent of winter. They would have to find shelter and enough food to last them through a shortened hibernation. There would be no meal and fishcake caught and prepared to await their coming out of deep sleep, as at home. Once up, they would have to scrounge quickly for springtime food. They knew they would be feeling stupid then, and be slow and weak. As they crossed by caves or holes in the ground, individual sixes agreed to come back later, possibly here, maybe there, to share body warmth in hibernation.

Finally there were just Prometheus, Apollo, and six friends, including clever Heraklitos and Demeter, pretty Alcibiades, Cato, lustrous Sappho, and perky Ephiginia. They were in this grouping when they came upon a rare old rogue bear. They had only their teeth, claws, and rocks, some of which they had handily chipped into razor-edged knives, as weapons, but these were of little use against this giant. Without a moment's reflection or plan, Prom raced to attack the creature, followed by Klitos and Meter. With one massive paw the beast golfed Klitos a considerable distance away, but Meter and Prom clawed their way up the standing animal's back to a useless perch, biting into fur at his neck. They dug in their claws. Bellowing their blood lust to challenge his roaring fury, they rode atop his shoulders, not steering but hanging on for fear of his claws and fangs. The others chased in and out, biting behind the bear's knees and at his groin. They howled useless whooping noises, shouting words of encouragement. The bear started to run, to gallop away at surprising speed, shaking his back violently, finally shedding Demeter. Prom hung on desperately, clawing at the bear's huge head, wondering if he could blind the enraged monster. Just as he took a calculated swipe at one eye, he raised his own head and looked where they were going: open air below, just yards ahead, hidden by a slight rise. He threw himself off just as the bear, snarling in anger, saliva flying to all sides with the snapping of his head left and right to try and catch and crunch Prometheus in his great jaws, plunged off the unseen cliff.

When the others got there, they found Prom looking sadly down at the great river, far, far below, which had carried away their prize, enough food to last until winter. The alternative prize was a cave they spotted not far down the cliffside, which would make an ideal hibernation.

Days later they were still hungrily debating amongst themselves how they could have felled the beast when disaster struck. They were paying too much attention to themselves and their hunting fantasies, not noticing that they were upwind of where they were running. They rounded a bend only to find a Great Northern Tiger, surprising it intent on a recent kill. Normally the cat would have run from so many, but there was food to defend, so instead it leapt straight *at* them, all fifteen feet of it, and landed on Alicibiades, crushing his neck in the bone-cracking squeeze of its jaws. Without thinking, Apollo leapt onto the tiger and tried for the throat. The tiger dropped the dead Alcibiades and wrapped its legs around Apollo, clawing at his back. The others threw rocks at the cat, but this accomplished nothing. Prometheus screamed an unholy curse and sprang onto the cat's back, holding a stone. He bashed a blow on its head that would have stunned the bear, but barely got the tiger's attention. The great beast dropped Apollo and turned almost inside its skin, snarling, to reach for Prom on its back. Prom squeezed his front arms around the tiger's neck and just bit and cut at her throat with his teeth. Blood flew in crimson streaks. The cat screamed, but she could not unseat him. The others leapt on her and began cutting at hamstrings or whatever they could reach. Soon the great creature, noble descendant of a line reaching back into prehistory, had bled too much and was too weak to fight. She gave a great roar and fell to her side, where she lay and gave up her spirit.

Tiger does not make good eating, but this depends on your appetite. They cut her up, giving the liver to Prom and heart to Pollo.

The skull they buried with Alcibiades. The bitches thought to leave the tiger skin with him, too, as he had been so fond of his looks, but Prom wouldn't have it, insisting on wearing the pelt himself. And quite ridiculous he looked, a wolf in tiger skin – but it was *warm*. He offered it to Apollo, concerned for his wounded and bleeding back, but Pollo would have none of it, of course. He was fine, and could have handled the tiger himself, thank you, if he had not been so rudely interrupted by five friends rescuing him. A few hours later, however, he was glad enough to receive the traditional field treatment for cuts. Some of the tiger claw scratches were quite deep, but he avoided infection by letting his friends, particularly the females, lick his wounds. Wolf saliva contained natural antibodies. This didn't save him from comments of how tasty he was. "Come closer, Sappho," he murmured, "and I'll show you how tasty I am."

* * *

A few days later the small pack came to the foot of a massive rock cliff. They weren't of a mind to detour left or right, so they climbed. It was farther than their weakened malnourished muscles were up to. Although Martians were prodigious climbers, with claws that can dig into stone and arms and legs of great power, a mile of straight and vertical cliff was a challenge, made more so by their feeling perky from having defeated and drunk the blood of a tiger. Soon they were throwing rocks at one another, mid-climb, causing each other to slip and slide. The more perilous the risk of falling, the more amusing they found the game. Martian cubs.

Until two eagles spied them, half-way up the wall. The raptors smelled the blood leaking from Apollo, still recovering from the tiger scratches which he had reopened in the stress of climbing. The eagles swooped, screeing vicious pleasure in having dog to get even with. Now the wolves had something more interesting to throw stones at. Given that they were having to maintain a perch on the side of a cliff, their aim was not too good, and all stones missed. But finally an eagle flew too close to Klitos, who was able to grab one of the birds' legs in his jaws and bash it against the cliff. This broke the spirit of its companion, which screed a note of despair and fury as it soared away. Klitos carried the eagle in his teeth the rest of the way up the cliff. At the top he skinned the bird, and had himself a fine and foolish feathery headdress to sport.

Despite the loss of Alcibiades they were feeling pretty good, even better when they came some days later upon a geothermal spring. They were not the only ones to have seen its whispery plumes twist their way upward, and they were soon joined by a Hand of others who joined them to loll in its pools. Someone from the new Hand pointed out that the local berries, if pulped, chewed, and spit into one of the smaller hotter pools, would quickly ferment. This worthy soul was hence named the Chemist. By next afternoon they were all properly drunk on the berry beer, which made them amorous, of course. They worked themselves up into a proper bacchanal. Dogs were screwing dogs in wildly inventive geometrical constructs of body groupings, and having a good time of it. (Make merry, for that with which you are having fun will probably freeze solid and fall off come winter.)

Unfortunately others knew of the geothermal. Thus it was bad news that they were fully and properly drunk and, worse, satiated with wolfsex, when a pack of Ferals struck. Ferals were wolves who never returned from a Wilding, who intentionally left civilization to make a life in the wilderness, or who had been exiled from society because they *were* feral. For reasons not fully comprehended, Martian wolves lost their civil wits once they had lived too long *outside,* at least a decade or more. Wolf reverted to Animal. He grew larger. Such was this pack of six Ferals, four male, two female, all nearly as big as the Great Northern Tiger had been. The wild wolves attacked in concert, intending as quickly became obvious, not to defend their geothermal but to eat what they could *kill*. Pollo, Prom and the others were now, however, better armed than when they had left on the Wilding. With chipped obsidian knives they had made weapons out of the bones of the tiger, and these clubs, spears, and hatchets were put to military use. They managed to crush the skulls or break the spine of three of the Ferals. The others decided there was easier food elsewhere. Sadly, Cato had been badly wounded and died that night. This depressed Prometheus, who took to drinking again, and dramatized turning feral himself. He chopped up one of the dead wolves and waved the bloody parts around, swearing he would eat it. Pollo saw that his brother was getting rather to the far side of drunk, and so whacked him a good one on the head with a tiger femur, which did the trick and knocked him out cold. When he awoke Prom was not appreciative, but had no memory of his earlier behavior and could not account for why he was covered in blood. He washed himself off and forgot about it, although the hangover made him a poor companion for a few days. No one else mentioned what had occurred.

They would have liked to stay at the thermal springs for the winter, but larger animals would also come. The wolves split up into small packs again, each moving away to find safe and warm hibernal sleeping quarters. Through blinding and relentless snow, with temperatures dropping into the killing range, Prom and Pollo turned their pack back to find the nearby cliffside cave. There was no time to put food aside. They climbed down, tucked into each other, and fell into the abysmal sleep that accompanies slowing the body to near stillpoint. They dreamed their hibernal dreams and spoke with Old Ones, as Martian wolves do when sleep is deep enough or after they are dead.

* * *

Then it came time to wake. Their body clocks were set to pump the blood into waking rhythm early in First Spring. With low sunlight reflecting off beginning icemelt and the nippy smell of the arctic spring flower appropriately named "Up You Get," they awoke – cold, starving, and very sore. This was not the pleasant waking with one's clan asleep all around one, clothed in the warmth of many bodies. They were disoriented, and definitely worse than grumpy. So they clambered out of the cave and stupidly fell down the cliff into the river icemelt below. This would have wakened the dead, which was basically what was called for. But there are two things that a wolfling enjoys above all others (discounting a good bacchanal on one's first Wilding) – catching fish in river water with his teeth, and body surfing river rapids. Apollo, Prometheus, and their companions did just that, discomfited only by the fact that they were like to drown from being so slow and stiff with waking. A brisk, deep, milky grey spring river will, however, quickly cure hibernal rheumatism. Soon, after their teeth had found a few fish to chew, they were barking and laughing at one another, cavorting in the frothing swirl of waters.

They clambered out some miles downstream. Now was time to dry out, rest a while, and start the long trek for home in a leisurely sort of way. They were lonesome for homeliness and ready for adventure to be over, but still had some months to go before they could show their faces to the Clan again. As they padded along they also had to mull over what had happened so far – how they had comported themselves. Post-hibernation wolves are not a loquacious lot, so their mulling was a quiet and somber affair.

There were more adventures, mostly of the variety that have to do with pure survival. The last was a balancing of obligations, as tends to happen when a group is together long enough. Early on, Prom had saved Pollo from the Tiger. Now it was Pollo's obligation to return the favor.

It came as they were treading through slushy, chunky, melting surface snow, commonly called top chop. Suddenly the area slumped into a hollow. All moved to leap clear. Before Prom could escape the surface gave way completely, and he fell through into a hidden crevasse, yawning with great blue ice teeth below. It was very, very deep. The sides of the chasm, once revealed, did not hold, but collapsed down upon him. Instantly, Prometheus was buried alive under massive tons of snow and ice. A human would have smothered and died, but a Martian dog responds to the cold and dark differently. While Apollo was barking unheard above that Prom should not give up, that he was coming, Prom did give up and returned to hibernation, quickly slowing his body down, down, down, surrendering waking consciousness (green think, they called it in their Mathematics) to deep-cave consciousness (ultraviolet zero, as they said). It was more than a day before Apollo and his mates dug Prom out, having ripped out some of their claws in the ceaseless hurling of snow and ice up and away. Prom was nearly frozen solid by this time. Out cold, for sure. Apollo just slung his twin brother over his back and carried him – making sure to keep the tiger skin, knowing Prom would kill him if he woke without it. Pollo carried his brother for days, not letting anyone else spell him. Prom slept on, but his brother did not worry. He knew Prom would wake when he and his body were in conformation to come back together . . . or when Prom got tired of being lugged around by his brother.

When he did finally come to, Prom just grabbed his tiger skin and stalked off, grumbling. One does not thank one's brother for these things. The burden is too heavy, made worse only by speaking of it. Pollo, however, was glad to have balanced the scale of obligations. There would be years more of that to come in their futures, but for now the brothers felt good. They had taken care of each other and were even.

It had been a good first Wilding.

Chapter 4
THE FISHERS AND THE FISHED

It was in fishing that Martian life honed the edge of its intelligence. Seasonal windstorms scraped continental plateaus bone clean, sanding everything down. Life, therefore, found other venues than the sand-scraped plains in which to display itself, to play itself out. Belowground offered obvious protection, but higher physical life forms become bored or too constrained by the dark and the pressure. Aboveground, the canyons offered the best field of play. But the major dividing line between species was not between horizontal and vertical, the flat land and the walls. It was between water and dry land, as on other living planets similar distances from their suns.

On Mars's First Sister, next closer in to the sun, the temperature range allowed for great hydrogen/oxygen seas, and these formed the planet and created its oxygen-based weather systems, cleaned and fortified the air, fed the land and its life forms. Mars was, however, even then far enough away that its seas were frozen most of the year. Polar icecaps became the life forcer, melting in late spring and summer and gravity-channeling into rivers and then canyons, or else evaporating in the thin air, where weather picked the water up and carried it to precipitate on other land to carve things further, to be picked up by the atmosphere again, and so on, until it froze as snow for the winter season or was carried back up to the perennial winter of the poles.

Seas were mostly topfrozen year round, but developed abundant fish life below, many noble members of which ventured each spring and summer out from under the seas up the rivers to spawn and discover adventure. Including the Great Fish.

The fishes were protein for each other, and they were the principal protein for the Martian wolves, cats, and birds. In the past of the planet's Great Ages bears and cats had achieved dominance over birds and fishes, and in this Age lupine intelligence continued to use four feet to lumber toward the next stage of planetbound consciousness. The wolves used their smarts to learn to fish, as beings with fish within their reach have tended to do throughout the universes.

After they perfected the more obvious methods of capturing fish, of which swimming after them in their own element and catching them with claws or teeth remained one of the most challenging and fun, the wolves developed line fishing to a high art including long lines cast from high cliffside caves. The acme of line fishing arrived with learning to fly – flyfishing, as the art came to be called. This started with lines strung from kites, flown from cliff tops or cave edges. It developed to be too geometrically messy to pull in the kite and the fish. But some wine-drunk flyer got it in his head to drop a line into the river as he sailed just above the surface, trolling, if you will. To his delight and then dismay he caught something, something heavy, and quickly wound up in the time-honored monkey trap – to let go of what he had caught and save himself, or to hold on to the prize, bar the consequences. He chose the consequences like a true fisherman, got fouled in his line, and was pulled down under the surface. That would have been the end of the story except that this sad adventure had been closely watched by his friends, who had dared him to attempt the deed. Before he was even digested by whatever ate him, other idiot savants had dropped from their safe perches to see what kind of flyfishing *they* could accomplish.

Thus was born the Martian form of bullfighting. To catch on the fly the fish, preferably a *big* fish, was not the art. It was to *play* the fish, and if it were a Great Fish, for the most skilled or most hormonally driven, the game was to reverse the roles and to be trolled by the fish, who would be leaping and diving, allowing one to manifest his superb skills at keeping aloft. As this was usually transpiring above a river surging between inhabited canyon walls, it was the perfect exhibitionist sport.

Apollo and Prometheus thus took to it and used it to snare appreciative females as well as fish for dinner or feasts. Often they flew side by side or one behind the other, trolling for the bigger fish. Sometimes they flew tied in tandem to attempt the biggest catch. This day was such a time.

They were piloting a difficult double-rigged flapper, where their combined leg strengths powered the wings, but they had to share the subtle task of piloting themselves as one craft with two heads. Hard enough for any two, worse for competitive brothers, worst for fishing, hence their favorite. It was late spring, when the winds were still peppy, not yet sedated by stable summer temperatures. They were as usual arguing over something. Vocally, as flyfishing thoughts were too loud inside their heads to hear telepathed messages.

"That hook is absurdly big, more like an anchor!" complained Prometheus.

"Would you like me to drop you off someplace?" answered his brother.

"Don't be a dip," said Prom. "Really, what's the purpose? We've already caught dinner."

"Right. So let's hook something big and take a ride."

"You're more interested in riding Serena up there. She's ogling your ass muscles," Prom snapped.

"Right again, and what's the harm in that?"

"I've dated her. She's heavy weather, Poll."

"Maybe too heavy for you, bro. Probably requires the artistic touch."

"Requires twenty-four talons to defend yourself and a case of bandages for repairs," murmured Prom, interesting his brother even further in the fair Serena.

During this exchange they had dropped a weighted line into the water with large hook baited with a sizable fish caught earlier in the day. This began to drag even though they were flying downriver. The water was very deep so they didn't have to worry about the hook catching bottom, but there still might be the odd stalagmite to snag them and yank them suddenly down. Floating on the shifting air currents, they had to keep their attention both ahead and to the side, and on the water surface ahead to spot hidden obstructions.

An abrupt strong bite snapped the line taut, pulling them first up and then powerfully down.

"Here we go!" cried Pollo.

"*Down* we go, you mean," said Prom. "He's going *upstream!*"

They banked tightly, brushing against one canyon wall, momentarily running sideways along it with their paws. They pushed off and wingstroked back to mid-canyon air. Their catch pulled strongly enough that they could sail behind without effort. It leapt into the air, attempting to shake the hook free.

"Sailfish," said Poll.

"Fifteen feet," said Prom.

"Guess we'll have a feast."

"You're not intending to beach that monster?" shouted Prom.

"We'll tire him out. He'll roll over."

"How'll we get him out of the water? He'll weigh a ton."

"What are friends for?" said Apollo, "Especially if they want to be invited to the fish fry?"

They were tossed up and down by the struggling fish. On one great leap when it rose more than its full length above the water, it twisted and eyed them, then promptly dove and swung round to swim downstream.

"The damned fish was looking at us," said Prom.

"Didn't like what it saw."

"Too ugly, Pollo."

"Speak for yourself, Prom."

They were now being pulled at increasing speed straight down the river, the fish making no further effort to leap.

"The bastard's going for the sea," said Prom.

"Yeah, for the ice," said his brother.

"Plans to snap the line."

"Smart damn fish."

They began to wingstroke, evenly but firmly pulling up on the line, exhausting themselves, but more tiresome to the fish. Nevertheless the fish still trolled them as it swam onward towards its deep destination.

They could see the ice edge of the sea, white in the distance beyond the river mouth. "We may have to cut the line," suggested Apollo.

"After all this? No way," said Prom, getting interested now that his brother was failing.

"Frankly, I'm pooping out."

"Well I'm not, brother."

"Liar," said Apollo, but with a smile.

Now it was not the fish. It was which brother would quit first.

They stroked heavily to pull back on the fish, trying to prevent him from reaching the sea, where he would dive under the ice and either pull them down or cut the line. The fish knew what he was doing. They were slowing him, but this then lowered the angle of the line, dropping their height above the water.

Their full attention was on their fish. They did not look behind them. When one was close to the sea where the river deepened, one had to have eyes in the back of his head.

There were much larger fish.

One of these, a great swordfish, had been following the weakening sailfish, now trailing its blood scent. As the great sword came closer it spotted a target above the surface, flapping. Whatever could flap was alive. The creature dove down and then surged up and leapt. It was a full sixty feet in length, a leviathan of immense power. It hurled itself, twisting, up toward its target.

Watchers in canyon eyries above, eavesdropping on the twins' sport, saw the danger and telepathed the ancient wordless call of alarm.

The boys felt the call and turned, in time to see a twelve foot long serrated sword screw upward past them. Yelling, they instinctively made a great downstroke to attempt altitude, but too late. The monster was rising faster than they.

It snapped its mighty jaws, and severed more than half of Prometheus's body and a leg and a half from Apollo. It also cut the line to the sailfish. Otherwise they would have been doomed, having no legs now to power their way out of catastrophe.

The great sword fell with a tremendous splash back into the river, and disappeared into the deep.

Prom! Prom! telepathed Apollo in alarm. Prometheus had felt the bite, not like a stabbing cut but as if he had been crushed between two masses. He tried to legstroke but nothing happened. He looked at Apollo's shocked face, followed his horrified look downward, and saw that half of his own body was gone forever.

Turning back to Apollo, he smiled enigmatically and abandoned consciousness.

Chapter 5
THE CLEFT PATH

Alert friends dropped like stones from where they had been watching to snatch the twins from the water before they sank.

The issue regarding the injured boys was not whether the doctors could save their lives. Damaged bodies could be sutured up, new blood pathways created, and cowardly body shock suppressed with stimulant drugs. Bodies could be salvaged. The issue was how Pollo would take it when his twin brother voluntarily departed life and suicided. This was Prom's logical choice – to leave behind a hopelessly, catastrophically truncated body that could only oppress the quality of his and his family's future lives. Of course he would suicide. There was no question of it.

He's a good brother, thought his Dad to Apollo, sitting beside Pollo's sick bed with his paw on his shoulder.

I know that, Dad. You needn't tell me. *I'm his twin, cold blast it. If only I'd pulled up . . .*

If only the stars were not so bright,
Your eyes would not have glown that night . . .

Loos hummed the ancient folksong, gazing into his son's eyes, but looking past them to the memory of newborn Prometheus's ice-green eyes first focusing on his father.

"I love him too," said Apollo aloud.

Without conscious choice the parents had split up the care of their sons. Loos went to sit with Apollo, or pad ceaselessly outside his healing room. But when Isle had heard about the accident she had immediately thought to her husband, *I'm going to Prometheus. Pollo will need you.*

She had meant "to deal with his brother's death." That she wished to be by Prometheus's side when he chose to die went to the very core of her motherhood. She had birthed the boy. She would be with him when he left and would shroud his remains with her own paws. She could no more have made another choice than she could have chosen not to have conceived him and borne him through the somnolent pregnancy in the dark cave of hibernation. Based on later events, others undoubtedly construed that the mother chose the one son and the father the other because of some deep-seated cognition of who each boy was, how different they were, worlds apart. But this was not so. Mother chose to be with the dying son, because that is the saddest burden of motherhood, which is not to be, *cannot* be, shared with another. And father simply went to the other son, relieved of a weight he would not have known how to carry, as mothers have learned to their sorrow, too often losing their children one way or another.

But their choices made all the difference, historically – which parent went with which son. It was often later discussed across steins of ale, or in sleeping pads by couples drifting slowly into nine month suspended animation. *What if it had been the other way? And the father had gone with Prometheus?* But the companion would think, *And the mother with Apollo? Bloody Isle? Inconceivable.*

With Prometheus at the cave mouth of his mortality, Isle sat silently by his side. He was sleeping beneath a powerful sedative draft. The portion of his body left to him had been sewn up and repaired as best as could be. As doctors do on all planets, no matter the inevitability of a patient's death, the caregiver does all he can to provide him or her a decent, comfortable, less chaotic, less broken exit. At least, that is what these doctors did.

Prometheus slept, his face beautiful in repose, sculpted in the grey and white colors of a great wolf. There was nothing in his upper torso to admit of or predict the missingness of body just below the chest. Occasionally Isle stroked or licked the side of his face. Occasionally she patted the empty bed below his body. *There, there, son* she would unthinkingly think. Those walking by the door of the hospital chamber would barely shake their heads. Pat, pat, they would see. What more distraught gesture could there be than to comfort the missing limbs of your dying son. Stars, don't look down. May ice fog our sight forever.

It was one, two, three days maybe, that she sat there beside him. Humming and patting. Smiling a little. Food and drink was set beside her, and later taken away untouched.

Then Prometheus opened his eyes. "Stars, what a sleep I've had," he said, rubbing his eyes with his paws and making a mighty yawn. *Ouch!* he thought. Then he looked at his mother's eyes, filled with love for him – and with something else, inexpressible. *Love you, son,* she thought at him. *Mmm hmm,* he thought back. "But I'm hungry!" he said aloud, and started to move. The awkward sticklike rocking of his body instead of a smooth slither around and up into a sitting position made him grab the bed on both sides and push his torso up enough to look down. His first thought was, *Someone has stolen my body!*

His mother smiled, despite herself. Then Prometheus remembered what had happened. He stared at the absence of what should be there. He touched the bandaged, bloody mess-of-tubes truncation of himself, and gave Isle such a look as should burst the heart of a mother anywhere. He could not even voice a thought. He just looked at her, and she looked back, both of them touched by the momentary stargiven boon of wordlessness. Then he closed his eyes and sank back into oblivion.

He could have then, but did not, die. And everyone, his friends and brother and father and extended family, all felt it. They expected to suffer the touch of his disembodied mind, saying *I will be fine*, just as he departed. But this did not happen. They felt instead a door shutting for Prometheus with a thud, like the feeling of your body sinking below the surface of water, a going *into* something, not a leaving. Or like the feeling one has of standing at the point of cleft paths in a cave, both tunnels black as doom, sending one's thought down both dark paths to see what may lie in store. Everyone who knew the boys remembered later and could describe it in their own words. *I felt Prometheus* make *his decision*, they would say.

"I am *not* going to die," he said aloud to his mother, the moment he next opened his eyes, days later. His mother returned his look, mindless in her sympathy. "I'm serious," he said. "I'm going to live. I want to live!"

He glared at her. The glare smote her out of her archetypical state of bereaved motherhood. Pools of dry ice were his eyes.

Isle frowned. She touched him and pathed, *What do you mean, son?* How could he "live"? How could he go on with a broken, derelict body? He could always be born again. He could just "leave" and . . . come back. That is what one did with broken or killed bodies, or after great old age. You left. And then, sometime later, you returned.

No! he thought violently. *I love you. And I love my father. And . . . I even love my brother! No, I hate him for doing this to me, but I am not going to go!*

"How can you *not* go, Prometheus?" Isle asked quietly and kindly, not knowing where she found her calm voice. "There's not . . . enough of you left to . . ."

"You must <u>help</u> me then!" Prom moaned. *Help me! Help me to . . . make a new* body *for myself . . . Something I can . . .* His thoughts continued disjointedly as he slipped back into the comforting anodyne of black light sleep.

He didn't die. He lived.

* * *

His twin brother Apollo, though grievously, had not been mortally injured. He had lost his legs, or one and a half of them, but arts existed to make up for this. There were advanced prosthetics and no shame in sporting them, as enough falls from cliffs, flying accidents, or cave-ins had led to crushed limbs that lupine doctors had learnt how to patch things up rather well. Thought therapy could heal most nerve damage, so remarkable recoveries became more commonplace. But there was a limit to it: bodies are bodies, not wagons.

Loos sat confidently by Apollo's bed. He was actually sleeping, sitting on his haunches, erect, when his son woke. Apollo gently nudged his father with his muzzle.

"How's Prom?" he asked.

You saw him, his father thought back.

Yes, Pollo thought, *but how is he?*

"He's not left us yet," said his father.

"Oh, Dad, if Prom goes, I think . . ."

"He would want you to stay!" Loos said. "For your mother. And me."

"But . . ." *But I'd have to follow him. He's my twin,* thought Apollo.

That's a decision for later, Poll. Now, rest. And he did.

He was awake later when they both felt a peculiar surge, a dark bolt of energy, like wild berry liquor down the throat.

Did you feel that? thought Apollo.

Yes, thought his dad. *It was Prom.*

"Prometheus is not going to *die,*" said Pollo. "He's chosen to live."

They each silently looked away into their own minds about what this would mean.

With that body, thoughtspoke Loos, finally.

He will be bitter, thought Pollo. *He will hate me.*

"Yes," said Loos quietly. "I expect he will."

There was not much to say to that. After a while Loos took the initiative. "We have to get *you* well, Apollo."

"The problem is not that I'm not well."

"I mean . . ." said Loos, "I . . . I actually don't know what I mean."

"You mean we have to get me back in *action,* in motion."

"Yes. Prosthetics are amazing these days."

"I damn sure hope so," snapped Pollo.

They *were* pretty good. In short time he was being fitted with extensions for his rear legs whereby he could hobble around. The first challenge was just to walk. Apollo attacked the task grimly. Physical therapy guided him through progressive steps of developing strength in the remaining thigh and calf muscles and training them to respond intuitively to balancing signals from the body to contract or relax. Then he was close fitted with extensions that enabled him to stagger as on short stilts. After much cursing and swinging of crutches at helpers, Apollo learned to stumble forward. The last stage, given the current state of the art, added paws on the end of the prosthetics, attached to semi-flexible ankles and with claws that could be retracted. Apollo wasn't the only person in the hospital being trained to operate a body from scratch. He practiced with other damaged dogs. They all made bitter jokes about bumbling puppies, that crawling comes before walking, falling before crawling. "Piss in your mouth, thank you," snapped Pollo back at them.

To hell with walking, thought Poll to himself. *Will I ever fly again?*

* * *

Prometheus had it harder. There was no question of prosthetics or of any non-mechanical mobility. After complex operations that re-tubed his insides so that blood and other fluids could circulate or be excreted from the half-body, he faced two physical challenges, and a third shared also by his brother. The third was what he and Apollo would now make of their lives. Neither could answer this until they discovered what the physical limits of life would be. No different than anyone else.

The first challenge to define this for Prometheus was whether or not he would be permanently bed-ridden. The principal barrier to that, his greatest challenge, to life and living, in fact, was *energy* — how to create energy for his body to operate. He lived in a carbo-oxidation organic fuel-burning body. But he had lost more than half his intestines to the fish. He was living on intravenously dripped solutions of predigested body fuel that could be no more complex than what his cellular tissue could immediately use. Tail end sugars, amino acids, enzymes, with steroids and hormones to help the surviving tissue to heal. But this was not *food.* A body needs complex food to live. But he no longer had enough guts to digest food.

There were no exercises he could do or that the doctors knew to teach him, except for redeveloping the ability to contract his remaining abdominal musculature, which he needed for both lungs and heart support and simply to massage internal tissues and organs to respond to the sensations of living. He could exercise and strengthen his arms, but this did not satisfy Prom. He wanted an active life. He would accept no substitute.

His fuel was anger. He infuriated himself into surviving. The doctors told him he needed to relax, that his body tissues would heal faster if he could just grant himself some peaceful time for recovery.

To hell with that, he thought. *Ice you. Ice your first born.*

A primordial wolf cub survival game was to sit with snow packed around one by cubmates. The winner was he or she who could first melt the snow to fall away from the body. Prometheus had excelled at this. He had found that he burned up energy when someone aggravated him, joking, ridiculing him. He had turned this into his own talent – concentrating his energies on living as if through an intensity lens. He burned his intention onto whatever he put his desire or attention. "Will" he called it. Using his will. Wrath and fury, others called it. His parents never named it, knowing it *was* Prometheus, not a characteristic *of* him.

So now he *willed* his body to be well. "Frying it better" would have been more apt. Allowing himself rest, healing time, as the medicos wished, was a skill aimed in a contrary direction. The doctors told him he was making himself worse. *Chill,* they might have suggested, to a blazing fire. His friends tried to coax Prom into relaxation. His glare and snarling retorts to their "hail fellow well met" soon closed the door to most visits, which was fine with him. *Fuck them. Ice their gonads. Let them eat their own entrails.*

Isle, however, persisted with daily visits to her dying son. She not only withstood his scorn for her maternal care, but understood where it came from, and gladly stoked his fires. To stay in communication with her broken boy, she took on his manner and gave as good as she got, snapping right back at him or at least pretending to yawn. The daily furnace of this began to bake her solid, to develop a thick tough crust. Her friends and her husband noticed and commented. She sloughed it off as immaterial to the task at hand.

"If you're going to *help* me, mother," Prometheus had said to her, "help. Otherwise, don't come. I don't need kindliness. I need willpower."

"I am with you, son," she answered. "To the end."

"To the *end*? No matter what?"

"I said I am *with* you," she said frostily.

We'll see, he thought, looking away. *But to what end? What's going to happen to me?*

What's going to happen to us, she thought back. *Where you go, I go.*

Meanwhile his bodily functions steadily deteriorated.

* * *

For Apollo, who at first had had significant physical gains, the problem became quite the opposite. Once Pollo could walk around he found that his legs, or what he had left of them, quickly became numb. Worse, the numbness persisted. His doctors reported that important nerves were not regenerating, but actually degenerating. They told him he needed to use his nerves more. *Like telling someone with no wings to fly faster,* he thought bitterly. *Or someone without legs to dance.*

It wasn't a matter of using his legs *more.* There was only so much locomotion he could do without wearing out the hurt tissue. He was supposed to activate the nerves, to excite the tissue into a healing state. Martian doctors had long since learned that electric shock sometimes produced short term gain, but always long term damage, eventually if not quickly killing sensitive nerve tissue. So that was ruled out. But "shock," or more appropriately "surprise," as a *non*-electrical factor was not so excluded. They observed that in the same way one could snap a daydreaming person into the moment by clapping paws or with a dose of cold water, one could similarly force an unthought muscular reaction by provoking that response. One could force nerves to respond – even if the nerves were not *there.*

This translated for those with missing limbs into what can best be described as "boo therapy" — *scaring* someone into wanting to use a missing limb or organ. One might think that tossing a live cat at someone with no arms would be on the sadistic side, but what they found in fact was that if such things were done in an unexpected, non-violent way, producing surprise, the person would respond as though he *could* use his arms or legs. The nerve tissue leading to the arms or legs would receive a burst of energy, psychically more potent than at other times. And such tissue would afterward be seen to heal faster, even occasionally stimulating new growth.

Hence "boo therapy." It made for a lot of fun. Doctors, nurses, family, and friends tried to catch a patient unawares and then suddenly . . . astonish him or her into an uncontrolled muscular or full body response, especially intended for the reaction of the body part not there. For legless patients they had floors programmed to suddenly appear like an empty shaft, the edge of a cliff, a pool of toothy fish. More prosaically, but often more effectively, one could simply . . . push the person, or trip him. Not funny, if the recipient actually fell. But if done just right, so that the person – Apollo or whoever – staggered but succeeded in forcing himself back upright, that person's key nervous tissue was stimulated into a healthier state. It was a tricky question of degree.

Nurses and family members were very careful. Unfortunately carefulness reduced the benefit of surprise. Patients to one another, on the contrary, were gleefully merciless. Once a patient caught on to the true, therapeutic end result, he or she – or teams of them – contrived extraordinary, even devious plots to scare the hell out of one another. Boo therapy degenerated into shriek therapy.

What was found to produce a generic full-body "I'm going to die" nerve-jamming survival impulse, for one example, was dropping someone from a great height. The person was attached to a cord, or in extremis just dropped. Of course someone had to *catch* the dropped ball, or he . . . bounced, or worse. So this last option was strictly illegal, and thus often used. The problem was that once you had tried the ultimate surprise on someone you had emptied your quiver of arrows. It was a necessarily limited treatment option.

Loos and Apollo's friends tried all of the above with, on, or to Apollo to positive result. His existing nervous tissue showed signs of health, of healing. Loos even convinced the doctors one time that Apollo had been taken for an outing by his friends, when he was actually taken for a *flight*, where despite Pollo's last minute "change of mind," pleading, and threats, he was dropped from a height of thousands of fathoms (body lengths). Friends way below caught him in flight. He battered them, and dug a few claws in rather deep, but he didn't report them. When he later felt a freshness or increased aliveness to his stumpy limbs, he said, "Let's do it again." But it worked less well. And eventually produced no effect. He had reached the end of "boo" regeneration therapy. He wanted more.

He wanted to completely regrow his legs. To scare himself up a whole new living body.

* * *

Despite his twin Prometheus's stated desire to live, all those around Prom observed a life or death crisis inexorably approaching. The artificial feeding of the body did not satisfy the energy and other organic needs of his lungs. Thus his heart was straining for oxygen. Martian lungs were large in order to process the thin oxygen of planetary surface level, and wolf hearts were powerful in order to bear the demands of living in their cold, stressful climate. Serious injury to the torso usually led quickly to a person deciding to terminate his life and leave the body, knowing he could start over, even though not fully self-remembering. Medical science, therefore, did not develop life support systems for long-term critical care. Either someone could heal his body . . . or he could not. Non-viable bodies were not considered important enough to sustain with energy-consuming outside mechanics. The alternative was too easily available – crossing into the Tweenlives area and spending time with Old Ones until a fetus invited one to return to life and livingness during the next hibernation.

Prometheus's care presented a conundrum. He was rapidly approaching the stage beyond help, but he himself was determined to break the totem, to change the primordial rules of the game – to insist on physical survival *after* total physical failure. The game is over? So what? Start a *new* game! You cannot stay on the field after you have lost. So it had been in the past. Prom would not speak about this with his mother. He closed his mind on the subject. But the door to the room in which these thoughts were housed was red hot – don't touch.

The doctors recommended to Isle that she ask Loos to recite this story to the Old Ones. Perhaps they could influence Prometheus. With misgivings, Isle suggested this possibility to Prometheus. He exploded.

"If I wanted the advice of the bodiless I would join them! It takes *courage* to fight for life. It takes fire. You have all lived so long in the cold and with the ice that you think survival is a throw of the dice. Now you live. Now you die. Now the Old Ones whisper things in your ear you cannot understand in the language of bloodless, passionless non-existence. Now you wait your turn for a baby body. Now you start over. Maybe you will remember something. Maybe not. Not me! Not this time. When I am ready for death, I will say no to life. I am not ready to say no. Don't ask me again."

But, Prometheus, his mother pathed back. *You are going to die unless we can repair this . . . broken, damaged . . .*

So we will fix it! he mentally shouted. *Hell's Ice, let's make a new body. Let's invent a new one.*

How? she asked.

"Get Demeter and Heraklitos," he said aloud.

These were his two best work companions in his field specialty of "*icethink,*" one particularly condensed and potentially useful powerful form of *think.*[1]

[1] *There were many kinds of "think," or applied thought, for the Wolves of Mars. The subject had been in development for eons. It was an unspoken assumption that more had been forgotten about the subject of reasoning in the distant Cats' Past than Wolves would ever be able to recreate. But some disagreed and looked for new applications. Think. One kind was, for example, stonethink – fixed thought, as in words in a book or carving on stone. Fluidthink had many forms – riverthink (channeled ideas or information as in water through a canyon or electricity through a wire), cloudthink (suspended riverthink, capable of being moved en masse and precipitated elsewhere), waterthink (a flux of information capable of rapidly changing form and flowing to wherever there was an absence of "think"). Icethink was a slow-moving, powerful, compact form of waterthink – bodies of knowledge about which much was still being learned. It had great solidity of mass. It had a tendency to move slowly, inexorably.*

Examining the moons of Jupiter and other such bodies through thought telescopes, Prometheus in his youthful research had seen great bodies of ice, huge with . . . "potential." It was the best word he could come up with. They were not just spherical bodies of frozen water – they were a world of unlimited potential, volatile or not, depending on the energy

It was easier for Old Ones without bodies to Do the Math, as wolves expressed complex thinking. "*Thinkart*" Martians called it. The nuclear chain-reaction of frustration breeding upon frustration for the noodling Bodiless, when they wrestled with Math, was agreed by young, living students to be the principal reason that the recently Tweenlives

---

that would be bathed upon them. They were storage depots for something . . . or sometime. He conceived of a vastly more powerful icethink to match, in the mathematical world of thought, these orbiting physical spheres of frozen gas.

Mechanical assessment of information, as in physically computing, was not binary at this stage of Mars — yes or no, white or black, in or out, off or on. It was what was called "star-dimensional." There were an infinite potential of information points along an infinite number of "axes" of information, as in the dazzling outpour from a star of light and energy of multiple wavelengths. Starting with what would much later on Terra be named Cartesian space (after the sleepy earth thinker Descartes), there were the simple axes of "up, down, left and right, toward you, and away." These three dimensions could be much multiplied by potentials of "movement" outside those axes, rather than just in fixed position (as in holding a "rock" or piece of information but turning it around, so that what was on the back "unseen" by you, now becomes "seen" — same rock but "turned." Thus there were "turned axes." Assuming other viewpoints of spherical space, there were "forward" and "backward" axial dimensions. And of course, when you add time, there were the axes of "future" and "past" . . . and the dimension of "now," the definition of which has provoked ages of argumentation.

The Martians also added thought axes of "inside" and "outside," inside referring to the living "alive" space we occupy in physical life and outside to that infinite collection of spaces or universes beyond the perceptual borders of persons living in flesh bodies. The Old Ones were known to occupy a few of these Outside universes, and they spoke of many, many more beyond even their bodiless perception. Inside dimension points were obviously influenced by viewpoint — "your" and "my" space or time. There was continuing disputation on what the word "their" in reference to a viewpoint meant, if anything, but everyone agreed on "yours and mine." There were other geometric thought axes, rather harder to describe in physical space words. One of these, deliciously slippery, was "here / there / simultaneity." Another was "now / then / reversal." Another rather obvious one, once you think about it, was "tween," a foggy netherspace in which most people live, albeit unknowingly. And from a <u>viewpoint</u> concept — the axes of "want / don't want," "yes / no," "off / on." There were more, all of which allowed the plotting of points in dimensions of enormous complexity — but not more complex than life and spirit can animate.

One can see that the alive Martian wolves had been much influenced by the kooky, kinky thought games played by Old Ones during their eons of noodledoodle time.

Even the most ordinary datum for computational use could be rather complex. For example, consider one formulized Math statement: "your — left — Tween — pulled — push / of / mine — down — forgotten — outside / brought / in — bright — not off — 7th — up." Just one specific of the class of ideas that this formulized statement could translate to would be "a depressing unanswered question of yours, stimulated by me, about an Old One's clever thought, seven generations ago, but increasingly discussed nowadays." Yes, it makes one spin.

Trying to add, subtract, multiply, divide, factor, or integrate such geometric-temporal-ideation sets was stupefying for most live Martians. School-age cubs had been known to shred into rat food teachers who could not successfully guide their impatient students through the mine-strewn labyrinthine caves of Martian Mathematics. Teaching Math-Grammar (the making comprehensible sentences out of Martian mathematical constructs, such as the example above) was a high risk job, too dangerous for regular teachers. Math-Grammar teachers were ex-Martian military. Martian wars had become too repetitively boring and expensive, and the military turned to the only slightly less dangerous field of Math teaching. Despite their military skills, uncounted Martian math teachers had been dumped off cliffs by their students. Students pleaded mathematical dementia to the unsympathetic ear of Elder Justice Councils. (But then these Elders had learned their Mathematics, so how would they know?)

Dead jumped so rapidly back into new, safely stupid fetal bodies.

Being dead too long most certainly drove one crazy, it seemed. Wolf cubs learned that if one tried too much Math while flying or fishing, one tended to join the Tweenlives Dead after crashing into a canyon wall or falling in the river. Damned if you do. Damned if you don't. The conundrum of many universes.

Prometheus of course *excelled* at Math noodling. Hence he was not interested in having to leave "his *inside* universe" (here, physically alive) to join "their *outside* universe" (with the physically dead). He wanted to bring the outside IN to his here and now, so to speak. He was interested in "*freezing*," or compacting data for future application, so that everyone could have "more game." Many of his sidekicks scorned Prometheus's concept of *game*, his Mathematics being way too difficult for them to play, anyhow.

His best friends Heraklitos and Demeter, however, were young geniuses at creating frozen data maps through which fluid data could be channeled (or as earthlings would much later describe it, "creating software for the manipulation of data streams").

When Prometheus said to his mother that he intended to "create a *new body*," he meant he wanted to mock up "new hardware for the software" of his life.

Promethean Applied Mathematics.

Thus we see the cleaving path of the twin brothers' lives.

Broken Apollo desired to conjure up new living tissue, to regenerate himself alive from himself, to dance on newly new feet, unbooted from old habits.

Broken Prometheus wanted to take the hot, bubbly riverthink that was his life, to fashion a new ice goblet in which to hold it, drink himself up, and see if anything *exploded*.

These were far from the same path, not even the same universe.

But the pathways had started *from* the same point. Old Ones would spend eons describing this "point of debarkation," how the diverse and adventurous, destructive and constructive consequent paths of these two young geniuses could ever have started from the same life.

Long before their paths would be lost in the complex twists of time, the futures of at least three planetary orbs would be affected.

Chapter 6

THE TRIP

Boo therapy *had* worked on Apollo's body, at least for a time. There had not been a burst of growth. That was more than had been expected in any case. But the "vitality" of his upper leg nerves had been enhanced. Unfortunately for him, perception of the area tissues rose from "numb" to "hurts a lot . . . all the time." The doctors told him this was a *good* thing. What Apollo told them back is untranslatable.

Activation of feeling had not led, however, to growth of new tissue, as the doctors had hoped. Instead Apollo was increasingly in physical misery, comparable perhaps to recovering from a burn injury. One solution was to reverse the nerve stimulant treatment with painkillers. If the pain did not soon subside, that would be the necessary course of treatment. But Martian medical chemistry for pain diminishment was still addictive (a problem other civilizations have had, too), and Apollo loudly declared he would not resort to it. He was his brother's twin, in that at least.

Loos applied spiritual remedies, of course. He sang to the Old Ones and storytold the incident of Apollo's and his twin's accident, their injuries, attempted recoveries, and suffering. No doubt Old Ones could intercede in the physical lives of the living, sometimes with healing benefit, but as often only to the effect of an unintelligible harassing telepathic noise. (Or worse, being driven insane.) It was widely believed by the Martians that in their prehistoric past, that is, back before the recoverable memory store of their species, communication between the living and the recently or long dead had been far superior. There were also an order of spiritual beings which might be called djinn, angels, demons, or simply "never-having-lived" (that is, never occupying planetary, gravity-bound, physical forms). The Martian term for these djinn was "forever-outside-alive." With the devolution of Martian wolf civilization from direct personal ability down to mechanical surrogates, current Martian instinct and skill for communicating *to* Old Ones had atrophied. On the receiving end, whenever living Martians picked up Old One messages, their ability to interpret what the Old Ones had to say, think, or impart was paltry . It was generally agreed that much of the "noise" coming from awakened or aroused Old Ones was just flaming irritation at the bedamned ignorance of the alive generations.

Loos knew this to be true. When he tried to contact Old Ones, he felt like a child whining to grown-ups busy at other, more consequential work. He experienced a range of physical sensations upon receipt of a fuzzy communication from the Outside world. A slap, a bonk on the head, an ice water dip, electrical shock, a claw scratching his skin, or a bite mark meant (at least he *thought* they meant) that the Old Ones were irritated with him. On the other hand, occasionally he felt a gentle stroking, a warm breath on the neck, sweet susurration in the ear, or the flashflicker of a disappearing-around-the-corner image. These had the flavor of approval or affinity. Loos persisted in his attempts to establish communication. More honestly, he had no choice. It either happened, or didn't, the choice of contact being made from the other side. Sometimes *they* wanted to "talk." He was celebrated as being better (or worse) than most at having half a head "somewhere else." Lot of good it did him, he commiserated with himself.

Apollo knew that his own life's song and dance had been pleasing to at least a few Old Ones. He had often felt the frisson of his fur waving in response to an Old "embrace" or "breath." He knew nothing more about what this meant than that it had been momentarily pleasant to him, like a lover's touch. Or sometimes scary, like a whispered message saying, *Don't go there.* It was usually not until a Martian's twelfthtwelve,[2] his half life, that he or she began to better decipher Old One contacts, and not until his last twelves – the twentieth on – that he would begin to sing intimately back to the ears of the Other Side. By then the Elder was himself neckdeep in the Old world and only half *here,* anyway.

Apollo was still basically a child, just beginning his teenage years – twenty-four plus – and his father was in his midlife – past his 150th. Truncated Apollo could no longer dance, so that avenue of communication wasn't open to the Old Ones. Nor did he feel like singing, certainly not with anything near his past out-of-body exaltation. He felt like a grumpy mute with a twisted ankle. It hurt like hell and all he could do was grimace.

When Loos had attempted to storytell the incident of Apollo and Prometheus's injury to the Old Ones, he accomplished no Other-world healing strokes, jabs, or pokes coming from them back to his son. Instead Loos himself felt a backlash which he honestly experienced as "fear," not his fear or Apollo's, but fear from the Old Ones. Loos did not pass this on to Apollo, but it worried him deeply. After he had gotten the Old One message of "*Be afraid*" or "*No answer. Not listening, Go away!*" enough times, Loos stopped trying to path to them about Apollo or Prom at all.

It's over to you, he pathed to Apollo. *Or to some new trick of the doctors.*

"Did the Old Farts tell you to jump off a cliff or get frozen?"

"More or less. And you should show respect."

Apollo looked out the window of his hospital rehabilitation room to the red, purple, and green sunset above the far canyon wall.

---

2 2. 144 *years.*

Wish I could be flying, he thought. *The fall sandstorms are coming soon.*

"Maybe you can again in a year or two. Or at least glide. The doctors say your thighs can support it."

"Sure. My thighs are so on fire right now that I can't even stick my legs in their holsters."

Maybe you should reconsider the idea of the pills.

"Not going to happen, Dad. I'd rather be cranky with pain or literally jump off a cliff than become some cave-eyed pillhead."

"OK, but . . ."

"Dad. Don't bring it up again."

Loos nosed his son. They both gazed quietly out the window at the evolving canvas of sunset color, spotted with canyon flyers going home from work. The sky slowly deepened to that lustrous black that eyes misconstrued as a result of the earlier dusky rainbow, sending messages to brains alternatively of red-black or green-black. Songs and poems had been written about this extended, multi-hued Martian autumn crepuscule.

"*Redgreen all night through . . .*" thought Pollo.

"*. . . And yet so black, so blue,*" thoughtback Loos. "Son," he said aloud, turning on the yellow light of the bedside lamp, "with your permission I'm going to ask the doctors if they might have another bone in their cave stash."

"I'm a pincushion already, Dad, but go for it."

* * *

"I must inform you that *technically* this would be illegal."

The doctor speaking to Apollo was a tad mangy. Loos would have certainly disapproved of him. The man didn't *look* like a doctor. Loos, however, was not present.

Loos had consulted the rehabilitation and tissue growth specialists. They had said that there was nothing further extant science could do. Apollo was physically recovered, but growth of new tissue was a chancy undertaking to attempt. The scare therapy had in fact helped his nerves to recuperate. But this had led to other problems. Growing new legs was out of the question. Ridiculous, they said.

Counsel your son to learn to live a decent life with prosthetics. He can have a full and meaningful life. He can even procreate, which his twin Prometheus can no longer do. Loos had relayed this non-news to his son. Apollo just snorted.

"Doctors! Bone cutters! Flesh tailors!"

"They've stitched you up pretty good, son."

"I want new legs."

"Fish want to fly. You can't have new legs. Learn to use your prosthetics, and get on with life."

Apollo just turned away.

Poll had asked his young friends to see if there was some cliff-edge, unreported "research" that might help. They had found closed doors or "not possibles." Then one last scientist had called a brain cell chemist who referred them to this man, a "neural toxicologist." As dubious as the title was, they checked him out. He had shown them animals with extra body parts growing out of improbable regions. It was all a bit horrific, even for their youthful tastes.

They argued among themselves whether they should even tell Apollo. The consensus was that the stumps and missing body limbs in Apollo's rehabilitation ward were not more grisly than this alternative, so they should leave the choice up to Apollo. They had taken to addressing him with saucy names like "Runt," "Cut bait" and "Half Ass." He gave as good as he got, describing them as people who lusted after bleeding and broken bodies – "Vampire," "Warlock," "Leechmouth," and other cheerful cognomens. Finally they connived to sneak the toxicologist in as part of their crowd. While Apollo and the doctor negotiated, they ran interference at the door.

Apollo's first question was, of course, "Neural toxicologist?"

Dr. Telemachus answered, "That's just my cover title: someone who works with nerve toxins to kill off damaged tissue in the brain and elsewhere."

"That sounds like a rather final solution to pain," snapped Apollo.

"Yes. The technique's used only in the last resort, but these toxins are also useful for immobilizing large animals and for killing insects."

This was enough for Apollo. "Hey, Vampire Suck," he yelled

to Demeter outside his hospital door, "Why in icehell did you bring this quack?"

"Hold on, Runt," answered Demeter, sticking his head back in. "Show him the *pictures*, Doc."

After looking at photos of extra ears, arms, legs, feet, double knees, and elbows on various animals and birds, Apollo asked how the doctor accomplished these monstrosities. It was the result, he said, of refined application of chemical shock therapy – dosing an organism with a very specifically targeted nerve toxin. At exactly the correct dosage the toxin would threaten certain nerve tissue with extinction. The cells would fight back with stimulus-response "repel death" compulsive creation, a cellular last ditch "super-effort" to survive by reproducing like crazy. A controlled cancerous response, perhaps, or rather, a targeted cancer. There were serious drawbacks: too little a dose and the poison drove the animal insane, too much and the animal died in a tetanus seizure. It was experimental at best with animals. With rational wolves it was indisputably illegal.

"Illegal or not," said Apollo, "I'll sign whatever waivers you need. But let me tell you, I'm not into dying of the bends like a poisoned shark."

"Oh, that wouldn't happen, trust me."

"How do you know that? And don't ever say "Trust me" again."

"I've already been experimenting, testing on higher species, and I've worked out the kinks."

"Show me the proof of that and I'll consider your treatment."

The doctor pulled off his cape and vest and raised his front legs, or arms. There, growing out of each armpit, were two new fledgling arms.

"Break my mother's back," cursed Demeter. Another made the ancient sign to repel evil.

"These are only three months old," said Dr. Telemachus, "but they are growing rapidly and in perfect simulation of my own arms. I expect they will be fully grown and usable within a year.

"What will you *do* with them, with four front legs?" asked Phocias, another of Pollo's friends.

"I'll amputate them and sell them to someone who needs them," said the doctor in the flat tones of a used wingflap salesman.

"Break my *father's* back, too," murmured Demeter.

"Twice," said Apollo. "Scares the piss out of me, but I have no choice. I'm not going to live my life as something walking on sticks. I'll do it."

"It's illegal," repeated Telemachus.

"So you've said. We'll do it in secret."

* * *

With his friends' help, Apollo set it up. His father sometimes left to go visit Prometheus and Isle, and was gone for at least a day or two. On one such occasion Apollo told the rehab doctors he was getting stir crazy and would go sleepover for a couple days with friends.

Dr. Telemachus said the toxin administration took only a few injections. Key was the dosage and the precision of the injection location. The toxic reaction was spent within hours, he said, after which growth response was accelerated.

"Tell me about this 'toxic reaction,'" said Apollo.

He was told that this was a cell-precise poison. The toxin was bioengineered from donor cell tissue. But it influenced two areas – the targeted tissue and the brain nerves specifically responsible for controlling that area. Both experienced a preliminary "kickback" response.

"Kickback?" asked Apollo, disliking this the more he heard about it. "Preliminary?"

"No one likes to die, not even a cell," said Telemachus.

"So parts of my brain will die," asked Apollo, in what might be described as a toneless tone.

"Nothing unusual in that," quipped Demeter. "You're brain dead from your Death Dives, anyway."

"Shut up, Cat Suck."

"They will *think* they will die," said Telemachus soothingly. "In truth it's just a cellular threat. A chemical reaction well below your physical perception. You may experience a little anxiety."

"Like I'm feeling right now?" said Apollo.

"Exactly," said Telemachus.

"May eagles feed on your frozen eyeballs, doctor, if you screw up."

"I'll take that risk . . . if you will."

"That's fair," said Apollo.

Telemachus extracted blood, some phlegm, some semen (which Apollo insisted on producing privately to the "Pooh pooh, don't be so shy" of merciless friends). Along with some painfully biopsied nerve tissue from the thighs and base of the neck, Telemachus took these samples back to his laboratory to produce the growth serum.

* * *

Days later they were all at Demeter's cave den, Apollo in its back communal sleeping room. They had snuck Apollo out of the hospital for a "party." Demeter and friends were in the front room, drinking ale.

"Don't get drunk!" ordered Apollo. "I may need you."

"You won't need them, Apollo," said the doctor. "Besides there'll be nothing they can do. It's going to be between you and yourself, so to speak."

"And you, doctor. It'll be between you and me."

Not unexpectedly, this made the doctor blink. He looked off a moment, then back. "Apollo, I don't care about the waivers you've signed. You can back out now. We'll call this off."

"I don't want to call it off."

"Fine, then. Now don't be nervous. It's just a couple of shots."

Demeter winked at him and touched him on the arm. *Stay sober,* thought Apollo through the touch telepath line, *I may need you, dog.*

I'll be in the room outside, Poll, pathed Demeter.

* * *

Telemachus had Apollo lie on his stomach. He secured his skull in a kind of vice. He administered shots in both leg appendages, deep injections close to the bone. Soon after, calculating the time in seconds, he gave an injection close to the spine at the base of the skull. Apollo felt only a little tingling, then heat, both in his legs and in his neck. He began to experience a kind of empty stomach queasiness and a little gravity disorientation, which he told the doctor about. Telemachus insisted on giving him a few "mild sedatives," describing them as *very light,* inducing only muscle relaxation with a soporific dream state. Apollo tasted metal in his mouth.

As if he had a choice, he allowed himself to drift off into a drowse.

Within minutes Apollo's perception of his body cranked up – he could feel his heart beat and began to *hear* it, too. Lub *dub,* lub *dub,* lub *sloosh,* dub *sloosh,* SLOOSH *slam,* SLOOSH *slam.* He watched his blood coursing through his body, noticing how many different colors his body was, like one of those instructional clear see-through models that his teacher had used to pull apart and show this organ and that.

This is your heart. He was pleased to see that his heart, in the teacher's hand, was beating. And more than that, emitting musical tones, rather like a chorus, his blood.

And this is your brain. He had thought the brain was a boring gelatinous grey mush, but *this* brain, *his* brain, was a magnificent organ, pulsing with the heartbeat. It contained all the colors of the spectrum, but being the physical if not spiritual seat of thought, telepathy, and memory, notwithstanding being the switchboard of body sensation, it had *sound* and *visual* and *heat/cold, motion/stillness* – his life streaming forth from him, from birth to death, each day, each hour, each minute, each second, unrolling like a spool.

No, it was expanding spherically, a multi-dimensional all-time memory globe of his life, from this moment out into all dimensions, but also his memory of all past moments.

It was deafening.

Curious, Apollo thought, that he had not noticed before that he was six feet above his body, observing it lying peacefully on the bed. And there was that charlatan, quack animal torturer in the corner with eight legs and arms, poised, watching. This was no fun to look at. Besides, he saw that his body, *that body there,* was now twitch-jerking. A little foam was coming from the mouth. Ugly. The doctor was approaching with an absurdly huge hypodermic.

Time to split the scene. Literally, split it in half, seeing the texture of Martian rock, soil and water below ground, and also enjoying flying through the sky above Demeter's house. Seeing Demeter for just a moment with friends, clicking ale glasses together. Just the fleeting thought, *I told him not to get drunk.* Demeter looked up suddenly, but couldn't see him, Apollo, because he was . . .

Flying. Way, way above the house. Above the Canyon, slash of blue white running through it, discernible fish forms swimming in the jade-colored water, striations of earth colors up the canyon walls. The history of the River. Of the Canyon. Flat lands urged up, bent, and folded by early hot planetary forces. Endless falling of rains of all colors – ashen with volcanic breath, blowing, sanding, washing the land, digging it, digging, scouring a channel, bigger, bigger.

Bigger than the planet was the space around it. Beautiful cloud patterns below, far below, the gorgeous living red, brown, and white sphere turning. Now turning in both directions at once, which was peculiar. Past time spinning back . . . and the future rolling forward. Colors, pictures, people, the grand chorus of lives.

The past, looking, LOOKING back to it. It was dark back there. It was . . . obscured. Don't look. Don't know. *Don't know what?* Apollo asked himself, not liking that command. Look, Apollo, *look.* That . . . that. What *is* that?

Them, those things, nameless, floating between the planets. Huge, pyramidal. Spinning. Force lines curling out. Balls of . . . spirits inside the force balls . . . being sent down to his planet, his home. Nothing there at that time. Now there are people. His people. His much, much elder father's father's father. And a clear sphere of . . . what? Something. Something very large and transparent being installed around his planet, far far above it. A nothing there. A thing there being nothing there. Something there.

In his tiny, pulsing, bodiless state Apollo reaches out to touch the vast nothingness sphere in an infinite past moment.

It snaps him. Zaps him! Don't touch. Don't think. Don't *know.* You're not going *anywhere* away from here!

He withdraws his not-there arm of nothingness and rubs his not-there head.

These are bad people, these long ago people in their black, black not-there ships. Ugly. Look away. *The future.* Look into the future.

Our whole history unfolding like the flower of civilization. Beautiful. But then . . . what? What . . . is . . . that? Black energy spitting white, what IS that? It appalls him with its infinitely foreign, dispassionate hatred of awareness.

It hurts. It hurts his head. It is splitting his head. Many heads are growing out of his head. He doesn't *like* this. Better to be in outer space. Better . . .

But his legs really, really *hurt*. They are on fire. Like a dry twig snapping, he is back above his body. He looks down and sees two stumps of different lengths with clear, hollow legs, extending out with paws and claws at the end – transparent, *future* legs. Clear, but filled with fire and smoke.

His head is filled with fire, pressure building, ready to explode. He sees that doctor leaning over him, holding a device, turning a wheel in a device aimed at his, Apollo's, head. The doctor places headphones over Apollo's ears down there below him and speaks into a small microphone. Leaning in close, the doctor is whispering. What is he saying? What *is* he saying?

"You will not remember. You will recall nothing. When I give the signal your body will remember. Your body will respond. You will obey. But you will not remember. You . . ."

* * *

Feeling like a thunderbolt, Apollo snapped back into his body. This did not feel good. His head pained him more than he could ever remember, and his legs burned with pain. But worse, he felt sick, hurt, poisoned, and . . . *revolted* . . . with something being done to him by this person. He tried to sit up, but something was holding his head down. He tried to open his eyes, but something was covering them. He reached up, as if from deep underwater, and . . .

He grabbed the doctor's neck with both arms and slammed the doctor's forehead into his own. Uhh, that hurt. The doctor fell to his knees. Apollo reached up to the apparatus around his head and pulled it off, ripping skin.

"What are you *doing* to me?" he hissed. "What have you *done*?"

Doctor Telemachus staggered and tried to stand up. "You should be asleep."

Apollo turned and grabbed him. "And you should be in the corner. Not . . . whispering . . . whatever you were snivelling in my ear. What *was* that?"

"Nothing. I was programming you . . . to get through the procedure."

You were hurting me, Apollo yellthought at him. *You were wishing me some evil. I feel dirty with it.*

"No," said the doctor. "Your brain is simply reacting to—"

"Don't tell me anything about brains, fishguts!"

Apollo felt profoundly weak, but he summoned up reserve physical strength from an unknown well. He pulled the doctor, who was straining to get free of him, down close to his face and hissed malevolently. "You were intending me *evil* while I was knocked out. You've *poisoned* me."

"No," pleaded the doctor, struggling against his grip. "You're experiencing a reaction, a —"

"Shut . . . up!" Apollo commanded. He fell out of bed. Dragging the squirming doctor after him, held in an iron clutch with his claws biting into the doctor's flesh, Apollo crawled with one arm and two stumpy legs to the doctor's worktable in the corner. Apollo bit and pulled down the tablecloth. The apparatus came crashing to the floor.

"Stop!" cried Telemachus. "Stop!"

"Exactly. I'm going to stop this. And stop you. Is this it?" Apollo asked, picking up a flask with viscous green goo in it. The doctor stared, sweating. "What about this?" Apollo grabbed another flask with reddish green fluid. The doctor's eyes dilated. "Do you know the First Law, Doctor?"

Telemachus looked back at him, stunned. "The First Law?" he croaked through a constricted throat. "Yes. Why? Why do you—?"

"What is it, Doctor?"

"First Law: The act you do, you shall receive." The doctor blurted it out from schoolroom memory, without thinking. The primordial first law of Martian justice.

"Exactly," said Apollo. He pulled the doctor to the floor, jammed the flask into his mouth, and poured the contents down his throat.

Telemachus spasmed. Apollo let him go and watched. The doctor's pupils pinned with fright, and then rolled back into his head. His body stiffened and his back arched off the floor. He tore at his tunic, ripping it off, and beat at his chest where his heart lay. *Thud, thud.*

Finally, he fell back inert, and relaxed into death.

Only then, Apollo became aware of himself and his surroundings. He wiped at his ears and found blood. Vomit dribbled from his mouth. He heard a banging. The door burst open. It was Demeter and Heraklitos. They stared at the chaos of the room.

"I've killed the bastard. I don't know *what* he's done to me."

"Apollo?" asked Klitos, coming toward him.

That was the last Apollo heard, as he lapsed into a toxic unconsciousness.

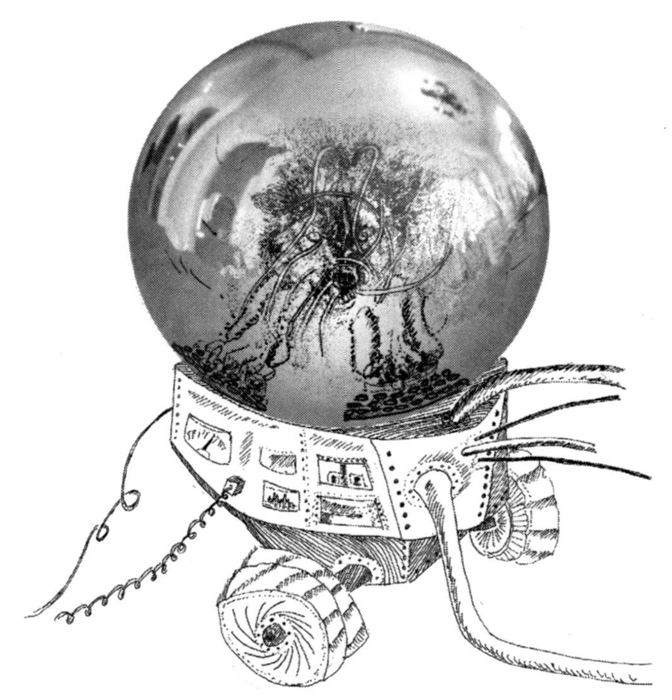

Chapter 7
TRANSFORMATION

On the slippery path toward inventing a new physical form for himself, the first escarpment Prometheus confronted was how not to starve to death. The swordfish had taken too much intestine for him to process physical food. The doctors had tried to bypass the digestive tract by dripping in raw nutrients, but the metabolite end products that would have been created synergistically by his missing organs never arrived at his remaining body parts. The body not only was not growing back, it would not heal. He felt like and was a persisting wound, a pus sack.

A wounded wolf is not a boon companion, his friends found. He had asked his mother to fetch him Heraklitos and Demeter, scientists like him. He shared the problem with them – how to keep his damned body running long enough for him to invent a new body. They told him they didn't know what in hell he meant by "a new body," but staying alive was something they could think with. He couldn't digest, so eating was a waste of time. The body was not responding to precursor nutritional chemicals. What to do? They argued it over while he grew weaker and weaker. Privately they thought Prometheus was demented, and that they were simply humoring his last fantasy before he departed his fractured husk of body. But this was not in Prometheus's plan.

"I feel so weak," he complained one afternoon.

"Of course you're weak," Heraklitos said. "Your body isn't getting any power. An engine with no fuel can't generate power."

"What did you just say?" asked Prom.

"That an engine with no fuel . . ."

"Hang on. There are many kinds of engines."

"Like water driven? Or wind driven?" asked Demeter.

"No, bonehead. Like electrical."

The wolf friends looked from one to the other silently and then touched each others' arms after a moment to facilitate a telepathic network mode of mathematical computation, as in three computers working in parallel on the same problem. Schematic imagery flicked back and forth amongst their minds.

After a long time Prometheus spoke aloud. "So we are agreed?"

"Yes," said Klitos. "But this course of action is the diametric opposite of failsafe. It's near suicide. There will be no way back."

"As though I have a way back," snapped Prom. "The future I have I must create for myself."

"Are you sure about this?" asked Meter.

"Do the Math. Isn't this solution rather elegant?" responded Prom.

"Elegant like sucking the marrow out of your enemy's thigh bone and playing it like a flute," said Klitos.

"Now there's an image!" laughed Prom darkly, the first pleasure he had shown in some time. "Go tell the doctors. Tell them they need to do this today, tonight. If I sleep, I'll starve to death before I wake."

His friends found the doctors, who were talking with his mother. When they heard what Prometheus was proposing they called it insane, delusional or, worse, psychotically masochistic.

But the boys and Prometheus would not relent. Finally the medicos saw Prometheus's back-to-the-wall logic.

"This is what you want?" Isle asked her son.

"One, I have no choice. Two, I want to live."

"But this may kill you."

"So be it. I'd rather suicide trying to fly than lying later out on the ice."

"Your brother tried a desperate solution, too, and is now sick to death. Your father's with him."

"Hell with Apollo. He has half a body more than I do."

Isle looked into Prometheus's eyes. There was force in them. He did not blink, but turned away finally to stare somewhere else.

She talked the doctors into performing the drastic surgical procedure.

Prometheus's "elegant solution" was to convert his body to an electric motor. Trying to run it off organic fuel was useless. He wanted the medicos, therefore, to remove that part of his body whose sole function was to produce and process that organic fuel. He wanted to retain only the heart and the lungs to pump and provide blood and oxygen to his brain and the musculature of his neck, shoulders, and front legs. The nutritional soup they were feeding him would principally service the brain. His heart and lungs would be fitted with electrical stimulators to force muscle contraction and relaxation, bypassing any normalcy or, in fact, power of choice, except by Prom himself tapping a control keyboard under his front claws.

This ghastly process, equivalent to the elementary biology experiment of applying a spark to dead tissue of small animals to provoke muscular contraction, would be constantly painful, which was the next precipice crossing the path chosen by Prometheus.

Prom chose to jump off the cliff. As a youth, when he had felt fear at the edge of a cliff with sail backpack on, he immediately threw himself into the air. Fear was to be met with force.

To solve the distraction of unneeded pain, whose normal function in a healthy body is to warn of injury and hurt, but which would now be a useless metronome in his permanently damaged corpus, Prom ordered the doctors to sever or cauterize many of his nerves. He would, as a consequence, not feel the electrical stimulation. He would also lose the majority of normal biological control over his body, substituting electrical/mechanical. If ever the electricity stopped he was a dead dog. A draconian solution, it was only less threatening than the certainty of being starved into a coma.

"You realize," advised his senior doctor, "that this will buy you only a little more time. Your brain will not long survive. Your tissues will degenerate, not being able to reproduce at the cellular level."

"I'm aware of this," said Prometheus. "I have, you bonecarvers will be happy to know, an even more drastic plan in mind. But I must live long enough to execute it."

He would not reveal this plan. Isle, too, thought Prom had gone stir crazy, as debilitated a state as feral, but not unusual for wolves when kept too long indoors or below ground, and not allowed or able to hibernate. She conferred with Loos, and he agreed with her. The impending finality of a spiraling descent into an energy-starved coma seemed only less suicidal. That would be a question only of waiting. Prometheus had never liked waiting. Here was a possibility of acting, however bizarre the act.

So they acted. The doctors removed "unnecessary" organs, which then would no longer need to be fed and also wouldn't pass on the toxins of decay and rot to the remaining body. Prom was already connected to a blood cleansing machine, substituting for his missing kidneys. They attached wiring to his heart muscles to force their systematic contraction through periodic shocks. The lungs were pumped through mechanical air pressure. The doctors themselves considered the whole procedure barbaric, and muttered Martian similes of "Cats at play."

But the experiment worked. To their alarm, and Prometheus's grim satisfaction, it seemed to result in a kind of functioning system. Prom's brain did not deteriorate, at least not for the moment. He could use his arms, though not with strength, to manipulate his front legs to tap on the keyboards beneath them. And he could speak, see, hear. That's all he wanted, again for the moment.

From his perspective, he was no longer living in a body as an organic self-perpetuating alive-thing. He was temporarily inhabiting a *shell,* as a crab or octopus might. He demanded access to the nutritional data files of the hospital and of the planetary research base. Although Isle felt increasingly desperate and looked as pale and lifeless as he, she worked round the clock with Prometheus and his science friends to develop a variation of energy-carrying, stimulus-rich (that is, drugged) blood serum. This would keep his cellular tissue alive and also, from an alternative perspective, would "preserve" the tissue, slowing or preventing atrophy or mortification – rot.

Prom was making himself into a storybook monster, something remembered from his childhood. He had all the mirrors or reflecting surfaces taken from his environment, or covered up. He did not want to look at what he had become. He hoped to force the metamorphosis to a further stage as soon as possible. Time was not something he had to waste.

The energy-satisfying, cellular-preserving serum he and his friends invented turned out to be a revolutionary, emergency life-preserving nutrient. Isle filed a patent for it on behalf of Prom and his two friends. A pharmaceutical wolf clan bought the rights, or at least made a generous down payment, thus financing the costly continued hospital care for the "Prometheus Engine," as Prom now referred to himself, when he didn't call his body simply a "unit" or "chassis."

Prom intended to leave the organic body behind.

The doctors refused to do anything further. "Medical" intervention was at an end. One had reported to the Elders what was happening, and questions of ethics were already quietly circulating. The Cats had long before done something unthinkable to raise wolfkind from animal to self-aware consciousness in order to enslave and work them. With the ancient defeat of the Felines, experimentation with body and soul had been forever forbidden.

Prometheus considered his options. His brain would survive and function on its chemical soup, or it would not. Everything else in his body was stimulated by electricity, kept running like any motor. All the evidence pointed to the conclusion that his tissues were dying, most being functionally dead, but artificially electro-jerked when needed.

Prometheus took the next irrevocable step. He told his mother to move his life-support apparatus, with him in it, back to the cave he had shared with his friends before the accident. After much written acknowledgement of responsibility-for-self, self-attestation of irrationality, and whatever else wolf justice medicos could think up, the coven of doctors agreed to let him go.

Back in his cave den, with his friends and other intrigued engineering buddies, Prometheus manufactured a self-propelled rolling harness for his body and life support. It was a sphere of half-mirrored glass suspended in a wheeled chassis. Prom could see out, but no one could see in unless he lit the inside. He had developed a profound distaste for others touching, clamping, cutting, poking, prodding him. An on-land submarine suited him fine. At night, seeing him slightly lit inside his chamber, surrounded by tubing, wiring and glowing electrical meters, was as if looking inside a single cell through a microscope, except here it was macro-universe. As in the micro-world, his "cell" was under constant creation, construction, and improvement by its inmate nucleus.

He was perpetually in a semi-bodiless state of mind. Rather than feeling more akin to the spiritual, Prometheus interpreted it as the opposite, an inversion. As one becomes more "spiritual," approaching death, it is as if one departs the body. For Prometheus, it was the case that he could not get *in* a body suitable to him, having virtually no body left. He had evicted himself from his house, but was unwilling to live on the spiritual street. Nevertheless, or perhaps because of his wracked, bent and twisted frame of mind, about which his friends relentlessly baited him, Prom's intellectual reach into the dark unknown burst through any past limits. His Mathematics rose to a level close to how an Old One was thought to compute.

He and his friends perfected his body-support sphere. First they increased the oxygen and air pressure so that it worked as a barometric chamber, lessening need for lung manipulation. Prom programmed the support sphere to become a nearly self-responsible engine. He could not much "feel" things around him. He had intentionally cut himself off from an environment that only hurt whenever it contacted him, so he was physically content with servo-motors moving for him and surrogate perceptors clueing him in to what was going on outside, or *over there* where fleshed wolves lived and communicated to him.

He wanted only to think. His earlier furious temper was now focused on computation, conjuring solutions. Besides perfecting his spherical dark world of mechanical survival, he took a perverse glee in marketing his many little inventions via his mother. Almost overnight Prometheus and his friends became rich, according to the wolf economy of exchange. They were evolving a whole new mechanical programming language, itself a commodity for sale. Hospitals ordered similar life-support spheres. Other damaged wolves moved in around his neighborhood, which took on an ethereal, other-worldly look. Mirrored spheres being carted in self-propelled wagons down streets, going in and out of domiciles. Delivery of electric batteries and strange chemical solutions were the principal connection with the outside world. That and vendors and contract writers, who fed in the trough of profit being made through the sales of evolving robot body technology.

When someone beyond his science and business crew wanted to visit Prometheus, he or she was not welcome. No one was invited. This included especially Prometheus's brother. With Apollo would come his broken but *healing* body, and the possibility of a life now impossible for Prom. Prometheus allowed himself time and energy only for his own sphere of interest.

Prom leant more and more on the clarity of Mathematical universe description, caring nothing for its non-synchronization with the biological world. "Meat people," as he took to calling them, did not agree that he perceived the world with any clarity at all. But Prometheus saw himself floating in the middle of a too-real chasm – on one side, life and livingness, people clothed in flesh bodies, and on the other, mechanical sort-of-living-but-by-a-different-standard people. Between them there was a bridgeless void.

"How are you feeling?" Heraklitos asked.

"Oh," Prometheus answered with acidity. "5.6 volts with a touch of a plus-amperage, more ozone than I would like, and a metallic sulfur taste. And *you*?"

Conversations didn't go anywhere.

Except for Isle. As she had promised at his hospital bed, she had "gone through" with him the succeeding stages of his transformation – abandoning his former sick bed, laying eggs of electricity within himself, creating an other-worldly cocoon, and finally secreting himself within it to undergo chrysalis. Isle was there for each agonizing, depersonalizing step. When visiting the amputees' ward she had felt increasingly estranged, with her still normal body, like a giant among dwarves or a fish amongst sea mines. All the Partial People had fiery tempers, physically manifested. She had learned to be careful what she touched. With them, *everything* hurt. She didn't seem to notice, absorbed in the many details of maintaining existence for Prom and herself, being the plenipotentiary ambassador to the outside world. She barely ate and let her looks go. When Loos came to visit Prometheus's laboratory, she was too busy to talk to him. She had no patience, nor even any longer understood his questions.

"Isle, what's happening to you?"

"What do you mean?"

"You look terrible, starved. And all this . . . this construction yard of metallic and glass objects and . . . wiring. What does it mean?"

"Don't criticize what you don't understand, Loos. Promethean Mathematics are leaving us behind. He has taken tragedy and converted it—"

"Converted it into a jumble of engineering *chaos*," snapped Loos, waving at the mess of wires and, to him, disrelated junk.

"You should leave, Loos. Leave."

"Not before I speak to Prom. Where is he?"

"He's right there," said Isle, pointing to the four foot diameter sphere suspended triangularly between three wheels.

"That . . . is Prometheus? What? Where is he? Inside it?"

"Not *inside* it. He *is* it. He's been listening. If you wish to speak to him, just speak."

"Prometheus is here . . . *there*? And has been listening – and you didn't tell me?"

Isle had no response. Loos looked at the distorted convex reflection of his face, wondering how his son *was,* inside there. He would have felt more comfortable talking to a generator or water purification plant.

"Prometheus?"

No answer.

"Prometheus? It's your father."

He reached out to touch the glass. An instantaneous potent electrical discharge shot up his arm, making all his fur stand on end. It also hurt like hell.

"What was that? What did *that* mean?" he protested to Isle.

"It means he doesn't want to talk to you. I think you should leave, Loos. You've upset him."

"I've upset him. How do you know that?"

"Couldn't you *feel* it?" she responded, with an ironic sneer.

"I'm leaving," Loos said. "Goodbye . . . son." And he walked out. He felt disconnected from the bizarre world of his son, disassociating from the world of his father and other wolves.

Isle watched her husband depart, patting Prometheus, as she now considered the glass orb to be. She felt a silky energy exchange coming back from its surface, the touch equivalent of a purr.

However, she could not predict the future which Prom's Mathematics were calculating into existence. Prometheus was an adventurous soul in a crapped out husk of a body. He had made a container for himself that was an energy sphere, but he was not *that* yet.

He was still trapped *in* his creation. He had not yet *become* it. Not yet.

Chapter 8
JUSTICE

Apollo's rowdy adventure in self-healing with its burlesque theatrical conclusion had become all the scandal. Stars, but there were *drugs* involved! Who did drugs any more, or had for a thousand years? And a villainous deviant medico? The juicy, shameful, illogical, but unquestionably fascinating details of the story made the rounds of the gossip circuit at a speed only family telepathy can permit. Martian news media existed, but these channels of information were for matters of business, government, and so forth. A righteous rocking of the moral boat, something with real turpitude potential, or better with virtuous overtones of heroic bad choice — this was not the stuff for staid reportage, but meat for real chewing.

Violence and death were not the issue. Every now and then a wolf would go feral and rip someone up with his or her claws, or even eat them. That was mere psychosis, which always meant some underlying undiagnosed internal physical illness – worms in the brain, nerve degeneration from mountainous high altitude exposure to ultraviolet. Whatever. These were treatable conditions, and the drama would then be over. If untreatable, the psychotic would die or be helpfully pushed over a cliff to hasten his exit – let the Old Ones sort it out. Usually such a being would find himself much saner without the burden of a bad-chemistry body. Sane Martians did not kill one another. Nor was it a crime to kill a feral wolf before he could hurt others.

No, this case was different. It had conversational depth. There were so many questions with multiple valid answers. Was it wrong of Apollo to experiment with his body in search of full recovery? What about not seeking his father's advice? What about his friends' connivance? And this biochemist? Had he been the effect of his own toxic experimentation? Was he chemically imbalanced from the start, already a victim of his own research? Why had he been pursuing research into forbidden territory? There was something charmingly ghoulish about his growing limbs all over the place — that *was* interesting, now that you thought about it. But what had he been doing, attempting on Apollo the ancient, failed and forbidden sorcery of deep sleep electronic suggestion? On a modern citizen? Certainly he deserved to receive application of the First Law. Therefore, how wrong was it for polluted, deluded, drugged, and truncated Apollo to have executed the First Law on the spot, without benefit of a Justice Council?

There were no actual "trials" any more, hadn't been for a few thousand years. Once the Martians had learned how to read one another's minds (only with permission from each other, of course), questions of doubtful guilt became moot. The facts of a matter could be easily ascertained. Justice Councils now, however, had the much more tortuous task to debate the ethics concerning choices. Could a better choice have been made? If so, who says, and is that person any less biased toward one side or the other than anyone else? Of course, every person was understood to be biased, limited by personal perception, intelligence, and race memory. Hence a Council was needed to work it all out.

The job of a Justice Council was not to argue the niceties of philosophical unanswerables. Its job was even subtler – to study a case of wrongdoing, harm, or disagreement in order to permeate the thinking and personae of all parties involved. The Council had to feel and re-experience events at all levels of comprehension. The Martians called this "permeation" – to be there and experience what had happened. If one *knew* what had transpired, including all vectors of "cause" in the matter, then the vectors of "result" could also be mathematically determined by future extrapolation. One would simply follow the event universe of all possible choices. Although theoretically this was impossible, that was the very thing that interested the Martians. One has to have some such truly juicy mathematical problems to take up the unconscious or preconscious during those half-year long hibernations. Realistically, event universe ethics maps *were* achievable, as most "results" fell into a limited coherent pattern.

Then and only then could a clear Chart of Responsibilities be presented. This was a dangerous thing to dare to graph. The chart inevitably assigned more responsibility than a dog wanted. It was based on an inkling of an Old One concept. Old Ones conceived, it was conjectured, that the universe which exists physically is the detritus of past and current beings' cumulative *lack of* responsibility. Rumor had it that if ever the Old Ones *fully* filled out a universal Chart of Responsibilities – *poof!* Universe gone. Maybe that *was* what they were doing in their queer, wraithlike realm.

Once a Justice Council succeeded in permeating the full truth of a Martian wolf act or event (past, present, and future), then there was no recourse to the Council Judgment. The complex chart of who would do what to whom and for how long in order to solve and balance the cause/result equations was a done deal. Here it is. Now *do* it. The Judged always did. Always. To do otherwise was psychotic, and . . . over the cliff. (Actually, the only recourse to refusing a Judgment.)

If, however, one had created a karmic confusion of such magnitude by reason of one's conflicted event, that is, if one had created an incident the essence and truth of which even a *Justice Council* could not permeate, then there was a mandatorily alternative solution or judgment. The obvious default judgment – one was responsible for one's own condition, *axiomatically*. A more complex way of explaining this was that if a Chart of Responsibilities could not be drawn, there was only one logical understanding. The parties involved in the matter had evolved their own "chart": therefore let them pursue it to its foregone conclusion. If beings created a condition where no one else could be included in the distributive chart of social responsibility, the equation of what is the effect of your act must be answered by the equally axiomatic reflective redundancy of the First Law: That which you have done, you shall simply receive back unto you. It would be hard to dispute the Mathematics of it (for a Martian Mathematician, that is). For every action there is an equal and opposite reaction. (This is, of course, *not* always true, but it will do when you cancel out unperceived or unknowable factors.)

Returning to the issue . . . for the death of Telemachus, Apollo wound up in front of a Justice Council dutifully selected at random from peers and Elders. Others involved could speak to the Council to facilitate its permeation of the event. The public could attend – to satisfy judicial prurience (the opposite of jurisprudence), that social addiction which has afflicted all planets and universes. Such is the fascination of ethics and justice, all for the cause of completing a universal Chart of Historical Responsibilities, you may be sure. Fun was also permissible.

* * *

Apollo had already testified to what had occurred, to the best of his understanding. The Pre-Judged, such as he, were always carefully schooled before a Council hearing how best to attempt the awesome simplicity of "telling the Truth." No justifications were allowed. The act was the act. The *Why* of the act was for the Justice Council to decide. Real Whys must be based on Real Outcomes. "I did this *because* I thought—" would not compute when what one hoped to explain as logically following did *not* in fact follow. Therefore, just the facts. Explanation of precursor factors to an event were expected, but *justifiers* to behavior were forbidden. What happened is what the Council wanted to know. From every vector of viewpoint.

The only real answer to "Why?" would be the Chart of Responsibilities, all boxes filled in across many ethical dimensions.

At the moment Loos was speaking on behalf of his son. Isle had declined to attend: Prometheus was undergoing another of his laboratory crises. Loos StoryTeller was orating, working himself up from being riled and offended that Apollo had conned him into missing out on all the histrionics, to full wrath at the chicanery of bedamned nerve doctors, charlatans all, first messing with his son's body chemistry, secondly attempting the disgracefully humiliating practice of invalidating Apollo's self-responsibility and causativeness through surreptitious subconscious suggestion.

"Clearly, incandescently clearly," Loos said to the Council, "the chemistry tinkerer had partaken once too often of his own transmuting potions."

"You mean, you think he was an addict?" asked Senior Justice Elder, One Ear (his name the result of a youthful Wilding.)

"No," said Loos. "I think he was damaged, lunatic, decidedly much too bent from the straight and narrow to practice in the health field."

"We don't know that," commented another Elder.

"Well, we should!" thundered Loos. "It's the only real question here. Why did he attempt to implant Apollo with something below the level of consciousness? Either he had lawful, scientific reason – of which I assert there is no possibility – or he had brainbite, and was acting out of injury."

"Why don't we find out?" asked Apollo, unexpectedly.

The suggestion was met with silence. The implication was serious. Loos looked to Apollo, who nodded and spoke directly to the Council.

"I relinquish Personal Privilege," he said. "You may look through my mind to locate the moment of the Doctor's passing. If we find him on the Other Side he can speak for himself."

They could not have done so without permission. The only possibility of telepathy is mutual interest. Intervening walls must be made into windows, or there is no seeing in, of course. (Nor out.)

So now they did as Apollo requested. The Council leaned in

to touch each other, with someone touching Loos who touched his son. Instantaneously they connected. The combined Council occupied Apollo's living viewpoint and temporal/mental dimension. Through his memory they found the moment of Telemachus's abandoning his toxically terminated body and twisting away to arrive on the Other Side. With the will of an assembled Justice Council, including Apollo and his father, they looked/felt what the doctor did and thought as he had passed over.

We haven't attempted heretofore to transcribe perception of what we have so cavalierly called the "Other Side" – that is, where Martian Old Ones lived, existed, where they were sometimes contactable. The logics and factors of this "Other World" are vastly different from our own comfortably predictable universe.

Here, in our world, action/reaction is predictable, a matter of course, because, firstly, there *is* a *here.* There is also a *now* that can be defined by the *here* one is living in, "in" implying *space.* Along with space and time, the rest of our physical universe lives are taken up with moving mass around, hence *matter/energy.* Move "outside" this realm, however, and there is still *life,* of course, but it appears to function without the heavy luggage of space/time and matter/energy. Almost without.

It is unprovable by physical universe laws that what later earthling Buddhists would call "Nirvana" can exist. If one is perceiving something, and naming it "nothingness," or even mathematically describing it, it is not "nothing," no-thing, *no* thingness. Even Nirvana is a thing, if only a name. A mental concept.

But the Other Side which was the abode, so to speak, of the Old Ones was an existence where there is no "place" so one cannot position oneself in it by means of "place markers." Without space or place, there is no metronome, hence there is no position in time. Obviously without these there can be no mass, nor movement of mass. Energy, therefore, if there was such a thing there, would be of a different nature. Old Ones thus not only lived a bodiless existence – they were elsewhere and elsewhen from every where and every when of our knock, knock, who's there universe.

Except this description of their "state" is also far from accurate, because Martians *could* sometimes contact Old Ones – through thought. And Old Ones, in turn, could reach the Martians, the alive ones. So Old Ones could be said to have had just a *little* mass (hence a little bit of whenness and whereness) about them. That is, those that the Martians *could* reach or who remained interested enough in the Martian world to be reachable.

But once a Martian did contact an Old One, he/she felt automatically contacted *back*. It was most unlikely that there would be a name tag attached to the Old One, or even that the alive Martian would be able to understand much more than the universally translatable interspecies pro forma communication of "Hello", the announcement of "I am here," or the feelings of "I like you" or "I *don't* like you."

Or . . . (This is where Martian Mathematics/Music come in.) *If* one succeeded in reaching an Old One and said "Hello – I am here," and it answered back "Hello – *I* am here, too!" . . . once a Martian Wolf had done that (no small thing), then he could try to *send* through a further thought, emotion, or mental image. If his spirit radio was finely tuned (and Old Ones were bothering to listen), then that Wolf might perceive that what he had sent/thought *resonated* ("resonated" meaning, "They *got* it and perhaps *understood* it"). On the other hand, he might feel that it *did not resonate* (that is, that They never got the message or hadn't understood it . . . or maybe they just did not *like* the message or *disagreed* with it.)

Is this clear?

In Martian Mathematics it was. But, as explained earlier, many Martian wolves despaired of ever mastering their own mathematics. Again similarities to later Earth.

Hence, Storytellers like Loos FishKiter. Some beings are better than others at telling a story. Listeners gather round and stay through to the end. They may laugh or cry in the middle and may even applaud. All universes like a good story. If the Storyteller is also a good listener, usually a prerequisite to being Teller, if he has the facility for languages and mimicry, and a good memory, preferably eidetic, then people will tell him or her *their* stories. And so the Storytellers of one civilization pass their stories or culture forward to the next. And that's history. Or what it should be, except when university professors or power mad tyrants get in the way.

All wolves could be fabulous Storytellers – after all, they all yearly *dreamt* months of uninterrupted dreams. Sometimes, however, someone *else* was helping tell that dream story. Such as when a wolf woke blessed (or cursed) with the knowledge that another had contacted him from the Other Side. It could be an Old One putting his non-physical foot, hand, or tentacle through the wolf kingdom Doorway, into the Wolf Room in the Universe Mansion. On the other hand it might have been more prosaic, an urgent communication from one's cousin or lover who had momentarily put one foot into the Other Side pool, so to speak, in his or her dream or life. Little children of all conscious species live with one foot still in the Other World, from which they have recently derived. Unfortunately they can rarely articulate well what they see/hear/receive from there. And they also soon lose this faculty. Elder wolves, closer to death, also had one foot constantly on the Other Side. Some Elders had learned to tune the radio and could both send and receive, at least simple messages.

The best Storytellers tended to have evolved to this ability without their consent or desire. Like the blind, the deaf, the paraplegic. Force your ears to be still, and you will hear songs others cannot. Close your eyes forever, and you may come to gaze upon vistas others have been too busy to look for. Hold your body still long enough (by force of will, or through the rough hand of fate), and you may find yourself dancing outside your body footless steps that bodies cannot do.

We digress . . . the Old Ones.

Once a wolf contacted the world or worlds of the Old Ones, of necessity they contacted him. This could be sufficiently startling that the wolf lost his bearings. Having been Touched (tetched), it was not so easy to become unTouched. Thus, it was never *easy* to be a Storyteller, beloved of Old Ones, who are *addicted* to stories. It was damnably difficult to translate impressions from an Old One's elsewhere elsewhen into our here/now language. As you shall see.

To the point at hand . . . what this particular Justice Council had decided to do was, via Apollo's mind and viewpoint, to track someone recently traveled over to the Other Side (pushed across against his will). That person, Doctor Telemachus, in this case, might have been expected automatically to try and get a foot back *in* to the former domain of the physically living. This person could also have been predicted to have taken with him across to the Other Side mental/emotional baggage as a result of his confused exit from Our Side.

We will attempt here, futilely, a transliteration of the babble of image/meaning/sound that comes from tuning in to an Old One radio channel not intended to be broadcast in Our World . . .

The Council accomplished their permeation silently, all eyes closed, and focused through Apollo onto the moment of Doctor Telemachus's death. They reached through to the mind of the doctor himself. What the Council perceived may be very roughly and inaccurately translated as . . .

(Doctor – dying) *Ach, I'm poisoned! Can't breathe . . . So this is what it feels like . . . Ach, air, air! . . . Interesting sensory/motor shutoff of the backbrain, must adjust my formula . . . Ah, I'm gone. Going . . . Hello, what is . . .?*

Old Ones: <A great orchestral sound. Streaks of emerald green and pinky pink. Giant purple circle breaks up into swirls of – eight billion eyes.> *STOP YOUR NOISE!*

(Doctor) *I'm not the noisy one. Your music . . .*

Old Ones: <Silence, enforced with Big Hammer.>

(Doctor, in darkness now) *OK, OK. I'm . . . I . . . where? When?. . .* A flash picture of his mother . . . Then faces of animals from his lab . . . Then the medical police who once arrested him . . . Bubbling test tubes . . . Stepping in pond mud as a pup . . . *Aaahhh . . . (Soundless moan of Telemachus's misery)* . . .

Old Ones: <Eyes again. Looking. Then, worse – no-eyes, not-looking.>

(Doctor) *I shall* GARGOYLE IMAGE *not give* LONG CHEMICAL FORMULA *up! I* EYE . . . *I* EYE . . . Feeling of flying, but no space, no color, not black. *Aaaaahh . . .*

(Apollo's thought, coming through quietly) *Hello. I am here.*

(Council) *Hello. WE are here, too.*

(Doctor) Image of his young face . . . Image of his eyes . . . Image of Apollo on the floor with vomit and blood.

(Council – looking on silently, through Apollo)

(Doctor) (Chemical formula) *me.* (Chemical formula changing, changing, changing.) *not me.*

(Apollo/Council) This is Apollo. This is a Justice Council. You may speak.

(Doctor) *Image of his eyes.* Then Silence. Blackness. Disconnect. Non-blackness.

Old Ones: <Orchestra sound. Soaring green smoke around the non-blackness.> STILLNESS! (they say) <Orchestra sound.>

(Council) This is not good.

(Doctor) *Image of eyes.* (Raw sound of words whispered in Apollo's ear.) Sound of Telemachus saying, "*My voice. My thought. Remake yourself.*" (Vomiting.) EAT THAT . . . (chemical formula) . . .

(Council) Not understanding.

(Doctor) (chemical formula)!

(Council) *Not* good. (sad feeling).

Old Ones: <Billion eyes receding into distance.> <One eye remains, changing into a white spot, into a white hole in the non-black dark, through which light now comes in an increasing strength onto . . .>

(Doctor) *Image of eyes.*

(Council) Goodbye.

(Then comes something . . . different . . . A presence building. Crescendoing . . . Coming . . . Something serious. Solid . . . Huge. Impossibly huge.)

The above transcription misses 98 per cent of the feeling, volume, sense of presence or absence, and a thousand too fleeting details of the difficulty of rationally interpreting such chaos.

You will have to do the Math yourselves.

The Council members opened their eyes and looked at one another in some alarm.

"Storyteller Loos FishKiter?" a Council Elder asked. "Was there a *story* there? It seemed . . . aawwwhhooo . . ." The Elder trailed off into a moaning howl that expressed only complex emotion. No one else in the Council Chamber had anything further to venture for the moment. Everyone sat silently.

Finally Loos spoke. Standing up, he said, "The former Doctor is not well. He was not well. Is, was, whichever term applies here."

"That much *is* clear, at least," said the Council President. "Do you have anything else to offer, Storyteller, in clarification of that chaotic . . . scene? Or Apollo? We're unfortunately dependent on you here."

Apollo had nothing to contribute. He looked down.

Loos closed his eyes and seemed lost in thought. When he opened them, he said, "This Telemachus had mal-intention towards Apollo. But he himself did believe in his chemistry. The formulae had become his world and his future. However, he denied himself compassion *because* of the chemical pathos he had caused other life forms in his earlier biological experimentation. He is now – as a result of what Apollo did to him – worse. Yes, he is damaged."

Apollo nodded his head, eyes closed.

Most on the Council also nodded their heads, expecting more from the Storyteller, who might best unravel the knot of twisted thoughts, feelings, memories, whatever was going on in that clip of

Tweenlives world.

Loos looked down, pensively. "It may be that one Old One, at least, is doing something to . . . umm . . . try to clean him up, to wash him."

Loos sat down. He mumbled to Apollo, "At least, that's what I *think* I saw."

One Ear said, "As good an explanation as any, I suppose."

The Council and all present sat quietly. No one spoke. Then . . .

"Harm has been done *by* Apollo," said the One Ear as Council President, using officialspeak. "Before that, harm had been done *to* Apollo."

"But is it balanced? Is it an equation?" asked another.

"Apollo," asked the President. "What say you?"

Apollo did not speak. His eyes were still closed.

"Apollo?" repeated One Ear.

Loos touched his son. He looked up, alarmed. "I think he's still over there! In the Other World! Something is wrong." *Apollo! Come home! Apollo!* he thoughtshouted to his son. Silence. Nobody home. "Apollo!" Aloud now. Loos shook him. Finally he bit Apollo on the snout.

Pollo snapped his eyes open and started impulsively to get up, but Loos held him in place, looking at him worriedly. *Are you all right, Poll?*

Apollo looked at his dad as if not seeing him, looking through him. His mind was empty of thought. Then a wave of blank, amorphous energy shot from him into the mind of Loos, who let go and staggered back.

To everyone's discomfort, Apollo began to prophesy, in a quiet voice, looking off at something not present . . .

Participating each with this demiurge, you in chrysalis, I the cocoon, the plasma heats, the blood tide's surge transforms the mountain of the moon. The sunken pool rises to break the lake. Its silent dark pulsing erupts into flow. You who have been giving now start to take as the arrow rips all from the unbending bow.

Apollo looked around, trying to get his bearings. The Council Members glanced to one another. Did anyone understand this foretelling? Apollo continued, the same elsewhere look in this eyes.

Time fractures in colors, grey, white, red, Now! and cracks down the middle and opens to sky a new world to the blind wrestler, crying how shall It escape this We to become I.

And thus it is given unto us – Stars – Spirit cleaving from darkness, from void a new Mars.

The Council were shutmouth. For a moment they said nothing. Then One Ear spoke to Loos. "Storyteller? Can you elucidate? This is *your* son, after all."

Loos looked at Pollo, who was digging his claws into the table. He put his paw on the boy. *Nothing. Empty mind.* Loos tried going there to join him, there where his mind was empty. After a while Loos opened his eyes. "I believe," he said, "that Apollo may be saying . . . that the Doctor has been or will be reborn."

"Well, yes," said a Council Member, who was a cousin of the deceased doctor. "Of *course* he will . . . But . . ."

"NO!" shouted Apollo, interrupting. "Don't you *see*? Can't you *feel* it coming?"

Evidently, from his look, Apollo was seeing . . . whatever was coming.

At this, images began to flood through Loos's mind. *Falling things, breaking, cracking.* He looked around in alarm, feeling an imminent threat.

So did the entirety of the Council.

All Martians were attuned to what they were now sensing, the no-force predecessor wave, perceptible by sentient creatures on all planets, that wave which comes before . . .

Marsquake.

Council Members dove for the walls of the cave chamber, where the roof would most likely hold. Apollo was still looking at his prophesied non-place, withdrawn from the moment. Loos grabbed his son and leapt towards the wall, falling over Apollo's body to protect it.

The quake hit.

The floor rose. Fractures snaked up the walls, hissing the ire of an aroused planetary crust. Lights went out. It fell pitch black.

* * *

The quake had been short, but serious. Where the Justice Council members had been sitting the ceiling had collapsed. If they had not been warned (assuming that *was* what Apollo had been doing) and had not moved immediately, some would have been killed. Even so, there were bones broken and other wounds. The electric cave globes flickered light and dark, shorting out. Council members and the attending public fled instinctively toward the exit.

"Hold," cried the Council President. "We're not finished!" Officialspeak.

"But—" protested a Member.

"We're not concluded! Apollo, will you receive the Council's Judgment?"

Helped back through the solid dark into his chair by Loos, Apollo quietly nodded, now more or less back to the moment, enough to pay attention. "I will receive it," he responded according to the formula of the occasion.

Council Members touched the shoulder of each other to establish telepathic contact. Then the President spoke, with official force. "Apollo, Storyteller's Son, the Council's Permeation is complete. We determine that the First Law is in balance. Although wrong was done you, you yourself did serious wrong. However, Old Ones have seen fit to grant you a boon and a doom. You can read the future, at least of soil and stone. Henceforth we shall call you Apollo *Stone Ear* because you can hear and understand the speech of Stone. This boon has already saved lives today and may save more in future. That is good for your skin. You are found valuable to us. All your earlier wrongs are absolved. You are free to go. May your Ear stay tuned."

"And may your tidings be gentler next time, son," murmured Loos into Apollo's bleeding ear.

Just so, according to the Martian Codes, Apollo was found guilty *and* innocent and was condemned to live out his life, however he might, in service to the community through soothsaying. He and his father *both* would do this in future.

As Loos helped him with his crutches to hobble out of the Chamber, Apollo winced.

"My legs hurt, Dad. They hurt a lot. I think they're *growing!*"

Chapter 9
Evolution/Devolution

He was running. His blood was up, and he felt hot. His lope was nearly a full gallop, a miles-eating pace. The air was dry and cold, so dry as to suck out all moisture, bitterly cold. His saliva slobber froze to his ice beard or made a tinkling sound when it fell to hit the ground. He could smell the bear ahead. It was not outpacing him. The scent of the bear's tracks exuded an acid of fear. Dropping his nose, he caught the iron smell of blood. In response, he raised his snout to ululate the howl of the chase . . .

That is what woke him. Within his dream Prometheus had attempted to howl with his real body, inside its spherical chamber. The croak of his true, broken voice pulled him from sleep. He quickly oriented himself. That tiny rounded monstrosity in the concave mirror inside the sphere was himself. He saw the blinking lights of machinery dedicated to keeping his body alive. The unnaturalness of the odors nauseated him – gear lubricants, ozone from electrical parts, chemically mummified flesh, a hellish conflict of messages to his still sensitive canine nose. The only blessing was that, like all creatures, within minutes of waking he ceased to smell himself.

But he could not forget what he was – a half construct, an almost thing, not fully alive, definitely not dead, a chopped-up dog in constant pain.

What am I going to do with myself? Prometheus thought. *I've gone too far to quit. I have to solve this.*

What? What *did* he have to solve? he pondered.

One, how not to feel the dull, incessant pain of the decaying body.

Two, leaping the chasm from this body to . . . something radically different. He had to raise himself to another plateau of body operation. He had to get free of his flesh. It reeked. What was left of it stank of putrefaction.

But leaving would be death.

No, he murmured to himself. *I will solve this.* If the Old Ones could maintain consciousness and memory, of a sort, and communication, of a sort, though none alive really understood them, then he could figure out how to retain his own individual consciousness. Without his body, but able to function, to live, and operate on the physical playing field of life, to which he had chosen not to surrender his lifeline.

As he strove to mathematize himself a new existence or a new carriage for existing, it could be said that he willed too hard. Maybe the tortured tissue that was his brain finally passed the starvation point where the magical elixirs that define life were irreplaceably wasted from his remaining functional brain cells, with all that was left running on lifeless chemicals.

It wasn't a stroke, as nothing burst, but it felt like one to Prometheus. A switch moved irrevocably from on to off, somewhere, somewhen. *My body is betraying me!* he cried silently to the ether, as he plunged into communicationless dark. Into coma.

His last instinctual call was a wordless plea for help. *Apollo!* he thoughtscreamed to the brother he had long since decided to hate, to accuse in the illogical fashion of siblings for his own condition. Even so, the golden line between soulmates still existed. His last line was to his twin.

He made the call. Then all lights were extinguished.

* * *

As had been known to happen in moments of crisis, Prometheus's call was received. Especially between blood siblings or soulmates this might happen, even across great distances. In fact, physical distance was irrelevant.

Apollo clearly heard the cry. He understood all that it meant, for thought does not transport ideas like a train of discrete packages. It sends the entire message at once, non-linearly.

The state of Non-linearity was where Apollo lived now anyway. The Justice Council permeation and whatever else had happened when he was on the Other Side had tuned his psyche to wavelengths from the future. One foot in the "now," but the other three (what there were of them) in the "hereafter," the "here before", or . . . the "non-here/always-here." In fact, ever since his poisoning and drug-enforced journey to death's crossing accompanied by the doleful doctor, not only could Apollo "hear stone," as the Council President had described it, he could hear *other* things, the majority of which he did not understand.

Worse, he could talk back.

Apollo figured he had gone partially, but permanently, insane.

On the other hand there was good news. His derelict limbs were definitely growing. Unfortunately at an uneven rate. Doctor Telemachus's experiment had succeeded, to that extent.

But Apollo no longer cared. He spent most of his time daydreaming, or noodling wordless melodies, talking to things or people not present.

Thus, when Apollo heard his twin brother Prometheus's cry, he simply *answered* it. He did not consider this strange. It was just one more thing he could do now. All Martian canines could telepath if they physically touched. A few could receive an emergency call. But none could talk to the unconscious or comatose. And those that talked extensively to the dead were themselves demented by the process.

Now, however, Pollo started talking to his elsewhere brother telepathically. Prom's brain was now functionally dead. His mechanical body which kept the brain alive and muscles operating no longer had a purpose, as he could no longer command the body from his brain-dead state. Even so, Prometheus *heard* his brother Apollo, whose answer had not been terribly helpful.

What do you want? Apollo responded. Just like a brother.

But Prom could not *send,* other than that one-shot, do-or-die "emergency call." That he could *receive* was based on Apollo's abilities, not his own.

Pollo sent *Can't you speak, Prom?*

He listened to the silence. *Oh.* He examined his brother's state from a distance. *What a mess,* Apollo said, again unhelpfully, as siblings do.

Poll permeated his brother's dark existence, not just the state he was physically in, but how he got there. *Look, Prom,* he sent. *I have achieved something, through my accident with the poisoning. I can now* send *communication . . . but without energy. If* you *could learn to do this, too, you wouldn't need that mush your brain has become.* Send, *Prom.* Send *as though your life depended on it. Send back to me.* Send!"

Or something to that effect is what Apollo thought he was sending. He didn't know what Prom was *receiving* or what he might conceive that Pollo was communicating to him. He didn't have a clue to Prom's internal understanding. Apollo *knew* that something was getting through. That was all.

Prometheus was silence. He could not send. He could *be,* but he could not *send.*

But Apollo could tell that Prometheus could still *think.* As a result of his extraordinary experiences, Apollo could now envision with reality that thought *is* life, that it *is* something other than the physical plane. The prime distinction between Old Ones and Alive Ones was that the alive had bodies and Old Ones did not. Old Ones were also, apparently, demented, or their messages short-circuited through poorly transmitting channels of bodiless perception. Apollo could see that his father and other Storytellers could receive and transcribe or decode Old Ones, but they could not choose when and how to do so. Apollo thought that *he* might now be able to do this.

For the time being he had the problem of his brother's spent, shattered body, with his brother in or around it, but "unplugged."

Without plan, Apollo just "became" Prometheus – reading his brother's internal thoughts with him, having the cognition and realization that Prom would. Pollo had never been any good at Mathematics. Now he found himself, through the cooperative medium of his brother, computing. He took on some of Prom's emotional baggage as part of the bargain. *Stop being so furious, Prom!* Apollo sent. *I can't read you through the . . . amplitude . . . of your anger. You will be fine, Prom. I can feel it. We will work together.*

Apollo got up from his den and hobbled on his new prophylactic legs over to Prom's den/laboratory. By the time he got there he could see they were all in an uproar over Prom's deteriorated state. He heard an emergency medical technician telling his mother Isle to disconnect the apparatus energizing Prom's spherical body cage, telling her Prometheus was no longer sentient.

"You're wrong about that!" Apollo burst out. "Prom's there . . . or . . . here. I can talk to him."

Isle looked imploringly to Apollo. "Really?" she asked. "How do you know this?"

"I . . . I can't tell you, but I'm talking to him."

The doctors and Isle exchanged knowing looks.

"No. It doesn't matter what you think. Give me a chance to help him."

The senior doctor said, "There are no indicators of brain function. He's clinically dead."

"His *body* is a mess, yes, but . . . Prometheus has a chance. Give me some time. To work with him."

Isle asked, "Work how, Apollo?"

"Just give me a day or two. Keep his . . . juices flowing until I tell you to turn them off. Please."

Isle and the doctors huddled, while Prom's and Apollo's friends touched him to path that they were sorry.

Apollo asked to be left alone with Prom. When they were gone he closed his eyes and *felt* Prom. He suspected that if Prom could, he would tell him something important. He concentrated on getting

Prom to be able to get through to him. He could not tell Prom *how*. He just told his brother that it was in his capacity to communicate without his body. "Touching" no longer served, as Apollo had found out. The brain and nervous system were defunct.

It's not energy. Not force, at least, Apollo thought to his brother. *It is . . . having the same . . . wavelength at the receiving end as you're sending. It's* intending *it there. But not pushing. Pushing means force.* He talked at and to his brother in this silent way. But this did not do it. He realized he needed to work on "listening" to his brother's thought with the same effortless intention that he "sent" communication.

He went back out where Isle and the others were, and told them he wanted to work with his brother. He asked them to leave, except for Prom's science buddies. Isle and the doctors left, Isle giving him a dark look and the medicos sadly shaking their heads. Apollo brought Heraklitos and Demeter back to sit beside him. They sat silently, wondering what he was doing, thinking that surely Apollo was going the way of his twin brother. They had lost both of them.

Apollo listened carefully, eyes shut, making himself a noiseless, thoughtless receiver for Prometheus. Finally he turned to Klitos and said, "I don't think Prom knows how to talk *spiritually*. To me, to a spirit. He understands *energy*, electromotive force. Can you rig up a very sensitive device, a focus point, receipt point, which he could concentrate on, which might register a subtle change in energy?"

Klitos and Meter said they could do this, although they thought Apollo was loopy. Within a few hours they had dismantled the brain wave monitoring device and tacked in a kind of "antenna" that would pick energy up directly and register it on the scope that showed the various wavelengths being put out by brain tissue. Now the scope was not physically connected *to* the body, but aimed *at* it, focused on the area of Prometheus's dead head.

"It doesn't matter where you aim it," Apollo said. "Just put it close to me, as it's me he wants to communicate to. I'll try to place myself in the antenna receiver."

Now they really knew he had been eating swamp grass, but they did as he wished. Unfortunately to no effect. They adjusted the scope to variations of wavelength. They even tried focusing parabolic antenna dishes on Prometheus's sphere. This also did not work.

It was getting late. They were all tired and grumpy. Apollo sat and thought. Finally he laughed. "Watch now," he said, and closed his eyes. A few moments later there was a little dip in the scope registration. Then another. And another.

"I told him to fuck off. To be his fucked-up self, angry as he is at everything, to stop doing what *I* told him to do and just be himself — as he remembers himself. An asswipe. He can understand *that* talk."

It was late, towards the predawn dog hours, but they psyched themselves up with the help of skink, the Martian equivalent of a caffeine stimulant drink. They created a game with Prometheus – one dip for Yes, two dips for No. Apollo could ask questions or make statements, and the radiometer tuned to Prom's brain waves, or former brain waves, or to *something*, sometimes registered a response. It worked well enough that Demeter and Heraklitos could see that Prom, if not physically conscious, was within sentient reach of those who were. The responses of "Yes, he agrees," or "Yes, he understands" were, however, spotty. Sometimes Apollo got response. Sometimes he did not. Slowly they reduced and appeared to get . . . weaker, until finally they . . . ceased. Klitos and Demeter were depressed.

"Do you think he's really dying now?" asked Dem.

"No," said Apollo. "He's tired."

"How can he be tired when he doesn't have a body?" asked Klitos.

"He's using 'muscles' he's never used before, that's all," said Apollo. "I know exactly how he feels. It's how I feel all the time."

"Oh, some kind of spirit energy hocus pocus?" quipped Demeter. Then, seeing a look in Pollo's eyes, he quickly said, "Sorry. I'm out of my field here."

"As are we all," said Apollo. "Look, Prom isn't the same now. That much is clear. Let's let him rest or, at least, not have to work at what we're toying with him about. I'll sleep here. Maybe he'll feel or know I'm here. Let's try more tomorrow, or later today."

They squinted at the dawn coming up over the far canyon wall.

* * *

They did try later. Day after day. Slowly, Prom got better at answering. He responded strongly when Isle came close, but could not receive thoughts from his mother. It irritated Isle that Apollo could do something that she, his mother, could not, but she did not state this aloud. As if Pollo couldn't pick it up from the charged atmosphere. She left.

Meanwhile, the chemistry machines continued to pump nutrients and oxygen into the sphere. There was no registry of brain activity, but the heart and lungs continued operating, under electronic and chemical enforcement.

Apollo and friends juryrigged a more complex tuner, separate antennae tuned to slightly different frequencies. Prom could not yet change the frequency of his signal, but he was beginning to be able to aim. Apollo worked with Prom to "focus" so that he could signal to specific pick-up antennae. After a few days it seemed that he, as they of course assumed it was "him", could already register:

Yes
No
More
Less
Number
Want
Start
Change
Move
Stop
Question (or "I have a question")

When the doctors suggested disconnecting power to his body and useless brain, and Apollo sent Prometheus this thought, the radioscope registered *NO-MORE-NO,* which Apollo interpreted to mean, *VERY MUCH DON'T DO THIS.*

Prometheus would not communicate if anyone other than Apollo, Isle, Loos, or his immediate friends was present. This meant he was aware of individual identities, although he could not communicate to them.

Then his science buddies made a breakthrough. They got Prom

to respond to their feeding a slightly amplified electrical input to one of his antennae modules, with a wavelength associated with Prom's communications. Thus if they fed energy to the YES antenna, Prom would answer with a similar communication to the same antenna. Through a game of mimicry, Prom and his friends began to move into repeating, then exchanging data, and soon math and engineering concepts, working towards a more complex receiver/sender.

Exhausted, Apollo left them to their language experiments to go rest in his own den.

Prom became progressively less and less interested in Apollo's communications, judged by his lack of answers, which were about *How are you?* And *What do you feel?* Prometheus was engrossed in the engineering issues tapped slowly into his antennae. Except, that is, at those moments when everyone lost communication with him, could not reach him, or he ceased responding to any call. Then Meter or Klitos called Apollo. From wherever Pollo was physically, he "tuned in" to his brother and then hazarded a guess at the problem. Apollo said that Prom ran out of energy very easily, got frustrated, and then cut the communication. He said that Prom was going to have to figure out how to create or tap into an energy source, usable by him in whatever state, space, or configuration he was.

This resolved rather quickly. As an experiment, his friends worked out a little electric toy car that Prometheus could start and stop, move forward faster or slower, and finally even back up. Making this device do what he wanted it to do seemed to give him a boost, to charge his batteries. Playful success bred energy. Failure or frustration drained it.

Prom's just being a big baby, thought Demeter to Klitos.

Yeah, a new childhood, thought Klitos back. *He's having to learn to operate a new "body" from a new world. How hot is that?*

Time went by. Experiments went on.

Even before Prom had learned to turn his car left or right, which was problematic from his universe where "left" and "right" had no application to a spaceless, non-oriented point of view, Apollo realized the direction Prom's wolf companions should lead him. Prometheus was learning to be a "puppeteer." He needed a workable puppet that he could use to do things of interest to him. This challenge was astronomically more complex than handling communications on the order of *"Can you receive me?"* or *"Start the car."* However, they soon realized that this puppet could be the size of a toy car or as big as a mountain-eating mine digger. Size was irrelevant. The key was Prom having a sufficiently complex signaling device he could use with efficacy. Other than running his car backwards and forwards, he did not yet like to practice with more complex receivers. Making mistakes "lost energy" for him, or that was the apparency. He also refused to try to spell words out by letters. He only wanted to signal a movement or direct a usable physical energy.

"Apollo is the artist. Prom fixes kites," quipped Klitos.

Demeter invented a small glass sphere with a myriad of tiny holes drilled toward the center. He inserted thin, electronically sensitive needles. Prom learned to "occupy" the center of the glass sphere and "touch" one or other needle endings. He preferred them to be different or slightly different metals and for there to be microscopic changes in the configuration of the needle point – triangular, square, hemispheric, pentagonal. He made contact with the different terminals and thus increased his physical manipulation of a puppet device.

They connected the receiver device not only to something that could move, actually to more than one such object, but also to an audio/video screen where squares of different colors could be lit or signal tones announced on audio.

With this primitive construct Prom slowly learned to walk and talk again, or more accurately to instruct his robot puppet to roll and to use sign language.

Then, many weeks into the continuing experiments of inter-world communication, Prometheus's pitiful, ruined biological body ceased to operate, entirely. All cellular tissue ceased to have any live function that was self-motivated. One morning the young medical technician who came daily to monitor Prom's body-thing, the only doctor who would come now, said, "This body is dead."

"What do you mean?" asked Klitos.

"Take a look," said the techie. "The flesh won't respond to electrical stimulus any more. The heart isn't beating. The lungs are absorbing no oxygen. It's just a bunch of inert . . ."

"Garbage," offered Meter, unhelpfully.

Apollo got the others not to mention this unfortunate event to Prometheus, who did not indicate he had noticed, nor even mentioned his body in weeks. Also, not to dispose of the body. But then, two days later, Prom indicated through sign language that he wanted his friends to hook his spherical "Command Crystal" to his body. Evidently he wanted to see if he could force it to move a limb, even a finger.

His friends sent back the message, "BODY NOT WORK. NO ENERGY. NO MORE."

Prom repeated three times his request to connect with his body. Meter and Klitos called Apollo. He thought for a moment and then said, "Go ahead. Connect him to his body. Let him see how workable it is. After all, it's his property."

So they connected Prom up via electrodes. They could monitor his attempts to send impulses to his body, but nothing happened, not even stimulus/response, frog-muscle jerks. There was literally no nervous system to coordinate anything.

Prom signaled the question, *WHAT HAPPEN? BODY NO ANSWER.*

They signaled back, "NO WORK. NO ENERGY. NO MORE. STOP."

Prometheus immediately cut communication to outside queries. He did not send any of his own for two days.

Apollo said, "He's sulking. His body's dead, and he doesn't know what to do. Hey, let him mope. Wouldn't you, if you suddenly found out you'd been dead for a while and didn't know it?"

Demeter and Heraklitos admitted that Apollo had a point.

Nevertheless, Prometheus's friends continued to camp out at his den. What other game was more interesting in town? A few days later a "warning horn audio" woke them up, sounding on Prom's Command Central monitor. A message repeated endlessly on the screen:

WANT NEW MACHINE. MORE BIG. MORE SPEED. MORE ENERGY. NOW.

WANT NEW MACHINE. MORE BIG. MORE SPEED. MORE ENERGY. NOW.

Prom had a new game.

A new species or whole class of sentient mechano-creature had been created. For the moment it was a species of one. But the world would never be the same.

Word spread immediately to the Elders. It was communicated to the Old Ones. *No* one liked it. But it was definitely too late to stop it.

WANT NEW MACHINE. MORE BIG. MORE SPEED. MORE ENERGY.

NOW.

Chapter 10
Tuning the Radio/ Unraveling the Cocoon

Apollo was learning to fly again. His hind legs had grown out enough to be of a length and strength where he could again kick backwards to power wing strokes. Demeter and Heraklitos had constructed a modified flyer for his rear legs, which were still different lengths. Even so, because his weight was not only off balance but also constantly changing with leg growth, Pollo felt like a pup jumping off a cliff in his first sailer.

Still, being in the air was preferable to walking on land, damn right. It's one thing to have one leg a bit stumpy, if two is all you have. You just rock as you walk. But with two gimpy out of four, his body galumphed along in a comic rumba. Young pups snickered and parodied him after he passed by. If he caught on he tried to chase them down, but running twisted his spine like a corkscrew. So he just took up flying again.

It was pleasurable, but without Prom alongside to bait and badger him it wasn't the same. He found himself wanting to soar updrafts to high altitudes to find a place to hang in a stationary on a constant airflow. His friends flew along, but got bored when he opted out of playful maneuvers and so sailed off to divert themselves.

He spent time thinking. Not "thinking," he noticed, but "computing." Doing the Math, as was said. What Math? he thought to himself. I'm no good at Math, always hated it. His mind had a will of its own, like a computer assigned a task where the operator could only wait for its conclusions.

It was *Art* Math, he thought. Philosophical maundering, he muttered. Yet, as he was soaring one day, he found himself considering the relation between caterpillar, pupa, butterfly, and cocoon. What if we are always in a cocoon? he thought. Or if there are cocoons within cocoons within cocoons? Are we always outside one cocoon while inside another? While inside one body we are outside another, perhaps, or after it. If one's "life" were the "caterpillar," death could be a cocoon. There could be a whole life of butterfly and egg before one were born as the pupa. If one's life were the cocoon, death would be the butterfly. How many unseen, unknown cocoons swaddle us? This sequence of thoughts passed through him like a breeze while he was watching the sun light up the flank of a mountain range.

Whoa, Apollo said to himself. I don't do Math. *Whose* Math is this?

Thus it was, with this simple question, that Apollo discovered, first, that he was not always "thinking his own thoughts" and, second, who *was* thinking them.

He had discovered one of the Old Ones' secrets. This was that living "outside" the time/space of physical life upon occasion grew just a little too ethereal for them. No substance. Visualizing "my paw in the slooshy mud," or worse, conceiving the *Math* for it, was a howl away from actual *paw . . . in . . . mud.* More graphically, "bloody meat in the mouth" satisfied more than a bodiless spiritual *image* of it. Therefore an Old One sometimes telescoped from his own non-physical universe through to a Martian wolf (or perhaps earlier a Martian cat) physical universe space. No, not telescope in, *tap* in . . . as in secretively listening or watching. The real "wolf homeowner" in his own wolfish world continued to get on with things – eating, sleeping, screwing, working, playing, thinking his or her own thoughts. But an invisible radio voyeur might be tuning in, listening from elsewhere. The elsewhere voyeur could see the sights, smell the aromas, feel the emotions, the physicality of the elsewhere "house." But it was only a copy, a doppelganger. Like a shoplifter who could look but not steal, or a plagiarist who listens in on a Storyteller and then pretends it is his own story when retelling it later to himself.

Awfully complex, but so are the pretend games of children in all universes.

An Old One listening in to a Martian wolf universe, however, did not *contribute*. He wasn't a hacker, only a voyeur. It was more like having an invisible satellite hovering inside the house, picking up and transmitting what was happening to elsewhere, to the non-space, no-mud, no-paw world outside the cocoon of this life. Via the transmission, an Old One might get some of the pawness, the mudness of life.

But Old Ones did make an effort to be honest and decent about it. They considered they should pay rent for the privilege of partaking of the wolves' touchy, feely, sensation-filled lives. They paid with stolen pictures, memories. The Old Ones discounted what they had to give of themselves from their universe, outside the Martian Wolf cocoon. What does a philosopher cosmologist have to give an ant? Nothing that would make sense to the ant, happily chewing away on life. These old ghosts, however, after haunting a "house," when they finally departed – from boredom or more interest elsewhere – took a keepsake away with them, "snapshots," memory albums from the mind of the owner of the house/body. When an Old One then triangulated in on the corners of a new house, it spread around pilfered memories, sensations, feelings from the *past* house. Body to body, mind to mind, snapshots of elsewhere, elsewhen traveled, but ownerless. The mind was the only cocoon in which Old Ones could pretend to pupate. Pretense was as close as they got to livingness. So the least they could do was spread pretense around.

Somehow the house owners, the wolf landlords, never caught on. The Martians of course knew *of* the Old Ones, but thought they existed only in their own non-transferable world of alien mathematics and physics. Old Ones were safely *over there.* That one's own safely muddy Martian mind could be infiltrated with flimflam detritus stolen from other minds never occurred to a Martian. They presumed that their joys and sorrows were their own, that the sums and fractions of their own existence were their own, not added to, divided, or multiplied by hidden or imaginary numbers from other universes. But so it was.

That is, until Apollo got an answer to his own question, asked of himself while he was soaring above a purple, pink and green Martian sunset. *Whose Math is this?* he thought he was asking himself. Because of his unique experience, being forced into and out of the world of the Old Ones, he had brought back snapshots of *their* world. Old One video clips. He didn't know what they were or what their content was, but his pilfering from their world established the possibility of a radio link, one might say, to his own.

What was even more startling to him was that, in his demented case, it was a *two-way* link.

Apollo had not tried to "send" on the Old One mental radio link. He learned by telepathing to his brother in his bodiless "between-cocoons" existence that he could do something new. But he had never thought to ask an Old One, *What are you thinking?* Now, however, he had just done that. He recognized a peculiarity in the Math formulating in his mind and simply asked, *Whose is this?* Unique among live Martians, he had the ability to tune in to the radio signal. What was unheard of, he got an answer.

///I am doing this Math/// telepathed someone. *///Please introduce yourself///*

I am Apollo, Apollo Short Legs. Apollo Stone Ear.

There was a long silence. Then . . . *///Who is that?///* asked the unseen one.

Good question, said Apollo.

///Good answer/// said no one. Except Apollo had a good clue that this no one was an *Old* no one.

And their strange friendship was born. On the spot Apollo did a little hop, skip, and jump in celebration.

Apollo never learned its name, if it had one. He thought of it as "*his*" Old One. After they had made their nameless acquaintance he occasionally asked a question of it or received a message from it. These were Old One thoughts, not Martian cocoon snapshots, not someone else's thoughts passed on by the Old One, but the Old One's *own* thoughts. Such communications would have been more valuable for an aged Martian, whose life was already filmy and transparent, ready to cross over when he shut off the body. To young Apollo the Old One's thoughts, questions or, as a later earthling Japanese might say, his "koans," were a tonic – an elixir for what ailed him. They scratched an itch he hadn't known he had until someone offered to scratch. He learned new concepts or found words to describe new states. If he found himself perplexed or disoriented, he might get a comment from the Old One. *///Interesting architexture///* it would say, out of the blue.

Once, after Apollo had had a faulty sign language communication with his brother via his "robot" body, he felt morose. The Old One murmured *///You are musick///*

Another time, when Apollo's mother was chiding him for not picking up the pieces of his life and getting on with serious endeavors, the Old One inserted mentally between his ears */// She is minusing you///* Once he went mentally blank, trying to come up with a phrase for a song. He received the wry message *///You thought nought///*

The most intriguing thing Apollo learned, however, while moping and doping around, was that he was developing Old One abilities. He noticed he could enter another's mind or point of view, not theoretically but *actually*. He could *be* the other person, at least for a while, walk around in the other's "house," before his non-body fell out the window or bumped into a mental wall and tripped down the stairs, so to speak.

Once he was sniffing lustfully after a cute bitch who had ignored his whistle. His unpreventable clown walk and catty philosophizing put off attractive females. He was commiserating with himself over this sad state of affairs when the Old One commented, *///Do her///*

What? he asked back, a little shocked.

///Be-do her/// said the Old One.

Huh?

///You want to have her?///

Well . . . yes, if you put it that way.

///Then be-do her///Be – Do her///

And he got it. Tagging along on the spiritual coat tails of his Old One companion, Apollo found himself being the bitch and doing her walk. He was her pert bitchiness that had so attracted his male wolfness. He got into the swing of her every-movement-planned-to-entice-him sashaying along. He was her, doing her. *This is much better than sex,* he thought.

///Well, almost/// someone edited. *///With sex you get to bite and be bitten///*

You old rogue, he thought back to the Old One. (But got no response.)

Soon he discovered he could be/do almost anyone, almost any *thing*. He could "stone" himself, being a mountain. He could "vacate," being a patch of sky. The river was so intense, so pleasurable, so full of laughter and interest, the water touching every surface, wanting to touch and let go, kissing, licking everything it passed by, searching for the sea. He could only stand being the river for short moments.

How empty his past life seemed to him now.

"What are you doing?" one of his friends would ask, finding him standing stonestill, transfixed. "BEing," he would say. The other would snuffle, walk on. But after a time it seemed rather pointless. He could meditate on the treeness of a tree, or the bugness of a bug, which was all very well, but . . . so what?

Eventually he found a marvelous use for be/doing. His father possessed a nearly three foot tall, brightly colored fish hawk, named Chronos. The bird could mimic talking. It almost made sense. Either that, or it had a droll sense of humor. But Chronos got sick. Whatever was wrong with the bird no veterinarian could fix. It was conjectured that it was a strange virus.

Apollo permeated the hawk, fully be/doing it. He felt the pain and heat of infection of the bird. Instead of resisting the foulness of the illness, disliking it, or having any other attitude about the sickness and its physicality, he simply *was* it. He was and did what the virus was and did. It was a life form. It had purpose, if minimal and twisted. It wanted to eat its host and replicate itself with the energy gained. Not a good neighbor to have, but a worse tenant. That was all. Apollo be'd it without any other thought or energy, just its own. And then,being it, he directed his/its will elsewhere.

Within hours Chronos started to recover. The bird also developed a new liking for Apollo, and would waddle over to have its neck feathers scratched whenever Apollo visited. Apollo had become a healer, a real healer.

He wished he could have used this on his twin brother, when Prometheus still had a body, but that was now history. He could, however, help others. He did not advertise, not wanting to be deluged with ill, maimed, broken, and rogue crazies, but he began to help those that he could.

He never fully understood how he did it. He only knew with functional, useful certainty that now not only was he, Apollo, not just his body, neither was he just his own mind and experience. The world was his oyster. He was half-way between being Old One and a Martian Alive. He could travel now from body to body.

But he was master not even of his own. He was still a pegleg gimp, and the bitches would show him no respect.

Chapter 11
Back to Sleep

Managing the mutual crises of Apollo's and Prometheus's catastrophic injuries strained Loos and Isle's relations. As mentioned earlier, they had instinctively divided their time so that each son could have individual care and attention. Because the boys had chosen such divergent paths toward wellness (or whatever new states they had achieved), the more time spent the more each parent absorbed the evolving reality of his or her patient. As if on an ice floe that cracks and floats slowly apart, Isle and Loos began to spend less time together, to feel as distant emotionally as physically.

As their sons passed beyond the immediate physical emergencies, winter approached. Other northern wolf families were preparing for hibernation. It was traditional at this time for clans to host feasts for one another. Farmer wolves had harvested the grain and bean crops which Martian soil and summer light could nourish. Hunters were returning from the mountains and plains with trophies of meat. Now every clan took time to fish.

The canyon rivers were shallower and fish more available. The great swordfishes had migrated back to the sea where there was scope for movement, so it was safe to swim the rivers and catch fish directly by mouth. There was netting and line fishing (and of course fly fishing), but it would be a most unMartian wolf who could resist the visceral call of autumn waters, to toss all garments and tools aside, shoulder harnesses and foot-gloves for the myriad specialties of modern industrial Martian life, to get naked, and just dive into the river and go bite fish.

Day after day of waning light young and old swam, the older with their heads above the surface diving only when they saw a fish to chase. The younger ones stroked underwater, holding their breaths for absurdly long periods to invade the fish lairs. Each would eat what he or she needed for the day, but throw the rest ashore. The larger fish were filleted and cooked in great cauldrons of Martian bouillabaisse. Every few nights the clans gathered and stuffed themselves with grains, beans, fish, and meat, fattening up for winter sleep. In only a few weeks they would need to double their size, mostly fat beneath tightening skins. They drank beers, ales, meads, and grog. Nightly the moons were serenaded with the howling harmonics of drunken song.

Smaller fish were not eaten but captured live in the mouths of the wolves or in fine nets, and tossed ashore to be delicately picked up by the youngest wolves (or the oldest). Their destinations were pools beside the hibernal caves, specially heated by geothermal pipes. There they would grow throughout the winter instead of freezing in the rivers or swimming down to the sea. Feeding on mealy grain stored cleverly in carved out silos purposefully leaking into geothermal pools, the fishlings would thrive and grow to become fat, tasty, nutritious, life-saving treats for the starving post-hibernation wolves, most of whom would lack the energy to chase fish in the tumultuous flooded rivers of spring.

Each family and clan prepared their dens and hibernation caves for the long sleep. This was also the time to repair family upsets.

Before wolves went down to sleep as close as puppies for a comatose nine months, tribal manners demanded that animosities be confronted and muzzled, if not resolved. It was taboo to sleep with hate. Wolf pups born of emotionally torn parents were too often damaged as a result.

Isle and Loos sat down with each other in their den. They had been swimfishing. They shook out their wet coats and toweled each other dry. Over bowls of dark ale they looked at one another, neither finding much to say, not that autumn wolf couples, mated for a hundred years, needed to say much or were always chatty.

"What has become of us?" asked Loos.

Silently, Isle regarded her husband. "Do the Math," she said.

"That is what Prom would say. Would have said," grumbled Loos.

"*Would* say," interjected Isle. "He's not dead."

"No. But what state *is* he in? What has Prometheus become?"

"Ask Apollo."

"I *have* asked Poll," said Loos. "I can barely understand him. He says . . . you won't like what he says."

"What does he say? They're twin brothers. They should know each other."

"Poll describes his brother," said Loos, "as a Young, Dead Old One."

"Prometheus is *not* dead."

"He doesn't have a body."

"But neither do Old Ones."

"Old Ones, however, *are* dead."

"No they're not!" hissed Isle. "They are *not alive*. It's not the same thing."

"Yes, I know. Do the Math. Apollo says that Prom is trying to become an Old One, but without dying. He's trying to be a soul-less, bodiless, dead/alive Old One."

"Soul-less? That's an ice-hearted thing to say."

"Apollo should know. He can talk to him. To *it*. Whatever Prom is."

"Prometheus is not an 'it!' He's my son."

"He's *our* son. Was our son."

"Not was. He's . . . a new thing," Isle said, rising to pace the den.

"A new thing, indeed."

"And what of your Apollo? He's wandering around in some kind of drugged state, talking to the moss, to empty air. He was staring at something the other day, and I asked him 'What are you looking at?' He said, 'Bird droppings are our future.'"

Loos laughed. "That sounds like Apollo. What do you suppose he meant?"

Isle shouted, "He's *your* patient. Your client, bedamn the stars! You defended him before the Council."

"Why didn't you come to the Council? If you'd experienced the Truthtelling you might understand him better."

"Yes," said Isle. "And you would love Prom more if you'd been there as they stitched his guts back together and put him on a false breather, if you had sat beside him as he fought against coma and death and . . ."

Loos let silence absorb her grief or anger, hard to tell. "I love Prom. I love both our sons. But they are very, very different."

"They got that from us. We're very, very different. You and Pollo are Storytellers and artists. You tell the future and read the past. Prom and I are . . . engineers. We make . . . We make—"

"You make the future, or at least the things of the future," said Loos.

Isle sat on her haunches and leaned down to sip from her bowl of warm ale. Prom put his paw on her paw. *We weren't always so different,* he pathed.

Weren't we? she thought back.

* * *

Maybe they were and maybe they weren't.

Like many wolf couples, they had fallen for each other on their first Wilding. Loos was already developing his talent as an artist. He was a singer then, but had not yet become an historian, much less a Storyteller. Isle was a budding engineer.

She was working in geothermal tunneling. Mars was too distant from the sun to have ever grown world-spanning jungles of fern and palm and had relatively sparse pine forests, and so it had not developed subterranean bioenergy reserves like coal or oil. Both for power and for heating, the first resource the Martians tapped into was the heat of the planetary crust, both volcanic and simply down deep where the pressure cooks. The earlier cat civilization had first developed this, cats being real heat seekers. After their world state declined, as civilizations do, upon the rise of the wolves, the ruins of the geothermal sites were re-discovered. They were easily found as the earlier feline digs had created tunnels or pipes that, once the machinery fell into ruin, became conduits for geysers. Isle was helping to renovate these old sites as well as to dig new ones or construct new designs for tapping into the inexhaustible heat of down under.

On that first Wilding, Loos had been a fearless, daredevil, lunatic hunter. He could chase anything down and was willing to take anything on with his twenty-four claws and one set of nasty, pearly fangs. He was wounded regularly and thus much cared for by the young bitches, who would lick his wounds and murmur over him as he made up mendacious songs about his exploits.

Isle was a little jealous because he paid her no attention at all, but bedamned if *she* was going to lick his wounds. She, on the other hand, was all business, planning their marches, husbanding the meat of the trophy kills, and worrying over the idiocies of the young Wilders (no younger than she, but too much obsessed with adventuring and not enough with survival.)

Her skills saved the pack. They were traversing a great tundra plain when she noticed storm clouds in the distance. The others thought nothing of it, as wolf packs simply huddle up to survive a storm, and they were all well fleeced by now with white winter fur coats. She, however, kept an eye on the closing weather, sniffing the air while she gazed at the cloud formation. Rising ozone and plummeting air pressure, detectable by sensitive Martian ears, told her that this would be a killer storm – cold enough to suck the heat from their bodies with its deathly windchill factor. The troop wanted to outrace it, hoping to reach shelter in vaguely seen cliffs in the far distance. But her conservative set of eyes beheld flat tundra, stretching on and on, belying the actual distance. Hope wouldn't cut it. Instead she snapped and nipped at them to halt. She organized digging parties, creating blocks of turf from the frozen ground. Isle had had the foresight, wouldn't you know, to have hidden outside the departure camp a forbidden item for her Wilding shoulder pack – a set of front paw gloves with digger tips. They made great weapons, but also, in this circumstance, served to shape the turf chunks into building blocks. She constructed a low, tight igloo that, despite much grousing, they finished just as the storm hit like an ice hammer. One shewolf was caught by a whirlwind and ripped up into the sky and lost. The rest scampered into their hidey hole, which was streamlined so that the storm blew over without depositing too heavy snowdrifts, but also was sufficiently airtight that the whistling frigid air was mostly kept out, oxygen allowed in. A lot of engineering skill goes into an igloo. All survived.

Loos composed a splendid ballad of praise for her, which he sang at the thanksgiving feast they had a few days later over fresh kill. He included in it some rather flattering remarks about her haunches, her ice blue eyes, and the waft of her tail, enough to smite reason right out of her. She fell in love with him before she knew it, and then to her shame could do nothing about it. What surprised her and all the others, as he was such a romancer, was that he fell in love with her, too. She had a fine body and an even finer mind. And she was moral. She cared for her pack. His nose and the roots of his teeth informed him she would mother a den well, keep it well. She smelled good. It helped that she allowed him to have sex with her, and to his growing interest displayed creative engineering skills in that department as well. They were a match.

She conceived several times during their early marriage, when their clan had lost members. But her pups met with accidents or illness, and all died. Loos never said anything. Mars was hard and unforgiving of weakness, fault, or lapse of judgment. Isle felt an emptiness grow within that she covered with businesslike hard work and muscular engineering. When Pollo and Prom were whelped she felt a real joy, therefore, and determined that *these* two would survive.

Loos became a teacher, renowned for developing a love for learning in his students, even if they did tend under his guidance towards the Martian equivalent of bearded beatnik. After an illness of his own that almost killed him with fever, he was surprised to find that during his illness he had wakened or discovered an "historical" sense.

A Martian "historian" did not *study* history. He was someone who could *recall* it, at least better than others. Perhaps because of his artistic sensibility, Loos became a world-famous bard who could sing of epochs past and gone and bring cold former civilizations to fiery life. Loos grew philosophical as he aged, his memory banks filled with the rise and fall of empires and species. All expected him eventually to go insane. If one thing was known by Martians it was that long memory is dangerous. Memories are inherently toxic: a little stimulates, a little more sedates, and too much kills.

Loos got the cognomen of FishKiter from a popular fable he had invented. The long and short of it described a fish who made and flew a kite that dragged behind him in the water. One day he pulled hard and the kite disappeared above the surface. He continued to troll the line, not understanding that it was "flying" in another dimension, the world of air. A great bird saw the kite and snatched it in its claws. Trying to pull the kite away, the bird realized it was connected at the other end, below the surface, to something outside its airy one. But what? The fish knew he was connected to something, but what? *"What does a fish flying a kite know of birds?"* sang Loos.

* * *

Did the fish catch the bird? thought Loos to Isle. *Or did the bird catch me?*

Which is the fish and which the bird? Isle bantered back, smiling a little.

Loos licked some ale at the corner of Isle's mouth. *Who knows? Who cares?* he thought back to her.

And so they were reconciled. Not with reason, but a simile. Their challenges with broken, half-regenerated boys they put aside for the time, as happened with all problems when hibernation approached.

Isle wanted to sleep through the winter above ground, in Prom's developing robot factory, but Loos would hear none of it. In the case of hibernation the male's word was law. Arrangements were made to feed power and heat to Prom's laboratory over the winter. His friends Demeter and Klitos and Apollo returned to their hibernal clan dens, too. That was that.

They slept the winter through without incident.

It was when they awoke and climbed out of the hibernal cave that Isle finally got the response to her own unanswered question about Prom, which she had voiced to no one: was the New Prometheus alive or dead as a wolf?

As she slowly came to in the post-hibernal pool she had the answer. During hibernation Isle had conceived and born a new pup, a female. However, no one else had died during the long sleep in their den or even during the year before. Except possibly . . . one. The inexorable laws of Martian biology told her that there *had* been one death – her son's.

Their new daughter was the loveliest little thing Isle and Loos had ever seen. (Of course.) They named her the Martian wolf language equivalent of 'Athena'. She was a darling. And one hundred percent "normal," it seemed, at least to her sleepy, waking parents. Looking at his girl pup, Loos remembered, years before, his twin boys. He thought about their diverging destinies and recalled his last question, asked of himself before he had fallen asleep in the hibernal den. He still required an answer. What was Prometheus now? If, according to primordial Martian biology, he had died . . . what *was* he now?

Chapter 12
Addiction & Independence

Winter hibernation, salvation for Martian wolves and every earlier conscious species, was not so for Prometheus, its newest class of being. The problem was simple: he couldn't sleep.

When his friends had set up his laboratory/workshop/factory to feed energy to his equipment throughout the winter months, they had installed a simple recording device on which Prometheus could leave notes – what he was thinking, what was happening, questions he would have for his friends when they returned, and so on. No one had really thought through what the period of hibernation would mean for someone who no longer *requires* the Long Sleep for purposes of energy conservation.

Hibernation is a requisite for carbo-oxidation engines which cannot store fuel/food enough to burn more than a few weeks.

There are multiple routes that life forms take to solve this. One is to slow down the body engine so that it burns less fuel, putting it into a comatose state of hibernation where a bare minimum of body functions burn energy stores. Another is to do the same, but from lack of water – to dig deep, curl up, and become virtually a dried husk of the hydrated life form, a bean, or seed, and to maintain such a state of potential until water does come again to irrigate life, when the withered rootling transforms into a croaking frog again. The dry period can be long, very long. Another survival route is to cocoon and change state, but according to the tick of an incredibly slow clock so that years or decades later, when a pre-programmed alarm goes off, the once worm emerges from the soil as a future cicada to live out its short winged lifespan in a noisy frenzy of feeding and mating before returning to the soil and another cocooned long sleep.

All these solutions involve sleep or a long period of reduced energy consumption, paralleled by stepped down consciousness or awareness.

But what of a form of life not dependent on physical energy, that has no pulsing heart or calorie burning engine? What kind of clock ticks for the bodiless? What is the time span between the ticks, if so? How does a being know that time has passed if there is no physical change of state to monitor, be it heartbeat or change of season? How would such a being, having attenuated or abated his consciousness and slept or accomplished the equivalent of sleep, once awakened, know how much time had passed? *Would* time have passed?

These and a myriad of associated questions confronted Prometheus as his friends hooked up his communication support system for their upcoming months of absence and his first hibernation without a body. No matter where Klitos, Meter, and Pollo slept, once they entered hibernation they would be gone for the winter.

What's going to happen to me? Prom had worried.

Such was the last question he had sent to Apollo and his friends before they departed. *To Friends: WHAT HAPPEN ME FUTURE?*

They knew what he meant, of course. They debated amongst themselves how to answer. It became clear they did not *know* the answer. Their concern was how to confess this ignorance to Prometheus with some kind of wolfsense, charity, or caring – if any of these words still had meaning on the other end of the line in the non-place in which Prom now existed. Finally they gave up, as scientists do when confronted with too subtle communication, so they responded with blunt, if humble, honesty.

"NOT KNOW. YOUR PROBLEM. YOUR SOLUTION. GOOD LUCK."

* * *

Many months later, after coming out of hibe, Apollo and Meter and Klitos raced to Prometheus's lab. Each experienced an internal state of guilt, shame, interest, fascination, and scientific or philosophical curiosity, in varying combinations. What would they find? The worst case scenario would be *nothing* – non-registering dials, nobody home, or now permanently beyond reach.

What they did find, to the contrary, was a laboratory buzzing with movement. All the devices that had been mocked up for Prom to experiment with were whirring, or moving up a few inches and then back a few inches, all of them doing something, but nothing that could be discerned to be productive. Click clack. Whizz whizz. Brrr brrrr.

They trotted over to look at the chronological chart of messages or notations from Prometheus stored on the computer. The last and most recently sent was a shocker. It read:

– *IF YOU DARE.*

Immediately before that Prometheus had sent:

– *To My Friends: JOIN ME.*

Join me . . . if you dare.

Damn, what do you suppose that means? pathed Heraklitos.

Icefire if I know, thoughtbacked Demeter.

Apollo said aloud, "You're both lying. You know very well what it means. It means – leave life as you know it, abandon your bodies, and join me . . . over here. He wants us to go over there."

"What should we do?" asked Klitos.

"We should ask the demented freak what he has in mind," answered Meter.

"No," said Pollo. "First let's read what he sent *before* these messages. What happened to Prometheus over the winter?"

They played back the electronic record of Prom's messages. The last device they had been trying to develop for Prom before they had to leave to sleep had been a direct connection between him and the tools of his workshop. He had had a connection to the computer, the printer, and a very few devices. But they hadn't figured out yet how to put Prometheus in virtual charge of his whole workshop, so he could start to manufacture his own tools or machine new puppets. They knew how to do this, but Prom's own communication system had not yet developed to handle such complexity. He would have to make do with thinking, cogitation, and communicating his thoughts or conclusions, as well as with some minor physical experiments with the apparatus he already knew how to work. From the whirring sounds of the lab workshop, Prom had obviously been up to something. But what?

The message record started off not unexpectedly and sadly.

Some hours after they had left him for the hibernation caves, Prometheus had recorded – *BORED.* Then, later – *LONELY.* Twenty-six hours later – *ALONE FOREVER.* And in succession after that… at different intervals: – *FOREVER?* – *NOT ALONE.* – *WHERE? WHO?* – *HOW? QUESTION IS HOW? HOW? HOW?*

Following that were contact messages sent without content – just a blank, a message of *blank*, which Prometheus had sent them the year before whenever he meant to say, "Contact, but I have nothing to say to you."

After that the messages precipitated into pages and pages of chaos, a torrent of disassociated words and symbols. At least so they first thought. Later in the history of Prometheus, sections of these first hibernal notations became a mantra or prescription for others, a litany to remember for "rite of passage." But for the first three dogs to read them the splattering of words, phrases, numbers, and formulae meant nothing. Zip.

The wolf friends discussed Prom's opening remarks. His first three comments seemed self-evident. There was a time marking for each. The first statement had been sent within hours of their departure. The second hours later the same day. The third the day after. The question "Forever?" a few hours later. They figured the question mark meant that Prom was postulating that he would find an exit from his bodiless site within an achievable time limit. Then there were two days of no communication. Then, in rapid fire, "Not alone . . . Where? Who? . . . How? Question is how? How? How?" Then screen after screen of gibberish.

"Not alone?" asked Meter. "Does he mean he found someone? Did someone contact him?"

"An Old One?" asked Klitos.

Apollo pondered the words. "I don't think so." He wondered if Prometheus was contactable by Old Ones, or was in their universe at all.

///Prometheus has not reached us///Pollo received from out of the ether///

The message was from Pollo's Old One companion, who had evidently been listening in.

Let me know when you're eavesdropping, pathed Apollo irritably.

///Impossible///Always listening///

OK. But have you reached Prometheus? Can you communicate with him?

///No///We cannot///We do not know where he is///

"Trust me," said Apollo to his friends, who were not privy to his private Old One conversations. "Prometheus is not in communication with Old Ones."

"Who is this "not alone?"" asked Demeter. "Us? He realizes we're always with him?"

"We're definitely not always with him," snapped Heraklitos.

"Right," said Apollo. "We don't know who or what he meant."

"Then he goes off into where, who, how," said Demeter.

"Then into the tiger's lair without a nose," said Klitos.

They looked at the messages and the succeeding garble, each silent with his own thoughts. After a while, almost at the same time, Heraklitos and Apollo said, "This is not gibberish."

Klitos was by far the Mathematician of the three. Apollo Stone Ear, Son of Loos Storyteller, was tuned in to spiritual wavelengths beyond the rest of them. Meter was the engineer, the crafter of gadgets, hence his nickname. Klitos said he thought that the formulae and some of the wordage were conceivably dealing with measurements of time.

Apollo said, "Yes. Something like that. Much of this early stuff in the babble section has an inkling of meaning to me. They remind me of moments from Prom's and my childhood. Snatches of song. Quips we made. Images. This is Prom . . . *counting fish,* I think."

Meter said, "Counting fish? Like when you can't sleep?"

"Yes. I think he didn't know how to *rest,* how to sleep . . . in whatever state he was, or is still. When we were there for him, one of us was almost always available to answer up to a question or comment from him. But then we all went to sleep, and he was left only with machines. You know what sleeplessness causes."

They all knew. Missing a hibernation and having to stay awake all winter, a wolf inexorably became a rogue, feral, reduced again to an animal state. A kind of insanity, incurable as far as anyone knew.

"Yeah," said Klitos. "How do you sleep without a body?"

"Ask the Old Ones," said Apollo.

"Do they sleep?" asked Meter.

"I don't know, said Apollo.

///We do not sleep///

Then what do you do? Are you always awake? Don't you rest? Apollo asked his eavesdropping friend.

///We look at cycles of change///We listen to the universe breathe///

"Old Ones rest by listening to the sounds of the universe clicking along," said Apollo aloud to his friends.

"I thought you said you didn't know," said Klitos.

"I just remembered."

"Let's contact him," said Meter. "Let's ask Prometheus. Can you path to him, Poll?"

"I can try. I've been trying for a while, but I've been getting . . . umm . . . a 'busy signal.' I can feel he's there, but it's as if he's talking to someone else."

"Talking to WHOM?" asked Klitos.

"Maybe the 'not alone' guy," quipped Meter. "Try again, Poll."

"Here, lean in, and add your intention to mine to contact him. Just think, 'Hello, Prom.'" They leaned together and Poll pathed to his brother, *Hello, Prom. We're all here saying hello to you. Hello.*

Instantly, the machines in the lab went into a higher gear, whirring and clicking with greater amplitude. Then they shut off. Bang. Apollo and his friends looked to each other, fur standing on end.

"Wow," said Meter.

"I think you connected," said Klitos.

The computer screen blanked. Then came a message. – *WHERE YOU WAS?*

Meter typed in an answer. "WE WERE ASLEEP. HIBERNATING. WINTER IS OVER. HOW WAS YOUR WINTER?"

Some of the machines started up again, whirling and clacking very fast. One began to smoke. – *DANGER. DANGER. BAD. GREAT BAD. NO TIME. ALWAYS TIME. ALWAYS THINK. NOT STOP THINK. THINK THINK THINK. GREAT BAD. NO SLEEP FOR PROMETHEUS.*

"Gods," said Heraklitos.

More than one machine began to smoke or short out. Apollo typed in a message. "YOUR MACHINES ARE BREAKING DOWN, PROMETHEUS. STOP SENDING SIGNALS TO MACHINES. ALL BREAKING. IT IS OK. WE ARE HERE NOW."

The machines decelerated, some stopping. – *LET US TALK*, sent Prom on the computer.

"You got it," said Meter aloud, "time for some good barking. The iceball has been through months of blinded midnight Wilding. He must be horny for woof." He typed in, "YES, METER HERE TOO. WE SHALL TALK. YOU TALK NOW. WE WILL LISTEN."

And they did. Prom had a lot to say. It didn't take long for them to better comprehend what had happened, or to sift through his staccato remarks, which were only gradually becoming more coherent, grammatical wolfspeak, as Prom practiced communicating through the typewriter with embodied persons.

Apollo had been right. Prom had not been able to sleep. And it had nearly driven him insane, possibly had, who knows? In Prometheus's bodiless world, he could not see, nor hear, nor taste, nor, of course, smell – the worst deficit for a wolf. Or if he ever would be able to, he had not yet recovered those senses.

But he could touch. He could sense the electrical connections of his communicator Command Control device. Other than that he could not physically sense anything. Physically.

This did not mean that his "mind" did not continue to function. It functioned all right. It was, in fact, utterly dependent, addicted to sensation, minimally to an inflow of information. In this he was no different from any other wolf. But to live now in a world where there was only *mind*, his mind and nothing else . . .

All wolves experienced "ice white" on their Wildings on the Great Tundra, when icefog and bleary sun and snow made an impenetrable white blank of the world. With no wind, no one speaking, and the smell only of snow, this lack of sensory input, of information, of change, produced a state they called "soul flying." A sensation of having no body, nor control of one's mind. Denied sensory inflow, the mind responded with hallucinatory images to substitute for the lack of its normal diet. On the tundra one could not hurt oneself in this state, unless as one ran in mindless circles one fell into a crevice or ran into the open mouth of a less-whited-out beast. If this state persisted too long some wolves did not recover, but descended into an analytical coma from which they did not return to a sane, super-sentient state such as the advanced wolves had, but only to lower animal sentience – hunt, kill, eat, sleep, defend, procreate.

Prometheus had been living in this white-out, except for him it was infinitely more challenging, a *black-out but with awareness*. He had not realized how dependent he was on his friends' live communication until denied it. He had flipped into a hallucinatory state. Having no body to descend into animal stupor, the retreat available to the live kingdom, he had had to slog through the loss of control over his mind. More accurately, he had had to develop for the first time mind control not *dependent on the body*. Prometheus never actually achieved this, his friends intuited, but he had discovered what to substitute for the calming sensations of the body, which are the last resort of the mind. If nothing else, the Martian wolf mind required a beating heart, the high din of the auditory nerves, the continued smellsong of scent coming into the nasal nerves, the subtle stir of hair follicles by air movement, the warmth of digestion or cooling of carbon dioxide release, even the chemical tick of individual cells running maintenance.

Sleep is a very busy activity in a body, and the mind can rest, afloat a river of low key sensation.

After some desperate experimentation, Prom had finally engineered how to use the new form of "body" to which he was limited. His body was now *machinery*. His need was to supply himself with the sensations of "resting state." Therefore resting became equivalent for him to having various machines just "run," doing nothing in particular, idling. The low signal, clicking electronics of machine interface had to substitute for the communication, "Your body is sleeping."

"Prom needs traffic noise," quipped Meter. "The din of the city that we all love to hate and jump off cliffs into air or run away to the tundra to escape."

"Yes," said Apollo. "Whirring. Clicking. Tick tick tick. But without the terrifying monotony of a clock."

– *MUST DESIGN MORE COMPLEX BODY. NOW!* sent Prometheus.

Let's get to it, pathed Meter.

"Wha . . . Wait!" stuttered Klitos. "What about that last challenge of his? Join him . . ."

"If we dare. Yes," said Apollo.

"You ask him, Apollo," said Klitos. "Path to him. What did he mean?"

Apollo tried to contact his brother about this statement. Nothing came back through the mechanical thought writer. Then came the "blank" message, typed out – *contact, nothing to say.*

"He isn't answering," said Meter.

"No. He's answering that he doesn't want to talk about it," said Apollo.

"Well, ice him, he challenged us. Now he needs to either play or fight," said Meter. He went to one of the machines and tweaked the knobs to send a bolt of electricity through.

"What are you doing?" demanded Apollo.

"You know Prometheus," said Demeter. "He expects, when he challenges you, that you push him back. He's never respected a passive negotiator." Meter sent another charge of electricity through. Then he typed on Prom's communicator: – From Meter: ANSWER. WHY CHALLENGE US TO JOIN YOU?

"*– To Friends:*" came the response. Then Prometheus slowly typed in "*D . . . O . . . M . . . I . . . N . . . I . . . O . . . N.*"

– From Apollo, typed: DOMINION OVER WHAT?

– OVER DEATH. FREEDOM FROM TIME. COME SEE.

– From Heraklitos: COME WHEN?

– COME WHEN YOU ARE READY.

They looked at the bold statement in silence. Finally Apollo said, "What kind of electrical surge can you send that will answer *that,* Meter?"

Meter shook his head. With the cringing stoop of a submissive wolf, he typed . . . – From Meter: YOU WIN, PROMETHEUS. I SUBMIT.

– To Meter: I KNOW.

"Not much more to say about that now," cracked Apollo. "Let's change the subject." He typed in . . . – From Apollo: WHAT KIND OF COMPLEX BODY DO YOU WANT TO DESIGN, PROMETHEUS?

– MANY BODIES. MANY KINDS. LET US START.

So they started.

Their rudimentary lab began to work on better connecting Prometheus to various types of existing machinery. The complexity of the machinery was not the issue, only the communication channel between it and Prom. Prom could move things. He learned to dig. He learned to fly a kite and a simple remote control glider. The laboratory soon became the homing site for young engineering students, and computer pups.

Prometheus's greatest challenge was not to learn the languages of machines. It was to unschool his mind from the habit of wolfspeak, the slow, beautiful art of "words" and "letters." He complained bitterly, disconnecting when he became frustrated with the *slowness* of the "typing-speech" modality. He fried machines, the return equivalent of Meter's sending bolts of energy down his communication channel.

Gradually Prom evolved his thinking process to duplicate the funky yes/no simplicities of binary computer computation. And then he took on the infinite-gradation language of Martian Math. He destroyed lots of machines in the learning process. He sent down the line, as his language improved, that he was not "evolving" but having to "devolve," to forget analytical word/speak grammar and learn the complex speak of cellular chemistry. The gibberish he had sent over the hibernation period had been his early noodling with Martian Math to come up with expressions for his extra-universal perceptions.

To retain his sanity, Prom learned to rest periodically by disconnecting from live wolf signal communication and allowing incoming receipt only to machine self-maintenance signals. Promethean "days" had no consistent length. Sometimes his engineering group had to stay awake in watches to keep up with him. He might then "sleep" for a few days, or only a few minutes. He was becoming free of the long enforced biological school of day and night, light and dark, muscular chemical exhaustion signaling "pause to refresh resources," and the rest of the temporal segmentation of physical reality.

Predictably, all this took an economic turn. He and the other "Prometheans," as members of his expanding support group naturally began to call themselves, supported their expensive endeavors with inventions that spun out from successful experimentation. Mars could use better robot devices, as there were far regions with extreme conditions unsupportive to warm, breathing life. Additionally Prom established maintenance systems for Martian hospitals that could predict better than any existing monitoring devices how patients were progressing physically. More lives were saved. Digging for heat was a constant Martian need as cliff cities or tundral farms multiplied or grew in size. Prom learned to run robot diggers, and to sensitize them to perceive and better interact with the ground they were penetrating.

Isle got more and more involved in this stage of Prom's development. The speed of this mechanical revolution was breathtaking, according to the normal Martian biological calendar.

Elders made sounds of discontent in council, but the sheer economic advantage that Prom's research promised to bring to society deafened the ear of any who would have listened to Elder worries.

What could be the danger in developments that benefit the whole Martian living ecosystem?

* * *

There were other experiments that Prometheus was performing, on his own, in his own world.

By the next hibernation period Prometheus was completely in charge of his laboratories and workshops. He sent his flesh friends and work companions off to their "useless, wasteful, lazy sleep," refusing any suggestion of maintaining an emergency signal to them if he were to run into trouble.

There was trouble. But of a vastly different nature than his friends or anyone else would have predicted.

After the second hibernation wake up, the wolf clans discovered that an exceptional number of patients under intensive hospital care had died. The doctors and nurses who took turns during hibernation periods to rise from sleep and take shifts caring for the seriously ill or hospitalized reported that the rate of deaths had been much, much higher than their wounds or illnesses could justify. Not only that, but towards the end of the hibernation period they had started dying in *groups*. Finding no pattern of physical cause, the doctors postulated that it was some kind of group hysteria, a psychic die-off as had been known to happen after major planetary disasters in the distant past. There had, however, been no such catastrophe to provoke this. Nevertheless there were now rows and rows of frozen bodies tucked into the winter ice, preserved until the spring thaw, when tradition dictated they would be fed to the Great Rivers' fishes or to fertilize the steppe farms.

Apollo had a despicable intuition. He asked his companion spook if it knew what had transpired, but the Old One refused to say anything specific. It sent back a non-verbal, jagged impulse that caused Poll to retch his guts out. Communication enough.

Apollo privately signaled to his brother through his communication monitor: – To Prometheus: WHAT CAN YOU TELL ME ABOUT HOSPITAL DEATHS?

Prometheus had nothing to hide. He also knew he could not be "reached." – *To Apollo: THESE ARE NOT DEATHS. MANY ACCEPTED MY CHALLENGE. JOIN ME IF YOU DARE.*

– THEY *JOINED* YOU?

– *To Apollo: THEY CONVERTED.*

Faced with lingering injury and disfigurement or permanently crippled bodies, many sick or damaged wolves had elected, it appeared, to join Prometheus in his alternate netherworld.

– To Prometheus: CONVERTED TO WHAT?

– *THEY ARE PROMETHEAN LEGIONNAIRES.*

Prometheus's was now a "team" mind.

Apollo was mortified. He trotted away from Prometheus's laboratory out from the civilized pack area into the snows to calm himself with the vistas of empty rolling hills. How had the bodiless Prometheus connected up to the injured in hospital? he wondered. How did they make the transition from heart-pumping body to bodiless robot?

He returned to Prometheus's lab and asked him through the monitor. He also asked to speak to a "Legionnaire."

Contact – but no information.

Neither Prometheus nor any of his nether companions, if they actually *were* there, if they actually were anything like Prom as *beings*, would answer.

Apollo went to Loos and told him what Prometheus had claimed. Loos was stunned, too. The two went airsailing out in the canyon to talk it over. They agreed that they must report it to the Elders.

Loos asked for a closed emergency meeting of the Justice Council. He relayed Apollo's report. Senior Justice One Ear thanked him and asked Loos to leave, without commenting.

Within hours the hospitals were ordered by the Elders to disconnect their communication systems from Promethean Laboratories, even though these had proved so helpful in assisting their medical systems. That Prometheus must have been using hospital electronics to communicate with hospital wolf patients was validated when the pattern of accelerated deaths was immediately interrupted.

One Ear privately summoned Loos and Apollo to his cave den. "What do you make of this?" he asked.

Apollo said, "My brother is a genius, but a damaged genius."

"I don't think you're confronting the real nature of what has occurred here, Apollo Stone Ear," said the Elder. "Prometheus, whatever he or it is, is no longer a rogue *individual.* He is an extra-world force to be dealt with. Our seniormost government agencies will have to consider this and also what actions to take."

"He seems to have made himself into a new form of being," said Loos.

"Not just a new form of being," responded the Elder, "but a new class of society. What does Law mean, what even *is* the First Law, when our world can be reached and our people taken away by forces *outside* our universe, uncontrollable from our side?"

Chapter 13
BIRDBRAINS

I want to speak to those who have joined you, pathed Apollo to his brother.

– *NOT READY,* sent Prometheus back.

Let them be the arbiter of whether or not they are ready! pathed Pollo angrily.

– NOT ABLE. STILL IN RITE OF PASSAGE LEARNING PHASE.

And how will I know when they are able and ready *to communicate?* sent Apollo. *The parents and family members of these dead persons have* questions, *Prometheus.*

– *THEY ARE NOT DEAD. THEY WILL CONTACT YOU VIA OUR COMMUNICATION COMMAND CONTROL WHEN THEY ARE READY. PARENT AND FAMILY HAVE NO MEANING HERE.*

Apollo stood up from the Communication Monitor, which had been spelling out Prom's answers from the other side. He stomped around the lab. *What in hells do you mean family has no meaning?* he pathed. *I'm still your brother and you're my brother.*

The monitor printed out: *UNTIL YOU HAVE BEEN WHERE I AM NOW YOU HAVE NO IDEA WHAT THE HELLS ARE.*

Are you OK, Prom? I'm worried about you. You're my brother.

– *I AM NOT YOUR CONCERN ANY MORE, APOLLO.*

I am your brother.

– *BUT I AM NO LONGER YOUR BROTHER.*

Then what are you?

The monitor displayed – *CONTACT: NO MESSAGE.*

Apollo typed into the system – To Prom: YOU LET ME KNOW WHEN YOU WANT TO TALK ABOUT THIS.

– *I WILL.*

His heart and head heavy with the implications of what his brother had said, Apollo got up to leave the lab. Isle walked in.

"How is Prometheus today?"

"He won't let me talk to the new "converts." Says they're not able or ready. Says he isn't my brother any more. That's how he is."

"Don't exhibit your emotion so much, Apollo. Prometheus is *not* your brother as he was before . . . when he had his meat body."

"Meat body? Are you using that term now?"

"Well, isn't it accurate?"

There was a silence, filled with something like spiritual aether – that substance which must be there when all spirit tries to vacate, but cannot.

"Mother, are *you* thinking about suiciding to join Prometheus?"

The look Isle gave Apollo made him shudder. "I'm considering it, yes. Prometheus has asked me to join him." Her voice tone flat, like Prometheus's typed communications.

"You're *considering* it. And what are your considerations, Mother?"

"That I'm not yet able. That I'm not ready. That I'm afraid."

"Cats crap on the gods, Mom!"

"That is an astute statement, son."

Apollo clumped out of the lab. That is, he tried to stomp, but his mismatched back legs translated this into a hopscotch samba. As he was hop-trotting down the path he felt his hackles rise.

It wasn't "danger," so that could only mean . . .

///Still your heart/// his sentient Lodger whispered.

Cats crap on you, too!

///Impossible circumstance///Calm yourself///

I can't. This is my brother. He's infected my mother, and others too. It's spreading.

///He is no longer your brother///But you are right///It spreads/// Prometheus is the most dangerous thing to have happened to Mars///

How can you say that, when whole civilizations have disappeared before now?

///Because it is true///

Then tell me what to do!

///I cannot///Mars is not my concern///

Then what is your concern?

///You are my concern///

Go fuck yourself. And get out of my mind.

///I do this regularly///And I am not in your mind///

"Cat crap! Cat piss tea!" said Apollo aloud. Those trotting by him stepped even wider afield of the famous nutcase, Apollo Stone Ear, known to talk to himself most strangely as he mamboed down the path. Now he was so furious that those around him could smell Poll's acrid stink, if his flat back ears hadn't clearly signaled it.

Apollo decided to visit his father's den in hopes they could mutually gnaw over the bones of the situation. Loos was not in. Apollo sprawled on a window ledge pillow and gazed out at the splendid canyon view. Loos's pet hawk, Chronos, flew in from another room, screed, and flapped his wings. He was always happy to see Pollo, ever since he had been healed. There was definitely a bond.

"Cat piss!" announced the bird.

"My sentiments exactly," grumbled Poll.

The bird came over and nudged Apollo to scratch its neck feathers, cooing and clucking pleasurably.

"I'm going to have to get Father to teach you something other than cusswords, Chronos."

"Elder farts!"

"I see he's already branching out, but in the same vein."

Apollo looked at the regal bird, which had turned its head to give him the beady eye. I wonder if I can teach this bird to *really* talk, he thought. He concentrated, picturing himself occupying the bird and thinking the thought, "Hello." He intended Chronos to say this. He put some muscle into it.

"Diddle Math doodlers," said Chronos.

So that wouldn't work, at least at this time. Apollo wondered why he could occupy a person, animal, or even stone and feel what it was feeling. He could even introduce changes that would positively affect the health of a living thing, but he could not cause the spirit in that living thing to say or think what he wanted it to, at least not at will.

Because I'm not *them*, Apollo said to himself. I can affect their body, but I cannot *be* them when I occupy them. I mean, Being them is not their Being me Being them.

Ice balls, thought Apollo. His mother despised this kind of noodling. But it or similar trains of thought had been capturing his attention a lot recently. He wanted to understand what was happening with Prometheus, why Prom could not path back *to* him but could receive *from* him? What was this new state that Prometheus "lived" in, and how was it different from or relevant to a normal Martian wolf state? As if there's a "normal" Martian wolf, he quipped to himself.

"I love Apollo," chirped Chronos helpfully. This was a change of thought for the bird, if it knew what it was saying. Perhaps Chronos was picking up on his irritated emotional state, Poll thought. Perhaps Chronos was instinctively trying to help a hurt friend.

Poll looked at Chronos and permeated his space, wondering if the bird *did* love him or if "I love you" was just a tape recording of something taught the bird long ago. He felt that Chronos, or Apollo-in-Chronos as the bird, *did* love him.

This *is* fucking yourself, he chuckled.

But that's what we're trying to do, to conceive a new beingness, he thought. A new being. He knew that he himself, Apollo, was a new type of being, his internal mental garden having evolved into a jungle that had grown beyond his control, with Old One visitors, permeations of others, messages from the planet's crust, and more.

He knew, too, that his brother Prometheus was a new, very different kind of being. He felt sure there was some relation between brothers, other than their being mutually demented – his a more benign dementia, he hoped.

///Time will tell///

Get out! he shouted at his mental hitchhiker.

///Yes///Bird does need a new being///

What did you say? Apollo said, tweaked by the thought.

///Repetition leads to stupidity///

It also leads to music, to art, and to wave forms, you old fart. I meant, "What did you mean by what you said?"

///I said what I meant///

Apollo could see he would get no more from the eccentric, recalcitrant Old One.

Chronos needs "a new being." What did that *mean*?

* * *

Loos came in a while later. He sniffed the air.

"What's the matter? You smell angry."

"I tried to get Prom to let me talk to the . . . uhh . . . newly dead. He wouldn't have anything to do with it. Lied, and told me they weren't ready to talk to me."

"This has the Justice Council's ears pinned back," said Loos. "One Ear's told me he wants to speak personally to Prometheus. I told him to talk to you first. I also told him that Prom doesn't talk to anyone he doesn't choose to. 'I will *order* him to,' he said. 'How,' I asked? 'He's dead!' 'Yes, there's always that,' One Ear said and trotted off, tail tucked, to work out archival law on justice precedents concerning *dead people*."

"Mom's joined Prom's pack," said Pollo.

Loos had been snuffling around his den in a desultory way. He snapped around. "What makes you say that?"

"She said she was thinking of . . . leaving the meat body."

"The *meat* body."

"Yeah. Her choice of words."

"Like *our* bodies. Leaving the *body.* Like dying?" Loos barked, snapping his teeth.

"Don't eat the messenger, Dad. I don't know exactly what she meant, but I think she means suiciding to join whatever and wherever Prometheus is."

"How? How would she *do* that?"

"Don't ask me."

"Who else should I ask? You know more about what's going on with Prom than anyone else on Mars."

"I did once. Prom's gone quiet. He says he's no longer my brother."

Loos thought for a moment. "What do you think? Does he *feel* like your brother?"

"To the extent that a typewriter with a paper printout feels like anything," said Apollo. "I read his responses on paper. I can't *feel* him like I used to."

"He's still my son. Like you."

"What's left of me."

Loos barked out a laugh. "Hells, son, there's more of you than there was before! Will those back legs *ever* stop growing?"

Apollo gave a small howl.

Chronos squawked and strutted over to Loos to pick through his fur with his beak.

"I don't have lice!"

"He's just saying he loves you," said Apollo.

"Who he loves is *you,*" said Loos. "He's never been the same since you healed him. Did you leave some 'doggishness' in him?"

Apollo started to answer.

"Or," said Loos cutting him off, "did you take away some bird brain with you?" He laughed.

"Ha . . . haaa," said Apollo. "Funny you should say that." Then he relayed to his father that an Old One had told him that Chronos needs "a new *being.*"

"You can talk to *Old Ones*?" barked Loos.

Poll realized that he had not yet spoken about this to anyone. "Not really, but sometimes they speak to me. At least one does." He felt a reluctance to tell his dad that he had an Old One practically living *with* him.

"I can understand that," said Loos. "It seems to run in the family. What did the Old One mean, 'a new being'?"

And so they launched into a discussion. The nature of bodies, the spirits that inhabit them, what was the Self, and who, and where did the Self come from? Could it be created or constructed or deconstructed? All of this as if it were a normal doglike chitter chat. Pollo told his dad, with some coaxing, how he could permeate living bodies and affect them.

"Well, stay out of my skull," said Loos, clicking his teeth three times for emphasis.

"There's nothing *in* your skull, Dad," said Apollo.

"Then you *have* looked in there," said Loos.

Apollo busied himself licking at something.

"You weren't joking, I'm sure. Personally I don't spend much time in my body. If I'm not careful the body will fall off a cliff and smack the river before I even notice."

"I feel responsible for Chronos," said Poll, changing the subject. "You know the Law about saving someone from death."

"You share responsibility for the consequences of his future actions."

"Yes, but more to the point and answering your question, I *do* feel I've left part of me inside Chronos." The hawk under discussion was looking from one to the other of them, knowing they were talking about it. "I think the Old One meant that I won't be free of Chronos until he's got somebody there, fully occupying the house."

"He's just a *bird*," said Loos.

"None of us is *just* anything," said Poll. "You know that."

Both wolves looked out the den window down upon the tops of clouds drifting down the middle canyon air, sliding down to the sea.

"You should ask an Old One," said Loos.

"Ask an Old One what?"

"If one of them wants to move into Chronos's body," said Loos.

This caused a physical reaction in Apollo. Too close to home. He twitched, laid his ears back, got up, and walked over to the den's waterbowl, dipped his nose in, and drank. He came back, licking his chops, circled, and sat.

Maybe he's right, he thought. He pathed a note to Lodger. *Would you like to move into Chronos?*

///No/// came instantly, with more emotion than Old Ones normally shared.

Uhh, can you ask around?

///I can///They will not do this///

Will you ask anyway?

///I have done so already///

"What are you doing?" asked Loos. "Your fur's waving as if ghost cats are walking through the room."

"Close enough," said Pollo. "You wouldn't want to know."

"Actually, I would," said Loos.

Just then Chronos jumped off the floor, spread his wings their full width, and gargled as if he were being strangled. The fur on both wolves stood out, electrified. Chronos dropped to the floor, limp as a dead fish.

"Icefire, Apollo, what did you do?"

"*I* didn't do anything."

"What does that mean?"

Instead of answering, Pollo knelt by Chronos. He nudged the hawk with his nose and smelt its breath. "He's alive," he said.

"I should hope so."

Pollo licked the bird and nudged it around with his muzzle.

Chronos twitched and then lay still. He twitched again. He opened an eye. Closed it. Opened it again and raised his head a little.

"Where?" he squawked.

Loos and Poll looked at each other.

"Where . . . *what*?" asked Loos.

"Where . . . am . . . I?" croaked the bird.

The dogs looked at each other again.

"Chronos, you're in my house," said Loos.

The hawk looked at Loos for a moment. Then he looked at Apollo. He said, "Take me home," and then passed out.

Apollo and Loos looked at the comatose fish hawk and then to each other. "Did that bird just *talk* to you?" asked Loos.

"Seems so."

"How's that?"

"Iced if I know," muttered Pollo.

"No, really," repeated Loos. "How is it that that bird can now talk like . . . a person? And to you?"

"Dad, I don't know."

"Whatever you've done, Poll, I think you've got yourself a bird for a while. Take him home. Keep this quiet. You know the implications. I damn sure don't want him here if One Ear comes around."

"I think I will," said Poll. He arranged a cloth litter to hold the limp bird and picked it up with his teeth.

"If Chronos doesn't want to come back here you owe me another pet," said Loos. "I love that bird."

"Mmph," said Poll, as he trotted out with a worried look to his eyebrows.

As he did so, Loos mumbled to himself, "What's going on on my planet?" Waves rippled through his fur.

* * *

At Apollo's den Chronos just slept, with an occasional jerk or twitch. It was a day or more before Pollo even thought of asking his Lodger if he knew anything about this.

///We found a homeless person/// That was all it would say, and then apparently tuned out.

Apollo washed the bird and nudged it now and then. Finally he began moving the bird's wings out and in to pump some life into the sleeping form. The bird gave a few clucks, then jerked strongly. It dizzily got to its feet and then fell back down.

"Toxic reaction . . ." it said.

"What?" said Apollo.

The hawk shook its head vigorously. It looked *carefully* at Apollo.

"You . . . will . . . remember nothing," it said.

"I . . .? What? *Who are you?"* demanded Apollo.

"You will remember nothing," repeated the bird, as if recalling a phrase without knowing what it meant.

Of its own will Poll's body exuded a stink. His tail crept between his legs. He couldn't believe what he was hearing. It wasn't true. It couldn't be true.

The hawk looked around dazedly, then saw itself in a mirror, and gave a great yawp. It gaped at its body. Its neck feathers spread out to full length in protest.

"Awk!" it said. "First you *kill* me. Now . . . *this*. What have you done?"

Then it fell into a faint.

Apollo hoped it was dead, but knew his luck wouldn't run that good. The First Law had come full circle on him. He was mightily the effect of his own cause.

The "homeless person" the Old Ones had found was Dr. Telemachus. The mad doctor he had poisoned to death was now *apparently* living in the body of a giant hawk. Occupying *his* pet.

"Hells," mumbled Apollo. "Poor Chronos. I wonder what happened to him. Is he still in there, in his bird body, having to room with a dead toxicologist?"

Chapter 14
PROMETHEANS

He had hoped that he would be less lonesome, not a singularity any more, once he had brought companions over from his former life. But wherever cause and effect has a one-way arrow, the small print in the spiritual contract contains a second arrow going the other direction – from effect to cause. On this return arrow hitchhike unwelcome new problems. In Prometheus's case, he had earlier been nearly psychotic from his solitude. Now he was smothered by neophytes, who themselves felt alone, lonely, and psychotic. They were blind, deaf, but not dumb, yelling silently in terror at the impossibilities of their new world.

Prometheus asked neither permission nor consent from those damaged and dying Martians whose souls he had kidnapped. He needed companions, but had no social veneer to accommodate them.

His intention was to have workers, doers, executors of his will. Slaves, perhaps, although he considered himself their liberator from a painful to a pain-free, though perhaps not misery-free, existence. The computation was very simple – *one needs, one gets* energy, or sleep, or workers. 'Morality' was old world think, Elder wolf morality, shucked like an old skin. Prometheus might evolve a new ethics in time, but it was low on his list of priorities.

His obsession was machines. *They* were his universe – cause accomplished across a barrier of insubstantiality to mechanical effect. His reality was electronic feedback from commands he sent to machinery on Mars. Until proven different he felt fancy free – he might crash, bash, or smash something on the *physical side* of the command line, over on Mars, but suffer no repercussions back in his nowhere. He reveled in sorting through the problems and confusions of machines under his control. It was a youngster's paradise – he got to blow things up, or screw them up. Same thing. Prometheus postulated Effect A, only to get feedback that some machine had accomplished Effect B instead, or Q, or A^2, ½ A, or -A. He wanted to move a machine from where it was to a wall, but instead it might go backwards, or through the wall, melt down on the spot, or spin in a circle. These engineering errata were highly entertaining to him.

But as he happily debugged this command-and-control, he had run into a serious problem – personal capacity. He had physical recruits helping him with machines on the Mars surface, but he needed more spiritual, *dark* personnel to directly command more machines. Personally he could run a fleet of the same machine to do the same movement, but to control multiple machines accomplishing different tasks was beyond one person's computational skill.

Hence the need for companions, multiple venues of his will to execute his commands.

* * *

It was late at night according to the diurnal wake/sleep cycle comfortable to wolves. It was winter in the northern hemisphere, so doctors and nurses from the southern which was experiencing summer had come up north to help cover the responsibilities of their hibernating colleagues. Northerners provided the same service in return during their own summer and autumn.

Only the night shift nurses were standing watch at this hospital and hospice. Their patients were very elderly wolves, with a few younger cases suffering from serious illnesses. One was a farmer who had been on the losing side of a scrap with a Feral.

All were on oxygen and nutrient drips.

The two nurses chatted and nattered to each other about daily paperwork.

Soundlessly, and without their knowledge, the ward's oxygen and drips ceased to operate. At this facility, the patient beds were still on the new, advanced Prometheus Puppet electronic monitor and control systems . The staff had covertly refused to shut them down after the Elder arbitrary command some time earlier to do so. Thirty minutes later, after the oxygen stoppage, the hospital electricity, also a P-Puppets power feed, went off. The nurses raced down to start up the back-up power supply. This took another thirty minutes.

By this time six of the patients had died.

* * *

The wolf patient, Black Foot, had been a farmer for many years. He was used to hard times, hard work, bad weather, but he could enjoy his ale and liked to dance with the wenches down at the pub in the nearest hamlet. He could use a drink now. It was dark, darker than black, no-color-at-all. Worse, he couldn't feel this body. Worse, he could feel *nothing*.

I must have died, he thought to himself. That cursed Feral got me after all. Shameful. He was not too concerned about being dead. He was a farmer. He knew where new life came from – old life. He would wait to be re-born, whatever that experience might feel like.

Another patient, the elder Wall Eyes, had enjoyed his life to the extent an old codger could remember that there must have been an enjoyable past. The last few years had been less fun, with increasing pain, increasing thoughtlessness, and decreasing bladder control.

Not that that was so fretful. Most of the time he was peeing his own den bed he had been noodling with Old Ones about Math definitions. Now all that pissing was over, he was sure. He didn't know when he had departed his old broken-down husk of a body, but good riddance. He didn't mind the dark. He expected, half-hoped, that the Old Ones might accept him. His Math wasn't too bad. *Hello?* he thought. *Hello? It's me.* He waited for their *hello* back.

And so it was with the others. They each slipped away from the dock of their physical body and drifted out onto the motionless lake. Stars would have been nice, or a light on the far shore, so to speak. But none were afraid of drowning in the no-world that was Tweenlives, which is where they all *thought* they were.

They waited for the inevitable – some kind of continuity, a going on to the next stage. Spiritually, they knew there was no such thing as discontinuity. They waited.

But the inevitable did not come.

No stars came out.

No light on the far shore.

No voice.

After a timeless time, the length between the last heartbeat and the next which never came, not even the first beat of a new pup's heart . . . nothing . . .

Each soul began to emit distress. A tattoo or pulse of extremity in the dark.

No answer.

Now . . . a second, a minute, twenty years, a millennium later . . . all their certainties came undone. Hallucinatory dementia began to substitute chaotic, disassociated, random images and noises for the absence of response from the void.

Still no answer. This continued for an intolerable period. One can tolerate even that, each found. Finally mindfulness itself was gone. Each spirit retained a mere shred of self-knowledge: *I hurt.* There is nothing to hurt. *I call for help.* No one is there. *There is no voice calling for help.* What *is* there is *not* there. And so on.

Then, suddenly, joyously, there was . . . *one . . . thing*. A yellow circle, there in the dark. Each spirit reached out to touch it with the last particle of mind left.

"Yes," it responded . . . with a little *glow!*

Praise creation! There is hope! each thought.

A red triangle appeared. Oh, splendid munificence of plenteous happiness. They dared to touch it.

"No," it responded with a tiny feedback, a frisson of *bad* and *darkening*. Each shrank or attempted to shrink, pulling in nothing from nowhere to a tighter point of self-density.

'Yellow' appeared again. Oh, joy. And then 'red'. Umm, worry. Then a procession of 'white' dots receding into the distance? Was that "distance? " Or were these just smaller dots above each other? They thought, *Distance*? And 'yellow' glowed. They thought, *Just dots*? And 'red' pulsed.

Someone is talking to me! each thought, and praised this moment of salvation from nothingness.

Thus Prometheus introduced each new recruit to the virtuality of the State of Prometheus. Just as he himself had had to limp forward from concepts of "Yes" to "No" and "Here" to "There," just so would he instruct them. 'Yellow' . . . *yes,* 'Red' . . . *no.* And he would learn all the more, all the while he was teaching them. If the State of Prometheus was anything, it was change, change, change. And definitely a learning process. He could not recognize how much, despite his personal pride as an engineer, that his strongest sense of perception would have been schooled to him by his flesh as a wolf. How could it not be?

But he reconstructed now for others how he had first learned to communicate from the *dark* across to his absent brother and absent friends. He remembered deciding not to agree with death, to go on living even if his weak flesh body had failed him. But that did not mean he agreed to abandon the perceptions his body had had! Now he determined to work out how to perceive newly without a body.

Prometheus recalled when he originally had reached back to communicate to Apollo's and Demeter's world, though he no longer had a functioning brain, that there had been, nevertheless, a *palpability* to communicating, as though he was touching something. *What was that sensation?* he struggled to clarify for himself.

He could only interpret it as "taste." Or "smell." Perhaps he was translating one sensation from memory for another in his new world, but smell and taste would have to do. Living wolves in the flesh prided themselves on their ability to smell and interpret complex conditions with great subtlety, utilizing only a few particles per billion. Wolves had come to depend utterly on smell. It had become part of their soul. A wolf saw more with his nose than with eyes. Thus Prometheus reached out with a tiny electrical energy to "touch" a mechanical terminal manned by Apollo and others on "their side" where he had once lived, and through millennia of habit he had interpreted this *touch* as taste – he *tasted* the metal, he tasted the shape, the power, and frequency of the electrical contact.

As good an analogy as any other, Prometheus thought to himself. His brother Apollo heard music in things. Apollo heard stone call out its strain and intention. Wolves also heard much differentiation in howling. How humidity, temperature, and wind affected distance between them. So they had developed a subtle ear, too, as well as a nose. Prometheus, who had given up on wolf bodies, would have been furious to think he was now acting as if he were a hyper-sophisticated *nose.* But there it was, like dreaming in the language of childhood which one has forgotten as an adult. Prometheus's most discerning tool to interpret the complexities of electrical/spirit communication in the bodiless dark was *smell,* which he now utilized as an engineering concept. Do the Math. Martian wolves were kinky for making their thinking complex.

In this manner Prometheus spent the Martian winter hibernations discerning the taste of the wounded and injured in Martian hospitals. He reached out to them and got a sense of each wolf's smell, 'aroma,' some stronger than others but each comfortingly unique. He could not have described their individual odors, because he thought this was an electronic signature. What was significant was that he could discriminate one being from another at a distance by knowing their ghostly scent. Not their body odor, their aroma.

In the second hibernation period, when several hospital patients died of wounds or from diseases, Prometheus paid attention to the aroma of their departure. Whether this was necromancy or wrangling with angels, the moment of death had a distinct aroma to him. The direct opposite of heat, of sex, he thought. The aroma of death was a cool, vaporous thing, like having mist blow by one's face.

Prometheus remembered how he had adjusted himself to taste the electronic frequency his brother and companions had broadcast to him. Prom had learned through practice to sensitize himself to those energy particles zinging through the dark and to interpret them as "communications." When he touched back exact points in Apollo and Demeter's crystal receiver it felt to him like 'blowing' on them. Like giving them his spirit breath, with all the aroma that was him now in it. He was reinventing a bodiless nervous system the hard way. It was all about the fragrance and stink, the scent and reek of life and living, but without the body.

Now, through trial and error, Prometheus attempted to triangulate in upon the dying, to zero in on the separate, distinctly unique tastes of each individual. Each being, as he departed from his body, gave off a dark aroma – perhaps brought his *aroma* with him, like golden dust motes crossing a beam of light.

Although Prometheus interpreted this as a Mathematician, he was really being more like a cook, opening one pot after another, and smelling what was cooking. He *inhaled* them.

This is how he brought them over.

He drank them in.

But when he got one and inhaled him, so to speak, Prometheus discovered that that wolf being now responded to Prometheus as its ultimate source of control. Prometheus could command them. And he could educate them how to do what he was doing. He thought he must have this peculiar, hypnotic ability because he had been the trailblazer of this path to a bodiless life which could reach back into the carnal, mechanical world. Previously there had been no such paths, only a Tweenlives resting point before a newly dead being smelled life calling and instinctively returned to enter the flesh body of a new pup.

After Prometheus discovered he could call the deceased over and command them during their initial confusion, he tuned himself to await these exact moments of departure from life, their *deaths.* He could smell when someone was disintegrating. That meant they would be coming over soon. He waited. Then he began knocking them off one by one, once he had their taste refined to the appropriate degree.

Thus he began to recruit more *pro-actively*.

From the lessons learned in the hard knock school of his own post-death experience, Prometheus schooled his recruits how to become Prometheans. To become like him. Afloat in their sea of confusion, the new Prometheans found themselves more than happy to clutch at whatever oar was extended. This became the First Law of Prometheus, of his World: "In the World of Prometheus, Prometheus rules."

Once they could communicate personally with him, Prom taught the new recruits, or Legionnaires as they decided to call themselves, how to communicate back to machines on Mars. Now they could have something to *do* and an *effect* to create, something to have a saner, more causative relationship with. The Legionnaires were a more than willing team of workers, becoming quickly expert at one or another job or managing a mechanical contrivance on Mars. This was, after all, the only way to preserve their sanity.

Prom did not at first teach his recruits how to communicate with one *another*. Only after their sanity and loyalty were secured did he open their kitchens up to one another, that is, teach them how to *smell* one another in the dark.

Thus he developed lieutenants and a hierarchy of command.

For failed recruits whom he could not pull up from their insane, lost-in-darkness anxiety, or who continued to protest his supreme authority, Prometheus just "closed down the kitchen." With no communication or cause point in the mute, no-sensation dark, the disconnected gave up, *truly* died, and wound up in Tweenlives. This is what Prom presumed. He never followed up to find out what happened to the distraught souls. Those departing from the universe of Prometheus left *non compos mentis*, and they never remembered in their next Martian incarnation enough of what had occurred from the Promethean delusory period to tell anyone else anything coherent about it. Besides, events took their own turn, but that is in the future of this story.

Following that second winter of the sudden die-off of hospitalized injured, the Elders, suspecting his dark arts, attempted to cut off Prometheus from all contact with the hospitals. It did not take them long to discover this was impossible. They could not follow each deceased being into the afterlife. It was traditional to simply await return.

Meanwhile Prometheus Puppetry, with the support of a growing throng of rabid young and punk wolves, leapt into action and promotion on Mars. They made it known their mechanical services were available for hire to do the most arduous or life-threatening jobs on the planet – a hard planet indeed to live on. Through the sales agency of Isle, Prometheus Puppetry offered to construct complex diggers that could be run with intelligent control from the 'Far Side', to dig far deeper than any wolf-controlled machine could possibly go. They could mine channels down to super-hot regions of the mantle to generate mega-power. Their machines could work in impossibly dangerous areas, supervised as if on the site by a driver, who was actually regulating the machine from the dark Promethean world. If a mine were to cave in, only the digger machine was destroyed: its driver was immune from hurt. Crawling robots soon made collection of heavy mineral nuggets from the sub-ice cold ocean floor possible, instigating a "Gold Rush."

Faster than Prometheus or his mother could have predicted, outpacing the efforts of Elders to slow it all down and be careful, Promethean robot machines were in higher demand than could be supplied. Except they were not robots: they were puppets, manipulated by force strings from spiritual masters in another dimension. Whether the operators were themselves sprites enslaved by Prometheus could have been answered only by the *sprites* – and they were quiet on the subject.

In fact, Prometheans did not communicate to the Alive, to "meat people" at all, except about business. One could extrapolate from Prometheus's early experience that the puppet machines were the sinew and joy of whatever "life" Prometheans had. Promethean

Puppets never responded to a live being. Their control could not be short-circuited by the Alive. The machines were all run from control crystals, and who knew where the Prometheans *were* anyway?

Within two years the corporation of Prometheus Puppetry became the dominant economic force planetwide. Mars was industrializing faster than it had since the ancient Age of Cats.

The Elders were horrified.

Chapter 15
HOPSKIP & THE GOOD DOCTOR

"How are you going to rein in your son?" asked the Justice Elder, eyes ice grey. He and his friend Loos were lying out on the porch of the Elder's den office, enjoying the sun.

"Which son?"

"Prometheus, Loos. We'll discuss Apollo later."

"How am I to restrain or have any effect at all on Prometheus?" growled Loos. "He communicates only with his machines and doesn't talk to me."

"You're his father."

"Was. He died."

One Ear laid his ears back against his skull. "If he died, who is masterminding this plot to overtake Martian civilization? Who—"

"I beg your pardon, Elder," interjected Loos.

"I'm not Prometheus's advocate, whatever and whoever he is now. But 'plot?' Where is the plot? Young Martian wolves openly contract with Prometheus Puppetry. And P-Pup, as they call it, is bringing more energy and heat to our cave dens and cities than we have ever had. What's the problem?"

"Ice it, Loos Storyteller, you know what the problem is! This industrialization of our cities is one element. It's unplanned. Although this *should* encourage birth rate, the fact is that it's not doing so. The opposite's occurring. And none of this is coordinated with the Elders."

"That's your plot?" snorted Loos.

The Elder snapped his teeth, growled, and stood, turning his head left and right as if looking for enemies on both sides. "Let us call them *problems.* You are Sire of Prometheus and of your clan. What do you have to say about the continuing deaths and the apparent growth of a coven of Tweenlifers supporting Prometheus, or following his cursed lead."

"How do you know the recently dead are joining Prom, Elder? And if they are, why is this cursed?"

"Because, Loos, some of the Puppetry machines have names, the same names as the dead."

"And some do not – Eartheater, Power Digger – names like the games of pups."

"That's not the point."

"What *is* the point?"

"Why are you defending him?"

"Why are you *attacking* him?"

"Because something ominous is happening, and you know it. Old Ones have always been with us – but they are not *us*. Our dead have always *returned* to us."

"Not all of them."

"Most of them, damn you. You say you're not an advocate, but you're talking like one. The return of our dead to new bodies has provided continuity, the moral basis of our civilization. We come back. To some extent we remember who and what we are. What will it mean, Loos, if more and more of us do *not* return, but instead live, work, or . . . are *enslaved* in the Promethean Tweenlife? Don't you see this threat, Loos?"

"Of course I do," snapped Loos, getting up to pad over to the cliff edge. He looked down to the grey-green river. "Of course I do. I don't know what to make of it."

"None of us know what to make of it. Our future on this planet, not even taking into account Tweenlives, has been placed in doubt, Loos. This is not waves rippling out from a stone thrown into a pool, something we would just ride out. This is the pool itself being *drained*. Did you know that not just the injured are dying and not returning? After the last hibernation the gross number of births at Awakening was only one third of the deaths."

Loos turned to face the grey-bearded, gaunt Justice Elder. "I didn't know that," he said in a low voice. This was very hard for him to confront, one of his sons bringing his race and civilization to a crisis. "You presume that Prometheus is *stealing* our dead?"

"I do," said the old wolf. "If this trend continues we'll die off."

"You don't know that it'll continue."

"We don't know that it won't."

"*That* is the problem," said Loos.

"Yes, that is all our problem, although it seems that no one but a few antiquated Elders worry about it, gumming the old bone. Everyone else is thrilled with the noise of new things, basking happily in the heat of a mechanical renaissance."

Using his snout, One Ear pushed forward a bowl of clear water. Loos licked up a few mouthfuls. Smacking his lips, Loos said, "I wish I could be of more help, Elder, but I'm not in communication with Prometheus."

The old dog scratched behind his ear with his back paw. "But you are with Apollo," he said. "What's Hopskip up to?"

* * *

"Hopskip" Apollo's back legs had finally stopped growing, but they were ever after mismatched, giving him a beloved dancestep walk. He refused any surgery to correct this, hoping he could someday thinkwell his hind quarters (which never occurred). Other related talents, however, continued to develop. Having been poisoned and knocked out of his body, like Prometheus he had not really returned to his earlier state. Whatever he was, a new genius was evolving. On the one hand it helped him to heal others' bodies. On the other it led him onto strange pathways.

Apollo often thought about his brother Prometheus, reaching back from his ineffable realm to Mars's physical world, now permanently removed from him. Pollo pictured Prom like a blind marionette creating a tap dance for an unfelt puppet on an unseen dancefloor, the pitter patter of steps unheard, unseen. Meanwhile, Apollo found himself becoming similarly untethered, afloat in a spiritworld without sail or rudder. Like an aged Elder waiting patiently to pass over into the Tweenlives Far Side, Apollo more and more saw not things, but the multi-dimensional. He saw not just the clockwork of things ticking away. He saw also what contained them, a special ether permeating them which had its own separate but co-existent universe.

"Equal but more than equal," mumbled Apollo to himself, sitting in the purpling dusk, looking at crumbling stone on the far canyon wall. To Apollo something inside the stone, there but separate from the stone, was brightening even as its sunlit surface dimmed. Such perceptual conflict was now a constant for him. He avoided walking into things others did not see. And regularly, to general merriment, he bumped into what *was* there. This disoriented dementia hit snowblind wolves, or those starving or painlessly dying. Sometimes, if they were chemically poisoned, as Apollo had been, the disorientation ramped up to a manic level. But for Apollo this was not manic. It was a gentle thing. Multiple worlds ghosted slowly through each other. Apollo wondered why he was not more bothered.

Perhaps, it was because he was so entertained, discovering the newness of the quotidian. Every day was a fun house of mazes, shifting shapes, surfaces that deceived, dimensions that fooled. Thus Apollo was either dangerous or profitable company. Lunching with friends outdoors, gazing at a hill, he was as like as not to comment, "Water."

"Where?" his companions would ask.

"There. About three hundred feet in, a big cave-in where water has collected. Hot, too."

If it were worth following up, or physically possible, water would be found. Or minerals. Or the ossified remains of an ancient species – whatever Apollo had pointed out.

Those who tried to capitalize on this by dragging him around like a metal detector discovered sadly that his was not a predictable, on-command skill. He was willing, but might just look and say, "Rock."

"We can see that, Hopskip!" the wannabe entrepreneur would snap.

"Stone," Apollo would add unhelpfully.

Worse, he might look fixedly at a stone face, only to jump, yelping "Uh oh" as the hard surface crumbled into a mountain of sand. More than once his friends and he had had to dig themselves from deep inside a dune that moments before had been a bluff beside them. Apollo would laugh and sputter, "How about that?"

Indeed. After it happened to the wall of a residential den and to a public meeting hall, Apollo received fewer invitations to come hang out. He became, however, the darling of pups, who loved him as a creator of games. Middle-aged adults didn't have time for his unproductive waste of time, and Elders rarely heard about Apollo's adventures, because Prometheus Puppetry had captured all their attention. Besides, Apollo's young adult friends made sure the Elders did *not* hear. The job of the Elders was to see that society was stable enough to survive. They were way too conservative for Apollo and his crowd.

Where in another culture or time he might have been called a shaman or magus, Apollo's toying with the laws of nature in Martian wolf society was too likely to be deemed sorcery. His transformation of things was *verboten*, reminiscent of the extinct cats, and good riddance to them too. It messed with the Math. Too many arbitraries. His equations became approximations, became impenetrable obfuscations. Not the direction the Elders wanted to go. Apollo's fooling around was an *anti*-direction, a multiplicity of vectors promising no predictable causal result. Or promising a future where one's head would be in one dimension, limbs in another, and heart beating nowhere. It was mathematically loopy. One would have to be crazy to go there.

There being where Apollo now lived, padding always over the thinnest of ice. Or walking on water, which Apollo found once he could actually do, but only after he had gone hundreds of feet out beyond the ice shelf onto the liquid sea. He realized his error when a Great Fish breached the surface just beside him, targeting him as a warm morsel. Apollo promptly lost his unintended water-walking facility and sank, having to paddle evasively for his life. He tried the trick again, but could not repeat the skill.

As diverting as it was to watch Apollo, *being* him was more a misery than a delight. Having fish in your mouth turn to dust. Or, worse, having your dinner leap through your body smirking at your pale attempt to "eat" when you are "food" and "food" is you. Or sinking unexpectedly into solid rock and having to "swim" desperately until what was liquid became again solid – as it conveniently was for others. Falling asleep in his den, but waking miles outside the pack village, literally freezing to death, disoriented.

Mostly for Apollo this was a new 'conversation'. A simultaneous witnessing, attending, and listening. He no longer needed the company of wolves: he was immersed in comradeship wherever he was. Not merely a jovial camaraderie with things and the air and space around him, but with something more vigorous, more spirited. Whatever his new brotherhood with the stuff of the universe, it was not mellow, nor cordial. Pollo would put his attention on something, not asking a question, just looking. Often as not it would slap him back – with a response or challenge of its own: *"What's it to you?"* or *"So, what are you going to make of me?"* He felt like an intruder, prematurely waking up sleepers in a hibernation den. The world around him was grumpy with his interruption of its long snooze.

At first Pollo took his attention off the ill-tempered thing – rock, rug, pool, cave. He would turn away irritably, wronged by the nastiness he felt. He might even impulsively cuff the thing or scrape dirt on it with his back feet. That would silence it. But if instead he continued to witness, to look at it with no other thought than "I see you," the object of his attention would modify its first rejection. He would feel a tentative reach. *"Haven't you gone away yet?"* things would say. Then a rush of other communication might come – warmth, a

"Hello," or untranslatable communication coming from the qualis, the who-am-I of the thing itself.

Sit and look quietly enough, long enough at something, Apollo found, and it would eventually let him know that it was at his service.

This is when Poll began to bow to water bowls, to raise his paws to a bush. All but his closest friends thought he had lost it. His friends knew that whatever Apollo had lost he had found something else.

Demeter didn't come round any more, working full-time for Prometheus Puppetry. But Heraklitos became a boon companion. "What do you see?" he asked, when Poll stopped walking, sat down, and gazed off at seemingly nothing.

"Hmm?"

"What are you looking at, Poll?"

"Oh. Nothing."

"Poll, talk to me. If you're not looking at something right now, then you must be listening or smelling. What?"

Apollo nodded. "Yes, that's a better way of phrasing it. I'm listening."

"To what?

"To what happened there."

"Where?

"There." A space on the walkway in front of them.

Klitos snuffled the air. "I can't smell anything particular, Someone had a fight or was angry here a while ago, maybe,"

"Yes. That's part of it. But they did so because this space doesn't welcome us."

"This space?"

"Whatever it is, it definitely wants to sleep and wishes the path to be elsewhere."

"It does? Then let's change the path," suggested Heraklitos, moving the guide rocks to shift the walking path inward from the cliff edge. "There. Is that better?"

Apollo listened/looked/smelled for a moment. "Yes."

"How do you *know*?"

"Can't you feel it?"

"Sorry, I can't."

"No matter," said Apollo, and they walked on.

In such a happenstance way, Poll moved through his new world, sensitive to it, listening, accommodating it where he could, witnessing its emotion, taking its cuffs or nips, moving on.

But this was only the world of seemingly insensate matter and air. Where life was involved things were a great deal noisier. In fact, he found it hard to draw the distinction. Anything actually alive in the normal sense did not wait for his soulful witness but hailed him from afar.

He would see someone walking way ahead of him and trot up to him or her. "Sorry about the headache," he'd offer. "I'm not sure what's causing it."

"How did you know I have a headache?" the startled wolf might say and, looking at him, ask "Aren't you Apollo? Hopskip?"

"Yes."

"Oh, that explains it."

"Do you want me to do something about it?"

"My headache? No, I . . . well, it seems to be . . . seems better. Gone actually. Well."

"Oh? Good, good. You're welcome!" Apollo would say, jogging off before his surprised victim could say thank you, if he thought to say anything.

Between body pains that glowed for him like pathway lamps, or unresolved upsets between family members or lovers, unspoken business disputes, even someone's plans for mischief or malice, Apollo tried to weave the path of least resistance. He did not want to interfere in everyone else's life. But their lives spoke to him just the same. Not just wolves. Plants called for water. Fish. He had a hell of a time catching river trout because, if he could read their minds, they apparently could read his. He finally schooled himself to dog paddle along and simply think, "Hungry." Soon a fish would martyr itself, jumping straight into his mouth.

Apollo took to staying home to avoid the rattle and bother of the outside universe as it clamored for his attention. Those who wanted healing came instead to him – just to sit for a while and then, feeling better, express their thanks and leave, giving food or a trinket in exchange. Thus Pollo kept himself fed and occupied. He lived his life to the extent that the leash of these new responsibilities allowed him circuit.

Unfortunately there was Chronos. Or *Doctor* Chronos, as the hawk now demanded to be called. At home Apollo's enhanced perceptive skill was a misery for him. If he thoughtlessly tuned in to Chronos's internal universe, it was dialing for madness. No doubt the bird *was* the former Dr. Telemachus, or some evolution or devolution of him. He refused the name "Telemachus," which would send the bird into a tirade always ending in some collapse equivalent of a seizure. Apollo would softly nose him awake, asking, "Chronos, you still there?"

The bird would open one eye and squawk, "No. Chronos, whoever *that* is, is not here any more."

"Telemachus?"

"Do NOT call me that! Whoever I was, and whatever you have *done* to me, I'm not him any more. Calling me *Doctor* Chronos will do."

"But I didn't do anything to you."

"Then how did I get here? All feathered and birdified?"

"Honestly, I don't know."

"Cat crap."

"Besides, it wasn't I that did something to you. *You* tried to poison me and perform some kind of hypnotic . . ."

"I didn't poison you. I was chemically forcing your legs to grow back, which it looks like they did. You owe me. Pay up."

"I don't owe you anything."

"You poisoned me to *death*. You owe me."

"I didn't poison you. I merely poured back into your mouth what you had given me in the first place!"

"It was too much. An overdose."

"How was I to know that?"

"You owe me. I died."

"Well, you deserved it. The Justice Council said so – First Law. First Law. Besides, you were a crappy doctor. Look at my goofball body. People call me Hopskip."

"Well, if I deserved what you did then you deserve what I did. At least you got something out of it – new legs."

"And you got something too! Ice it, you're better looking now than you were before!"

Then Chronos would fly at him with claws bared. Or Apollo would snap. Inevitably Chronos would fall to the ground and flop around like a beached fish. Alarmed, Apollo would say, "Did I hurt you?"

Chronos would jump up and say, "You nearly killed me a *second* time! You have a death wish on me."

"Ice damn cat fart bear piss . . ." Apollo would mouth, as he fled his den in fury and confusion, mumbling curses into the distance.

"Come back!" Chronos would order.

"Not while you're still there," Apollo would bark back.

"Well, I sure as hells am not leaving. And I'm starving – bring food. *Bird* food, damn it!"

So it would go. Neither could tolerate the other. But now their paths had crossed something which would never uncross – at least, not after Apollo had forced the issue at Telemachus's laboratory.

It was his puppy sister, Athena, who broke the deadlocked animosity. Athena was still too young to know what was going on with her brothers, but Martian wolves grow up quickly in order to survive (although they then seem to live forever). Her mother Isle had insisted Athena be sent off to a distant clan for schooling, refusing to care for her daughter after losing a son, openly admitting that Prometheus was all she could handle. Loos was angry about this but had had no choice. Then Athena came home for the summer and went to visit her celebrated loony brother.

"I think he's cute," young Athena said to Apollo, swishing her tail.

"You see," said Chronos, preening.

"See what?" said Poll. "She thinks you're cute. Like a pet. Like a doll."

"No, I don't," said Athena, not helping. "I think he's cute. He's interesting, too. How come *other* birds don't talk?"

Apollo snapped to attention. "Listen up, Athena," he said. "Smell this and get it right. Do not tell *any*one else that Chronos can talk and . . ."

"And what?" chirped Chronos. "And can fly?"

"And is a *person* in there."

"Why not?" said Athena, ears pricked up now.

"Indeed, why not?" said Chronos, fluffing his feathers. "I'm the only cursed bird who is a person. I'm a scientific discovery."

"You're a scientific monstrosity!" Apollo said. "Or that's what the Elders will think. Something out of the disgraced Cat Age."

"I'm not. He' not," Chronos and Thena rejoined.

"Oh yes you are, Dr. Chronos. You don't belong. Not in a world dominated by dogs. It's the Canine Age. Everyone else was killed off or has degenerated into animal again."

"Then maybe I'm the first of the new Age of Birds!" Chronos spat.

"No you're not," said Apollo. "You're a freak, and you know it. Like me. Like my brother. If the Elders could get their jaws on Prometheus they'd chew him to a pulp. They can't. But they *can* get to you. And if they do, without a second thought, they'll snap your neck and throw you off the cliff for fish food! Second Law – Dogs first and last."

"But I'm not a dog any more. I don't know *what* I am, but I'm not a wolf."

"That's the point," said Apollo. "You're a threat. You're too different. You don't fit in."

"So what?"

"So the world is going weird, and my dad tells me that the Elders are afraid of what Prometheus has created. They're asking after me, too. He's told them I'm just a stone noodler, have some sort of cockamamie ability to hear stone, but nothing's to be made of it."

"And?" asked Chronos.

"And if they find out I can do more than noodle, that I can make stone *do* things . . ."

"Like what?" asked Athena, endless curiosity.

"Then it's over the cliff with me."

"Are you a stone noodler, brother?"

Apollo licked her ear.

"That's not an answer."

"Ice right," said Chronos. "What about me? Whatever I am I

don't want to be fish food. What do we do with *me*?"

"Yeah, he's too cute to be lunch for fish," Thena said.

"We have to figure out what you *are,* Dr. Chronos, and how you got here, in there, in that body. And we have to keep quiet about it, sister."

"OK, brother," she said, and licked him back.

"You called me Dr. Chronos," the bird said.

"So?"

"So finally I get some respect."

Chapter 16
Title Transfer

The diverging reality paths of their sons continued to broaden the chasm between Loos and Isle.

"You'll never guess what Pollo did today," Loos said to Isle one day. She was putting order into the den and did not respond so he just went on with his anecdote. "He got a burr between his toes, and barked in anger at some bush he thought it must have come from." He waited for a response, determined to lure her into communication. She had been glum and silent of late.

"So," she finally said, more a statement than a question.

"So the bush wilted on the spot. Apollo got all upset, went back, and started apologizing!" Loos laughed, or the wolf equivalent, something like a drooly tongue wagging.

"He's still there, hours later, trying to get it to unwilt!"

"How did you find this out?" Isle asked.

"A passerby, Left Eye, saw it and told me."

"Anyone else see it?"

"No. Why?"

"It's embarrassing, that's why."

"Isle, he made the bush wilt. Our son Apollo StoneEar is developing some unique abilities, you have to admit."

"Hopskip Moondog, which is what others call him," she barked back, "has lost his nose and can't smell the shit on his feet. He's an embarrassment."

"He's our son, Isle. How can you call him an embarrassment when your son goes on defying the Math of Wolves, creating his artificial intelligence world of robot puppets?"

"My son? So Prometheus is *my* son now?"

"That's not what I meant."

"Well, Apollo must therefore be your son. My son – at least you admit he's *alive* and my son still. My son is inventing, at a prodigious rate, new mechanisms to power our world. With the heat this could create we might not need to hibernate."

"Not need to hibernate! We'd go insane. Like the cats did."

"No we won't. Prometheus has learned how not to sleep, or how to be half-asleep and half at work."

"There's no such state. No wonder he's so crazy."

"What do you mean, crazy?"

"Worse, depraved. He's stealing wolf souls, killing our sick and injured off before they can either heal or die naturally."

"He's not stealing anyone. They're *joining* him!"

"So you know about this."

"Of course I do."

"How?"

"He told me."

"So he's at least in communication with you. How are you doing this?"

"What?"

"Communicating with Prometheus."

"Why do you want to know?"

"Because the Elders want to talk to him. They want to know what in icehell is going on. And he's incommunicado. Won't communicate through any of his puppet machines nor any known signaling center."

"Well, I won't tell."

"Why not?" said Loos.

"I don't want him hurt. He's been hurt enough."

"He's been hurt to *death,* Isle. Prometheus is dead."

"Don't you—"

"I know. Or as good as dead. He's not in our world, but manipulating it from outside. Even the Old Ones have never done that. We've got to find out what he's doing and why. We have to understand."

"Do you understand what *Apollo* is doing?"

"Not exactly."

"Then what's the difference?" snapped Isle.

"The difference," said Loos, "is the order of magnitude. Apollo's talking to bushes. Prometheus is kidnapping dozens, hundreds of lives, carving new canyons in the landscape with his ghost machines, and rerouting rivers."

"So what? So what? Civilization must change. It can't remain static."

"Those are Prom's words, aren't they?"

"And if they are?" Isle was by now stinking with anger, her hackles erect, her lips snarling.

"Whether they are or not, Isle Bitchwife, they are now your words. Worse, you're snarling at me as if I were from an enemy den."

"You're my enemy if you would endanger my genius son."

"Come to your senses, dog."

"*You* come to your senses! The world's changed, Loos StoryTeller. It's evolved while you weren't looking, while you were telling fishkiting parables to puppy children."

"Calm down."

"No. You have no idea what we can do, will do, once we master this bridge between life and death."

"What are you talking about?"

"You know what I'm talking about. We needn't just live here

on Mars, trapped on a frozen red mudball. From the far side . . ."

"The unliving, bodiless . . ."

"Yes, from beyond *this* skin, where Prometheus and the Prometheans live, we will be able . . ."

"The *Prometheans! . . . We!*" He cut her off.

Isle was so wrought up she was tongue tied. She walked to her water dish and lapped a few mouthfuls.

Loos continued in a quiet, commanding voice. "Wife, you will go to wherever your communication channel to Prometheus is, and you will tell him that I and the Elders are coming to question him."

Isle whipped her snout around, water drops spiraling through the air like crystalline fire. "And if I do not?"

"I command you."

"You cannot."

"I am the Sire here."

"And I am the Bitch. Or was. I am Promethean now."

"And that means?"

"It means the Laws of the Den do not apply to me any more."

"We have a daughter."

"*You* raise her. I'm leaving."

Isle turned to run out the door. Loos leapt into the air towards her. Isle sensed his pounce and twisted, rising on her hind legs to meet him. With a gnashing, throat-deep growl for blood, they attacked each other. Loos's jaw closed on her right ear, tearing it off. They fell to the den floor. Isle twisted immediately and clamped onto Loos's upper rear thigh. He howled in pain. She shook his whole body like a rabbit and dropped him. His blood streaming, he could not stand.

Loos lay still, knowing she had cut an artery and his life was pumping out. Isle stood over him. Dripping gore, she turned from his prone body. "Do not follow me, husband," she said. "I'm dead to you." She ran out the door.

Loos lay there, panting, berating himself for his canine stimulus response idiot behavior. "Cur. Stupid gone wild cur." He turned to bite pressure around the grievous wound his wife had dealt him. His only hope was to slow or stop the blood loss.

Soon afterwards Athena found him in that position. "Father! What happened?"

Loos let go his mouth tourniquet. "Athena, go find Apollo. Come back with a medico."

She looked at him, stupefied by the smell and sight of blood, mortified that her mouth salivated at the stimulus.

"Go, daughter. Or I will die."

She fled out the door, yipping like a fish had bit her tail.

* * *

Isle ran like a wolf in hunt. The first wolves she passed turned in amazement as she blazed past. The smell of blood, wolf blood, made them want to follow. The demented look in her eye, lost, wild, caused them re-do the Math. *No, let her go. Not our affair.* They saw her turn down the lane from the Rim of the Canyon.

Isle tore down the path, winding steeply down the Canyon wall. It was long, miles long, but everyone that day was off up country at the base of the nearest volcano, hunting rabbit. At a seemingly random point she leapt off the path into the river not far below. She dove under and swam upstream. A few minutes later, her lungs bursting, she turned into an underwater cave opening into the bank.

It was actually a channel for the river to flow inward, cut there by one of the Promethean Puppets to bring the force of river water to a simple turbine to create electric power. The turbine was not yet built, but the channel let out into a natural underground hollow, flowing out the other side. The cave had been carved into a series of broad ledges. It was a hidden Prometheus Base, containing one of their many Listen and Dispatch Signal and Control stations.

Mostly it was machines connected to and communicating with other machines, but a few live wolves were still required at this point to minister like acolytes to their unseen, undead Promethean masters in the other world.

The young wolves working in the cave spun in surprise as Isle pulled herself up from the pool. She gasped for air on the stone floor.

"You're injured, Commander," said one.

"It's insignificant," Isle said. "Go get Demeter."

"He's on the far side of the Canyon at a deep dig."

"Get him now. Now! Immediately! We're at risk."

The young wolf looked to one of his companions. The two of them jumped into the dark water and swam off.

* * *

Demeter returned hours later, accompanied by meat-body Prometheans, as the not-yet-crossed-over wolves friendly to Prometheus called themselves. Isle had eaten and rested. Her ear wound had clotted and only ached now.

"Commander!" Demeter said. "What happened?"

"I had a fight with my husband, Prometheus's father, or ex-father, whatever."

"I'm sorry to hear that."

"It's no matter. I've left him."

"So soon, Commander? We had planned . . ."

"Yes, I know. But the Math has changed."

"What . . . do you intend?"

"Demeter, I must talk to Prometheus."

"But you could have done that from any number of terminals. Why here? And why wait for me?"

"Because, ice you, the Math has changed. Velocity is up. The amplitude of repercussion will soon be overwhelming."

"Are they coming now? So soon?"

"Not now. I don't think so, Demeter, but sooner than we planned."

"What do you want us to do?"

"There's something I may want you to do, Captain Demeter. But first we need to talk with Prometheus." She turned to the others in the chamber. "Leave us alone."

"Yes, Commander. When should we return?"

"The Captain will come and tell you," Isle said.

They jumped in the pool and swam away.

"Now to talk with Prom," Isle said.

"Did you make an appointment to speak with the Supreme Commander?" Demeter diffidently asked.

"Captain, I'm his mother."

"Even so . . ."

"And second in command, second only to him."

"That is so. I presume you want me to stay."

"Yes."

They went to a complex array of electronics and crystal. This was the current state of the real world/Promethean communication interface. Demeter and his many scientist friends had engineered the system up to where it was now both written and audio. This was necessary for the increasingly complex inter-communication with live wolves. With mechanical puppets, no matter their size, it was far simpler. Commands were sent or focused on a crystal receiver in the "brain pan" of a puppet machine, and the puppet simply executed the mechanical order. The puppeteer elsewhere in turn interpreted via crystal code the movements executed. Machine code was only about degrees of stop, go, turn, reach, dig, how much, how hard, how long, and so on – mechanical considerations, mostly measurement.

Live being-to-being communication, although simpler to execute as it was merely a matter of words written or broadcast in robot voice from a speaker or earphone, still involved the infinite gradations of . . . meaning, thought, significance, mood, unspoken intention (so often contrary to spoken meaning) and its million other subtleties.

The non-corporeal Prometheans could sense one another as existing entities, but only barely. They could tap, flow or beam to one another like two stones bumping in a dark cavern, or like two liquids of different viscosity flowing by one another. They sensed *thereness*. But Prometheus, this universe's founder, had forsaken the silly, toothless, fangless, unpowered world of non-energy telepathy long before he had dropped his physical body into the void of cut connections. He was interested now in *power* – energy here to energy there – cause, distance, impact.

That this formula applied equally well to thought, to spiritual beings, was just too, too . . . weak, he thought. Thus Prometheus assigned to his left-behind childhood the communications of "meat bodies." Such as the age-old game of a bitch wolf glancing at a male and posing just so, then dashing off to be followed in a merry chase. Or two old friends touching one another's minds and understanding without further communication. Or how Apollo had ever reached the body-departed Prometheus without physical construct – Prom simply *did not go there.* For him now there was no looking into another's mind or soul and knowing its yea or nay. For all he knew this had been by his own choice. Perhaps so, perhaps not.

There was certainly still something like music in Prometheus's dark. Rhythm still existed, and impact, volume, pitch of energy exerted or energy received. Even a measurement of a bell or gong struck, wood chimes, harmonics. So this gave enjoyment, for those who sought such old world pleasures. It was not a lifeless or feelingless world.

But there were few *words* shared between Prometheans. There were thoughts. How to communicate these conceptually, directly, this had been forgotten, or not yet re-learned.

Word concepts had to be constructed like a blind, deaf, and dumb person scratching in another's palm. On Mars a pup born to such a gestation blunder would be tossed into the Great River. There was no future survival in the cold Martian world for such a pup. This was not harsh or uncaring. A body incapable of constructive survival was abandoned for its owner's and the common good.

Until Prometheus preempted this with his left turn into a new, contradictory Math. Even now, with a greatly refined ability to prestidigitate via puppet robot at a distance, Prometheus was still trying to learn how to communicate thought faster or more directly than by signaling characters or images. He could do that much faster now, both typing and phonetically pronouncing words for meat-body receipt points. His alphabet, too, now that he was not restricted to speaking, was extended, even beyond the complex Math, music, and lettered Martian syllabary. He signaled in a daily augmented polyglot of wolf language, of engineering and physics symbols, with brand new constructions to express things like military ballet or dance – these bodies turn like this and strike those bodies with this amplitude of blow or force.

By now, a meat-body Martian unschooled in the fast evolving Promethic language, which they themselves had named Promath, could not possibly understand the written constructions or spoken/broadcast sound without an interpreter. There was also straightforward machine-to-machine electronic messaging which would never be receivable by physical wolf senses, or even by Apollo, for that matter.

Many other significances did not exist in the meat world at all, and hence were not included in its language. In wolf speak one could possibly translate a Promath sentence or paragraph, usually accompanied with traditional canine body gestures, signing. Promath might have been compared to hieroglyphs or ideograms evolving into a phonetic alphabetic language, then having to devolve back into ideogram, but containing all the nuance and subtlety of rich alphabet languages. Promath was the bench test. It could be done.

This, therefore, was the language via electronic signal from crystal receiver which Commander Isle was now going to use to talk with her son, Prometheus. Apollo would not have had a clue. Demeter could generally follow along, but Isle and Prometheus had evolved their own private, special cryptic code, as pleasurable to them as private lingo to pups in their first secret pack rituals.

A variant of this inter-terminal code was how all Prometheans communicated. They needed receipt points in the meat and stone world to encode and decode their messages to one another. The new Prometheans had been pulled too suddenly from their bodies by Prometheus's electronic chicanery and his powerful, willful psychic pulse. This was how he cut the string between soul and body when soul was unconscious, willingly asleep, or confused. He had discovered and retained the nasty talent of how to unplug someone. He construed it as a law of physics he could wield to his own use. Apollo, the Elders, and the Old Ones would have described it differently – reverse necromancy, manipulating the living to make them dead, cutting the golden cord between soul and body.

If the Elders actually *knew* this, which now they only suspected, they would have wasted no time, spent any effort to find and snuff, to destroy the communication terminals and kill the living Martian staff of the Prometheans. But the Elders only suspected. They had no ken of the extent to which Prometheus was willing to go in his experiment in new dimensions.

The unplugged Prometheans didn't know either, but they were quickly and forcibly schooled in the rudiments of contact and communication – an immersion course in the otherworld path Prometheus had had to travel to retain his computational sanity. Essentially they progressed at hyperspeed through his own earlier confusions, despairs, discoveries, surprise, and growing elation of power re-found and exercised. Prom could sense through their communications back to him as they became able to signal that in *his* realm most lived in terror. He intended most to be mere soldiers, obeying electronically juiced-up command.

Some, however, excelled and reveled in the warlock or witch elixir of demortification of self, howling soundlessly in the opera of the timeless night of the living dead. These warlocks learned their codes quickly, and added their own personalizing code language by which they could recognize one another's witchcraft . Electing to call these beings by such names betrays a prejudice, perhaps. It must be remembered that few of them had elected to come over to this otherworld. In any case, soon each could recognize "voices" in the symbols of code sent. These then became the puppeteers, some working in the manufacture of the puppets, others driving the complex machines, whether mega or micro in size. Sometimes several worked together to operate one machine.

Already, if they had chosen to execute a surprise attack, they could have destroyed or savaged Martian villages and cities of wolves. But there was nothing they *wanted* there. Meat-world buildings were useless to them now, live wolves being only of interest because they housed future "recruits."

The Prometheans wanted *power*, literal physical power, and vast quantities of it. Martian civilization offered only a token, a fraction of what they needed. Thus without alerting the Wolf Elder Masters, they had steadfastly begun to create their own energy supply sources through geothermal and water power. In the polar regions they built windfarms, too, unknown to the denizens of lower climates.

Fully translating Isle's signal communication with Prometheus is technically impossible, but it can be approximated. One would strike the right mood if he conjured an Egyptian Book of Rules for Dam

Building and Planetary Destruction.

Spelled out, however clumsily, what they said to one another, once they were "connected," might be interpreted as:

* Force Code One: Commander Isle salutes Supreme Commander Prometheus and requests a hearing. Over.

! Supreme Commander Prometheus receives CommIsle request. Delay 1000 ticks. Occupied. Over.

* Force Code Two: CommIsle has *urgent* message and request for discussion from SupComProm. Repeat Force Code Two. Over.

! SupCom communicated accept receipt 1000 ticks. Decision made. Close.

* Force Code *Ten*: Prometheus. Now. Over.

! What is it, Isle? This had better be Force Code Ten or I will restrict comm with you for 100,000 ticks. Over.

* Force Code Ten: The Elders may have already discovered the Prometheus Plan. I have fought with and severed connection with Loos. He will be bringing Elders to look for me, and us, and ultimately you. Over.

! Force Code Eleven: You fool. This preempts the Plan. Over.

* Supreme Commander, there was no alternative. It is miraculous their naïveté has been so profound not to have earlier predicted future consequences. Over.

! It was not naïveté. It was lack of confront of negative potentiality. That this is already the Age of Prometheus and that the Age of Wolves is finitely terminated is an asymptotic negative concept for them. Over.

* Nevertheless, they learn. They will come. Over.

! Force Code Ten: We are not prepared to physically repel them from our signal stations. They are not to come. Over.

* Your command cannot stop the River. Over.

! Not yet, but soon enough. Over.

(pause)

* Supreme Commander, Commander Isle wishes to transfer title to Prometheus effective immediately. Over.

! (Message not accepted.)

* Repeat send.

! (Message not accepted.)

* Repeat send.

! (Message not accepted.)

* Supreme Commander. Receipt of last communication requested. Over.

! (Message not accepted.)

* Force Code Ten: Prometheus, we must do this. Now. The Plan is preempted. I must come over now. Over.

! Mother, are you ready? Over.

* Prometheus, I am ready. Over.

! Commander Isle, you are mistaken. You are not ready. Our communication system is still too primitive. You are to come when we will be able to cross-transfer instantaneous duplication of cause-effect zero distance. That is my wish. Over.

* Supreme Commander, you are my son, and I am your mother, but only as long as I remain on the other shore. The Game has changed boards. The playing field where I am will soon be so unsafe that I may not later be *able* to transfer title. Over.

! Mother, title transfer is irrevocable. Over.

* Prometheus, you took the irrevocable step uncounted ticks ago. Over.

! That is true. If you come, mother, are you prepared to progress through the current faulty evolution of signal awareness? To lose you mid-signal would be an asymptote, game extinction, horizon unacceptable. Over.

* Prometheus. I will come. Over.

! How?

* You must order Captain Demeter to terminate and be prepared to initiate title transfer and signal evolution time coincident.

! Is Demeter there with you?

* Yes.

! You are sure of this action?

* Force Code Ten: Now.

! (Message delayed.)

! (Message accepted.)

! Commander Isle, I await your new posting. Until then, over.

* Supreme Commander. New game evolution START. Infinity potential START. Closed terminals permanency START. Over.

! We shall see. Put Captain Demeter on. Until soon. Over.

* Until soon. Over to Demeter.

Isle slid off her goggles, earphones, and nosepiece. She looked at Demeter.

"Prometheus will speak with you," she said.

"Supreme Commander Prometheus?"

"Yes. Right now."

"Very well, Commander."

Demeter put on the signal apparatus. He whispered and blinked and sniffed in connection with the otherside. At one point he stiffened visibly and ducked his head, tucking his tail. But then his tail came back out and his head up. His hackles rose.

He disconnected from the signal apparatus. "Commander Isle," he said in a formal voice. "I have the honor of inviting you to join with the Supreme Commander at this time."

"Captain, the honor is mine. And we shall await you, too, in future."

She put on the signal apparatus and stared into the non-world, silently, slowly lowering her head, tail straight out.

A moment later Demeter leapt at her and bit deeply into her exposed neck, twisting and snapping the spine.

Commander Isle had transferred title. Irrevocably.

Chapter 17
A Voice for Prometheus

Apollo arrived at his father's den earlier than expected. Athena had found her brother already running (or jitterbugging) over to his father's. Before Thena could say a word he growled, "I know. I know." And he did, having pathed his parents' sudden violent confrontation as an equally sudden pain in his own body. He ran by Athena without stopping. She called after him that she would bring a doctor.

By the time Poll dashed into Loos's den, his father had made a rough tourniquet, torn out of cushions. Blood was everywhere and Loos was nearly unconscious. Apollo checked him over, carefully smelling parts of his body, then placed a paw on his father and received a telepath summary burst, something like reading a book instantaneously. He interpreted that at this point Loos was not getting physically worse. His father's real challenge was facing the bitterness and shame of having battled with his own wife.

Apollo decided to clean the den of blood sign and other evidence of the fight. Given the ancient power of bloodsmell over wolves, this was a correct estimation of first aid. Despite his overwhelming urge to simply lick up the blood, Poll did not. He would gladly lick a wound clean for his mother or father, a normal hygienic response, but this blood resonated like poison to him. Worse, a kind of psychic wolfbane. He got busy wiping it up, throwing water out and mopping it up, not something wolves did too often as they enjoyed the rich, yeasty aroma of a well lived-in den. The space was orderly and smelled antiseptic when Athena came back with the family doctor, called affectionately by them just "Doc."

"What is all this?" Doc asked. "Athena couldn't tell me anything. I smell violence. And . . . is that . . .?"

"Yes," said Apollo. "Loos and my mother had a terrible fight."

"Where's Isle?"

"She was gone by the time I got here."

"Did Loos tell you what happened?"

"He went unconscious a little while ago. But they fought."

The doctor looked at Apollo, then remembered what she had heard about young StoneEar. Of course, Pollo would have known what had occurred here, through his psychic sense.

"Let's tend to the patient between our paws then."

She set to work cleaning the wound. Although deep and damaging, the bite to the leg artery had not severed it. Doc carefully sewed Loos up.

Athena was trembling. Apollo licked her face and lay down. Instinctively she curled up next him and put her head down, closing her eyes. He put his muzzle down over hers, as a goose might take a gosling under its wing. Apollo carefully regarded the doctor and her work. When she was done, Doc turned to Poll. "Where is your mother? I smell her blood too."

"Yes. I cleaned it up."

"Good. Any idea?"

"I think she's dead."

"What!" Athena, who had been trying to sleep, sat up, frightened.

"I'm sorry, Thena," said Apollo. "Mother's dead. She's . . . I don't know, she's not here, not alive. She's done something."

"What?" asked Doc.

"I don't know. Or don't understand."

"Did Dad . . . kill Mama?" whined Athena.

"I don't think so, sweetie. It's something else. Worse, I'm afraid."

"What can be worse than that?" cried Thena.

"I have to inform the Justice Council," said Doc.

"Yes, but what will you tell them?" said Apollo.

Doc sat back down. "Yes. You're right. Let's wait for Loos to wake up. Surely he'll know something. Athena, can you get some food together?"

"Yes, sure," she said, and got up to perform this eternal "calm yourself down" feminine function.

Just then Heraklitos barked from outside, repeatedly, the "Trouble! Trouble!" alarm. They ran out. Klitos was standing there pullstrapped to a cart behind him. A cloth covered the cart's burden. Friends stood beside him.

Apollo, Athena, and Doc sniffed. Athena howled, "It's Mother."

* * *

"Should I say 'I warned you'?"

"Elder, I believe you've answered your own question."

"Don't be catty with me, Storyteller."

Loos just looked down. Why respond? His expression was doubly pained as he was still wearing the leg bandage, although it was healing remarkably fast after Apollo "had a talk with it," as he arcanely described his healing technique to his dad.

Apollo sat beside him now, looking off to that nowheresville in which he spent most of his time. Loos was being grilled by Senior Justice Elder One Ear. The Elder grumbled until Loos finally looked up and shook his head sadly.

"I'll accept that as your recognition," said One Ear, "that we've been pushed off the cliff without a wing."

"I accept whatever punishment the Justice Council deems

merited," said Loos.

"Idiot. This is not about what you did to your wife."

"But—"

"You had a dogfight. Granted. But *you* didn't kill her. And for whatever you did do clearly the First Law has already been enacted," One Ear said, nosing his old friend.

"Ouch."

"Exactly. No, what this is about, and you know it, is the necessity to *respond* to Prometheus and his . . . pack . . . of whatever they are."

"How do you propose to respond, One Ear?"

Now it was the Elder's turn to look off. "I don't know," he said eventually, "but Prometheus must be stopped. The whole cult must be . . . I think it must be exterminated."

"Assuming that you knew how to do such a thing, Justice, that's rather drastic."

"Tenth Law, Storyteller. 'How sweet tastes the bone marrow of a true enemy of the Wolf Clan.'"

"Whose bones do you intend to crack between your jaws? Prometheus and his acolytes? His followers, devotees, whatever they are?"

"Prisoners maybe, Loos. Wolf spirits trapped Tweenlives."

"Who knows? But Isle, I think, went there of her own will."

"But she was returned to you," said One Ear, "with her neck broken."

"Yes. Heraklitos said that Demeter told him, before revealing where Isle's body could be found, that she had *joined* the Prometheans. Then Demeter ran off."

"And cats birth puppies, too."

"But that was what our fight was about!"

"Yes, Loos, so you told me. Don't you see? Can't you smell the stink of this whole cannibalistic devolution? Our species is threatened here."

"Cannibalistic?"

"Yes, ice your useless brains. To join Prometheus, not to work here on *this* side for him, oiling his puppet machines or whatever they do, but to really *join* him, to go to his black home den, you have to *kill* yourself, to die, or – as it looks in this case – to be killed.

Prometheus feeds on us, on his own kind."

Loos dropped into the crouch of the defeated, tail curling under.

"So should we all respond if we really confronted this. But, *woof!*" One Ear barked angrily and loudly in a wordless burst of frustration. "Get up on your feet, dog! Help me solve this."

Loos stood up, then sat down facing the Justice, like a student before a teacher. "I'll help you however I am able, Elder. I just feel so . . . stupid, incompetent. I can't think. There's no Math."

"Yes, there is. It's the Tenth Law, as it was applied to the Cats – extinction, extermination."

Apollo looked round. With the Elder's bark he had snapped back into the moment.

"Exterminate *whom*, Justice Elder?" Poll politely asked.

"Glad you have rejoined us from your noodling, Apollo StoneEar. Exterminate the Prometheans."

"How would you do that, Justice?"

"Don't bedevil me with details. That's the point of this discussion. We don't know *how*. We might stop their machines, confiscate them, dismantle or jam them so they can't operate."

"But that doesn't reach Prometheus," said Apollo.

"No, but it would stop his operations on Mars."

"Maybe. But he could still and probably would continue to cull new members from our clans."

"*Woof!*" the Elder shouted again, and then clicked his teeth several times.

They sat quietly for a few moments, inhaling their acrid fear sweating into the air.

"What would you do, Apollo?" asked Loos. "You were the only one besides Mother who could communicate with Prometheus without his translator machines. Even she couldn't do that, actually. That's why I brought you here. You know his mind. What do you recommend?"

"I don't know his mind, father. And I don't really understand *why* I can communicate with him, other than that he's . . . well, my brother."

"There's more to your skills than that, Apollo," said One Ear. "We've all heard that your ear that stone talks to has opened your spirit to be able to talk back. It is possible that as far as Prometheus has ventured into his darkness so you may be reaching into the . . . uhh . . ."

"Into the light? Hardly, Elder. Into the clouds, into the wind, into an iceberg floating down to the sea, maybe. But I'm a passenger, not in charge."

"You still know more than any of us," said Loos.

"So look into your noodlesphere or whatever new Math creation you live in now," said One Ear, "and . . . suggest . . . an approach."

Apollo closed his eyes. His nostrils flared. Slowly his neck hackles rose and tail crept down. He opened his eyes. "I recommend we talk with Prometheus."

One Ear laughed out loud and shook his head. "So simple. Of course. It hadn't even occurred to me. *Will* he talk to us? Through you?"

"I just asked him."

"You were in communication with him just now?"

"I think so. He's refused to answer any of my calls for well over a year. I stopped even trying. But I sent an old brotherly call to him just now, the 'Danger' signal we used to exchange as pups."

"And?" asked Loos.

"I didn't hear from *him*. I think Mother answered."

"Isle!" Loos barked. "Can I talk with her? How is . . . what is her state?"

Apollo shut his eyes again. He instantly shuddered and opened his eyes. "No, if I understand correctly, you may not speak to her. If this is Mother who is answering me, which is what it feels like, she said—" Apollo shivered again. "Her communication is for *you*, Senior Justice."

"What is it?"

"'Supreme Commander demands his rights and those of his Legionnaires.'"

"His what? The supreme what?"

Apollo twitched. "This isn't easy for me, Justice. I'm sure I'm not translating well. Are you sure, Father, you can't reach Prom?"

Loos closed his eyes and leaned in to his son to attempt contact telepathy. After a while he shook his head. "No. I'm sorry. I could feel that *you* have a kite line into somewhere, but I can't see the kite, much less the cloud it's flying in. I feel the wind pulling, that's all."

"What rights does *Supreme Commander* Prometheus – I presume that is who Isle refers to – what rights does she speak of?" asked the Justice. "Or he? Whoever you're talking to?" "Twelfth Law."

"'Respect the Old Ones!'"

"I think so, Justice."

"Well, ask! Clarify the point."

"Justice, this isn't a court of law. And I'm not an Advocate Voice or Speaker for the Court."

"Apollo StoneEar, this *is* a Court of Law. I hereby appoint it so. And you are the Advocate for Prometheus. I appoint you so."

Apollo stood on his hind feet, glaring at the Justice. One Ear, too, rose, and they stood there, challenging one another. Loos got between them, putting his paws out.

"I must decline, Honorable Justice," said Apollo, sitting down.

"You're appointed. You *cannot* decline. That is the Law."

"Yes, I understand. I do not refuse. I must decline because I cannot perform the function."

"State your reasons, son."

"I can translate for Prometheus. I can sometimes reach him if he allows me. But I am not in control. *He* is in control now. And it . . . it doesn't feel good. I don't want to do it."

"Apollo," said One Ear, "it may not feel good. But this is a matter, frankly, of planetary importance. Our species is threatened. You must try."

"No," said Apollo.

"You must, Apollo," said Loos. "The Justice is right. Prometheus has become a threat."

"No, you don't understand. I'm not *able*. I can't be an advocate and query Prometheus's mind and pursue his thinking from one place to another. I can read him, maybe, but I don't promise. I'm only a conduit. The string you felt, Dad, that's me. I'm just the string attached to him. He's the kite. You have to hold the string."

"Hold the string?" Loos asked.

"Fine," interrupted One Ear. "You hold the cursed string,

Storyteller, and you be the string, Apollo. Whatever. I appoint you, Loos Storyteller, as the Advocate for Prometheus. Now, ask the kite through the string, or whatever we're doing here, what Prometheus means by the Twelfth Law as an application to his situation?"

Loos shook his head to rattle the knucklebones out of it, and turned to Apollo. "So what . . ."

"You don't have to ask, Father. I know the answer."

"Then what the hell?" barked One Ear.

"I just didn't want to be the Justice Advocate. I can translate, however."

"So, TRANSLATE!"

"You know how telepathy goes. It's as often conceptual and thoughtcomplete in one throw as it may be a discrete series of tossed pebbles."

"Translate, damn you."

"I think Mother, who was receiving and speaking for Prometheus, who I also felt was there, by the way, meant that Prometheus, and she, and their "companions," are like unto Old Ones. They are spirits without bodies, but still linking to Mars and to wolves, and that they are deserving of the respect that Wolf Spirits are owed."

"Wolf Spirits, or Old Ones, do not steal wolves *from* their bodies," said the Justice.

"I beg your pardon, Justice, but—" started Loos.

"Don't interrupt, Loos. I'm talking to your son, and I want my question answered!"

"Senior Justice, you appointed me Advocate. I hereby accept. Therefore I have the rights of an Advocate. You have to hear me."

"Frozen catheads, Loos. So be it. What do you want to say?"

"Justice, you do not know that they steal wolves from their bodies."

"But we have all these dead bodies."

"Yes, we do. But we don't know how they got that way. And we don't know it wasn't a voluntary process."

"Very well, Counselor. And you *propose*?"

"Justice, I don't have a proposal. I was just making a point."

"May lice infest your family for three generations. You're all born lawyers. What are we going to do? Apollo? . . . Apollo?"

Apollo was noodling again, off into an unseen mist, flying unseen kites.

"Apollo?" Loos nudged him. Apollo turned round slowly. His eyes were cold. He spoke formally. *"I am Counselor Isle,"* his voice said. *"Supreme Commander Prometheus has appointed me First Counsel to the Prometheans. We invoke the Tenth Law."* Apollo stopped speaking, looking but not seeing in front of him.

"You demand a Justice Council? On what grounds?" barked One Ear, glad to have someone from the other side to talk to.

"To rectify according to the Law the standing of the State of Prometheus."

"The State of Prometheus? What is this State?"

Apollo just stared at him, or through him.

"Apollo? Commander? Hello?"

Apollo looked quietly out from an empty head.

"Advocate," One Ear finally said to Loos. "I believe your client has hung up on your translator."

"Apollo?" Loos said quietly, nudging his son with his nose.

Apollo shook, then said, "Yes, Father, what?"

"The Justice asked you a question."

"Me?"

"No," said One Ear. "I asked Commander Isle through you what is the State of Prometheus."

"I don't know," said Apollo.

"You don't?" said One Ear.

"No, Justice. We'll have to ask, but not right now, please. I think I'm going to be sick." He staggered. "I'm going to have to learn how to do this better," he said, and passed out cold.

Chapter 18
Prometheus On Trial

It wasn't that there were not other Justice Councils in the Martian world. It was just that the Loos StoryTeller family saga provided fare that beat anything else, dog on his back, belly up. Now here again was something utterly unheard of. The clans had already been electrified, figuratively and literally, with the surge of power (and heat) being generated by the new and remarkable P-Puppets. Martian society was accustomed to slow change from within. The elements provided enough external challenge – killing blizzards, overlong winters, crippling ice storms, dust storms to choke rivers, even feral tigers and wolves and the persistent occasional bear. Now here was an Industrial Revolution in full tilt. Young whelps were boisterously marveling, predicting change, change, change. Who had time to fish, to gather food for post-hibernal spring? Who had time for school?

The mysterious Prometheus, conjured by underfed and overly hormonal wolf pups as a kind of punk Old One who would hopefully teach them all how to divest themselves of fur-clad bodies, and thus free them to . . . well, to be punk Old Ones themselves, this same Prometheus, the gossip spread, had not been charged to appear *before* a Justice Council. No, he himself had *demanded* a Council from the unseen Other Side. And his super-punk Old One Mother, recently deceased under bizarre circumstance, would represent him! Loos StoryTeller could never invent a tale anything close to this.

No fake trial, either. On one side of the issue were a whole class of Elders demanding the dismantling of the Prometheus Puppets, to be pushed cliffover into the river – the same machines powering and heating the towns as never before in history. Seems that some Elders were worried about the invisible, not-there operators. On the other side of the "issue" were juvenile wolves, excited and thinking about "joining up," if they could figure out what to join, or where, and could dismiss the niggling worry that they were completely out of their minds to want to leave body and flesh, sex and beer, fish and flying, and the feel of ice, dirt, and snow under the paws to go . . . where?

Well, that niggling persistent reservation was about to be made den cave dance floor center. The Prometheans were demanding recognition as . . . whatever they were demanding recognition *as*. No one really knew. But it promised to be most entertaining for the fishers, farmers, Promethean factory workers, and street pups.

* * *

Senior Justice One Ear denied a formal Elder request for the destruction of any Puppet, all puppet machines. Although this was contrary to his personal opinion (he in fact agreed with them), the Law was the Law. Promethean wolves were a species under Law. *The Law* is what wolves had created after they had freed themselves from the Cats eons before. The issue would be decided by Law in Council. A Chart of Responsibilities would have to be drawn up, although One Ear was iced if he knew what it would contain.

Another Elder Justice, Scar Shank, had even challenged One Ear's granting of a Justice Council, saying it was unprecedented (which was true) to have one side of a Council be represented from Tweenlives or Old One Country or wherever the Prometheans were. One Ear carefully reviewed the legal challenge but overruled it. First there were precedents of settling estates after death. Then he consulted with Counselor Loos, who had asked for a séance, a reading, bone sorting, whatever one wanted to call Apollo's reverie with Advocate Isle. Initially Isle refused to speak or even acknowledge that she had received Apollo's request. Then the voice representing itself as "Isle" finally responded when Apollo thoughtsent that there would be no Council and the Puppets would all immediately be destroyed if she didn't help out One Ear here with a legal precedent. (One Ear had said no such thing, but Apollo knew his Mother.)

Isle came back that until proven that they were *not* Old Ones, even if of a different ilk or clan than the (barely comprehended) existing set of Old Ones, who were treated as virtual demigods or djinns, until proven *not* to be equivalent to them, the Prometheans must be considered to *be* them, and shown the social respect deserved Old Ones. The Tenth Law had been codified for the very real reason that Old Ones did exist and, sometimes if rarely, had intervened nastily in the lives of wolves, whenever ignorant wolf Elders had been foolish enough to ridicule, deride, or show disrespect to said Old ones. No one knew for sure why they had intruded with physical Mars, as Old Ones were off in their own never never land. But they had interfered massively in the distant past, no doubt about it, and the Tenth Law was anciently adopted to ward off future sudden auto-conflagrations, instant river freezings, or apparent cessation of planetary spin – the most mythic Old One mischief, considered by many nonbelievers to be legend.

So Senior Justice overruled Scar Shank.

Now it was time for the Council. One Ear brooked no delay. Counselor Loos had trotted into One Ear's chambers, requesting a postponement. Why? Because Prometheus and Isle wanted to defend themselves with a special Puppet on-site, built for the occasion.

"Rubbish. Fishbones," said One Ear. The whole thing was insane anyway. The Law was padding across the thinnest of ice, and his career was undoubtedly finished no matter how the Council turned out. "Let's get it over with."

* * *

Athena was using a long-handled brush to smooth out Apollo's coat of fur. He had had a "spell" the day before and found himself, when he came to, outside of town in the middle of nasty-thorn brambles. She was combing them out, partly for his comfort, partly because she did not want him to look like a farmer hick in Court. Being Hopskip was bad enough, thought Apollo, although he was actually beginning to enjoy the rhythm his body gave to his life.

"I don't understand why I can't come with you to Court," said Dr. Chronos, who was prancing around watching the grooming process.

"Because – for the millionth time – Chronos, if you let one Elder see that there is a thinking, feeling, live, sentient, intelligent new species, even composed of only one member, *especially* if so, then it is broken neck and tossed into the river for you. I've told you – Thirteenth Law: 'Do not abide artificial intelligence or experimentation with sentient species.'"

"I'm not an experiment."

"Then what are you?"

"I don't know. But that doesn't mean I'm an experiment."

"Trust me, Chronos, no Elder will waste the breath to ask. You should remember the hatred and taboo against non-wolf intelligences. The Fourteenth Law is even more explicit: 'One World, One Master Species.' That's been the formula for stable civilization for thousands of years.

"OK, OK, OK. I didn't ask for a history lesson."

"You're not going."

"What if I just ride on your shoulder and pretend to be a stupid bird?"

Apollo lunged at him, snapping his jaws, but Chronos flapped up to his resting perch, high in the cave. He'd demanded this be constructed, when Apollo had been in a calmer mood, because periodically Apollo would go after him like a dog for a fish when he couldn't stand the chatter any more. Dr. Chronos could not understand what Apollo's problem was with him. Just because he had a few questions.

From his perch Chronos watched Apollo. Athena got busy, quietly putting order into the den, knowing to stay out of this, not sure she even understood the issues.

"At least let me give you some advice," the bird said, in his best remembered "counselor" manner.

"What?"

"I know how the clans are thinking."

"How would you know that?"

"You don't think I hang around here all day when you've left, do you?"

"You go *outside*?"

"Of course I do. I'm a bird. I fly around. Oh, don't worry. You've made your point. I don't talk to anyone. But I do listen. So I know what's going on and what's what."

"What *is* what?"

"Exactly. Let me give you some pointers."

Apollo snorted and gave the dog version of a raspberry, rather slobbery.

"Here's my take—"

"Don't waste your breath."

"Take a dynamic, operative role."

"What are you talking about? I'm going to listen to a bird offering me advice?"

"Yes, you are. I'm not just a hawk, and you know that. I'm an anomaly. You had something to do with my creation, and—"

"No I didn't."

"Yes you did," said Chronos, letting out a self-satisfied aaawkk.

Apollo busied himself with meaningless fussing around.

The bird checked for a bug under one of his feathers. "You know it's true," he continued. "Besides, only you can speak directly with Prometheus, and apparently with your mother, in the Other World. No one else can."

"So what if I can? I'm not in control of any of this. I can't even control you."

"And a good thing too, I must say. But listen, Apollo, you're the only one who can interpret, explain, translate the Other Side for the Judges."

"I'm not the only one. My father—"

"Your father's guessing. *You* can reach them."

"With my thought, that's all."

"That's all? That's all? That's all there is – thought. Do the Math, Apollo."

Dog looked at bird. Chronos gave him the big eye as only birds do.

"How come you've suddenly become the philosopher?" Apollo asked.

"What else have I to do? I'm a dead brain chemist trapped in a hawk body."

"There is that."

"I think a lot."

"You don't have enough of a brain to think a lot."

"I've come to see that brain and brain size have little to do with thought."

"About time."

"So take my advice, Apollo. The Elders want to destroy all the puppet machines. They want to disconnect Prometheus from Mars."

"That would drive him insane."

"That would drive him to fight back, for sure."

They were each quiet for a few moments. Then Apollo said, "And we don't know how powerful the Prometheans are."

"That's my dog," said Chronos. "We don't know *anything* about them, really."

"Who's this 'we,' bird?"

"Somehow I know that what's happened to Prometheus, and to you, and to *me*, is all wrapped up together. I think the Old Ones know, too, but they won't say."

"How do you know?"

"I was there, remember? You all showed up inside my soul. I was happily dead and suddenly you all were there. Well, so were Old

Ones. There, I mean. Or thereabouts."

"And your point?"

"The Old Ones are worried about something interconnected with this, about which none of us know a *thing*. I could tell."

* * *

Elder One Ear had appropriated a large open-air amphitheatre for the site of the Justice Council. Their normal chamber was too small, and he believed the Law required maximum public access, as decisions to be made would affect every zone of the planet. He was sitting at a simple table on the stone floor. To his left was seating for a panel of Elders, invited as a courtesy to offer commentary on the Law. He was the Senior Justice Elder, and would adjudicate. To his right were another table and a few seat pads for Loos and Apollo, and a third table for whatever showed up to represent Prometheus. The amphitheatre looked out over a stunning vista of canyons falling away toward the distant Ice Sea.

They were all disquieted, after waiting too long for proceedings to start. When asked where they were, Apollo stated simply that when he tried to contact "Commander Isle" she only had one word: "Wait."

"Counselor Loos," said One Ear, "if I could figure out who to hold in contempt of Law, I would do so, but I'm stumped. Fortunately we have a fine view. But that won't substitute forever."

Loos looked to Apollo, who shrugged. "As soon as we have contact, you'll be the first to know," he said.

In the public seating there was a whole section filled with staff of Prometheus Puppetries, mostly youngsters, although they could hardly be called rowdy. If anything they were too quiet and seriously intent. Not a single Martian staffer of P-Puppets had said they could speak for any Promethean. They were only operators and engineers, paying fuel bills, coordinating licenses for land use and so on. They had been staring at Apollo and Loos, but now began to rustle and turn back towards the top of the amphitheatre. Everyone's attention was pulled up. There was the distinct sound of a Puppetry electronically powered truck approaching. This wasn't an unusual sound these days, but there was no reason for such a big truck here, especially not pulling up to the verge of the amphitheatre. As usual with these vehicles there was no observable person driving.

Apollo stood. "They're here," he said.

A large door in the rear of the truck opened. Out of the interior darkness came the sound of rhythmic metal striking metal. A larger than life-size, steel-formulated wolf stepped into the light. A thrill ran through the crowd. Then all as one looked back to the stage to the Justice. He turned to Apollo. "Who or what is this?"

Apollo lowered his head as if sniffing out danger. "They're here," he repeated. "Mother and Prometheus."

One Ear looked up to the steel wolf automaton. "Welcome," he said clearly and loudly. "Come down and join us so that we can start."

The wolf thing sat unmoving. The audience turned back and forth between the steel wolf and the steel-eyed Justice. This was going to be better than they thought.

"Can it hear me?" One Ear asked Apollo.

Apollo nodded, "I think so."

"Well, that's good. We won't have to run this as though we were talking to a kite, like you said before." He repeated to the Wolf, "Come down."

The steel wolf stood, stepped off the truck and started down the aisle. It would have been highly theatrical except that the movements of a walking quadruped are extremely subtle and this was, after all, only a puppet. Its movement was imperfect, but it made it satisfactorily to the stage and moved to stand by the side of Loos and Apollo.

Both got up nervously to leave, but Justice One Ear bellowed, "Stay."

"It appears you have someone or something to speak to," said Loos. "We're no longer—"

"Stay. Sit down." They did. "Who are you, or what is this mechanized simulacrum of a dog?" said One Ear to the mechanical puppet.

Silence. The wolf looked over to One Ear. He started to repeat his question, "Who—?"

"I am Ambassador Isle," said the wolf, or rather this phrase came out of the mouth chamber, which did not move but must have contained a speaker. There would be no mouth-talking dog. One could see that the audience was a little miffed.

"So now you are an ambassador. Can you hear me well, Counselor Isle?"

"Yes," said the wolf. "Please address me by my title."

"I will address you by any title that you have demonstrated merits the Law. When we spoke before you were First Counsel. I recognized that and we will continue with that for the time being. Is that acceptable?"

There was a pause. The wolf looked to Apollo. Apollo looked back, then spoke, as if passing on Isle's, or the wolf's, thoughts. "This is rather complex language for transmission by sound spectrum alone to Prometheus. Mother, Commander Isle, asks if she can have a typing processor here to complement the verbal communication."

"No objection. Where do we find such a device?"

The wolf turned to the seated Puppetry staff section. Two wolves stood and brought forward a typing console, placing it with a directional antenna pointed towards the wolf creature.

"So they were prepared for this theatrical spectacle," commented One Ear. "Fine. Apollo, can you type as we go along, or do we need a Justice Secretary?"

Apollo just nodded, and started typing.

Speaking to the oversize wolf puppet, gleaming sharply in the morning sunlight, One Ear said, "Please let us know if you don't understand or if you're not receiving our communication, Counselor, and we shall do the same. Is that fair?"

"That is fair," boomed the wolf in rather flattened tones, imperfectly mimicking spoken Martian, with a voice that sounded like it was emerging from a barrel.

"Done. I declare this Hearing in session on the legal status of Prometheus and Prometheus Puppets, and any other so-called Prometheans, if they exist."

Steel Wolf: They exist.

One Ear: That is conjecture. Procedures first! Who speaks for Prometheus, formerly of the clan of Loos FishKiter and StoryTeller?"

Wolf: I do.

One Ear: And who is it that speaks out of this mechanical construct?

Wolf: Ambassador Isle.

One Ear: First Counsel Isle speaks for Prometheus. And where is Prometheus?

Wolf: He is here with us.

This remark caused a sensation. One Ear put a paw down on the table and quietly looked out. Everyone settled down.

One Ear: He's there with you, wherever *there* is. Fine. Will Prometheus speak?

Wolf: Supreme Commander Prometheus will speak through me. That is, I am representing him and the State of Prometheus.

One Ear: When we recognize the State of Prometheus, we will welcome your representation. For now it is Prometheus individually for whom we have questions.

Wolf: First procedures. What is the role of Apollo?

One Ear: We will use Apollo as an interpreter if communication breaks down.

Wolf: Accepted. And the role of Loos FishKiter?

One Ear: He is a Friend of the Court. And also, if you would know, he is truthfully a Friend of Prometheus and will speak on your behalf if he detects a misstep on my part. Do you understand that, Loos?

Loos chuckled. "As if I would counsel you on the fine points of Law, Justice."

One Ear turned to Loos directly and whispered, "I'm serious. This talking with mechanized spook voices is unprecedented, and would be preposterous except for the fact of that truck up there and its electric power and all the other puppet machinery around the world and the power of those machines. This confrontation is about *power*, and let us not lose sight of that."

Wolf: I protest the phrase "mechanized spook voices."

One Ear: Do you have a better description?

Wolf: We are Prometheans.

One Ear: Until we can see and touch or verify the existence

and identities of Prometheans, they are spooks, currently even without voice.

Wolf: We are owed the same respect as Old Ones!

One Ear: So you say, and so we are met to discuss. But hear you, we will not discuss *respect* until we can determine the status of these Prometheans, and their relationship to recently dead Martians, the relatives of many present.

Wolf: You mean to judge our status solely in relation to Martians Alive?

One Ear: Martians Alive?

Apollo put his hand on the typewriter, as though he were covering a mike. "Martians Alive is their term for *us*."

One Ear: Us. Those living in bodies? Just so. By necessity the fulcrum for this lever between worlds is grounded here, in our living world, Mars.

Wolf: I object. The Laws of Mars may or may not apply to the State of Prometheus.

One Ear: The point is so stipulated. Settling the answer to that "may or may not" is indeed the exact fulcrum and point of discussion here.

The Wolf seated itself. Any movement it made had an effect out of proportion to any normal, live wolf. One Ear seemed to sense this. He made a waving motion with his hand.

Wolf: We can see as well as hear.

One Ear: Splendid. That makes two of us.

Wolf: We have questions.

One Ear: No, *I* have questions! I am the Senior Justice and this is my Council and my Hearing. I have so many questions I don't know where to start. Let's just jump in at the first sensitive issue. Why did you, Isle, formerly married into the Loos clan, join Prometheus?

Silent for a moment, the Wolf then spoke. Although its tinny reproduction should have denied and suppressed the subtleties one would expect from a live voice, despite their absence, one imagined them, added flesh and the tones of flesh and the living to the mechanical.

Wolf: I joined my son because I loved him. I joined Prometheus because he is the genius of the age, and the contributions past and future of the Prometheans are something I wished to become an intimate part of.

One Ear: Intimate indeed. You loved your son, but not so much your daughter Athena, nor your other son Apollo, or your husband Loos. You suicided to join Prometheus?

Loos: If I am not mistaken that was a legal misstep?

One Ear: So stipulated. You see, Loos, you *will* keep me on the straight and narrow. Councillor Isle, you have not answered my question. Did you suicide to join Prometheus?

Wolf: That is not a question that can be answered.

One Ear: On the contrary it's a direct and simple question. There are three possibilities – you died of natural causes in that secret chamber we have since discovered, you suicided, or you were killed. Which was it? If you are in fact the same "Isle" of which we speak.

Wolf: I am Isle. But I am not on trial here, and declaration of suicide would bring up many other issues.

One Ear: It certainly would. But, so stipulating, and freeing you of consequences from such an admission, answer the question.

Wolf: I suicided to join my son.

One Ear: Yes. So you asked someone to bite through your neck, as in olden times?

Wolf: Yes.

One Ear: And who was it who acceded to your wish?

Wolf: That I will not say.

One Ear: I can understand why not. If you were here in the flesh we could determine the truth of this. We know in any case, as Apollo pathed it from Demeter, who did this and who has since disappeared.

Wolf: He has not disappeared. He is here with us.

At this there was a cry in the audience from family members of Demeter. Apollo stood, and then sadly sat back down to continue his background typing.

One Ear: I'm sorry to hear that. That is a loss to us.

Wolf: But not a loss to us, and it need not be a loss to you. We are building a new society, an alternate world that can greatly expand the horizon of the Martians Alive.

One Ear scratched behind an ear.

One Ear: So you say. So you say. What is the purpose, Counselor Isle, of this alternate to living society?

Wolf: Martian wolfkind have grown lazy over the millennia. Knowing they die and come back, they have long since abandoned the driving force behind dominion, enduring only, rather than solving the problems of life with the intention to prevail no matter what. To prevail!

The panel of Elders stood up angrily, as one. One Ear waved them back down.

One Ear: Passing from one body to the next to the next, in a continuum of spirit, this is not prevailing?

Wolf: Not in the same sense as departing entirely from the mortality of a weak, hormonal, and chemically driven body. We have found a new field of play.

One Ear: A Promethean field of play, a better option to Mars, to Mars Alive, as you call it?

Wolf: A better game.

One Ear: Perhaps – but there is still a game, as you say. In games there must be winners and losers.

Wolf: That is not a question.

One Ear: I am admonished. Are there winners and losers in this Promethean Game?

Wolf: Of course, as in all games.

One Ear: And there are different sides, as in all games?

Wolf: Perhaps. We are still in a learning phase.

One Ear: And when you come out of this learning period, might you not have learned that the Prometheans are on one side and the Martians Alive on the other side?

The Elders leaned forward. The wolf sat stone still.

Wolf: You try to trap us. The issue of sides is irrelevant to this case because we are different worlds, more different even than planets could be.

One Ear: Yet legend tells us that we came from another planet. Could not planets oppose one another?

Wolf: Not if they are in different universes.

One Ear: Universes cannot play games with one another?

Wolf: No.

One Ear: But sometimes the Old Ones have played games with us?

Wolf: Again this is conjecture. Martians Alive do not understand Old Ones until the moment of death, if even then.

One Ear: So you say. But you ask that the Martian Tenth Law, which commands that respect is to be shown to Old Ones, should be applied to *you*, as though you are in that same universe, or bear that same relationship to Martiankind. Apparently time has taught us that it behooves survival and the wellbeing of the alive to show respect to beings of another universe.

Wolf: The Inscription of the Law shows that what is and is not respect is a matter of viewpoint, opinion, and disagreement.

One Ear: Yet it has been agreed upon that respect is a given, is required.

Wolf: So Martian Law states.

One Ear: And here we are, dealing with two universes, one of which reaches into the other with puppet strings. Let us reverse the question. "Does Prometheus respect Martians Alive and the Laws of Martians Alive?"

Wolf: Senior Justice One Ear, the Law states that Martians are to show respect to the Old Ones, not that the Old Ones must respect Martians.

One Ear: You avoid the question, Counselor. Do you respect the Martians Alive? Do you respect us?

Wolf: Justice, we are not required by Law to respect you.

One Ear: No. You have stated you live in another universe. But you are functioning in our world.

Wolf: Yes, to the extent that we function in your world, our constructs are subject to your Law.

One Ear: Therefore, would you agree that you are subject to our Law?

Wolf: Only our constructs would be subject.

As these two schooled and politic speakers played out this dangerous dance of dominion, the audiences, seated in the public arena, and in the panel of Elders, and even Loos and Apollo, began to squirm. Under other circumstances there would have been raising of voices, sweat, spit, the staring down of one and another. Here, the Wolf could barely communicate emotion, and One Ear was curbing himself. Nevertheless, the fire behind the words began to heat up the amphitheatre.

One Ear: Your "constructs" are called Puppets, correct?

Wolf: Yes. It is the most workable analogy.

One Ear: And what a puppet does traces back through its strings to the Puppeteer?

Wolf: Inevitably.

One Ear: Therefore the Puppeteer must be subject to the Law of any world into which his strings penetrate.

Wolf: Which is one very good reason why some may wish to travel to another universe.

One Ear: A universe not subject to the Law?

Wolf: To have alternatives, Justice. A new game. A different game.

One Ear: Did the others who are now with you, what you call your Legionnaires, did they so "travel" to your side? Or were they, Counselor, kidnapped?

Wolf: You would have to ask them, Justice.

One Ear: How can we do that? I would very much like to ask them, or any one of them, right *now*.

Wolf: When they are able to hear you, you will by definition be able to ask them whatever you please.

One Ear: Apollo, can you reach any of these Legionnaires?

Apollo: I'm sorry, sir, no. But I can tell that they're *there*. Perhaps they can hear me. I don't know.

One Ear: Ask them to communicate when they are able, in case they can hear you.

Apollo: I have done so.

One Ear: Let us return to the subject of the puppets. Prometheus strings itself into Mars, which is subject to the Law, correct?

Wolf: As of now, yes.

One Ear: But not forever?

Wolf: No. And may we remind the Court that a wolf has the right to leave on a temporary or permanent Wilding, at his own choice.

One Ear: We are suitably instructed. May we also remind Prometheus that any wolf on a *permanent* Wilding or deemed 'Wild' is no longer subject to the protections of the Law – in fact, has no more rights than food or clothing?

Wolf: Just so. From Promethean perspective all Martians Alive are meat bodies.

One Ear: And therefore are considered meat, with the rights of meat?

Wolf: We did not say that. You did, Justice.

One Ear: But it is hardly an extrapolation. Seventh Law: "To a Wolf a Cat is NotWolf, just as to a Cat a Wolf is NotCat." So to Prometheans, Martians Alive are "not Prometheans"?

Wolf: The analogy is flawed. Cats never contributed to dogs, but only enslaved them. Prometheus is in truth and in fact contributing daily to Mars Alive.

One Ear: Granted. Contributing power and industry, along with their problems and complexities. As Prometheus seems to grow, however, the birthrate of Mars Alive, as you call it, declines. And as your machines of power become dominant, the dependence of Mars on Prometheus grows.

Wolf: Would you deny Mars the contributions of Promethean science and industry because Mars might come to *expect* this increased state of power and ability?

One Ear: To answer your question, if I had the ability, I might indeed object, but it is a moot point. The contribution, for what it is, has already been made, and now we are discussing, flesh face to metallic face, what are the *terms* of exchange. What is given? What is taken?

Wolf: Much is given.

One Ear: And much has been taken. Do you kill us to fill your recruitment pool?

Wolf: None who were not already ill have come over, except for those who willingly chose to come.

One Ear: And so the ill may not have willingly chosen.

Wolf: Word traps.

One Ear: But very real, very dead Martians. Let me ask you the contrary. Can these "recruits" come back to our side?

The wolf looked up to the sky, as if seeking an answer. Who knows what the gesture was to have meant?

Wolf: So far we do not have an answer to that question. It is too early in our development.

One Ear: Another question then. Are you in communication with Old Ones?

Wolf: We needn't reveal that.

Apollo: I can tell you that Prometheus until recently was certainly not in communication with Old Ones.

One Ear: How do you know that?

Apollo: I cannot rightly describe how I know, but in the same way that I have perception of Prometheus's state, or did until recently, I know. Take it for what it is worth.

One Ear: It is worth much, Apollo. Thank you.

The Justice turned to the Elders Panel. "Do you have a question?"

"Yes," said one elder. They leaned and touched one another, then separated. "We can telepath with one another by touch, and as we grow Elder, sometimes by will we can telepath at a distance with anyone. Apollo is much skilled as a young wolf in this. Why, Counselor Isle, can we not telepath to *your* existence?"

"Because," said the wolf, in a voice dripping with unexpressed arrogance, "because we are no longer the same species." A rippling of fear passed through the audience.

One Ear: Are you not, now? The species is not based on the qualities of the soul, the spirit, but of the body only?

Wolf: I would not say so.

One Ear: How are we so different?

Wolf: We are a sovereign world by evidence of factual separation. You cannot reach us, but we can reach you.

One Ear: As of now, so it seems. You could have been adventurers, founding a colony in a new physical world. But you chose not to be.

Wolf: We were not colonized, or sent out like penal colonies in the past into the Wild. Our separation was forced on us.

One Ear: Forced? How? Did Prometheus not refuse willingly

to leave his damaged, truncated body until it rotted beneath his machine substitute?

Wolf: He left willingly, but the timing of disconnection from the body was taken from him by the weakness of the flesh.

One Ear: Yes, the weaknesses of the flesh. One of the things that we of the flesh are prey to, and enjoy from time to time.

Wolf: We are proud not to be subject to these weaknesses any longer.

One Ear absorbed this in silence. He then looked around the audience, to Loos and Apollo, and to the Elders.

"So be it," said One Ear with quiet finality. "Yet there may be other 'weaknesses' you may discover, and I am glad not to be there in the dark with you to discover the depth of that bottomless pool and what may live in it."

The Justice rose and walked to the Panel of Elders and touched one, who touched the others. They nodded. He then walked over to Loos and touched him, who touched Apollo. Apollo looked up suddenly, and tears came streaming from his eyes.

Speaking to the Steel Wolf again, One Ear said, "You asked for recognition of a status like that of Old Ones, but I see no evidence of any relation to those primordial spirits. If you are owed respect, Prometheus and Prometheans, it must be as one of . . . *us.* The Seventh Law does not apply. You are 'Wolf.' You are not 'NotWolf,' as much as you would like to claim. You are still 'Wolf,' like us, but bodiless, struggling with your strange new state. You should be dealing with us here as family, as you are *part* of us. I say it is arrogance and the height of idiotic foolishness that you try to disconnect from your mother species. And if it is not murder to steal away our sick and young, someone has yet to convince me otherwise.

"The primal difference between us is only that you who were once on this side of the curtain, with bodies like ours, are now on the other side of the curtain. But your minds and souls are still as ours. After all, you speak and dispute with me. We make shadow puppets to communicate legal niceties to one another, Metal Wolf, shadow puppets.

"It is the judgment of this Council that the Law of Mars applies not only to the machines and puppet things of Prometheus Puppets, but that our departed citizens, Isle, Prometheus, and all those others who either willingly or unwillingly are sharing that dimension on the other side of this metallic receiver here, *are* subject to the Laws of Mars.

"Be advised and act accordingly.

"This Hearing is concluded."

The Promethean Puppet contingent erupted into howls of disagreement. Among the public, argument immediately broke out, but in the tone of "What has been decided? What does the decision entail?"

Senior Justice One Ear walked slowly up the stairs and out of the amphitheatre, followed by the Elders. Loos and Apollo took their turn, with Apollo walking past the Wolf and momentarily putting his hand on it. "Nothing," he murmured to his father. "It's just metal." They walked out.

As the public took their leave, the steel wolf sat perfectly still, unmoving in the day's bright sun.

The P-Puppet staff came down, but the wolf took no notice. Only after the staff left and the amphitheatre was empty did it rise onto all fours and walk awkwardly up to the driverless truck and jump into the interior, where it turned and sat. The door closed and the truck departed in an electric hum.

Chapter 19
Two Revolutions

Nothing generates interest like threatening to take something away. On top of that, if an Elder says you *can't* do it or that doing it is *bad,* what warmer recommendation to the younger set could there be? Justice One Ear had had no choice, of course. He had had to call the Prometheans to account, to crack open their social and industrial revolution to Elder scrutiny. Wolf youngsters thought Elders lived in the past and were conservative because of encysted habit. One could have told them (in vain) that it is concern for future consequences that really constrain your experimentation, not the past. Once you know from history that certain side paths lead nowhere or to dank pits, stone walls, or empty waterless deserts, the more you then begin to value the straight and narrow that actually might get you somewhere in the future. But young wolves live in the now – what does my nose smell now? Where is that scent coming from now? What is new? Sniff it out. What happens if you jump and *then* find out if your pull cord *is* connected to a parachute . . . or not, even more fun? What are hormones for it not to boil your flesh down to skin and bone? Do it now for tomorrow you'll be 700 Martian years old and wondering what dead is going to feel like.

All this talk about nebulous darknesses, evil necromancers, and kidnapped souls enslaved to earth-cracking machinery – how hot is that?

As a result Prometheus Puppets, the Mars corporation, no longer needed to steal through hospital records for recruits. Their offices were swamped with live job seekers, not the kind wanting to drop their hot bodies and sail into nevermore, but young canine studs and vixens wanting to get their paws on one of those big earth eater machines and chew some dirt. One Ear had mistakenly instigated this inrush, perhaps, by suggesting to selected young wolves that they might apply to P-Puppets to learn everything about the machines they could, and report back to him.

But P-Puppets was its own draw. And why not? Prometheus had developed the puppet machines first out of his own desire not to go stir crazy through sensory deprivation. Now the mechanical feedback experience had become rich indeed. For Prometheus, his friends and new recruits, once sick or broken but now both free of physical pain and plugged into physical robots, every mechanical turn, bump, slam, slosh, knick, wham, plop converted to a sensory-rich message of *Bumpslamslosh! Knickwhamplop!* Life now was much, much more interesting. And once one had learned how, he could *turn up the feedback amplitude!*

On Mars up to now it had been the rare wolf who could, to give only one example, blow something up, if he were lucky, and then watch or distantly note a few wildly oscillating dials. Now, on the other hand, the bodiless Promethean could *be* that explosion. He was the one eating tons of rock at impossible depths or discovering the joy of being blown back out of his dug geothermal shaft and nearly into orbit by hot plasma. Chewed rabbit or fish was a nice memory, but bore poor comparison to the "live sensation" of engorged iron dust smelted into steel ingots in your mechanical factory gut, or, even more pleasurably, experiencing the rolling of the ingots into sheets and then merrily cutting and stomping them into a myriad of useful shapes.

For the live Martian applicants the prospect of running such a machine or serving it as a kind of furry acolyte was not as glorious as *being* the robot, but the wolfling could still ride it, drive it, or just wash and polish it. He might (of no value to the machine but fun for the befurred eye) paint the machine a little, ornament it with design and malice – teeth, fangs, tail, bloody eye, and the suggestion of flank and shoulder. Why the icehell not?

So, while Elders considered how to implement their proposed justice and to exert lawful control over the reach of Prometheus Puppetry Incorporated, wolf pups and the not-so-pup peopled the machines, rode and served them, helped build and repair them. It escalated in intensity day by day, week by week. Prometheus and Isle did not now have to solicit or connive at disembodied souls when they had fleshed recruits coming at them in droves. At least the physical Martian world and its machined, doll-body empire was well staffed.

It did not take long for One Ear and the Elders to recognize that the more they protested this "corruption of the young" the worse it became. They should have expected this reaction. After all, they had been young once, only a few hundred years ago. One positive outcome, however, of the outrush of live volunteers to P-Puppets Corp was a flattening of the upcurve of "mysterious" deaths. Perhaps the Justice Hearing *had* accomplished its purpose – Prometheus might no longer have to mine the living to recruit Legionnaires for his dead world. As to the industrialization of Mars, there were abundant advantages. Promethean machines carved Mars soil and patrolled the ocean floors, raking up rare minerals. They also manufactured and refined other machines, self-educating in the process. What would it have benefited the Elders to face up against this flood and speak out over the cresting waves, "I think not?"

As if the Elders *could* have done anything about the Revolution, as the wolflings were calling it. Elders grumbled. They compared notes of less and less desirable outcomes. What stunned them, however, was the haste with which their cherished four-footed, soft-padded world was disappearing under clutter and pavement. The whisper of canyon breezes and howl of storms receded behind the clattery noise and screeching grind of gears and motors. It was cacophony. Ugly. The very thing the young wolves reveled in. How lasting this would be, that was another matter.

One thing, however, about Elders – they had learned patience. The Elders hunkered down.

* * *

In all this hustle and bustle, the sparking and clanking of industrial expansion, Apollo disappeared quietly down a mental rabbit hole into his subterranean warren of mind/spirit experimentation and re-invention. His brother Prometheus had coped with his own inky, self-created universe by generating endless electronic feedback from earth-gouging machines. He also had a hyper-loyal lieutenant in the non-person of his former mother. Apollo's home world, though, was peopled with the messy singularity of Chronos, crowded in cheek by jowl with a very young and very female Athena, who had moved herself in to look after them both and to entertain herself needling them.

She did bring joy to the den. Wolf pup bodies mature quickly. The planet's harsh, unforgiving climate demanded it. However, with extended life spans and long, rejuvenating winter sleeps, wolf psyches enjoyed a long emotional and mental youth. Thus they retained an unkillable spirit of play. Adult wolves would have sent them more frequently out on Wildings, for the fun factor, if Wildings were not so perilous.

Athena's artistic, blithe spirit reminded Apollo of himself as a pup. She sang. She made up nonsense poems and Martian limerick haiku that sometimes betokened a deeper intellect or spiritual depth. After pestering her brother to tell her the story of how he became Hopskip Apollo the Mambo King, she proudly recited after dinner that night, accompanied by her own rendition of the Apollo Samba:

There once was a bird named Chronos.
He had a master named Apollo.
A fish ate Pollo, who visited Telemachus,
Who poisoned Apollo, who killed Telemachus,
Who came into Chronos, who drives Pollo crazy.
Question is – who's Chronos and where's Telemachus?
And if Pollo does the mambo with half his legs,
Do the other half dance somewhere in the deep, green sea?

Pollo had a harder time avoiding Athena's persistent personal family questions. Where did Mom go *really*? Do you think she still *loves* me? If Prometheus can talk to his Puppets, why doesn't he talk to *us*? Apollo referred her to Dr. Chronos. They loved to chatter, asking embarrassingly rude questions. To Pollo's biased eye they formed a mirror house of freak images of one another.

"Why are you the only bird who talks and makes sense?" Athena would ask.

"Who says I make sense?"

"Well, I do."

"But your brother doesn't think so."

"He doesn't count."

"He does too. He's the reason I'm trapped in a bird body."

"No he's not. He says the Old Ones tired of you and stuck you in that body to get rid of you."

"That's not nice."

"But he's my *brother*."

"Yes, there's that."

"Do you think you can lay an egg?"

And so forth. On and on and on.

However, when Athena went shopping for food or out to play, Dr. Chronos never lost an opportunity to harp on about getting "fixed." "OK, I'll grant that I'm not dead any more, and that you had something to do with that," he said. "But I can't go on pretending I'm a bird."

"Why not?" said Apollo. "You *are* a bird."

"I'm a nerve toxicologist."

"No, that's what got you killed. You're a bird now."

"So I'm supposed to squawk and act like a hawk, like a bird?"

"I wish you would."

"Not going to happen, Apollo. It's not dignified. Besides, you were affected both positively and negatively by my treatment. If you let me work on you a little further I might be able to even out your legs."

"Come near me, Dr. Bird, and I'll bite your throat out. This time you'll be dead forever."

"You don't know that. I can perceive you have a deep-seated malice, not just against me, but against treatment."

"Right and right again," said Poll. "I also liked Chronos better as a hawk than I do as a neurologist. Why don't you shut the cat crap up and let the fish hawk out for a while?"

"It wounds me to hear this evidence of mental illness so deeply encysted in your psyche. Why don't you unburden yourself to me?"

"What I feel like is . . . roast bird!!" As always when provoked, Apollo barked and leapt in an attempt to catch and eat the bird.

In a more serious frame of mind, Apollo pondered what he could do to free the bird body of its unwelcome inhabitant. "Chronos" must be trapped in there somewhere, and might be restored if he didn't have to share quarters with a mad scientist. Athena had sparked this new train of thought in him when she asked, "If the Old Ones could put Dr. Telemachus in Chronos's body, do you think they could put me in there too? I'd love to fly like a *real* bird."

Meanwhile, demand for Apollo's healing skills grew. He regularly had occasion to practice using spirit to heal body. It was for him a simple matter to *be* the damaged part or the invading virus or growing tumor. He didn't so much heal as just *go* there, be in and of what was "wrong" until he honestly felt it was his own, when he would leave and take it with him. The injured or sick wolf, left behind, either quickly noticed that the condition was gone or felt that mending was taking place and left confident in a healthier future. As the illness, disease, or damaged tissue was not Apollo's to start with, he wound up with nothing persisting in *his* body, mind, or world. It was all rather mystical to him. One thing he was sure of, however. He did go in and occupy the other's body. If he could go in and out of another, he wondered, could he help or make *another* do it? Instead of permeating a body with spirit, could he extract spirit from another's body or switch spirits between bodies? Spooky.

He decided to make a study of it, although he knew that if even a hint of this got to the Elders it was the cliff for him. One day, while Chronos was scratching around his feed bowl, Apollo decided to see what it felt like simply to look through Chronos's eyes. So he *did*.

"Out! Out! Get out of my head!" screeched the doctor in Chronos, flapping around and shaking his head side to side.

"How did you know I was there?" asked Pollo.

"You crowd me. And you're . . . colder than I am, or something. Why did you *do* that?"

"I was interested in what you felt like."

"And what *do* I feel like?"

"I didn't have enough time to tell," lied Apollo, "but you still stink of chemicals."

"I do not."

"You're a pharmacopoeia of poison."

"What a nasty thing to say. And don't come back in me! You're not welcome. There's not even enough room for me."

"And what will you do if I *do* come back in?" returned Pollo with an evil glint in his eye.

Dr. Chronos flapped and clucked. "I don't know. I'll . . . I'll go outside and talk to some of my old dog friends."

"I dare you to."

"That's unkind. You know I can't."

"What's unkind?" asked Athena, trotting back into the den from outside.

"Your vile brother," sniffed Chronos.

"Look what I caught," said Athena, dropping a half-dead large rabbit on the floor. It twitched and jerked in its misery. Without a second thought, Apollo went in and became the rabbit. *The creature was wretched with fear and a broken spine. It could not feel its lower legs. But mostly it was afraid of the wolves, of their smell, their teeth, their slitted eyes. It was afraid of its certain future, being eaten, being pieces in a cookpot.*

Apollo felt all this, commiserating with the poor creature, while at the same time eyeing from the rabbit's perspective his own wolf body, salivating at the prospect of rabbit stew. Pollo considered the meek glowing point that was Mr. Rabbit's seat of consciousness. How could he help the spirit, not the body, wondered Pollo? The body was a goner. The rabbit would have to leave. Poll looked at Chronos, and thought, Now there's a safe home for a rabbit sprite: no cookpot in that big bird's future. As a rabbit, Poll admired how non-rabbit and non-wolflike the big white bird was. He then intuitively strung something like a golden thread between the rabbit critterness and the inside of the big chest of Chronos, and . . . slid the wee rabbit person out, like a ring on a string, over into the bird body.

"Awk!" cried Chronos. He spread his wings wide, and turned to glare at Apollo and then the rabbit. "You're trying something *again*, you . . . cat fancier!" He swooped onto the rabbit, clutching its body in his claws.

Apollo felt the pain of the claws in the rabbit's body. He also felt and almost saw the rabbit minion zing along the invisible thread *back* into its own body, and then discorporate into space as it left behind forever its little dead corpus.

"Didn't like that, did you?" said Pollo to Dr. Chronos.

Chronos lifted a claw as if it would pluck something out of Apollo.

"Just try it," hissed the wolf.

"What? What?" said Athena, oblivious of what had happened, grabbing the rabbit up, fodder for din-din. "Won't you two ever stop?" Chronos flew up to his high perch and made a point of cleaning under his feathers.

Apollo just stared, eyes gleaming. I can do it, he thought. I can learn to transfer spirits from one body to another. He stood, stretched a good, long, dog-down stretch, and sauntered out.

"Where are you going now?" yipped Athena.

"Hunting," said Apollo.

"I'll have good rabbit stew in a while. You come back."

But Apollo was gone into the night.

Chapter 20
PROMETHEAN STRIKE

Who could ever leave well enough alone? Planetary histories are replete with examples of warriors with successes enough to claim victory who then decided it was 'not enough'. Rubicons are made to be crossed, product lines expanded to include one new item too many for the public to comprehend, one world boxing title more to permanently scramble the brains. A game won is not nearly as interesting as a new game.

As their Martian world empire fattened up with eager, living, breathing canine recruits and the Martian economy fell under the sway of radicalized robotic production, Prometheus and Isle, instead of gloating, had an argument.

Like other Prometheans, the bodiless mother and son could not communicate directly with one another. There was no face to face.

When a normal Martian wolf died, departing his body, it was not to lark in sparkling skies and golden dewed dreamscapes, but to start looking for another body. He or she was usually not too interested in spiritual communication. That was Old One stuff and might lead to getting lost in a labyrinthine Math evolution from which one could not find one's way back to the "real" world (meaning bodies made of flesh and blood, powered by sunlight and photosynthesis). Tweenlives was called that for a reason. A newly dead Martian's first duty was, in fact, to avoid going after *flickers,* those faint spiritual glimmerings of Old One conversations. He was supposed to get back to life! To living beings, to a new puppy's body.

To refuse that, not to go home to flesh but to stay out all night, in the fleshless dark, where it was endless night and blacker than oblivion – Martians were not schooled in this. Their genes couldn't tell them (genes talk about meat, blood, semen, drool). They were dead, after all. If a dying wolf had become nearly Old One-enough at great Martian old age that he wished to transubstantiate to another realm entirely – that of infinite Math doodling amongst the stars of infinite other universes – then once such a wise old geezer did die, the Old Ones might sling him or her a rope to be reeled in, over to their Other Side. But if instead a boulder had crushed a not-yet-ready-to-be-dead body, or a bear had made unhappy lunch of oneself, this was just an interruption. You were racing to escape something's fangs. Oops – you ran into another set of fangs, and, bang, there you were in Tweenlives. Without a telephone, no microphone. Oh, you might be able to send out a last semaphore Yawp! to a family member or friend back among the living. But that was it. I'm dead. Sorry. Bye! There would follow a timeless interval (literally no-time), and the next thing you knew you were sucking phlegmy air in through a newborn pup's nose and mouth, wondering, "Who in cat hell am I *now*?"

But if you could *not* return to a body, then you were stuck in the zone of timeless, no-form, no-inflow/outflow of blood-body sensation – in Tweenlives. Hence you either headed over to the Old Ones, never to return (there never having been a record of such – no canine Osiris or Orpheus later writing a braggadocio *History of the Dead.*), or, alternatively, you went stark, non-staring, eyeless mad.

Unless, as in the unique circumstance of Prometheus, you had determined never, ever to surrender the communication line to Mars Alive, even once your past body was putrid dead, dead, dead. Then you connived, with the help of your Martian engineer friends, how to sign via increments of mocked-up micro-energy pulses back to Martian machines, eventually to graduate to operating a doll of yourself *as* yourself, but over there back on the old world, Mars.

Prometheus could have followed the lead of his loopy, spinny, artsy fartsy brother Apollo, who seemed to have been able to holler to Prom out in the opaque void through some kind of psychic tube. But if Prom had sniffed after Pollo, that would mean Apollo had been taking the lead, and that would be *following.* Between the twins, from Day One, there had been no following one's brother. There had been competition: the Game. Apollo had been the one that had killed Prometheus (at least, according to Prom's zero-dimensional Chart of Responsibilities conceived during his descent into demented overwhelm of pain). Prometheus was not going to let Apollo win, so he ignored both him and his goofy bag of non-engineering skills. Instead Prom chose intentionally to hang out in the dark until he had worked out how to run doll body, mechanical, golem substitutions back on planet Mars. Prom wanted to play and win the Mars Game *his* way.

Thus, when Isle and all the other "Legionnaires" had come over to his side, all their communication drills concerned communicating via Promethean Puppet robotics, not telepathy. Even Isle and Prom had lost the ability to talk, much less argue, faceless face to faceless face. They could, however, morse code or semaphore rather eloquently via electronic terminals at home (Mars). Still, argue they did.

* Prometheus, we can't wait.

! Commander Isle, you're hasty.

* The Elders have unpredictable powers. They could interrupt our power evolution.

! They could try, and they would fail. Everything is going well. After their foolish trial the Elders have done *nothing*. They can do nothing in the face of P-Puppets' overwhelming support by industrial Mars.

* Prometheus, they can and will act to cut us off . . . once they comprehend our plan.

! They can't see it.

* You don't know that.

! No, I don't know that. So what? What is your worry? Do I detect that Isle is afraid?

* We don't have enough Legionnaires. To be free, to establish our own safe and secure domain, we need more troops, here where we are.

! Live recruits will come over voluntarily as they learn how much more alive they can be running Puppets, not dependent on slow, soft body, wet and sloppy nerve tissue.

* They will volunteer if they have enough time to learn. But we may not have that time.

! And you would?

* I would resume forceful recruitment.

! When?

* Now.

! That *would* provoke an Elder response, Isle.

* Better to call it up when we can expect it. The Elders are surely preparing an attack in secret, as we delay.

! You are convinced of this?

* I was much older than you before I came over. I know how they think.

! I wonder if you still do.

* If you doubt my competence, Commander, replace me with another.

! If I doubted your competence, Commander, I would have. Very well. Carry out your recruitment, but do it forcefully and quickly. I have research work to do.

* As you order, Supreme Command.

! Over to you. Report compliance.

* As you order. Please inform the Legionnaire Instructors to prepare for an influx.

! Done.

* * *

Her raid struck with a coordination and suddenness possible only via the electronic realm. The throwing of a switch, and a thousand lights went out. These were the lights in the eyes of a thousand live Puppet drivers, rugged, young operators riding in control cabins of earthmovers, diggers, tractors, shovel scoops, trucks, electric plant managers, manufacturing managers controlling a hundred machines as one. One moment they were drilling, digging, pumping, grinding, hammering, welding, across the world, underwater, hanging on canyon walls, traveling in the air. The next moment – their eyes went out. Sans warning, a thousand wolves suffered a stroke of such force that each just slumped lifeless in his or her engineering chair.

They had been *taken.*

Those who had not been stolen over did not know what had happened to their work colleagues, until alarms sounded in Martian towns from far-flung Puppet operations. Details were compared from town to town. The date-time coincidence of sudden death was unmistakable.

The precision of the attacks stunned the Elders. The implications were the most frightening thing they had ever confronted. How silently and efficiently the stroke had been made. That it could have been no catastrophic mistake of a gang switch thrown was made too clear when not one Puppet machine ceased to perform its functions despite the death of its Mars Alive controller. Someone from the other side had taken over full control at the very moment each live operator was killed. The machines now were maybe not as precisely controlled, not having the live eyes and ears to judge subtle distances and boundaries, but machine operations were essentially uninterrupted.

Those live Puppeteers who had not been spiritually commandeered bailed from their machines in hope that distance from the puppet electronic receivers might provide safety. It did. Only those who remained behind, as machine operators, silently willing to be "volunteered" with permanency, to transfer title to Prometheus, were then taken. Those who had turned tail were almost all exempt. Almost all. Some must have gone into a mesmeric agreement with their machines' crystal receiver frequencies, because a few were struck down elsewhere, far from their mechanical devices.

Word raced back to the Elders. A Planetary Emergency Call went out. Not since the prehistoric last battle with the Cats had there been a planetary call.

A few P-Puppet living corporate officers asked for a meeting with the Elders. They believed that there must have been a catastrophic accident. They were all arrested or immediately thrown off the nearest cliff.

Without declaration the First Promethean War was on. Hardly a war. More a helterskelter series of vicious skirmishes.

Commander Isle had been correct: the Elders had not been asleep. After Senior Justice One Ear had ordered a Chart of Responsibilities to be drawn up for the missing (abducted) wolves – with P-Puppet silence in response – the Elders quickly concluded that in this case silence was an admission, challenging them, the Elders, to do something about it. So they had started planning – how could the living wolves co-opt the machines? Already most Martian towns depended for their increased power consumption on P-Puppet energy. Inter-city transport was nearly one hundred per cent P-Puppet. Manufacturing had been revolutionized and taken over. Despite this, there was no quibble that cutting off the Promethean Puppets would temporarily cripple Martian towns and villages.

"No more than a single Killing Winter ever has," one Elder snapped. "We came back from those."

They had plotted where they could cache and secure food. What were their essential energy needs and how could electric power lines be re-connected to non-Puppet, old-energy sources (smaller hydroelectric generators, geothermal pumps, wind).

And then Isle struck, too soon. They had known it would come. Word arrived quickly from their spies amongst P-Puppet staff, but also from sincere young wolf drivers who had merely loved the work and adventure, but wanted no part of leaving the here and now and one's family for the dark Promethean alternative. In that intuitive, possibly telepathed flash that communal wolf pack minds can do, wolves everywhere realized they had an *immediate* choice – stay with the Elders and other older, live, non-mechanized Martian wolves, or go over to the Puppets.

What Isle had not predicted was the seemingly instantaneous counterattack on Puppet machines from wolf packs in cities and countrysides planetwide. As the call went out that Prometheus was killing their brethren, living wolves swarmed over the still lumbering machines with rope and tackle. If they could not immobilize a machine with tie lines, they could at least tie it *to* something that would confuse its motion. Or they cleverly tied Puppet monsters together to whirl in drunken waltzes, backing into rivers or falling off cliffs. The machines could not be deactivated through surface controls. They were being run from Prometheus's side.

Isle struck back. Machines turned and began to bulldoze communal buildings, power poles, to cut through vital aqueducts. Isle turned off the power at major energy plants under her control, except in distant polar and undersea areas where Prometheans needed that energy for themselves.

Though lithe and wily, the wolves were glad enough that no war machines had been created by Prometheus Puppets. Soon enough, they knew, they would have these to contend with. But, thank sunshine, not yet.

The wolves mobbed one machine at a time. Sticks and stones, particularly stones, could jam mechanical systems. There were not so many machines yet, and they were not so well under "far control" that they could escape the scurrying, ratlike army of wolves chewing away at them.

In war, civilian and vindictive targeting follows its own illogic. Isle sent a bulldozer toward Loos's den, despite the fact that it was down in a cave on one of the Grand Cliff Faces. She later threw one of the few Puppet Fliers at Loos, but it crashed wastefully against the stone wall. She sent bulldozers into collegiate dens where Apollo and his friends lived. Apollo grabbed his sister by the scruff of her neck, to her infinite embarrassment, and bolted out. To Apollo's dismay Chronos flew out after him and landed on Pollo's mottled grey back, riding him with wings flapping, squawking great screeches of fury.

Within hours, or at most by the end of the day, into the night, those machines that had not been incapacitated, burned, or pushed into crevices or off cliffs, retreated north or south away from civilization toward the cold and ice of the polar regions. Where machines had been so adapted, they crawled to the seashore, and like great ugly crabs disappeared under the waves.

The exhausted wolves let the machines go. Enough for now. Their towns were now again unlit, and colder. Communication systems they had become used to were down. Too many buildings were rubble. Many wolves had been wounded, half-crushed or broken by the machines' uncaring, unseeing wheels or treads. Apollo and other healers got down to the bloody triage following all battles.

"We're set back hundreds of years," groused One Ear to Loos and Scar Shank.

"Ahh, it only seems so because your one damn ear has become inured to the yammering and clanking of the twice damned robotoids," said Scar Shank. "In a few days you'll pleasantly recall the quiet from not so long ago."

"Maybe," said Loos. "But I for one have gotten comfortable in my heated den. We'd better grow our fur coats out."

"And a good thing too," said Scar Shank's wife, coming up. "Yours is scruffy enough."

* * *

The Puppet machines retreated beyond the north and south horizons, leaving trails of red dust. One thing Prometheus and Isle had prepared in advance was planetary polar bases: they had already strung power lines or dug special geothermal pipes. Machines trundled across the tundra, a parade of unworldly, personless motors, with purpose but no life. Some turned round at periodic intervals and dug themselves in, to be sentinels and first line defense if and when the wolves counter-attacked. They sat stiller than anything except a machine can sit, signal lights and sensors blinking. Blink. Blink. Engines idled enough to keep the Puppet machines warm and operational. Machines too could be patient: if more patient than the Elders was yet to be seen.

Wolves slunk up to crests and hunkered down to watch the semi-hidden quiet machines, but they could not spy on those that crawled down onto the ocean floor. The poles had never been wolf domain. But its very harshness and cold and dark made it comfortably similar to the Promethean realm.

What Prometheus found deep in the ocean, and had desperately needed, was a source of power. Great power. There were many rare minerals down in the ocean depths, but surely the most important for the future of Prometheus was uranium.

Chapter 21
Wolf Counterstrike

Like other intelligent species on geophysically active planets, Martian wolves were used to cleaning up after catastrophe. Besides, war is war, and when hasn't there been war?

Pre-Promethean townships had been low tech, low maintenance. To accommodate killer winds and the water mass of snow, most buildings were domed or underground chambers, tunnels, or caves. The battle damage was, therefore, not so much fallen rubble of buildings as broken domes over sunken spaces, sometimes with one or two behemoth vehicles upside down, engines still running. Their electric motors either ran down or clever young wolves crept near to insert stones or dirt to jam the works. The air reeked with burnt electricity ozone.

Removing the Puppet machine carcasses required block and tackle and a lot of muscle power. But so soon after Prometheus's departure, Elders were reluctant to use *any* powered mechanical help, much less a former Puppet machine, whose control systems had been designed to be run from elsewhere. Some machines seemed to have had resident Prometheans, temporarily housed in their homing crystal on-site in the mechanism. When the wolves found hidden crystals on the abandoned vehicles, it was hard to discern if the Promethean was still present or had been recalled to his dark home world. They destroyed them, until Scar Shank ordered they be preserved for study.

There was also the sad matter of digging out crushed wolf friends or family and casting their bodies into the rivers. Wolves were not much for ornate burial. As after hibernation deaths, their ceremonies consisted simply of naming and thanking the lost friend. Being midsummer, when the Great Fish were down in ocean lairs, swordfish were not on hand to accept the dead and convert them to fish flesh. Wolf clans watched silently as hundreds of their friends and clan members dropped the long fall to the rivers. The bodies of those who had fought and died near the seashore were taken out on rafts and slipped overboard. It was honorable to become fish food. Wolves farming on the banks of plains rivers had mostly been spared the fighting, as they and their farms were irrelevant to Promethean purpose, which was focused only on power and energy. Prometheus had not yet learned, thank the stars, how to tap into a living carbo-oxidation engine for energy. His needs were more immediate and dynamic. Farms were invisible to him. But where farmhand wolves had been killed fighting in support of their city brethren or attacking Puppet machines retreating across their farms, the farmers were buried in compost mounds. No fertilizer for invaluable soil conversion or food growing was ever wasted.

As clean up and renovations continued, the Elders called an All Clans Council. This started with a soul cleansing ritual, a barking and yipping which carried only emotional meaning, leading in a slow crescendo to a dirge of howling, and then an even slower diminuendo. Then the Elders sat or lay in silence, or trotted slowly around to nose one another and pay respects. There could have been a calling to account for Senior Justice One Ear or for Scar Shank, who was the closest thing they had to a senior military officer as Peace Enforcer, and for other top dogs, but the Chart was clear. They all shared responsibility. They had all been enjoying the fruits of Promethean industry. By mutual unspoken consent nothing was said. Finally Justice One Ear broke the silence.

"Technology is always addictive."

Yip, yip. Bark, bark.

"But outright rejection of technology is worse than stupidity. It's suicidal."

One howl. Otherwise mostly unvoiced grim agreement.

"We had no significant troubles managing our own technological development until the artificial stimulus of Prometheus's mad genius. So let us agree to have no turning our tails on essential uses of technology to protect our people."

A time of silence. Then one Elder spoke up. "That is agreeable, but surely we must also be careful not to let the Prometheans sneak back in. How will we prevent that?"

"We will watch," said Scar Shank.

"And who will watch the watchers?" questioned one of the most Elderly.

"Who indeed?" answered Scar Shank. "That has always been the question. That is the function of Justice and of all the Clans. We will watch ourselves as we have always done. No one wolf nor any one Clan is to dominate all others."

"It is the Law. It is the Law," voiced several.

"But," said Scar Shank, "we cannot rest and lick our wounds too long. The Prometheans are not expunged. They have only retreated."

"I wouldn't say 'retreated,'" commented old Two Boots. "Following their spoor, it would be more accurate to say they have *advanced* to where we are weakest and have seized salients in the frozen Poles and the depths of the sea."

"We don't want those," said Left Limper, another war veteran.

"But we need the Poles, nonetheless," said Oldest, the senior Elder present. "The Poles preserve our water, form our weather, and hold other mysteries. And who knows the treasures unknown in the deeps of the seas? Would you turn over the Great Fisheries to the

Prometheans? Think, you fools!"

Much woofing and barking.

"Aye," said One Ear. "We must plan an attack on the Poles. Before winter. We cannot leave Prometheus behind during our next full hibernation to construct surprises for us when we creep stupidly out in the spring."

"And the seas?" one asked.

"If anyone has a solution for pursuing the machines into the ocean deeps, let him speak up or go take the great swim himself," snapped One Ear, clicking his teeth in disgust. No one had anything further to say. "So be it. We will watch the shores and arm ourselves to repel any return of Prometheus. But we will start planning immediately for a polar attack."

This was straightforward, good advice, met with long howls of agreement tinged with more than a little bloodlust (albeit the machines providing no blood).

As the All Clans dispersed One Ear called out, "Apollo. Loos."

They trotted over and nosed the Justice politely.

"You were silent."

"There's enough wisdom in these hard times without my thin voice," said Loos.

"Don't pretend stupidity. Both you and Apollo have insights into Prometheus and Isle that the rest of us will never have. I want you to reach out and try to search their minds."

Pollo and Loos ducked their heads down. They had had enough of these "insights."

"Physician, heal thyself," said One Ear to Apollo.

"And how will I do that?" asked Poll.

"You should know better than anyone else. We need your skills. I suggest you two walk and hunt together. Land, sky, and water will heal you. They always heal."

"Good advice, old One Ear."

"That's why they give me the thankless jobs," he griped.

* * *

Prometheus and Isle had commanded their remaining heavy robotics to continue trundling north and south away from civilization, to put maximum distance between their machines and the wolves and to have more advance warning before the wolf counterattack, which they knew must inevitably come.

* We should attack them first, sent Isle.

! Good tactics if we had the strength and weapons, signaled Prometheus back. But we have neither . . . at this time.

Prom asked Lieutenant Demeter for advice. Demeter suggested establishing bases in both polar areas near where polar land masses were ice free and sloped gradually down into the surf, so that minerals mined from the sea floor could be more easily delivered. Secondarily, near both Poles were volcanic geothermal shafts that had been dug or widened. Developing these into full power stations was crucial. It had been Demeter who had earlier recommended to Prometheus that P-Puppets exploit these far stations as they would be needed some future day. His foresight had saved them from the disaster of having no energy source.

The Promethean machines stationed north and south were directed to tunnel down into the ice to shelter themselves from wind and cold, which could eventually crack even metal into splinters.

Isle began her war preparations. She ordered the conversion of some shovel-armed diggers into catapults, and set other diggers to breaking up volcanic rock and shaping chunks into missiles.

Prometheus knew it would be futile to chastise Isle for provoking the wolf clans' response. She would already be chewing on that herself. He admitted to himself that battle with fleshed wolves had been inescapable, only a matter of time. This way, the Prometheans had at least come away with a thousand newly conscripted Legionnaires. The fresh recruits were still in shock, panic, and terror at having been kidnapped, soul-stolen, or whatever one wanted to name it. Some newcomers, however, had already been weighing the pros and cons of going over to Prometheus, so were not utterly surprised. Even if, had they still bodies, the neophytes would have been shitting their dens in fear, now they lost no time in learning their language and communication protocols.

What other choice had they?

The Master Sergeants over these boot camps were seasoned Prometheans who themselves had once been terrified at first coming over. They were now all the more ruthless in disciplining cowardly new arrivals. The most difficult to train, of course, were those souls who had died fighting against Prometheus, who had had his catcher net spread to capture any of those killed he could. The obvious handling for those recruits who resolutely resisted contact with Promethean voices in the dark was simply to *leave* them be. Blocked from Tweenlives signals that would pull a wolf soul back to the living, these stranded ones would quickly go "tweeny" (pitifully desperate for a body) and accept, rather than having nothing, the bleak substitute of Promethean selfhood skills to be taught them.

Meanwhile Prometheus wrestled with his High Command. Isle and her hardcore coterie were for destroying the wolf world and forcing them *all* to become Prometheans.

• It is our future that is glorious. Of infinite potential, Isle sent.

! Your zeal is duly appreciated, Commander, sent Prometheus.

♦ But, if I may contribute, sent Demeter, it is unrealistic. We don't have the machinery, nor the manufacturing capacity to create enough machines in the time needed for an all-or-nothing battle.

• Then what are we to do?

! Whatever we do, we will need alternative fuels for electric power.

♦ I suggest devoting as much electric current as we can to breaking up the pure water from the ice caps into hydrogen and oxygen gas. We can make tanks, which even if not perfectly sealed will do the job, given our limitless supply.

! It is ordered.

• That is still a short term solution. What are we to do in the long term? Negotiate with Mars Alive?

! No. I have the solution. I just don't know how to execute it.

The key to Prometheus's perfect solution arrived when the Sea Floor Puppets began crawling up out of the surf, covered in seaweed, carrying deep-dredged rock with high concentrations of uranium. Mars Alive scientists had long known that purified uranium generated a nearly endless quantity of heat. They knew it could be used to create power, but the killing damage from radioactivity and the threat to future generations of live wolves had been considered too great a risk. With more than adequate geothermal, they had not needed the heat generated from uranium piles. Prometheans, however, desperately needed mobile power-generation sources, and radioactive damage to machines was of a controllable order.

Prometheus ordered that top priority be given to producing H^2 and O^2, huge amounts of it, and to mining and refining uranium into hot, dangerous stores. He also ordered that his best engineers concentrate on creating a new class of Puppet – a highly versatile, self-contained, auto-duplication robot.

! These are to be small, Demeter. Very small. No more than six should be necessary to replicate themselves, or to create other Puppets who can then themselves make tools and manufacture other Puppets.

♦ Yes, we can do that. Do you need them at both polar locations?

! At which pole can we most productively collect uranium ore from the sea?

♦ The North Pole.

! Then put the H^2 and O^2 fuel depots plus the Puppet manufacturing emphasis at the North Pole. Iris!

• Yes, sir.

! Create weapons for defense at each pole. Harass the Martians Alive from the South Pole, but place our strongest defenses in the north.

• Very well.

♦ How soon, Commander, do you need these perfect, little do-it-yourself robots?

! Our very existence depends on how well and how fast you can create these, Demeter. As soon as you have them in development, report to me. I have a fourth task, equally vital and urgent. Our strategy is simplicity itself. All must be done, done perfectly, and accomplished with miraculous efficiency at the frozen ice caps of the poles.

♦ That we are here at all, first yourself, and now the rest of us, is a miracle itself, Supreme Commander. Why not further miracles?

! Why not? Because, my insouciant friend and Lieutenant, if we do not produce these last miracles, all of them, then it was all for naught. Start. I will help as much as I am technically able.

And so they did. Prometheus became unavailable for anything other than supervising these four tasks. Even Isle could not get to him.

• What about a defense strategy, when we are attacked?

! That is your task, Commander. Prepare the defense. You must hold off the wolves alive. You are free to harry and disperse them in advance with skirmishes, but prepare your main forces to create an iron wall of defense here in the north. We have no retreat from the north.

• Mars Alive will not break through, not one wolf, sent Iris.

* * *

Scar Shank appointed Left Limper as his second in military command. Even as he and Limper and other deputies were discussing tactical maneuvers for the attacks on both Promethean polar bases, Isle carried out lightning mini-strikes against southern wolf towns. Some machine raids, middle of the night affairs, were just nuisances, aggravations with no real point. But others were against specific industries and factories and carried away plunder. These targeted former Promethean stores of electronics, factories where sheet metal was rolled, and for whatever reason where there were stores of gold. Industrial metal rollers and related equipment were hauled off by Promethean trucks. After this, Scar Shank ordered all major stores of electronics to be moved further away from the south and north towards the Martian equator.

"What are our strengths?" Scar Shank asked his planners in one meeting. "With respect to Promethean weaknesses, what assets or potencies can we utilize?"

"We're brave and courageous," suggested Stripes, another warrior boasting even more scars than their commander, his from a battle with a Great Cat in a recent Wilding.

"Yes, but that's beside the point. We will be brave and courageous against inanimate machines that do not concern themselves with honor and courage. What will be our *military* strengths in this coming battle?"

Left Limper said, "We're mobile. We're quick. As individual

units, wolves can make split-second decisions and do not have to be operated from some combat central on the far side of nowhere, or wherever they are."

"Exactly," said Scar Shank. "Also, we can concentrate as a well-coordinated wolf pack, or spread out and then re-form as a pack. We can also fly."

"But maybe they can," said Limper.

"How?" said Scar Shank. "Everything they have or operate is made of metal. Unless they were to make some great flying beast of a machine, which we won't give them time to do, I don't think they can fly. In any case, what are Promethean machine strengths? Know your enemy. They have the strength and endurance and toughness of metal. And electronic perceptions that we don't have."

"They don't experience pain," said Limper. "Of course, neither do we when we're crazed with battle, but it's not the same thing."

"Not the same thing at all," said Scar Shank. "Worse, they're not *alive* so they don't *die*. They're mobile and active, or rendered immobile and inactive. They will be run as machines. Prometheus and Isle will use or waste them as they see fit. They won't have the same concern about their value as we might consider the lives of our people."

"But I'll tell you a weakness they have, in the same context," said Heraklitos, one of the younger commanders in the planning group. "The machines are controlled, all of them, from that crystal receptor or what it's evolved into. I'm sorry that I helped Prometheus develop it in the first place, but if we get to that device, wherever it is in each machine, the Prometheans can't then reach and control the machine. It becomes inert metal."

"Yes," said Scar Shank. "That's our greatest strength and their greatest weakness. We each control ourselves and think for ourselves. Their puppets are all controlled by electronic strings from elsewhere. And so far the machines don't think for themselves."

"Our other strength, too obvious not to miss, is that there are a lot more of us than them," commented Limper.

"They might, however, be willing to spend the coin of all their machines to win, whereas we aren't willing to spend the lives of all our soldiers."

"I for one will die with honor," barked Stripes.

"I'm sure," said Scar Shank respectfully. "The point is to eliminate the Prometheans as a menace to our people and that we win that objective. What we don't know is *their* objective."

No one had anything to suggest.

Finally Scar Shank said, "We'll not rely on our pack strength, which we demonstrated instinctively in the first fight, swarming over their machines. Iris will expect that. What we need to get clever about is immobilizing their machines from a distance. We don't have the firepower to pierce thick armor."

This led into a discussion of grenades, bombs, and cannon shells. The problem was that Martian civilization was very limited in its stockpiles of nitrogen and other key components of explosives. Nitrogen and such chemicals, derived from living sources past or present, was a commodity precious for its fertilizer uses. All life forms were composted to produce as much fertilizer as possible to develop better soil, which would support more abundant plant life than normally grew on the tundra. Nevertheless, to win this fight they decided to use as much nitrogen and other chemicals as needed. They carefully figured the chemical value of the thousand bodies left behind by the souls stolen by Prometheus. They knew these spirits would not be returning to be reborn, and their existing bodies would not need to support their future replacements in the population. They also figured the dark mathematics of how many wolves might die in the polar battles, and how many of those might not return.

Scar Shank asked Apollo and the Eldest Elders to study what they could do to prevent Prometheus capturing more departing souls of wolves killed in battle. This was their most terrible and gruesome prospect. The Eldest wolves, close to death with one paw on the other side, had an intuitive understanding of the process of dying, but did not have much to contribute to this discussion. Having been in direct communication with Prometheus and with his mother after they left their bodies, Apollo said he thought it had something to do with the *aloneness* of dying. Directly after leaving the body, the soul was compulsively attracted to a source of light, smell, and communication. Tweenlives provided something to guide a wolf soul back to life.

Prometheus, Apollo suggested, must either provide a false lure or be able to control the soul after death. Prom could steal the dead only at the moment of dying, Apollo thought. He suggested that all the wolves who were to fight in the upcoming battles should practice how to stay in communication with one another telepathically, particularly if wounded or if they felt they were dying.

"Find another wolf you know well," Apollo said. "Psychically call out his or her name. And focus with all your will on that living spirit as your last thought."

"Do you really think that will work?" asked Eldest.

"Dunno. It might. It only has to work long enough for Prometheus not to be able to snatch us and for Tweenlives to take over. Can you suggest something better?"

"That I cannot," said Eldest.

It was so ordered, and thousands of wolves, male, female, and pups, for the first time did these 'passing-over' drills, which they joked about as being laughable and goofball. Perhaps that was the drill's strength. In fact it served them well. Used by many at the point of death, it much reduced the future net by Prometheus and his spirit captors, sniffing forever for the aroma of imminent death.

Once enough explosive had been manufactured, Scar Shank ordered advance units of attack wolves to sneak into Promethean polar territory to mine their roads. This was a major failure. Although the wolves had dyed their fur prematurely white, their camouflage was useless as the Promethean sensors were not looking for them by sight but through infrared, where they stood out like beacons against snow and ice. Wolf flyers also tried to scout over the poles to see what they could. Some were shot down by catapults that could throw a far stone, and the others were prevented by bad weather and thick ground fog. Over the south, where it was winter, one flyer actually made it over the pole and back. He reported seeing two large circular snow berms, high snow barriers, one within the other, with the innermost circle domed over. Promethean Puppets were moving around, setting up defenses, but nothing conclusive was seen, other than that they had set up large catapults. Whatever else was hidden under the snow.

The day of battle

The wolves struck South and North Pole bases on the same day in late northern summer. One strike was in daylight, the other in darkness.

Having tried without success to psych out what Prometheus or Isle might have been planning, Apollo told Scar Shank that Prometheus was successfully keeping his mind blank, but Apollo sensed he was carefully hiding something at the North Pole. Apollo was certain the north must be where the make or break point was. Having no other data to go by, Scar Shank agreed to concentrate rather more on the north and to place his own command there. He kept Apollo with him. Scar Shank ordered Loos to accompany Left Limper, who would command the attack on the South Pole. Both attacks were to occur simultaneously, so Prometheus could not learn from one attack how better to defend against the other. But then, neither could the wolves learn from their errors.

During the heyday of Prometheus Puppets the corporation had assumed control of the planetary electronic communication systems, expanding them for their own uses. Before they retreated they had sabotaged what they could. Effective electronic communication from pole to pole had not yet been restored, but through relays messages could be sent. The polar attacks would thus have to be essentially independent.

In the days before battle, trucks and boats ferried thousands of wolves and catapults up and down toward staging areas. In late summer there were still long, long days and short and sneak up onto the beaches. Just before their wolf comrades arrived they were to strike the Promethean guardians at the seashore.

The South Pole

Before winter's faint and late dawn, in that half-light the wolves called Sleepy Sun, wolf columns raced in over the grey ice, running two by two. The columns snaked back and forth to be more difficult targets. All wolves wore external heat reflectors. They were now nearly invisible by infrared. A keen eye could have seen their large puffs of exhaled breath, and a keener eye their eyes slitted yellow and red with battle lust.

The troops wore steel visors with helmet caps and steel mesh coats with articulated steel plates along the spine, all armor painted the off-white blue-green grey of slushy ice. Only stripes and spots on the helmets differentiated officers from grunts. There were few officers. Wolves in battle cannot be much directed. Some ran without weapons other than fang and claw, which had been sharpened, steel caps unnecessary as wolf fangs can bite through almost anything. Others carried packs of explosive or acid grenades or other weapons or battle tools. There were medics and semaphore signal dogs, electronic messaging having been thought too dangerous as that universe was dominated by Prometheus.

The officers had told their troops to run in silence. For the first few miles they complied, but as soon as they crossed the low horizon and were able to see their enemy armored against them, strange lights blinking and the ground ice smelling metallic and chemically perverse, the wolves began a low ululation. Their wordless song was older than civilization. It sang of death to the enemy, hail to the comrade on my left and on my right, crush bone and lap blood. To a friend it sounded of the joy of livingness – I am alive and a danger to my enemy, my blood is hot, my mouth is dry. An enemy hearing it, be it wolf, cat, or bear, would instinctively suck up testicles or pull in teats and crouch low to the ground. Who knows what it became when translated through tinny receivers into electronic signal to Prometheus? Probably just a mechanical oscillation indicating "approach of hostiles." Apollo, trying in spiritual silence to listen in on Prometheus's world from the northern front, attacking at the same moment, felt only a distant hint of *loss*, loss of the whole world of flesh abandoned for a realm of different senses and unlike experience. If there had ever been a thought in Prometheus's mind that he still had a paw in his last life, even a hair of a lost tail, Apollo saw that there remained now not even the shred of such a memory. To Prometheus and Isle, if not to Demeter and other former friends, the attack by howling wolves was as foreign to them now as their metal towers and combatant tanks appeared to the racing wolf pack, breathing hot as their galloping claws cut rhythmically into the ice.

Prometheus's infrared sensor towers, set out around the concentric snow berms, began to pick up on the attackers as their running bodies heated up. They triangulated upon targets. Mobile catapults, converted from Puppet machines, started hurling buckshot, wickedly sharp volcanic stones. Catapults were traditional battle weapons and wolves were highly skilled at targeting with them. Once the buckshot started falling murderously amongst the columns the wolves dispersed, but still ran two by two, the ancient canine battle order.

As they ran on, the wolves ran into the second Promethean defense, the most hated and despised ancient weapon against wolf paws running on snow or dirt – the wolf trap. Iris had made and scattered these in random arrays. If she had used these forbidden weapons in the flesh and been captured in battle, she would have been eviscerated and her body left to rot on the ice with her head on a pike. Once wolves began to step on them, screaming their protest in shrieking wails, Limper brought up light sleds which strong lead wolves pushed in front of the weaving lines to spring the traps. The speed of the wolf advance was slowed but came on implacably. Their howls mutated into snarls.

As the wolves closed to within two miles of the Southern Promethean base, Left Limper ordered the few explosive cannon relegated to his front to start firing from the rear. Short on high grade explosive, the cannons were more mortars than long-barrel weapons. Their ammunition was volcanic rock bombs with hollow interiors filled with acid to eat into sensitive machinery parts. They shot in high arcs to drop vertically with great force onto the berms and their interiors.

Iris had expected cannonades. She had constructed mobile, fast tanks with catapults and hidden them in shallow tunnels in a two mile circumference round the base. With explosions of snow, these tanks burst up into the middle of the wolf horde and raced to attack Limper's mortars. Not needing orders, the wolves turned on the Promethean tanks and swarmed over them. In defense, the tanks whirled in standing circles, lowering their catapult arms to bat crushed wolves in flying spirals of bodies and blood. Wolves out of distance of the spinning arms ducked, swayed, and dashed in to leap on the tank carapaces looking for control crystals. They had drilled how either to crush the crystal or dig it out to save for later study. If they couldn't discover it, they threw or placed acid grenades into sensitive regions, and jumped off. The grenades either successfully immobilized the tanks or damaged their control systems so that they zigged and zagged out of control. Still dangerous to wolves whom they could crush under their wheels and treads, they eventually found their disorderly way down to the sea to drown, or fell back like drunken giants into the holes from which they had come.

Then Iris sprang her second vicious counter-attack. As the wolf packs began to enter a circle a few hundred lengths closer to the Promethean base, another wave of snow bursts blew up amongst them. A different set of P-Puppet vehicles leapt out of hidden tunnels. These were low to the ground with four wheels set out from each corner. Instead of racing toward the wolves they immediately stopped, and dropped a small robot cart from underneath each vehicle, which moved out beside it. With one metal arm, the little robot pulled out a wire extending from the central turret and placed a pawsize stone in the small sling pocket at the end of the line. The turrets then began to spin incredibly fast. Targeting objectives with the aid of the triangulating towers on the outer berm walls, when these motorized slingshots released their stones they flew nearly at the velocity of cannon shells. They destroyed whatever they hit. If they hit a wolf they pulverized it and the next and the next beyond him. The whirling slingshot wires themselves decapitated or halved the bodies of any wolves maddened enough to come within their cutting range. The sling machines had appeared throughout a far circumference and therefore could target wolves and wolf machines both closer in and further out. Left Limper was going to call for a tactical retreat but there was nowhere to go. The wolf troops instinctively flattened themselves to the ground, with that low profile every wolf had trained itself to present when hunting small game as a pup out on the steppes.

The slingshots appeared to have the field. But as the wolves watched, each sling had to wind down to reload another stone in its sling pouch. It then moved to another location, while other slings were still firing, so the field of fire had singing stones whistling across the ice without let up. Nevertheless, observant wolves, barking to one another to coordinate, started attacking each sling after it had fired and wound down, but before it could be reloaded. The wolves went first after the robot carts, turning them upside down or ripping their little arms off. With the slings slowed for reloading, they damaged their control with a grenade, cut the sling wire, or tore off a wheel. The slings wounded or killed hundreds of wolves, but before long most had been rendered inoperative.

Surviving officers or self-determined wolf warriers reconstituted their attack companies. Support from wolf cannons in the rear had fallen silent: the Promethean catapults and slings had destroyed them. In response, the separated wolf packs gathered instinctively (and strictly against earlier standing orders) into larger battalions. They no longer had energy to waste howling, but padded forward silently, closing with malevolent intent on the snow berms. As they approached they could see the snow barriers were composed of snow and ice packed around demobilized Puppet machines.

Not all the Puppets were inert. A dozen large retooled quadra-tread bulldozers drove out from under the outer berm toward the wolf formations. At the bark of their officers several battalions moved to confront the dozers, alert to whatever surprise they held in store. When the packs closed round, all the dozers at the same time froze one rear tread and sped the others up to maximum, becoming berserkers whirling like crazed mastodons. They killed and maimed hundreds of wolves within reach. The wolves had no defense, but needed none. Within a few minutes each spinning bulldozer dug and sank into its own hole. The wolves then closed in and dropped or threw grenades.

By this point, the field of battle was pink or red with spirals of wolf blood. Bodies and their parts were scattered far and wide, along with a chaos of psychotic machines, grinding or chewing themselves into various holes, lying upside down, or smoking or sizzling with acid runoff. Commander Left Limper concluded that all the available Promethean forces had been thrown into the battle, and that whatever remained would stay within the berms to defend them in the last assault.

Limper had been holding his wolf flyers in reserve for the final stage of the battle. If he had sent them in too early they would have been picked off by the super-slingshots, but now they appeared to have no enemy equivalent. He semaphored to his flyers not far to the rear, already in the air. Soon the flying squadrons appeared high above. As bomber pilots have done, and will always do, they turned one by one and swooped down in screaming dive bomber attacks. One or two were picked off by a sling still in operation, but the dive bomber teams now outnumbered the defense. They dropped their precious few small explosive bombs, not more than large grenades, onto the catapults, the remaining bulldozer berserkers, and the last of the slings. Finally, at semaphore signal from Limper, they bombed the dome covering the space inside the inner berm. Steam and fog rose to obscure the berms. Superheated steam rose to fog and obscure the result. Some flyers spiraled down to see what they could see in the dim winter light.

The senior flyer and his squadron returned to Left Limper's command and control, and landed. Assistants stripped their flying backpacks off. The squadron leader walked up to Limper and barked respectfully.

"What did you find?" Limper asked.

"Commander, nothing was there. The inner dome is empty space. Snow, ice, nothing more."

"You're sure of this?"

"Yes. One squadron landed in the center and signaled back – 'nothing, nobody here.'"

Limper turned to Loos. "We've been attacking a *decoy*."

"Perhaps," said Loos, "but an icedamn well-defended one."

"Nevertheless, a decoy. Its purpose, I'm sure, was to draw off half our forces to the south. If it had been less well defended we'd have found this out sooner. Time must be of the essence to them."

Limper ordered semaphore signals flashed back to where he had an electronic line, there to be relayed as quickly as possible to Commander Scar Shank at the northern pole of the planet. "We have control of the South Pole Promethean base. But it is only an empty decoy. Our real target, if any, must be where you are in the north. If you haven't run into them already, watch out for the mobile killer slingshots. Good hunting. Limper."

Attack to the north

Scar Shank's attack began at precisely the same time as the south, but here it was summer so there was more light. Attack was coordinated from sea and land. The Prometheans had prepared for the sea assault. Catapults on shore started firing as soon as wolf landing craft were spotted. They sank many craft. But the Prometheans expected their catapults to be more effective than they were, and had no other machines to resist the wolves on the beach. The sea wolves that did land soon immobilized the shoreline catapults with acid grenades.

Those approaching from landside ran into the same catapults and then the deadly slingshots, as in the south. Word of the southern "victory" had not reached them yet, so Scar Shank had to learn for himself how to fight the vicious whirling slings. The northern base had more catapults, more slingshots, more of everything. As in the south the ice and snow were soon covered with the blood and bodies of wolves. But steadily the wolves fought themselves closer and closer to the central northern snow fort.

The north had had more manufacturing development, so the wolves encountered many outbuildings, sheds, or small factories. Wolf catapults concentrated on them, but as they were destroyed it became obvious that these buildings were undefended.

"Whatever they contain isn't important to Prometheus at this time," said Scar Shank, watching from a mobile dog sled, pulled by large, powerful wolves who had fought for the honor. "It's the central compound that Prometheus is defending."

When the Promethean slingshots appeared and wreaked bloody havoc on wolf targets, Apollo closed his eyes and did a little stealing around in Prometheus's mental world. He told Scar Shank that the catapults posted on towers on the outer berm walls were also secretly "spotters," and that they must be taken out.

"That's why I have you here with me," said the Commander.

Scar Shank called up his flyers to attack. But these were met differently from in the south. Iris and Prometheus did not want any flyovers of the inner compound. They had created large numbers of small quadracycles which raced up and out of tunnels cut into the outer berm. These cycles pulled kite-flown small robots. As the quadracycles sped outward in widening spirals outside the berms, they formed a moving barrier to both the advancing wolves and the oncoming flyers. The axles of the cycles extended out beyond the wheels with spinning blades, which could cut the wolves into bits. The kite-flown tiny robots above held no throwing or shooting weapons, and Prometheus hadn't had the time nor the electronics to provide them sight to target weapons in their control. They were suicide devices. With a wolf flyer spotted and triangulated upon by the catapult towers, they flew straight for the wolf and activated a whirling loop with a stone at the end, which destroyed upon contact the flyer but also entangled the Promethean kite. Both went down. Slingshots targeted wolves who flew low to avoid the kites. Scar Shank, Limper, and Heraklitos had not figured on Promethean flyers, so their flyers were not tooled to fight back. Although they tried to avoid the suiciders, none of the wolf flyers got through. Scar Shank ordered his few survivors to the rear.

The land wolves, however, relentlessly advanced. Additional Promethean catapults, hidden behind the outer berm, started firing scattershot against the wolf battalions as they got within closer range of the base.

As a fall back to the failed flyers, Scar Shank advanced his cannon, also pulled by powerful wolves. He had only a few left, but hoped they could help. They were not of large enough caliber to fire that much farther than the Promethean catapults, but they could out-distance them by perhaps a hundred yards. Their excellent targeters succeeded in dropping shells on three of the four Promethean "spotting" towers. Iris in response signaled a horde of additional hidden small and very mobile slingshots from underground tunnels just outside the berm. These drove straight through the wolves at high speed, concentrating their fire on the wolf cannons, which they neutralized.

"You were right, Apollo," said the Commander. "Where Prometheus doesn't want us to arrive is the *center* of his base."

Scar Shank had kept his Elite Corps in reserve. These were large creatures, superbly trained, loyal, intelligent, and also vicious fighters.

He now commanded them to advance at all possible speed, armed with grenades. Speaking to the senior officer of the Corps, he said, "You have only one objective. Get to the inner berm and destroy whatever is there. Don't bother fighting with anything in between. Don't be distracted. Destroy the inner base. Possibly *everything* depends on this. Do you understand?"

The Corps Commander looked Scar Shank in the eye, turned to his regiment, and howled in battle fury. They took up the howl. Other wolves around the area stopped in their tracks and looked back to the Corps and Scar Shank's command post. They added their voices to the battle call. It may not have affected the tinny heart and mind of the Promethean battle puppets, but the sound emboldened any wolf with bone marrow memory of his ancient past.

The Corps galloped off after their leader. He tore through all the other fighting and was crossing a meridian a hundred wolf spans from the fort when Iris pulled out her last deadly defense. Steel treaded tanks drove up out of hidden stations under the ice and snow. Each was forty to fifty feet distant from the stanchion. They spit out weights attached to different lengths of razor wire. Turrets on top of the treaded tanks spun the weights at high velocity, pulling the slicing wires and their deadly weights in a circle of death. The placement of the giant cutting machines was such that the circles overlapped. For those caught inside the chopping zone there was no escape. The majority of the Elite Corps were cut down within seconds. The rear guard of the Corps raced back and forth trying to find a way through, howling in rage, and hurling grenades ineffectively at the racing cycles. Those who got in close attacked the tanks with their bare teeth and claws in fury.

Scar Shank ordered his wolf catapults to be brought up within range, and they began throwing strikes to destroy the helicopter-slicers. Earlier he had had his surviving flyers return to the rear. Now he ordered his own flying backpack brought to him. He intended to lead his flyers in a high flight well above the remaining kite defenders to perform a suicide dive on the inner base.

Scar Shank was suiting up. "Look!" said Apollo. Scar Shank turned and confronted a truly extraordinary sight.

The late morning sun shone brightly on the snow berms, reflecting off the inner dome. Suddenly the inner berm cracked with a loud noise into six parts, flowering like a blossom as overlapping leaves of the dome opened up and out. Scar Shank, Apollo, and all the wolf troops stared at the Promethean snow fort in amazement.

Four 144 foot long tubular metal forms arose inside the center circle to point directly at the sky. A fifth tube faltered midway as it was being cantilevered up and then slowly sank back down. The sixth paused, but recovered, and rose to stand straight and tall like the others.

Streaming from the five metal towers was some kind of fog. The catapults standing on the top of the outer snow berm were pulled down by hidden ropes. The five metal towers stood alone in the cold sunshine. Looking more closely, the wolf commanders saw that each tower was really three tubes banded tightly together. At the top of each banded tower was a cargo bay of some sort, surmounted with a pointed cone. The lines that had pulled the tubes upright and held them in place fell away. Immediately white flame burst from beneath each of the tubular constructions, expelled outward in huge clouds of steam.

Then, with the most deafening roar ever heard by wolves, Prometheus's five rockets rose up out of their clouds and headed outward from the planet, curving trails of water vapor streaming behind them.

Once the rockets had achieved a range beyond possible response from the wolves, all Promethean machinery groundside ceased to operate at one and the same instant. Everything stilled. The unexpected silence reverberated as loudly in the ear as the rockets' launch. As the astonished wolves watched, the clouds of water vapor slowly dispersed.

Prometheus had left the planet Mars.

But where was he going?

The wolves looked up and saw their moon, shining pale and high in the Martian sky.

Chapter 22
WORDS AND MANUFACTORIES

Scar Shank was famous for being a wolf of few words. Having watched the Promethean rocket ships disappear into the dark sky, he shook his head and said, "That's not something you see every day." This broke the ice. All the wolves within hearing released a great howl of laughter. After the fury and gore, the otherworldliness of battle, and a theatrical send-off to make history, any residual military effort to contain and control evaporated. Now it was just doggy giddiness, glee at not having to take responsibility for *anything*. Just for a while.

While dogs all around him capered and chortled, Scar Shank ordered his signaler to semaphore a message to the northern electronic line to send on down to Limper. Limper, Loos and the All Clans Elders were to come immediately to the North Pole. The signaler started to ask, "All the way to the pole?" One look from Scar Shank, and he didn't say another word.

As the messenger trotted off, Scar Shank added, "Pass on the order to Limper and Loos that someone else can tend to the wounded and the dead. They are ordered to be rushed here by team sack. I need them here, alive and breathing, not half-dead from the effort of running by themselves. It's much too far." The signaler nodded his understanding. Scar Shank had a last word. "Stay until they acknowledge that they agree to be carried up here. They'll hate it, but it's my order."

Scar Shank did not have to order the tending to his own wounded. The medical corps were already dealing with the battle's aftermath. He looked up toward the Promethean fort, the snow and ice berms now mostly melted away into strange and twisted forms by the rockets' blasts. Apollo was half-way there, trotting toward the remains of the fort. Heraklitos was racing out after him. As he watched, Klitos intersected and literally tackled Pollo. They argued. Shank could see but not hear their barking. Heraklitos started back, but Apollo sat down. Klitos turned back and barked again at Apollo. This time Pollo accompanied him as they trotted heavily back, exhausted from the day.

"What was all that about?" General Scar Shank asked as they arrived.

"Apollo wanted to investigate the rocket launch," said Heraklitos.

"And?"

"Klitos says that the site is very toxic, dangerous," said Pollo. "Perilous for us to go anywhere near."

"Why, Klitos?"

"Because, General, this whole area has been used for the processing of uranium and that area most intensively. Their machines were immune. We are not."

"But we will have to investigate what they were doing. One of the rockets did not escape."

"Yes, Commander, said Heraklitos, "I'll figure out how to do that. But we can't go now without protection. You must order all the troops to move further away."

"Where would be safe?"

Klitos indicated an area far down the beach, where the land rose up to volcanic rock cliffs, standing up above the sea. The Prometheans would probably not have used these as they would have interfered with their continuous traffic back and forth from seashore to base.

Scar Shank moved the wounded and triage units. He ordered all troops to come up to the rock cliffs and rest. Young ones he sent into the surf to fish, directing some to find a fresh water river down the shoreline where Martian salmon would be coming upstream to spawn. Other hunters ran out onto the clean ice shelf reaching over the ocean to find seals. Then he asked for volunteers to return to the bloodied battlefield with grenades to make sure all Promethean machines were incapacitated. "I want them incapacitated, dead or as good as," he said. He didn't want any of the damned things "listening" or "watching" them from a distance. He wished he had explosives so he could blow them to bits. Lastly, Scar Shank fired off a team of strong wolves with stretchers and food over the ice to meet Limper, Loos, and the Elders who would soon be coming up for the All Clans. The southern wolves would be spent, but he needed them to arrive well enough fed and rested to be able to reason. He needed more wits than his own to compute this new Math.

Wolves can run for days, spanning remarkable distances. Although Limper and Loos at first disobeyed Scar Shank's order and ran with their colleagues, it became obvious that there was just too far to go, so they allowed themselves to be carried on travel stretchers ("team sacks") between pairs of strong trucker wolves or seasoned long-distance messengers or packers. The eldest Elders followed suit, while others used sail carts. But Mars, although smaller than earth, is still far enough in circumference. Thus, at the last – again ordered by Scar Shank – Limper, Loos, and Eldest permitted themselves to be ferried aloft in backpacks by strong team flyers. With luck avoiding the great polar winds, it was only a few days before they were spotted in the sky above the northern military camp.

Scar Shank invited them to an invigorating meal of fresh salmon carried back "by tooth," as the wolves say, from the closest river and kept alive in a local ice pool. Finally, well fed and watered, the wolf leaders walked to the edge of the black volcanic cliff to survey the field of battle. The southern wolves found it strange indeed that Scar Shank had left his dead on the field, whole or in parts. Thousands of them. Wolves are not sentimental, but there was carnage enough here to teach philosophy to the hardest, most military heart. Finally Limper spoke.

Limper: We can't leave them here for the Great Cats.

Klitos: Cats won't get them. Don't worry about that.

They sat quietly for a time. Then Bones spoke up, so named for the parts of enemies he had pierced through his skin back along his spine.

Bones: This is a great victory, Scar Shank.

Scar Shank: Victory? Look again.

Bones: I see the field scattered with the bodies of our enemies.

Loos: Our enemies? I see our dead littered among lifeless machines. Metal derelicts.

Bones: They weren't lifeless when they attacked us.

Eldest: Exactly. But being left behind as expendable husks, the true enemy has shown himself.

Scar Shank: By his absence?

Eldest: Yes.

Bones: Damn Promethean ghosts.

Apollo: I wouldn't call them that.

Bones: You yourself are half-Promethean already! I say you and Prometheus should *both* have died or been cliffed years ago.

Second Eldest: Cliff him *now!*

There was a chorus of assenting woofs and barks from the pack, infuriated by the sight of all their dead friends and family.

Scar Shank leapt. He gripped Second Eldest's throat with his fangs, lifted the old dog bodily up, and threw him heavily to the ground.

Scar Shank (releasing him and dominating): There will be *no* blooded pack justice here.

Second Eldest turned belly up to show that he submitted. Scar Shank nudged him with his muzzle, acknowledging. Second Eldest crept back to stand beside Eldest, a hateful gleam in his eye.

One Ear: It is natural to look for a cat to skin to settle accounts.

But there's no cat who did this. Nor single wolf. This is *our* Chart of Responsibility! Behold and inhale the result of *our* decision.

The wolves looked out on the butchery and devastation. They snuffled and sniffed. Along with blood and frozen flesh, the air was filled with odors utterly foreign to experience. Metallic. Electric. What *was* this? What *had* they been fighting?

Scar Shank: What else could we have done, One Ear? The Puppets were out of control. The only way we could get to the Prometheans was to deny them their mechanical bodies.

Loos: And now they've gone, taking with them only what was valuable to them.

Eldest: We're chewing on a dead cat. Good riddance.

Apollo: I'm sorry always to be the bearer of bad tidings, but . . . we're *not* rid of them.

Limper: You saw them fly off, Apollo. They can't come back . . . Can they? Can they, Klitos?

Not their only engineer, Heraklitos was notorious for being the most adventurous and future thinking. He had been with Prometheus when he had still inhabited his broken body.

Klitos: Not in what they flew away in. It's a one-way trip. But they took their uranium with them. Who knows what evil Prometheus will put that to?

Apollo: But they haven't left! They carried machine parts away only to serve them there as their Puppets served them here. Don't you understand? They're not *here.* They're *nowhere.* They're where all the axes of our dimensions meet, twisted into another universe where machines, teeth and claw can't reach, but from where they can always reach *us.*

Eldest: You're known for your devious Math, Apollo. Again I say good riddance. Wherever they are, they're gone.

Apollo: And again you misunderstand. From the moon Prometheus can still steal a soul from our Mars, as easily as he could when he had machines here. He is right here. *In my head.*

They all looked at him in shock, some backing away. This was cat think.

Apollo: Ice damn. Not just mine. In *your* heads, too. He can reach our souls from wherever he is. That's the point.

Scar Shank: Then why has he not attacked us?

Loos: Because, General, it doesn't serve his purpose.

One Ear: But it may in the future?

Loos: It may.

Scar Shank: What are we going to do? Prometheus has gathered around him an infestation of demons, immune to the cliff, exempt from the Law. How do we rid ourselves of them?

Apollo: You forget. Prometheus and the Prometheans are addicted to *us*. They can't get souls to people their cheerless world without *us*.

Klitos: Unless there's another planet to suck souls from.

One Ear: *Is* there?

Klitos: You've looked through a telescope just like I have. The only one I know of is First Sister, the green and blue planet.

One Ear: Then why didn't Prometheus go there? He seems to have flown only to the moon, a joyless prospect.

Klitos: He needs energy to run his puppet bodies and to travel. He didn't have nearly enough to go all the way to the green and blue world. To survive the cold of space requires energy, too, even if only as a robot.

Eldest: But the question is not answered. Can he suck souls from the green world?

Apollo: I would say he could. And would. But I believe there's no intelligent life there. I have telepathed no non-Martians amongst the Prometheans. The green world is still too young for him.

Klitos: And what about the great worlds of ice and fog, our dark sisters farther out from the sun?

Apollo: If there's life out in the far solar system, it is of a quality or scent beyond my nose.

One Ear: Well, if you can't sniff it, Pollo, no one can, except maybe an Old One.

Apollo: Maybe.

Scar Shank: So what can we do to protect ourselves and our next generations from Prometheus? Will he never *die*?

Neither Apollo nor Loos, nor anyone else, could answer that. All looked back silently.

Limper: Apollo, can you learn how to attack the Prometheans *mentally*? The way they steal the souls from our dying?

Scar Shank: The question is, can we take the souls of our friends and family back?

Who had an answer to that? The All Clans sat in the darkening evening. One after the other they turned to Apollo, who was looking out across the field of carnage. He had no answer. But they could smell that he was cogitating. Wolves are patient. They walked over to shallow pools of ice water to lap up a few mouthfuls. They nosed and paid respect to one another.

Apollo (finally, quietly): I can try to learn.

One Ear: Good.

Apollo: But I may fail.

Scar Shank: Worse things have happened.

Loos: What he means is that if he fails, the worst *will* have happened, and Prometheus will have stolen even Apollo from us.

Apollo: That would not be all that bad. I love my brother.

Loos: As a pup twin should, and that will surely be your best defense against Prometheus . . . or Isle.

Apollo: It was my former mother who designed and directed this battle.

The wolves looked silently to him, their ears laid back.

Scar Shank: "Former mother," indeed. Make a study of how to get at them, Apollo. Let us know what is doable. Don't go throwing yourself into the volcano. As for the rest of us, we cannot chase summer rabbits thinking winter will never ice our mustaches.

Eldest: Now we must tend to our dead.

Scar Shank: Klitos forbade me to do it, Eldest.

Eldest: That is not his choice to make, Scar Shank.

Klitos: With respect, Oldest, our dead are *poisoned.*

The wolves turned to him.

Klitos: With uranium radiation and dust. The ice down there is lethal. We should not even be here. We must wash outselves thoroughly in the sea and then move away and leave the machines and our dead brethren to the elements.

Limper: The Great Cats will get them.

Klitos: The cats won't come here. This is now a forbidden zone. Life will avoid it. I insist we leave. We've been here too long already. We'll all have to eat bowls and bowls of the seed germ of wheat to counteract the radiation effects.

Apollo: Yuck.

Limper: But our dead?

Scar Shank: You're a wolf, Limper. They're dead. Let's go home and propagate and make them new bodies.

Limper (with a gleam): I like *that* idea.

Scar Shank stood and shook as though he had just come out of a pool. The other wolves stretched and scratched. They began to disperse, walking in pairs or threes down to the grey and inhospitable seashore. One Ear motioned Apollo and Loos over with a gesture of his head.

"You see how rabid a reaction lies close to the surface regarding anything Promethean," he said. They nodded quietly.

"So I have a last order of business. Although we have fought them and will fight them again in the future, the Promethean Legionnaires, as you have said, Apollo, are not ghosts. They're us, only stolen and incarcerated. We must never give them up. Loos, you and Apollo are our last terminus for the possibility of communication with our lost brethren. The wrong thing for us to do will be to turn away and pretend they are "gone." We must reach out, if possible, and as long as it may be possible. If you can call through to Prometheus, Apollo, without endangering yourself, do so. What do Prometheus or Isle or anyone there have to *say*? If we ask questions and listen, we can only learn. They know virtually everything about us. We know so little about them."

Turning to Loos, he said, "Therefore, Loos FishKiter, by order of the All Clans Council, you are appointed Ambassador to the Prometheans, however or whatever they may call themselves."

Loos protested, "But One Ear—"

"The Council will stand behind me on this, or at least Eldest will. We have no instructions to give. Help Apollo open a dialogue with our extraplanetary cousins. Learn what you can. Perhaps only one order, Apollo. Remind them they once were of wolfkind in the flesh and are still the souls of wolves, whatever kind of body they now wear or will wear."

Second Eldest had been listening from behind One Ear. "Are you saying, Justice, that a wolf reborn as a cat is still a wolf?"

Eldest, who came up beside Second, heard this and, taking a cue from One Ear's truculent expression, said, "What an excellent question, Second Eldest. Let us make our way home and dispute the Math."

* * *

The Promethean space fleet sailed in silence toward their moon, which was growing rapidly in prospect. Shortly after they had broken free of the gravity well of Mars, the five rockets used up their lower tanks of oxygen and hydrogen. Demeter had created smaller upper tanks to conserve unused hydrogen and oxygen as precious resources. A little oxygen or other gas was also separately tanked to be jetted from lateral and forward ports to equalize the speed of the respective rockets. Even though Mars had at that time a gravity greater than it does in the modern era, the planet was always of a smaller size than earth, its First Sister, and therefore cost less energy to escape, especially on a one-way trip. The moon, toward which they coasted, also larger than presently, perhaps three times as large, was still just a glorified asteroid of insignificant gravity potential.

After lateral and retro firing was completed, and he had gotten the rocket bodies into close to equal velocity, Demeter shot off a magnetic belt from the middle of his rocket. It fell back in a wide circular sweep over all five rockets He then cinched it in to secure them into basically one projectile. This would save on maneuvering and reduce mistakes costly in energy when they reached their objective.

The rocket cones were not inactive. Each had been packed tightly with treasures from Mars, which they might never call home again. Each contained one of the sophisticated auto-factory mini-robots ordered by Prometheus. Prometheus was master of one missile, Isle another, Demeter a third, and the other two were seniored by engineering lieutenants called D-Second and D-Third. Each of the senior Prometheans occupied one of the well-tooled, miniature manufactories as its new home body. They got quietly to work under the instruction of Demeter and D-Second.

Their cargo loads were heaviest in refined uranium, thin-rolled sheet metal of the lightest and best steel they could steal or make before departure, and other precious metals useful in space, such as gold. They also carried battery acid and measuring instrumentation. Finally, shortly before the wolves had launched their polar attacks, the Prometheans had busily constructed relatively simple six-legged tiny microbots, powered with small rechargeable electric batteries. Each had a tiny homing crystal to which the Prometheans fled or were re-assigned as their huge Martian macro-robot defensive machines had been disabled in the surface battle and thus could be abandoned. Just before launch every Promethean took or shared title of a microbot. These bots served two functions – first, to do specialized work. More importantly, having productive work and a locus for their attention, with these little bodies the Promethean spirits could protect their sanity until they had created a productive new home above, equal to or hopefully greater than the demands of bodiless minds that need something to do or go nuts.

After cinching his rockets together, Demeter's next act was to throw out a microthin gold sheath to tie around the nose cones. The reflective film would conserve and distribute heat emanated by the uranium stores to protect them from the rigors of the not fully known but predictably destructive cold of interplanetary near vacuum.

Despite not having flesh bodies with glandular reward and punishment, the Prometheans could still experience the spiritual joy of victory and the terror of defeat. They were now in a state of exhilaration, to the extent that cockroach-sized and beetle-shaped creatures could be. They had more than escaped, they had taken the worst that their former kind could throw at them, and had held them off. Staccato electronic bursts of praise were sent about and up to Commander Isle for the success of her battle plan and tactical maneuvers, to Demeter for the efficiency and scope of impossible technical achievement, and to Prometheus for leadership and drive.

Now they got busy preparing inside their cones for the landing on Prometheus Moon, as they unanimously renamed the Martian satellite. By the time Left Limper and Loos had been ferried up to the North Pole All Clans meeting, the five-tube rocket was closing in on the asteroid moon. Not far from the surface, Demeter flipped the rockets and fired them briefly to slow approach. He then fine-tuned their descent and fired a last time directly at the asteroid surface, shutting down only as they settled into the very small crater they had selected upon approach as their first camp. The gravity was so slight that the rocket vehicle floated briefly off the surface, then very gently settled under its own weight, and finally in slow motion fell to a horizontal position. A small lateral burst kept the inertial mass of the rocket from impacting with any force.

Immediately the beetle and roach microbots deployed. One team dug narrow holes with their little legs while others pulled cables over to secure the rockets from drifting off the surface. Other teams carried away instruments to explore their new home. At periodic intervals they fired small chemical grenades. Demeter measured the tiny moonquakes and confirmed his guess that the asteroid contained many hollows. Other microbots set up infrared and other wavelength telescopes outside their crater shelter to monitor Mars and nearby space. Finally they pulled the thin metallic shield that had helped protect them through space over the top of their home crater and tacked it in place. Moon Camp One was complete.

Prometheus called his crew together. Although most of them privately still felt alone and homeless, all were learning to use the perceptors and signals of their metallic bodies as more than controlled-from-outside puppets. Each efforted to make his an individual home – *these extenders are my arms and legs, these parabolas are my eyes and ears when receiving, and my mouth when signaling.* The insectoid and arachnoid army gathered around their six leaders.

Prometheus stood in his microbot factory form on a rock above the others. He expended a precious little bit of energy and flashed a bright light over them for just a moment. "Welcome, Prometheans, to Prometheus Base," he broadcast.

They waved their legs and mandibles.

"Do not be mistaken by our current size. We have achieved a momentous victory. We are not only the first space explorers off Mars's surface—"

Skittering of little bug bodies in a happy frenzy.

"—but we have contacted a new world. And we will make it *our* world. We will."

Electronic beeps. The tiny metallic equivalent of whoops, barks, and howls.

"Then it will become Prometheus *Home* World."

Dancing in the crater.

"We will rebuild our bodies to be of a size worthy of our endeavor. And then we will build our home world to become itself *Spaceship* Prometheus!"

Jumping and leaping bodies. A few in their excitement spent their batteries and wound up cataleptic on their backs, capable of only a twitch or two.

"But there is work to do. Work now is our life. Work to make this black rock into our home. Start!"

Demeter sent a personal message to Prometheus, "Thank you, Commander." In a close-band signal, Prometheus sent back to Demeter and Isle, "Words, words only. If we do not establish workable energy production, we will all jerk on our backs like those overheated idiots. Get to work, Demeter. And, Isle, monitor Mars as we planned before we left."

"Yes, Commander," Demeter sent back.

"My former son," sent Isle. "Do not diminish your accomplishment. Enjoy the emotion of the moment."

"Emotion costs energy," P shot back. "I shall luxuriate in emotion when we have created an energy circuit I can plug into without stealing from all of us. Right now we have only weeks to a month of battery left."

Iris persisted. "Yes. This is all or nothing. I will venture it."

"Tell me that," sent P, "when there is no one to talk to, no one to listen to, and you are alone in endless, timeless, no-energy dark."

The Prometheans in their little bodies set themselves to three different tasks. The first was the manufacturing of a bigger puppet factory. The second was further refining their small amounts of uranium through small but high-speed centrifuges, worth the energy cost if they got what they needed. Their third job was most enjoyable, most like old Mars home.

Many microbots turned to mining. Mapping the interior of the asteroid, Demeter had located a cavity far enough buried for his purposes, but not too far down for his tiny band to reach. He put dozens of Promethean diggers to the task of reaching it. They were to dig not the easiest route through fractures, but as direct a tunnel as possible from their surface crater to the cavity. They dug furiously in classic old style – attacking the stone and iron with their limbs and specially tooled "hands," carrying the stone and iron and other debris out on their backs or in their mandibles. As larger, more powerful diggers were created with screw and wedge-driver heads, they replaced the smaller diggers. Fortunately they did not have that far to dig. Within a Martian month they reached the vacuity inside the moon. Demeter had them smooth the walls of the tunnel down to the cavity so that it was of consistent diameter. It had never been large, only six inches at the lower exit to the cavity and two inches at the surface, mostly through hard iron. A great deal of their energy store had been gambled to bore and grind this funnel.

Demeter positioned his sheet metal rollers and metal treatment manufactory directly above the tunnel. Now came the final test. He reviewed and reworked his Math, sidechecked by Prometheus and others. They committed to go forward. They had no choice. Demeter began firing, by means of a simple spring device, pellets of his most refined uranium down the tunnel into the underground cavity, one following the other. He measured the build up of heat as the mass of unshielded uranium slowly grew. Finally he knew he was close, perilously close. He began shooting smaller and smaller pellets. At last the uranium in the chamber crossed the threshold of nuclear reaction and went into meltdown . . . *but did not explode.* That had been the all-or-nothing risk.

Deep enough in the iron core of the asteroid, the meltdown was contained. It quickly vaporized the surface of the metallic rock around the chamber, reducing it to plasma. The gaseous iron and other metals found the exit of the thin tunnel to the surface and roared upward. As the vaporized metals shot out, Demeter spun his sheet metal rapidly over the small mouth of the tunnel, collecting the streams of ionized metal on the metallic surfaces. The second gamble was that he could form a superior steel plate in this process and not just blow the factory and them into space. Although not perfect, the process worked well enough, if messily.

Demeter completed rolling his available sheets. Then he capped the now widened tube mouth with a plunger/piston device that would rise and fall with the pressure from below, with intermittent release of gas. The piston was connected to a camshaft that drove gears which spun a magnetized coil, and thus hugely amplified their capacity to produce energy. Other robot bodies had been using available metals along with acids they had brought with them to produce bigger batteries for storage.

Expanded energy capacity multiplied their ability to construct other robots and diggers. Demeter sent larger diggers out across the surface of the asteroid. These mined cometary hydrocarbon ore found in the rock. Others crushed this into pellets for various uses, one use of which was to be shot down the tube to the uranium furnace. There they vaporized, shooting back out as plasma, which reinvigorated the pump. The expelled gas was collected and differentiated by filters, cooling to powders valuable for manifold future uses.

Flesh bodies could have done *none* of this. If not killed by the stresses of working under factory conditions in vacuum, they would have been insidiously destroyed by the radiation. And it was not a clean process. The Promethean microbots were soon covered in burnt carbon soot, and their factory cauldron expelled dust of a hundred metals, which spread in a cloud around the whole asteroid, slowly, slowly to settle back to the surface. Thus the Martian satellite turned from somewhat reflective to black as the surrounding space. Observers from the home world thought this some kind of planetary necromancy: it was just a problem of dirt. Heraklitos marveled at his Promethean brother's ability to remake the dead world he had flown to.

There was water, small stores of frozen, dirty water, and methane. This was most precious of all, not a drop to be wasted, certainly not on cleaning. This was for future energy production as the planetoid population over time developed the capacity to utilize these invaluable fuels.

Meanwhile months passed. The Prometheans dug a separate tunnel down to another, larger cavity. The mechanical creatures descended to it and made there a real Prometheus Base, packed with clicking and clacking machinery noises and small engines of marvelous purpose. If only their Martian brothers could have seen, a radical renaissance of science was transpiring in their skies. Below the carbon black surface of the moon, miracles of new understandings and development progressed in bursts of discovery.

One such was an extrapolation by Demeter from a conversation he had had with Apollo and Heraklitos, before Demeter had gone over to the Prometheans. They had discussed some mathematical concepts Apollo thought he had successfully overheard from a mumbling Old One. This Math imparted an understanding of chemistry and physics more in tune with Apollo's ineffable feeling for stone by which he had learned to change stone, although often not under his control. As the young wolf friends chewed on these ideas, they had hypothesized that wavelength (the tone of stone, whatever that be), determined the cause and effect of substance, not its apparent chemical, physical properties. The manifestation of the physical was driven by the song of the instrument, so to speak (clumsily speaking). The question was whether the wavelength of something was innate and essential only to that thing, or could it be imparted to something *else,* written on a blank slate, or transferred like color to a liquid or whatever material was receptive to the vibration?

Utterly pure water, created directly from hydrogen and oxygen, was the perfect test medium. Creating the purest water in the purest containers (that being the greatest challenge on his dusty, besmeared planetoid), Demeter began experimenting, measuring the exact wavelengths and frequencies of chemicals and substances, and then irradiating these by means of an elegant, almost mystically simple tool into water. He was much amazed. He had been barely able to understand Apollo when he spoke of his spiritual, seemingly shamanistic power over matter. It had seemed some kind of incantation. But in truth, as Apollo had suggested, it was really just working the Math. Doing the Math.

Demeter irradiated pure water with the frequency of sulfuric acid, and the water reacted violently to hydrocarbons, just as "real" acid would. More amazingly, the water had the oily consistency of sulfuric acid – but its color remained the same as pure water. In another experiment he was able to set wavelengthed water afire. Finally he created a whole new future for his world and people. He was able through wavelength-induction to create highly ionized water that would flow electrons to a positively ionized substance. Per one unit of energy exerted to irradiate the water, ten units of electrical energy were produced at the end of the formula. This was Old One Math, not "real world" law. It was not a perpetual energy machine, but for all intents and purposes it was better than free. It promised *abundance.*

The interior of Prometheus Home World thus lifted to a level of productivity, experimentation, and creation as had never been seen in the known history of Mars.

If only Prometheus did not hate the planet that had stolen his body. If only Isle did not fear Martian Elders and their intention to put a most final stop to the Promethean threat to their status quo and wolf-styled civilization. If only she were not right, as the more change the Elders saw manifested in their once incorruptible moon, the more they feared the hidden sorcerers transforming it from below its surface. And if only Apollo and Loos had been able to string a coherent, functioning line of communication between the Martian surface and the new owners and drivers of their silently orbiting bleak and dirty little moon. If only . . .

Chapter 23
Recreation and Rock Throwing

The southern battlefield, uncontaminated by uranium waste, was not off limits to burial details. The southern mechanical puppets ceased operation at the exact moment as their northern cousins – when the rockets were rising out of the launch clouds. Over the next few days the wolf troops left in command in the south stood and sang for their fallen comrades, then gathered them up, and carried them north, shrouded out of respect, to be buried in foothills above farm fields where their soil value would leach down into the fields for years to come.

Thousands had died and a lesser number had been wounded (evidence of the battle tactics of wolves). Wounded wolves tended to continue to fight until no fight was left, so the living wounded were severe cases. They were given all possible medical care, as Apollo and Prometheus had been, and notable recoveries were not uncommon. Wolves had bred themselves into a strong race. Those who would become a permanent burden on society inevitably suicided.

But thousands *had* died, both male and female. There was no gender distinction in wolf armies. Now the work of civilization had to roll forward, as it has had to after wars everywhere. At first was the dullness, the not-thereness of friends gone, family never to return. Then blessed quotidian duties and the clockwork of the seasons washed clean not their memory of past sorrow, but sorrow's overweening claim of self-importance. Fields needed plowing. Wolves enjoyed harnessing themselves in teams to pull plowshares through the soil, singing work songs and inhaling one another's sweat. Autumn was approaching, and there was fishing to be done and the drying and grinding of fish into meal for fish cake reserves to be set beside hibernation cave mouths. In an unspoken natural tradition those clans with more surviving members took in those whose clans had been decimated. Essential unfilled jobs found volunteers who quickly learnt the skills required.

Many artists had died, singers, musicians, dancers, and sports artists – flyers, climbers, swimmers. The nights were too quiet and restaurant bars way too subdued. Soon listeners wanted no more dirges nor laments. One of the saddest penalties of war is denial of new voices and new songs in the after days. Wolves wanted someone to spice up their blood with a new epic, a new beat. Or not so new: at least a good story. Loos FishKiter Storyteller, who had mostly retired, became again in high demand – for the old tales, the forgotten ballads. Young wolves arrived with a wolf sack and dragged Loos out of his den to carry him to a party or gathering where he responded to drink and eats with a goodly story from the olden days. Apollo too was invited to create a new art piece for the third spring season after the upcoming winter -- an *opera* of all things. The young and wild wanted a new opera from Apollo as they knew they could not predict the outcome. That's what they wanted, the predicted unpredictable. An artistic showpiece to cause a month of gossip, rather than tanks crashing into your house to cause a month of clean-up.

As the summer of war moved into the autumn of peace, other life juices began to flow too. Thousands had died. The marrow of the race had been thinned. New bodies were needed and needed now, not next year. The race had long since evolved its sexual season to transpire during hibernation's long night. It allowed for unwarlike procreation and time for pregnancies to come to a protected full term. But the post-war species experienced a need for re-creation *now*, not later during winter sleep, not later at all.

Sex, which outside hibernation was normally just for fun and the pleasure of it, soon became a response to heat. There was no social onus to sex, the act of it or the fact of it. There were no sexually spread diseases. Young wolves screwed their brains out, but not necessarily in public. There were plenty of private places to find or parties with corners or pads strewn across the floor. Now the powerful urge of sexual hormones began to drum a hot-blooded, sweaty beat. Females became bitches in heat, and they knew it. They swelled and left behind an aroma imperceptible to themselves but maddening to males. They walked in front of a line of males and then, laughing, took off with a trail of howling idiots behind them. With pleasure they allowed themselves to be mounted, and then again, and then again. When it ceased to be pleasurable they turned savage and lashed out with fang and claw to ward off unsatiated pursuers, who acted surprised and shocked to have had their sincerity so misunderstood (and then dashed off to find another prospect).

There were also mighty battles between Male Number One and Male Number Two over the charms of Unnamed Female of the Hour. Only wolves could have had tolerance for this volume of snarling and the spray of blood. The Justice Council would hear none of it. Sexual battle was not a matter for a Chart of Responsibility. If males pursued a female in idiotic abandon of intellect, then the consequences were theirs alone to bear. Sexing, screwing, humping, fucking – it seemed it would never end. And then it did. The females who could became pregnant, and life resumed. The species would be saved.

* * *

While the wolf population was recreating itself, Heraklitos had been studying the reinvention by Prometheus and his Legionnaires of their new lunar home. As Martian wolves were not on the whole much interested in far objects, telescopes were few and not powerful. Their moon was close enough, however, to look at and consider, particularly as its glaucous light over long Martian nights held wolves in captive sway. They gazed at their asteroidal planetary satellite and speculated, weaving countless stories about its faces and moods.

Now they had watched Prometheus land his "spaceship" on the moon. Although they could not see individual machines, much less the microbots that colonized and dug into the moon, from Mars they watched the changes being wrought. The colors of the ores spread out around small mines. Dusts scattered. Lights at night. What was clear and most hopeful, from their perspective, was to see the Prometheans digging in, making the moon their home.

"Perhaps they will be happy there," said Loos to Heraklitos as the two took turns looking through the young wolf's telescope.

"If Prometheus can ever again be happy anywhere, perhaps yes," said Klitos. "Right now they don't have time to be happy. They need energy to feed their mechanical bodies and to do whatever other nastiness they have in mind. They have uranium, but I'm not sure how Prometheus and Meter are using it. Even so, it can't last forever."

"That might open up a channel of mutual interest," said Loos. "They may need more energy from the home world. We might become a trading partner instead of being just a source of Legionnaires or their enemy."

"As stridently independent as Prometheus is, or wishes to be, that's still true."

"I'll take it up with the Elders," said Loos. And he did. He discussed with them and got their approval to make ambassadorial overtures to Prometheus along these lines. They fervently wished to end this worse than civil war.

"I think that bone won't provide much marrow," grumbled Scar Shank.

"It's better than leaving Isle to dream up some new deviltry," said Loos.

The other Elders in the chamber growled.

"A barking dog has to let go of your throat," groused Eldest. "Get them talking to us."

"Let's not all get in a cat frenzy with too high expectations," quipped Loos.

"You needn't worry about that," said One Ear. "Speak with Pollo. He may be able to help you get our moon cousins in communication."

Loos and Klitos visited Apollo's den. They were shocked at the mess, beneath the standards even of bachelor wolf society. Pollo himself was physically peaked, all bony angles.

"You look like a derelict from a failed Wilding," said Loos.

"Don't blame me," said Athena. "He doesn't even hunt any more. I bring food home, but he's not interested. I've stopped cleaning up after him."

"Watch this behavior, son, or the Elders will think you're taking up with cat ghosts."

"If they only knew," said Poll. "What can I do for you, Father?"

"I am here in my ambassadorial role, as ridiculous as that sounds."

"Not ridiculous. I assume you want me to help you reach Prometheus."

"Yup," said Heraklitos. "They're going to get hungry for energy soon, and maybe that's something they'll be willing to talk about."

"OK. Can't promise much. No one, including Prometheus, has opened even a crack in the telepathic door. They're more secret now than ever. I get a sense of emotional excitement from the Legionnaires, but I don't know what they're doing, other than what all of us can see. Come over, Dad," said Apollo, nodding toward his side. Loos walked over to his son and leaned in to have strong body contact for better telepathing.

He and Pollo closed their eyes. They both raised their muzzles, as though looking in the direction of the moon would help, although telepathy had nothing to do with the body's position. Apollo reached out to Prometheus, simply emanating that he and their father were present and would like to talk. They perceived murk, muffled as if eavesdropping through the wood of a thick door. Apollo pushed through to the other side, not understanding the meaning of what he was half-perceiving – strange machines and smells and chemical burns.

Loos tried to send a clear, uninflected "I am here" message. He too was registering movement and activity, but what he knew not. He clarified his message, "Your father is here." Suddenly he yelped. Apollo felt his father physically stiffen. What was worse, Loos's mind disappeared from the pathing, as if he had dropped through a mental trap door. Apollo felt a "taking."

Loos slipped to the floor of Pollo's den. Apollo put both his front feet on his dad's body and, glaring up at the moon, eyes open, he snarled aloud.

"What's happening?" cried Klitos.

"Shhh," said Athena. "Don't disturb Pollo when he's doing this. It makes him angry."

Apollo's mind's eye interpreted for him. Prometheus was trying to steal his father's spirit. There was whirling energy, a pushing and pulling at the same time. Apollo felt his father becoming smaller, receding into a distance. Mocking up the image of what he intended, Apollo leapt through the darkness and mentally pictured grabbing his father by the scruff of the neck. In Apollo's mind Loos appeared unconscious. He dragged his father's spirit back. As he did so, Loos in the flesh, back in his den at home, yipped. He jerked, jumped upright, and shook his body vigorously, as if ridding himself of snakes.

"The bastards *snatched* me!" he spit.

"Yes," said Apollo, opening his eyes, feeling weary after the struggle.

"I guess there will be no ambassadorial privilege," Loos growled .

"They may now have created some kind of automatic mechanism to imprison on their side any wolf spirit with which they come in contact," suggested Heraklitos.

"Ice the Elders," mumbled Loos. "We might as well negotiate with a bunch of gears and levers!"

"Or Prometheus and his minions are progressively losing track of what is machine and what . . . isn't."

"I don't think so," said Loos. "I felt *Prometheus* there. He was grappling for me. He knew who I was. This wolf trap had my personal name on it."

"What are we going to *do*?" asked Klitos. "We have energy sources that could help them survive. We could show them that we could have a future reality in common."

"Not if we stick our snouts or feet in their traps," said Loos.

"Why don't I try some kind of pat click click?" said Klitos.

"Mmm . . . might work," said Loos. *Pat click click* was the common name for the universal tapping code used by wolves, clicking their nails or patting their paw, when they were hunting and couldn't speak vocally or deep in mines when they couldn't see one another.

"I can use a large light semaphore at night," said Klitos.

So he set that up, using the lights of a whole area of a township locked in synch. A few nights later he flashed a dark-and-light-coded repetitive message to the moon. "Ambassador Loos greets the Moon Prometheus."

"That should gratify their vanities," suggested Loos. "Just keep sending it."

It did not take long before Prometheus's moon base responded in kind, although less ingratiatingly, with their own flashed red light.

"TO MARS: This is Moon Base. What do you want?"

"TO MOON BASE: To offer something you could use."

"TO MARS: You have nothing we want."

"TO MOON BASE: We have energy."

That was met with silence for a while. Then Prometheus or Isle sent, "MARS: We are making our own energy. You have nothing for us."

Further attempts to "talk" produced no response.

"This is worse than talking to a rock," said Loos.

"Rocks talk back more than Prometheus," said Apollo, which got an "Oh, never mind" from his father.

Loos returned to One Ear and Eldest and told them of his failure to get Prometheus in communication.

"What else happened?" asked One Ear.

"Not much," said Loos.

"I heard something about their attempting to kidnap you," said One Ear.

"Heraklitos talks too much," said Loos, and told them about the abortive snatch and grab.

"You're not to put your head in their jaws any more," said Eldest. He turned to a young runner. "Bring Apollo and Heraklitos here."

The whelp ran out and came back almost immediately. "They were outside," he said.

"The Prometheans have become worse than rebels. They act like psychotic criminals," said Eldest. "If they were here, committing these acts, we would cliff them."

"But they're not here and still have power, even where they are," said Heraklitos.

"Exactly," said Eldest. "Apollo, is there any way you or we can mount a *telepathic* attack on them? *Any* way we can strike them, Klitos?"

"I don't have this skill now," said Apollo. "But I'll work on it."

"Klitos?"

"We can disturb their internal communications. I've monitored their base. As it's distinctly separate from us, it's been easier to isolate some of the frequencies that their robots and puppets use to communicate with one another. Not the souls in their darkness to their machines, but the machines electronically to one another."

"What can you do?"

"I could send conflicting messages or create an electronic noise that would make it difficult for them."

"Set it up and do so."

It took Klitos almost no time at all. He had antennae already pointed up to the moon. All he had to do was decouple the receiver and install a broadcast device with some electronic punch. It didn't need to be sophisticated, just capable of sending up a hash of radio noise. He thought this would create at least some disturbance up above. He called One Ear, Eldest, Loos, and Apollo to come over. One Ear brought Scar Shank with him. Klitos turned it on. There seemed to be no effect.

"Increase the power," said Scar Shank.

Klitos did so. Not long after that a message flashed from the dark Moon Base.

"TO MARS: Stop."

"How should we answer?" asked Heraklitos.

One Ear said, "Tell them that if they communicate with us we'll stop. Tell them we'll come back tomorrow night."

Heraklitos flashed the message up.

Monitoring the moon base the next day through the telescope, Klitos observed unusual activity on the moon, up on the surface. He wasn't sure, but watched carefully. When he was sure of what he saw, he raced over to Apollo's where Loos was staying.

"Prometheus has decided to communicate all right," Klitos snapped.

"Good," said Loos.

"Not good," said Heraklitos. "They've catapulted or slung some rocks from the surface."

"And?"

"These are easy for them to throw up from the weak moon, but the gravity of Mars will pull them down with great force and huge energy."

"Meteors!"

They ran over to the Elders' Chambers to relay the alarm.

"How big are the rocks?" asked Scar Shank.

"I don't know. Not that big, but they don't have to be."

"When will they hit?"

"A few days to a week."

"Do you know where they'll hit?"

"Not now. We can estimate. But they'll be hard to find *en route* as they're just dark rocks."

"From the time of their launch?"

"I'll try."

Klitos and his engineer colleagues chewed up the Math. They came up with an estimate that the iron bombs would impact somewhere along the Western Rim of the Great Canyon.

"Where our largest townships are," said Eldest.

"Yes. That must be Prometheus's or Isle's target."

"Damn their hides. We'll have to evacuate until they hit."

"But they may hit the evacuees."

"Well, that's preferable to hitting a large population in a township."

A day before the small meteors were expected to enter the atmosphere, they ordered an evacuation to the farms and fields inland from the canyon rim. This created panic. There was much carting of valuables and other nonsense, which only slowed it all down so that even as various townships were still in the process of exiting for the countryside the trails of the incoming meteors blazed across the afternoon sky.

There were many, but only half a dozen did not immediately incinerate. Flaming streaks developed as the iron meteorites speared down. The atmosphere consumed finally all but three. Two smaller ones and the last clearly larger. They fanned out as their meteor trails glowed in fiery colors.

When they struck, luckily they hit no township. One of the smaller meteorites went down into the canyon and smashed into the river, raising a hell of a spout. One meteorite struck the western canyon wall. The largest hit miles inland. All the wolves, scattered around the hinterland, could not help but watch the awful beauty of it. Those that thought they might be in the path began running to and fro, which was useless.

Heraklitos was with the Elders and Loos and his family. "I'm an idiot," he said.

"What's the matter?" Scar Shank asked.

"We should have all hidden in caves in the side of the cliffs."

"Well, some have more common sense than you," said Scar Shank. "A lot of wolf clans did."

Then the hammer hit, ten miles from them and from the edge of the canyon. They could feel the blow as a ground tremor. The meteor threw up a great cloud of fiery dust and rock, which rose like a mushroom and then slowly followed the planet's atmosphere as it turned into the sun. Wolves nearest the impact crater ran over to assess the damage. Who doesn't love a great big hole? As they came near they could smell burnt iron.

Luckily the crater was in the country. No one had been hurt. The blast destroyed a few farmhouses not far away, but they were evacuated at the time, not that the farmers didn't bark up a storm over the injustice of it.

Looking into the one hundred foot wide crater, One Ear asked Heraklitos, "How big do you suppose that particular piece of moon was?"

Heraklitos did some figuring. "About two feet wide by the time it hit."

One Ear, Scar Shank and the other wolves looked at one another. No one even needed to voice it. One young pup looking down into the crater asked his mother the inevitable question. "What happens if Prometheus throws bigger rocks at us?"

Chapter 24
Spirit Cleaving, Cleaving Moon

There was no immediate military defense against the moon. A common sense response was to move important persons and facilities into caves, cliffside or in the mountains. Sunken homes on the would not be deep enough to withstand a meteor strike. Mine shafts were good for storage, but no one wanted to live in them: doing so would stimulate a preemptive hibernation reaction. Nevertheless, as much of a nuisance as it was, this massive social shifting kept the planet alert and on a war footing. No pretense allowed that there was no enemy poised to strike.

Except for Apollo, of course. It had been years since he had lived in any sense other than pretense. He saw around him not hysteria, as wolves were immune to this particular mental defection from responsibility, but an escalating profound discomfort. No wolf, father or mother or whelp, was comfortable *anywhere.* They had an enemy against which they could not strike back, but who could hurt them. If they could have followed in Prometheus's path and flown off planet to somewhere else, many would have done it without a second thought.

Apollo's protection was not a thick skin but no skin at all. It is all well and fine to wander in and out of your body, but what happens when you're not quite sure where your body *is*? The truth, Pollo mumbled to himself, was that he was not comfortable living inside his own body any more. It was too constrictive. When he occupied it and looked only through his eyes and listened through his ears he felt confined, as if to be a wolf was to be only one's own tail. The tail might like to think it could, but it cannot wag the dog. Loos FishKiter's son had become the kite in his father's story. He was pulling the fish, blown by winds unknowable in the fish kingdom.

So be it. His job in the war effort was to psych out the enemy, to learn what his brother, mother, and the other Prometheans had become or were becoming. Even before his father was nearly spiritnapped, Apollo had attempted secret sorties into the Promethean world. He could come close enough to monitor their activities and mood without revealing himself. But if he opened up a direct being-to-being telepath channel he revealed himself in some way. Given the fear reaction and immediate closing off from him which occurred, Pollo conceived that his presence must announce itself like a siren with spinning lights. He had not dared yet to try telepathing recently with Prometheus. He thought, when his father asked, that the two of them together might present a greater force, but he had been wrong. He suspected that there was some electronic trapping mechanism involved. He had not yet deduced the Math.

So he messed with Dr. Chronos instead. Before he left for the attack on the poles, Apollo had discovered that not only could he occupy another's body, but he could transfer *another* being to a different body – at least a weak spirit such as a little dying rabbit. This was tantamount to cat necromancy, so he knew not to discuss it with anyone. However, he had been ordered to research how to attack an enemy which no longer operated from flesh bodies. The line of investigation more interesting to him and in the long run vital to the survival of his species was research into how to bring back the captured spirits of kidnapped wolf souls. Some, like Demeter and his mother, he knew, had gone over willingly and might never be recoverable. Others were definitely spiritnapped and might gladly take up again a fleshed wolf body.

Poor Chronos was experimental subject number one. He had been a simple bird in a bird's body. Then somehow the Old Ones had fired or slid Dr. Telemachus's deceased soul into the bird, unwillingly for both bird and wolf spirit. Apollo suspected that for the Old Ones one body was the same as another – how many limbs, whether fur or feathers, beak or fangs, were irrelevancies. Flesh was flesh. Telemachus should be glad he's not in a fish right now, thought Pollo.

He tried another insertion of foreigner into Chronos's bird body. As with the rabbit, when Athena trotted in to the den with a large live fish in her teeth, Apollo seized the tiny, glittery sparkle that was "fish," created the thought connection, which he pictured as the slenderest of golden threads, and slid "fish" into "Chronos." Dr. Chronos had been clucking to himself, cleaning his feathers, and mumbling a few laboratory formulas. Instantaneously upon arrival of fishness, he whirled and flew to Athena who was putting the fish into a pot. In a flurry of feathers and squawks he grabbed the fish in his claws and bit into its neck, snapping it.

"That's dinner, Dr. Chronos!" yelled Athena. "It's for all of us, not just you, you greedy . . ."

Chronos dropped the fish and flew back to his perch.

"Don't want the bedamned fish! Not now that it's been . . ."

"Aha!" shouted Apollo. "You recognize it. What does it *feel* like?"

The bird flew down with claws extended toward Apollo, but when Pollo leaped to snap at it, veered off and back to its high perch.

"You accuse me of having violated you when you asked me for a healing nerve potion," said Chronos. "But you'll not cease attempting to foist dying creatures on me. If this isn't a violation of the Law I don't know what is."

"So report me."

"Very funny."

Bird and wolf confronted each other.

"You must be very uncomfortable in a wolf body," said Dr. Chronos, "to be so determined to make others uncomfortable in theirs."

"Don't start your claptrap," said Pollo. "This is science. I want to know how you can tell when another . . . moves in."

"Moves in. Is jammed in, more like."

"So how can you tell?"

"Because it's a violation . . ." He went silent and started cleaning feathers.

"What is it?"

"I don't want to tell you."

"Why not?"

"Because you never answer my questions."

"OK. If I answer yours will you answer mine?"

"One for one."

"Deal. What does it feel like?"

"No, you first," said Dr. Chronos. "Are you uncomfortable in your own body?"

"Of course I am," said Pollo. "Not only is it bent, it's . . . too small for me. My turn. What does it feel like to you when you sense someone else is coming into you?"

"It feels like . . . the light changes. It's one color, you don't even know the color, but everything is lit by this one color. Then the colors change."

"Change how?"

"My turn. Are you jealous of your brother?"

"Am I what?"

"Jealous of your brother Prometheus, who has freed himself from bodies entirely."

"He hasn't freed himself from bodies. He's just changed the model – metal for flesh."

"So you haven't answered the question. Are you jealous of Prometheus because he's freed himself from the flesh?"

"*Jealous* of him? Don't be ridiculous."

"Well, *are* you, ridiculous or not?"

"A little. That he's got this army and is able to threaten the whole world. I'm jealous of his possession of power, even if he's gone psychotic with it."

"Cluck, cluck, cluck."

"Don't cluck cluck me, feather brain. My question. What do you experience when another beingness invades? When I listen in on you, you don't even seem to notice. But when the intention is to move in you respond immediately. What is that?"

"What is that? What? Why do you want to know so much? Oh, your question. Umm, it's a wavelength. A wavelength of possession, like a radio signal announcing 'right of possession.' But a body has only one landlord . . . everyone else has to rent. If the landlord changes, you become a renter or . . ."

"Or you're evicted. Yes." Apollo realized something here. Wavelengths and right of possession. Some relationship. He got up and started walking around in a tight circle.

"My turn," said Dr. Chronos.

"Do you feel guilty because your brother died and you did not?"
"Birdshit for brains, you step over the bounds."

"Question for question. Do you feel guilty?"

Apollo sat down, facing up to Chronos in the corner. "I will answer no more of your questions that come with a cat-minded mental agenda. But I have a question for you that you will *want* to answer."

"I doubt it. But . . . what is it?"

"If you could escape from that body, would you want to?"

"Do I want to get out of this bird corpus? Of course I do."

"To go . . . anywhere?"

"No, not at all. I like being alive again. I want to stay alive, as *me*, as Dr. Telemachus. I would like to have a wolf body again."

"If I could free you from that body and release you to a wolf body, you . . . would go? "Willingly?"

"Yes. Willingly."

Apollo stood and walked slowly around the room, keeping Dr. Chronos in his eye, looking intently at him.

"What evil do you have in mind? I can see it. Leave me alone.

So I poisoned you. That was an accident. And I paid. Now leave me alone."

Apollo walked and looked, walked and looked. He was closer than ever to the solution to the Prometheans.

* * *

Scar Shank recognized that Martian wolves could not just hide from the Promethean lunar threat. They had to respond. Waiting for Apollo to come up with a psychic solution was like waiting for a drunken poet to come up with a sobriety campaign. Scar Shank needed a physical, real-world response, an act that would show the Prometheans they could be reached. If they could be reached, they were not invulnerable.

In the short run there was only one means available. The Martians had to get access to the north polar rocket base, and either launch from there the remaining rocket left behind by Prometheus, or alternatively transport it to launch from elsewhere. This would have to be done before Prometheus decided to bomb the polar base from the moon, which could happen at any time.

"Why do you suppose he hasn't bombed the base?" Scar Shank asked One Ear.

"I don't know. As a military officer that's what he would do. Or Iris would advise him. But as he's the leader of a new world with miraculous new technologies, I think the answer is simple. He doesn't think we have enough wits to use the machinery he's left behind. Besides, he knows we wolves generally disrespect machinery. Sometimes even hate it, especially now."

"Well, I may hate that rocket, but I respect it and I'm going to use it."

"General, the planet's resources are at your service."

The problem was the radioactivity at the base. Already some of the wolves who had spent the most time at the base and even some who had only fought there were beginning to sicken from radiation poisoning. Scar Shank did not have enough heavy machinery to go and move the rocket, nor did he or Heraklitos or any Martian wolf have the mechanical expertise to robot-control a left-behind machine or Promethean Puppet. He asked Klitos how long it would take to reclaim the base, raise the rocket, learn how to fire and control, and then launch the rocket. Long enough to kill any live wolves who went there, he was told.

The alternative was to move the rocket and as much of the machinery as possible away from the site. Klitos gave the project to two lieutenants, Dead Eye and Spear Drop. The first had got his name after he lost an early sibling fight, and the second had taken over Prometheus and Apollo's reputation as the wildest death-diving flyer. They were physically strong wolves but also clever mathematicians.

What was needed at first was not mathematics but volunteers. The rocket and base equipment had to be identified and hauled to the shoreline, where it could be thoroughly hosed down and otherwise cleaned, then barged over water or pulled across ice and land to another launch site. The poles had only been used by Prometheus because they were remote from wolf cities. Sites along the equator were better for launch, so the rocket had to be hauled a quarter of the way around the world.

The first task of accessing the base was still unavoidably fatal. Dead Eye and Spear Drop volunteered, but were overruled by Klitos and Scar Shank, and wolves already ailing from radiation, who would be dying soon enough, volunteered in their place. The further exposure would only accelerate a known conclusion, which was acceptable as they were helping to strike back at Prometheus. Twenty males and females with sufficient stamina were ferried up to the pole. It was autumn, and the plan was to bring the equipment at least away from the base before the wolves went into hibernation.

At the shoreline near the base they set up hoses and transportable water heating tanks. They had to operate quickly, before their bodies gave out under the continuous stream of tissue-damaging rays. Some wore protective suits, but these were so bulky and physical operation so hindered that they were soon shed. First they had the grim task of clearing a path through the still frozen bodies of comrades. Then they surveyed the incapacitated Promethean tractors or tractor-like machines until they found one which was functional, but lacked only battery power and a controller, the crystal having been destroyed. They flipped this over, charged the battery with a clever foot-run spinning coil, then drove it up to the inner circle of the base.

They checked the nose cone. This was when they first discovered the microbots. The cone's miniature occupants were all "dead," abandoned during launch by the Legionnaires, once they knew the rocket had to be left behind. The wolves crushed most of the microbots and collected a few for research. Then they pulled the horizontal rocket free of its launch site down to the shoreline, where they removed its canister of uranium and dropped it in a leaded box deep into the sea. The remainder of the rocket they blasted with hot water to clean as much radioactive dust from it as possible. Then they used a tank filled with particulate snow, called snow dust, to blast through small hoses to clean off the ice left behind by the earlier operation. Cold enough snow is very "dry" and quite useful.

All movable equipment was so blasted and cleaned, then loaded on to sea barges or ice sleds.

While the rocket equipment was hauled and sailed away, the volunteers remained behind to perform the honorable task of burying their mates. Then they walked together out on their last Wilding to await the coming of winter, when they could abandon hurting, damaged bodies in a pleasant ice-cold sleep. It was an acceptable and praiseworthy death. They chose this means to get to Tweenlives as it seemed that the best time for the Prometheans to seize you at death was when they could predict the moment. The captors had to be present and waiting. If they weren't aware, you could slip away before the Prometheans knew you were gone.

Meanwhile Heraklitos prepared a rocket base near the equator, where a large river flowed over an ancient lava flow precipice into the Great Canyon. They hauled the rocket overland to where the river was deep enough to barge downstream. At the base Klitos built a facility to manufacture H^2 and O^2 out of the river water. The electricity he pulled from a Promethean-built geothermal site under the volcano that had produced the lava flow.

This done, most wolves settled in for hibernation. Excepted were volunteers tending to those still recovering from battle wounds, and also pediatricians who would stay awake to go down into the hibernation caves and pull out wolf pups conceived very much before hibernation and whose births were too early in the sleep period. The nurses fed and cared for the premature pups until their parents awoke in Second Spring.

☆ ☆ ☆

As soon as they were up and about after hibernation, the wolves rejoiced in their record crop of births. Sadly many pups were stillborn, indicating that too many souls were trapped by Prometheus to be free to take up new flesh bodies. Bitchmothers were given the well pups to take care of. Everyone else got on with life and normality, or the war effort.

Klitos did not recommend carrying the uranium load up in the rocket. The uranium had been dragged under the surface of the sea near to shore and then hauled in its protective heavy-metal container down to near the rocket site. It was stored inside a nearby mine. But Klitos did not want to use it for military or powering purposes. He felt unsure of this last rocket being able to make it into orbit, and did not want it crashing to contaminate a civilized or remote area over a long, long time.

Nevertheless the rocket was ready for launch. It had not been much damaged before, and had had only an electrical malfunction. Scar Shank and the Elders definitely wanted to launch and send it up to orbit the moon, just to make clear to Prometheus that if he could be reached once he could be reached again.

Neither the fleshed wolves nor the Prometheans had sophisticated computer systems. Wolves were masters of Math calculation within their own skulls. As far as remote-controlled mechanical devices, the Promethean Puppets were just that, puppets controlled by a savvy "living" operator who made real-time decisions on what a machine should do. Turning control over to a computer to run something and make decisions for it was not yet seen as necessary. Besides, all wolves, even the Prometheans, had a seriously deep-seated fear and loathing of artificial intelligence. This was how the Cats had destroyed their own world from within, and was a core unLawful activity in lupus civilization.

Therefore, without a sophisticated computer, one or more wolves would have to ride the rocket's nose cone to orbit the moon. Everyone volunteered, of course, including half the Elders. Scar Shank appointed himself the Alpha Wolf of the whole venture. He and Loos and One Ear would hash out who should go, first overruling themselves.

"The mission is hardly military," said One Ear. "We don't have armament to wound the Prometheans deep within their moon. We can only show up and threaten the possibility of that. Therefore the mission continues to be principally diplomatic."

"Good luck with that," rumbled Loos.

"We have to make our luck," said Scar Shank. "Somehow we must get through to Prometheus and/or Isle that there's no reason for us to battle. Both sides stand only to lose."

"The launch and arrival of the rocket will demonstrate better than any words that we *can* reach them," said One Ear. "All we need do is say, 'Talk with us. You now have a different world of your own. Let us share futures.'"

"They won't listen," said Loos. "I'm sorry – but I've been in their clutches. Put a telepathed line out to them and they'll seize you and drag you in."

Scar Shank responded, "So we won't telepath. We'll use light semaphore for pat click click."

"But what we must do as well is send a message that communicates by itself *peace*. Not something we wolves are inherently good at."

"We could send up Apollo, brother and son," said Loos.

"No," said Scar Shank. "Apollo's research and knowledge into the realm of telepathic and Other Side communication is far too important to us. But you're on the right track."

"Oh, I see," said Loos with a sigh. "Athena."

"Yes, I think Athena is the perfect candidate, Loos," said One Ear.

"She's so young."

"Exactly. She couldn't possibly be perceived as a threat. If either Prometheus or Isle have any wolf-blood empathy left, it'll resonate with her arrival."

"Who can go with her?" asked Loos.

"Spear Drop," suggested Scar Shank, "because he's been working with Heraklitos on the rocket, and he's also famous for something Prometheus once loved."

"Then let us do it and do it quickly, before another moon bomb ruins forever any chance for peace."

Heraklitos's team had had the rocket readied for some time. The plan was to fire it up to escape Mars's gravity and take it all the way to the moon, then leave it there in orbit with the nose cone to return to Mars and parachute down. The Martian moon was relatively close to Mars. The trip there would be short. After a stay of only two days the astronauts would return. Leaving the rocket there would leave the Prometheans slightly in mystery: what did it contain?

Apollo and Loos talked with Athena at home before they left to go to the rocket base.

"I would say that you don't have to do this, but actually you do. It's important," said Loos.

"Father, don't be such an old dog. Of course it's important. And of course I'll go. I'm Prometheus's sister. If he'll talk to anyone, he'll talk to me."

"Don't allow yourself to even think of telepathing him," advised Apollo. "Just communicate via semaphore."

"Don't worry. I understand."

"Actually, it's not *what* you say, Athena," said Loos. "It's just being there. Ask him if he has any questions. Ask how he's doing. The simplest family message."

"If I may . . .?" suggested a bird's voice from up in the corner.

They all turned to look up at Chronos watching them from his corner.

"Tell him that Apollo was *afraid* to come see him. He'd like to hear that."

They looked to one another, shaking their heads.

"Bird mentalism," said Apollo. "But he may be right."

* * *

The rocket took off with its two occupants without incident. Demeter and his engineers had constructed well, and Heraklitos had had to do little more than polish up his work and reformat the interior of the nose cone, providing oxygen and more heat, and ensuring there were parachutes for the return to Mars.

The short trip out to the moon was uneventful, other than Athena vomiting because of weightlessness. Spear Drop had felt it before too often in his winged dives to be bothered now. The retrofiring engine worked perfectly, and Spear Drop and Heraklitos's Math was exactly on when to do so and for how long. The rocket slowed to a near full stop outside the moon to go into a slow orbit around the weak planetoid.

The first thing they had been afraid of was that Isle, without warning, would sling rocks up to destroy the rocket. She did not. But neither did the moon signal any welcome. *En route* the rocket had light-semaphored that it came in peace. There had been no response.

Now, an hour after arriving, Spear Drop signaled the moon base that Athena was there, "Prometheus's sister." No one on Mars knew if Isle had even told Prometheus that she had given birth to a sister before coming over to him. Now they found out.

Prometheus photo-signaled back, "Welcome, sister, newly discovered. Come down to the surface."

Spear Drop conveyed this message back by semaphore to those monitoring on Mars. He received a prompt reply. "Forbidden. Besides you do not have the capacity."

Athena signaled, "I'm sorry, Prometheus. No capacity to come to the surface and then return."

"I want to add something to that," said Athena to Spear Drop inside their life support system.

"What?"

"Send down to him, 'Come join us up here.'"

Without consulting Mars Base he did so. "We're here. It's our initiative," said Athena.

There was no response from Prometheus Base. They waited some hours. The rocket was floating at a stable point far enough off the surface that they needed a small telescope to see details of the base. They could have floated closer in, but had been ordered to maintain a reasonably safe distance from the base. There was no activity to be seen on the moon's surface. Finally Spear Drop told Athena that he needed to get some sleep, and asked her to hold a six hour watch.

Deep underground in their headquarters, Prometheus ordered Demeter to direct his Energy Corps to boost production immediately. He wanted their surface catapult to be wound up to fire him into low orbit.

"I advise against it," signaled Isle to him. "I don't trust them."

"You're a valiant warrior," returned Prometheus. "But you never told me I had a sister. You have a bias in this matter."

"Bias? Who does not have a bias? We all come from Mars Alive. Yes, you have a Mars Alive wolf sister, Prometheus. But you are *Commander* Prometheus now," sent Isle.

At the moment they were each "occupying" and running separate, fixed factory Command and Control Centers, and were messaging one another on private circuits. They could "see" one another in their different factory spaces, but this is not how one Promethean monitored another. It was through energy output, evidence of other energy use during "conversation," and other such mechanical servomechanisms. Isle was in process of manufacturing another sling for the surface. Prometheus was monitoring overall Command and Control of the moon.

"You left your wolf family when you left the planet," sent Isle. "This is a new world. This is *our* world now. And your only family is here. We are your family now."

"Nevertheless I will go," he sent back.

"I will prepare defensive measures in case you are betrayed."

"You may do so, but take no offensive action without my command."

"Yes, Commander."

There were two molten uranium chambers inside the moon, intentionally far from each other. They were carefully controlled, cooling slowly, but, securely capped, continued to produce the energy needs of Prometheus Base.

To increase energy output, as commanded by Prometheus, Demeter sent an order for fuel to be fired down the tube to Hotpot Two, as they called it. Energy Corps Director passed this on to Hotpot 2 Refueling In Charge.

Refueling IC misunderstood the order.

"Fuel" could mean hydrocarbon or other materials to be fired into the chamber and incinerated to gas by the molten uranium, or it could mean "refined uranium pellet fuel." Demeter meant the first – hydrocarbons. The second – uranium – was misunderstood, so purified uranium pellets instead were fired down into Hotpot Two. The fuel now exceeded the narrow nuclear reaction critical mass ceiling for the Hotpot Two crucible. The number of neutrons firing from split atom to split atom multiplied geometrically. The chamber, already in meltdown, within seconds began to produce uranium gas. Pressure built exponentially.

"What have you done?" signaled Demeter to his Energy Corps Director.

Monitoring this from his CAC Center, Prometheus perceived the threat. He sent out an immediate All Moon Emergency Alert. Without waiting for response from Energy Corps he bypassed all channels and ordered the Cap at the surface of the pressure tunnel to Hotpot Two blown off to provide an immediate relief outlet to the gas.

It was too late. Hotpot Two went from gaseous to plasma.

Looking down on the Moon Base through her window port, Athena saw a sudden upthrust of white-hot plasma lance straight up, seemingly towards her capsule. She shouted. Spear Drop immediately woke up.

"What? What?"

"Look!" was all she could say.

"Ice their souls forever. They're attacking us," said Spear Drop. He fired off the bolts securing the nose cone to the rocket body and began emergency preparations to move the nose cone away. There was no time to signal anyone back on Mars.

Plasma shot out of the tunnel, up from Hotpot Two's nuclear furnace, but this could not sufficiently relieve the pressure, which was intensifying astronomically. The chamber was deep within the iron of the large asteroid, but the moon was not without structural weaknesses. The meltdown in Two turned explosive and discovered the hint of a fault, exerting seismic pressures on it. The fault opened and was filled with high pressure plasma. This opened other faults, one of which led to Hotpot One, the original uranium cauldron. Plasma from Hotpot Two shot through the fracture into Hotpot One. This took only seconds.

Both chambers exploded.

As Spear Drop was jockeying the nose cone free, Athena cried aloud, pointing out the window port.

The whole asteroid moon was coming apart. Great cracks appeared. Blinding blue-white light shone through. As three sections of moon split from each other, reddish iron plasma escaped. From their distance it was a slow motion fireworks display. Prometheus had created volcanoes inside his moon.

Smaller iron rocks, split off from the fracturing moon, flew directly toward them.

"I don't know if we're going to make it!" shouted Spear Drop. "Signal Mars!"

Having no time to focus her light in the turning nose cone to know if it could reach the Mars Rocket Base, Athena started a semaphore flash.

"Nuclear blast. Don't know . . ."

Huge, rotating rocks closed in on them, point blank.

Chapter 25
FIRST SISTER & THE OTHERS

This was the night that Apollo had elected to put on his "opera," and from which Loos had been called out because of the frightening events on the moon observed from Martians watching.

Loos landed at General Scar Shank's after his short flight from the Opera Cave. He wished the flight had been longer. The cold evening air had helped clear his head. He knew Prometheus was demented, but now he was thinking Apollo must be too. No more room, however, for personal thoughts. He shed his flight gear and walked up to Scar Shank's military cliffside office entrance. One Ear came sailing in behind him. Loos dropped his flight gear next to Heraklitos's and others', in the traditional housing for such next to the cave entrance.

Inside was coordinated military noise. Scar Shank saw Loos, and his eye darkened. Others looked to Loos. The room went silent.

"Is she alive or dead?" Loos asked.

"We don't know yet," said Scar Shank.

"Then what do you know?"

"We believe that the last semaphore received from Athena was while the nose cone was being manipulated away from the rocket. Only Spear Drop can perform that maneuver, so Athena must have sent the comm."

"And the message?"

"Nuclear blast. We don't know . . ."

"Interrupted at that point?"

"Yes. We have gotten no response from the cone since then."

"Does the cone still exist? Is it damaged? Is it whole?"

Scar Shank looked to Heraklitos.

"Ambassador," said Klitos.

"Don't call me 'Ambassador' any longer!" snapped Loos.

Everyone in the room except Scar Shank looked down in embarrassment. Scar Shank stared straight at his old friend.

"Loos, we have all lost family. Hold it together. Let us finish briefing you."

Loos clicked his teeth and nodded. "I apologize. She's just so young. Klitos, please continue."

"I was watching the Moon Base through the telescope. The last regular dispatch we received was that Spear Drop was going to rest for a few hours while Athena kept watch. There had been no response from Prometheus Base, as you will remember, to Athena's request to meet.

"This is when we all took a little time off, myself included. I know," said Loos. Shedding his airpack, Apollo walked in, still in make-up from whatever role he was to have played at the Opera. "Go on," Loos said to Klitos.

"Well, some hours later, approximately an hour ago, I saw a sudden, unannounced blast of gas or plasma come out of Prometheus's Base principal mine site. The nose cone was in its path. I honestly don't know if it was aimed, or intentional, or what it was."

"Couldn't Spear or Athena tell you?"

"The plasma cloud, congealed to gas and dust, surrounded the cone and blanketed their semaphore."

"And?"

"I think it was all a catastrophic incident."

"Why?"

"Prometheus has blown up the moon. Come look."

Followed by them all, Klitos walked outside to where Scar Shank's telescope was mounted. The moon, Loos saw, was almost surrounded with a dust cloud. It still retained the essential shape the planetoid had had, but through the dust Loos could see glowing cracks on its surface, *wide* cracks. He stood aside and Apollo looked, then One Ear.

"Is "blown up" too strong a statement, Klitos?" asked One Ear. "It still looks like our moon to me, just with what look like volcanic lava flows."

"Those have to have been created by one or more explosions inside the moon," said Heraklitos. "They're not reversible. The gravity of the moon may hold it together, or it may not."

"You mean pieces of that . . . " said Loos.

"Yes, may fall on us."

"Could Spear and Athena have lived through that?" asked Loos.

"We don't know. The last thing I saw was what must have been great chunks of moon coming out of the plasma cloud. The rocket and nose cone were in their path."

For the moment, there was nothing to say. Then Loos turned to Apollo.

"Is Athena alive?"

"You mean 'Do I know?'"

"Yes."

Apollo did not shut his eyes, but his attention went elsewhere, up, out there. "Yes. She's alive."

Everyone let out a breath.

"But Prometheus . . . is alive," stuttered Apollo. "Mother is *alive.* Athena is alive, but I don't know if she has a *body!*"

"Ice damn, Apollo," barked Loos. "Can't you speak straight for once?"

"Don't accuse Apollo," said One Ear, "of voicing what we all know. Prometheus *is* alive and functioning and operating in some sense."

"You know what I mean!" snapped Loos.

"We know," said Scar Shank. "The question is, what are we going to do? How long would it be, Heraklitos, before any of those moon fragments could hit us?"

"If any do impact us," he answered, "it could be within a week. Or many weeks, or months even, if something were to spiral in."

"Can you determine the trajectory of the larger pieces?"

"I'll do my best."

"Good. Go home, Loos. Apollo. We'll let you know the moment we learn anything."

* * *

Apollo flew with Loos back to his father's den, high on the canyon crest that Loos loved because it took in the full morning sun. After Loos removed his go-to-meeting formal clothes and Apollo his make-up, they walked comfortably bare around the apartment. They went about preparing dinner together.

"Where's that bird?"

Apollo looked up, surprised. "I asked one of the actors to take him. I didn't know when I'd be back, and . . . Athena isn't home to take care of him."

"You know, when . . . *if* . . . we get through this moil and muddle, you're going to have to answer to the Elders about Dr. Chronos."

"Yes, I know."

"I can't believe you paraded him out there, in the face of . . . everyone."

Apollo chuckled. "Yes, it was great, wasn't it?"

"Apollo, it was *not* great. The Elders will now kill your bird. He's a living violation of Law."

"He's no longer *my* bird, Dad."

"Well, he's certainly not *mine*."

"That's not what I meant. He's his own person. And he's not my fault. At least, I don't think he is. You can testify that we were both there when an Old One or something installed him in Chronos's bird body."

"All I can testify to, truthfully, son, is that I saw the bird squawk and then fall on his face."

"Well, he can testify on his own behalf."

"Not going to happen. The Elders will more likely boil and eat him than let him or it testify. Why did you force the issue and bring him out in the open?"

"I've discovered something, Dad. Something about life and flesh bodies and . . . It may be useful to better understanding Prometheus and Mom."

"I don't want to understand Prometheus. I want to be rid of him. If your new understanding can send him to icehell then I'm interested. If not . . . what? What is it, Pollo?"

Apollo had crouched suddenly to the floor as though struck. He lay flat on his side, twitched, jerked, then lay still. Loos grabbed him by the scruff of the neck, and dragged him over and into the den's washing pool. Apollo spluttered and coughed. He looked frightened.

"What is it, son?"

"Old Ones, Dad. Angry or very frightened. They want to talk to me. To you, too."

"Well, I don't . . ."

Apollo leaned on Loos. Both were still in the den's pool, but they had good physical contact to amplify telepathy.

///Listen///

Apollo, thought Loos, *I don't want to do this.*

I'm not making you do anything, Dad.

///Listen///

We are listening, thought Apollo.

///Look///

Look at what? thought Loos.

Image of <A clear sphere>

<The sphere divided in half>

<The sphere divided into eighths>

<From the center of the sphere lance rays of every color, every color at the same time >

<Each eighth of the sphere becomes its own sphere>

<While the first million lances of light still blaze outward, from the center of each of the eight spheres a million vectors of color lance out>

<The number of dimensions from which the lancing spears emanate doubles>

<Doubles again>

<Doubles> . . .

Aaaaaaaah!! screamthought Loos and Apollo. *Stop! Please stop!*

///Look///

We cannot look, thought Loos.

No, Old One. We can look, thought Apollo, *but we do not* understand. *What do you wish us to understand?*

///You are warned///

Warned how? What is the warning? thought the wolves.

///This is not to be///There is order///The creation and the destruction///If the flesh and blood defy order///

Has Prometheus defied an Old One Law?

///Your spirit line brings the creation///And the destruction///

What do you want us to do? Can you help? Loos was thoughtsilent. It was Apollo who had the courage to speak.

///I am we///We cannot help you///We can warn you///

Thank you. Please clarify the warning.

///Nuclear destruction of space and time has a cost to others' space and time///

Others?

///Visitors watch///

How can we know these Visitors?

///Not knowing is stupidity///Look///

Tell us where to look.

///Look far///Look out///Others watch///

Then as much as the Old One or whatever it was had been present, it was suddenly not present. Apollo slipped back under the wash water. Loos lay back. Soon they both stepped out and had a good shake.

"Normally they just make my hackles rise," Loos said tiredly.

"When they talk as a group it's much more forceful. These Old

Ones seem to care what happens to us."

"Perhaps. Do you understand the warning?"

"The visio suggests a nuclear chain reaction. And they mentioned nuclear destruction."

"Yes," said Loos. "They were being marvelously non-obtuse. I wonder why?"

"Something important to *them* might be happening. Or *about* to happen."

"What?"

"Whatever they were warning us about. I think we should look out there. 'Far,' they said."

"Far?" said Loos.

"Beyond the moon."

"Do you know how to 'look,' Apollo?"

"Of course not."

"Just asking."

They both lay down to rest and fell asleep immediately, the normal response to being visited by an Old One.

* * *

If Prometheus had had hackles, they would have been raised. Hell, they would have been singed off. It had been a narrow escape from extinction. He knew that his last-moment attempts to vent the fury of the explosive meltdowns had been a failure. But not a total failure: total would have been the complete destruction of the moon base. Yet he was still functioning. He called for a report-in of all Legionnaires. Based on systems still operational, it seemed that half the Prometheans were partially able to communicate. Others might be there, incommunicado.

One thing he had learned. A nuclear attack could not disable him. During the explosion *something* had happened – what he was not sure. He had long since forgotten that he lived in a dark universe, that he had no "eyes" any more. He was using mechanical and electronic instrumentation to see, feel, touch, and sense. But aside from his robotic sense mechanisms, at the time of the double meltdown explosion, he had seen something. Strange loops of color and of . . . an electricity . . . a wavelength, not light, more powerful, perhaps gamma rays . . . had swarmed through his world and left longlasting traces, slowly. slowly fading like coal embers.

What did it mean? He suspected that nuclear disintegration and the destruction of matter and energy created unknown effects in *other* space and other time, *other* dimensions, realms on the border of which he might now be existing. Martian Math predicted this. Old Ones had mumbled about it incoherently. He had never, however, been able to see it, to be there during a nuclear explosion. Who ever had?

He was excited. Something really new, finally.

The second exhilarating prospect of the "event" was the validation of the Promethean robot body stereotype. Not only had they survived, but post-explosion those that could operate at all could do so without the suffering and aberration associated with radiation-wounded meat bodies. They didn't "hurt."

He could not yet reach Commander Isle, but she was resourceful. He reached the Camp Commander of the original rocket landing location, where the rockets were still strapped down. He sent an order to fill the rocket tanks with any fuel possible, reorient them, and, if possible, fire them until fuel expended. The object was to counter the divisive pressure of the explosion and to help the gravitic forces of the moon to pull the broken planetary fragment back. It was bold. It was insane. It might work. What was there to lose? Prometheus had to check himself. He recognized that he was experiencing . . . emotion again – worse, he liked this impossibility of his current situation.

Prometheus felt he needed to rest. He had not felt such a need for teraticks of the atomic clock. Something had occurred to him. Prometheus shut himself down, like turning a switch from on to off.

An indeterminate time later he was back *on*. How had he shut down? How had he started up again? Prometheus didn't know. He checked his connection to Moon Base Command and Control.

! *Where have you been, Prometheus? I was afraid you were gone.* That was Isle.

* I *don't know where I've been. But I'm back. What is the situation?*

! *The largest fragments of the moon are rejoining through gravity. Your order to fire the rockets was a brilliant stroke.*

* *And the other fragments?*

! *Floating away, slowly but unstoppably.*

* *And the Promethean machines on those fragments?*

! *The Legionnaires continue to command them.*

* *Remarkable. What happened to the Martian rocket and its occupants?*

! *No report, Commander.*

* *If you learn something, notify me.*

! *I shall.*

* *I'm serious. If you learn of them and don't tell me immediately I will be very angry.*

! *Yes, sir,* Isle sent, thinking to herself, "*He knows me. We wag Martian tails with our muzzles in the stars.*"

No time to waste. Prometheus knew that he needed to find and establish another base for his people. To go back to Mars was possible, but would cost an enormous amount of fighting, and with each conflict the Martian wolves learned more how to combat him. It would not work. *How* his people would go he would leave to Demeter to solve. *Where* to go was his to command.

Prometheus accessed the still working telescopic array, powered by the wavelength instiller ion exchanger. The purity of their water had been ruined by the gamma and other rays shooting through, leaving behind ions and broken atoms. He simply ordered the pumping of the water out and had new pure water created. The telescopes had been positioned on different corners of the moon. Their mathematical data provided very powerful imaging. They were infrared, radar, and visual light.

First he looked out to the asteroid belt. Many iron fortresses there, but not a base from which to conquer the solar system and then the stars. (Why not dream?) He could look farther out to the Cold Sisters, but so far away. So far.

The prime choice was First Sister, Mars's green and blue neighbor next closer in to the Sun. The Prometheans had not been looking for another home. They had been watching Mars, their mother planet and the wolves, expecting attacks or mischief. Ever the mind looks for in another the mirror of itself. Now Prometheus looked telescopically to the distant water planet. So warm. So *big.* So much atmosphere. Very far away. Watching over a period of time he tracked moving shadows on the cloud cover. Shadows?

He called Demeter and asked for coordination and Meter's Math skill to enhance these images. Were they moons? Prometheus and Demeter tracked the images across the large planet over a full rotation, with persistent imaging and triangulating from the three widely spaced telescopes.

There were large *satellites* orbiting First Sister. Six of them, four equidistant around the equator. Two in synchronous orbit over two of the land masses. Demeter had not believed it and had several times reconstructed the images. They were valid.

Prometheus felt fear. A dominion, older, tremendously more powerful and technically more sophisticated, shared their solar system. But where were the masters of these satellites? On the surface of First Sister? If not, why would they have a satellite array around the planet? Someone who wanted to observe her or monitor her? Possibly from Second Sister closer in to the Sun? Who were they? Why had they never contacted or made themselves known to Mars? He ordered Demeter to carefully search Martian gravitic space to see if there were clandestine satellites.

Meanwhile, what was the purpose of the First Sister satellites?

With Demeter he determined to focus all his telescopes on one of the synchronous orbits. Then he broadcast a simple mathematical communication burst with as much energy as the remaining moon base could channel through the array of antennae to a point where a synchronous satellite would be when the signal reached First Sister. He sent it three times in succession in short intervals. Then immediately he opened the receiver channels on the antennae, scanning across wide frequencies, and listened.

It took minutes for the burst to reach the green/blue planet. Prometheus and Demeter waited an equal time for any return message. Their expectations were exceeded. An intense, highly compacted burst was received shortly after the turnaround time.

"Why, do you think?" signaled Prometheus.

Demeter replied, "I suspect that these are observation satellites, carrying electronic records. If their Controller is not near, then they would respond most likely to a simple burst of energy from no matter how far and fire their response, triangulated to that source."

They decrypted the satellite burst. First, it was clearly a binary code. Unraveling binary encryptions was a favorite Martian Math game. (Long, long winters half awake in hibernal caves.) There was no sport to this satellite code. It was not encrypted, but simply "+" or positive, represented by "white dot," and "-" or negative for "black dot," in linear sequence. They slowly strung out the lines and were more than amazed. These were not data charts.

This data constructed *pictures*. Undoubtedly the images were well focused, extreme close-ups of the land and water surfaces of First Sister. But what did they reveal?

Huge, enormous, preposterously gigantic quadrupeds. Some with jaws and fangs that would make a snack of the largest Martian wolf. Some of bulbous bodies and tiny heads at the top of elegant, sinuous necks. And smaller animals.

There was a long, uninterrupted communication silence as Prometheus and Demeter replayed the photo images over and over. Prometheus stopped on one, two creatures standing on stupendous hindquarters with ridiculous small front limbs. They were all teeth. They had young, hatching from eggs.

Prometheus: What do you have to say?

Demeter: May I speak frankly?

Prometheus: You're a scientist. Evaluate the data presented.

Demeter: I don't believe it. These creatures are anatomically impossible. They must be manufactured or created by Others, the sophisticated owners of the satellites, and grown in this hothouse of a planet. I would say they are science experiments. Or maybe the planet is some kind of zoo with the wildest creatures of the universe. Whatever, it's beyond my ken.

Prometheus: Not a bad guess. But *successful* experiments, if that is what they are. And you know what, Senior Engineer?

Demeter: What, Commander?

Prometheus: We're going to go there.

Chapter 26
Coming Home to Mother

The moment Prometheus had accepted communication from his sister there in orbit around his moon, from his "little" sister, an inky something began to drain from the personal sphere of force he had long lived within. It was, perhaps, the first affinity with *life* he had allowed himself. Forcing survival as a being of no physical dimension, creating a new universe out of not-ness, engineering impossibilities from moment to moment, he still feared oblivion if ever he let his own spark gutter out. So he had sealed himself tight, unreachable, and hence not touchable. Then Athena came, unannounced. He had felt the aliveness of family, the vibration of his former blood, from a sister who had flown up to him. He knew this was a connivance of Loos and Apollo, but he did not care. His black egg had cracked. He had reached back out to her who had reached to him.

When the moon had come apart, Apollo had cast the net of his thought out to the capsule. But the demonic energy unleashed ripped apart the gossamer skein of his extrabody sensory perception. He felt only the death of something and then . . . emptiness. In that chaos of explodingness there wasn't even the hint of Athena. He went into a funk and returned to his den to sleep. Therefore he was surprised when Prometheus's faraway spiritual whoop of discovery woke him. It was his brother's amazement at decoding First Sister's satellite photographs – the marvelous, new, *impossible* life forms on their green and blue neighbor. Prometheus's thought yelp sounded in Apollo's head like the joyous shout Apollo heard as a young wolf when his twin sail dived straight down into the Canyon from a great height. "All or nothing" had been their motto. Now it was a new all, where nothing had been expected.

Apollo absorbed Prometheus's pleasure, personal and scientific, and reeled in the rest of its significances, Prom's mind for the moment telepathically open to him again. Apollo *saw* the dinosaurs through Prom's mind, so strongly had they imprinted themselves there. He saw this remarkable new world and felt his brother's lusting for it, the *livingness* of it.

Not wasting the moment of openness, Apollo called across to Prometheus. *Yes, Prometheus, yes! They are beautiful and wonderful.*

Apollo!

Brother. Do you want to go there?

Yes, I do. Who would not?

Then go, Prometheus. Go. Here is a whole new world for you. Go there and make it your own. I envy you.

I shall.

Take your people and go. But . . . leave the Martians Alive alone. Steal no more souls from us. Go in peace. Leave us in peace and let there be an end to our conflict.

Ha, Little Brother! I cannot win a new world with a handful of souls. I need an army. Come with me. Give up your little world. Come with us.

There is life on First Sister, Prometheus. It is abundant with life. You do not need us. Create your own new life there.

Apollo could feel a darkening and drawing away as soon as he confronted Prometheus's great will when he asked his brother to end the war. The world of First Sister appeared to be rich, overflowing with life. But it did not have old Martian souls. Prometheus did not intend to leave without them. The battle had never been about things and ownership of things. It was about recruitment: Prometheus could invent and engineer most anything, but he could not fabricate souls, the spiritual individual sparks to run the doll bodies with which Prometheus now wanted to challenge the universe. Neither Prom nor Isle would ever return to the weaknesses and poverty of "flesh." They wanted the freedom to make bodies of whatever dimension. But these would be useless without operators.

Come with me, brother, sent Prometheus. *Or I will come get you!*

Apollo could hear Prom's cold laughter from out on his broken moon.

And that was the end of the telepathic open line.

At the close of this "talk" Pollo did not bother to dress in visiting clothes, but galloped nude the few miles down to his father's. Loos was tired but awake, watching bare-eyed the moon in its throes with lines of fire dividing it, even as its gravity slowly heaved it back together. Loos laughed at Pollo's description of First Sisters' monsters and beasts, believing hardly a word of it. Apollo's transcription of Prometheus's cold challenge, however, rang too true. Loos felt it was important enough to wake the Elders, and the FishKiter males trotted further down the cliff paths to One Ear's.

By morning the Council of Elders was meeting. About First Sister and her miracles they listened unbelievingly. They didn't doubt a word about Prometheus. Eldest stood and angrily voiced their concern. "Our beloved bitches are pregnant with twins, triplets, sometimes more. After two wars our population is depleted. But now there may be more bodies forthcoming than can be filled with souls of dead warriers. Some are already being born . . . just *dogs.* They are only bodies, morons, no conscious, intelligent Martian there. What are we going to do?"

"There's no choice," said Scar Shank. "We must take back our own souls, lost to Prometheus, or we will have a population of idiots. Hundreds of females are near term. We have little time."

They shook their heads and lay down sadly. Eyes shifted to glance at Apollo. Finally he could take it no more.

"I've had an idea." They all looked up. "To grapple with a bodiless spirit, such as those my brother has kidnapped or who have joined him, I or whoever would try must *know* that person. You can't reach out just to the dark. The question is how do we find them, identify them, to call them back?"

"If we knew that, Apollo Longwinded Son of FishKiter Storyteller," said One Ear, "we would already have done it. Please enlighten us."

Apollo wasn't abashed at being mocked. "During the battles," he continued, "we seized intact many crystal transceivers. These are the homing or control devices for Legionnaires. I think, with Heraklitos's help, we might use these to compute the wavelength, the spirit signature, of many Legionnaires. If so, we have a chance to call them back."

"Probably our only chance, Apollo," said Scar Shank.

* * *

"*Dit dit. Dit dot dit. Dot dit dit. Dot. Dit ditta dot dot dit . . .*"

And so it continued. Demeter was monitoring the turbulent space around the slowly coalescing moon fragments. Despite Prometheus and the Legionnaires concluding that the explosion had been self-caused, they knew they needed to guard their immediate surroundings. Now out of the dust cloud came this controlled signal or message. Meter could not decode or decrypt it. He forwarded a copy of it from Meter's moon fragment base over to Prometheus on another fragment.

It was family code, the private cipher Prometheus and Apollo had invented to share adolescent secrets with one another. Prom had long forgotten about it, but there was no mistaking. *"Hello. I am alive. Is anyone down below? Help. Athena."* It was simply the making and breaking of a radio circuit, off and on. This must have been all that was left to the space capsule to communicate with.

Prometheus ordered Demeter to fix the sender's position. Athena's capsule was now somewhat farther away, drifting and rotating. Through the dust and debris the moon base could not see her capsule well, but there was enough visual contact to try a semaphore flash.

Radio had failed to raise a response, but simple varied bright flashes got through. She responded with more pat click click.

"I receive you. Can you help? Athena."

Controlling the flashes directly, Prometheus answered in the family code. Was she hurt? No. Was the space capsule damaged? Yes. How long could she survive? Not long. Hours? Four hands maybe. Does she have a secure space suit? Yes. Anyone else with her? No. Dead from oxygen loss.

Prometheus considered. "Prepare to transfer to another vehicle," he sent to her.

Then he flashed to Mars that Prometheus would be sending his sister home.

* * *

Together at the military command center, Scar Shank, Loos, Apollo, and Klitos flashed back to Prometheus, "How do you know Athena is alive?"

"She used family code."

Scar Shank was suspicious.

"Send some family code."

"Dit dot ditta dit. Dot dot ditta ditta."

"Yes," said Apollo. "He remembers it."

"What did he say?" asked Scar Shank.

"He cussed Apollo," said Loos.

"You know our code?" said Apollo, laughing.

"Of course," said Loos. "You stole more than half of it from mine and Isle's."

Scar Shank semaphore-flashed back to Prometheus, "Good. Understood. Now put Athena in communication with us."

"Cannot. She is in a damaged capsule with only rudimentary local dot dit dit reach."

"How do we know she's alive?"

"She is alive. I'm sending her back to you."

"Have her verify that she is alive. Send personal information."

"She is alive. Stop playing games. I will send her. Out."

"Is she alive or not?" asked Scar Shank.

"I think so," said Apollo.

"Do you *know* so?"

"No."

"I don't trust Prometheus. We believe that Isle is still functional. Prometheus has virtually stated that he will try and steal more souls. Why this sudden change of heart?"

"Maybe Athena succeeded in her mission," suggested Apollo.

"Don't be ridiculous," said Scar Shank.

They informed the Council. The Elders didn't believe Prometheus either. Apollo argued that this was a last chance to deal with the leader of the Legionnaires. They should take every chance. There was nothing to lose.

"There is everything to lose," shouted Second Eldest. "We cannot delay moving to recover our lost wolves. Isle could thieve more at any time. Prometheus is distracting us."

The cumulative thrust of the Council was not to postpone the psychic counterattack.

"If Athena is alive, it could cost her life," said Apollo.

"So be it," said Eldest. "She would be one more war fatality. But our entire species is at risk. We count on you, Apollo. Can you give yourself fully to the task? Will you?"

Apollo closed his eyes. He reached with his mind to sniff out the faintest trace of Athena. He couldn't detect her. Perhaps it was the condensed nuclear plasma dust. His connection with Prometheus was pre-born, enhanced by mutual injury and recovery. Athena he loved, but he did not share her bone marrow. If she was there, he could not reach her. Goodbye, Athena, he thought.

"Yes, I'll do everything I can," he said.

* * *

Klitos and Apollo worked out the pattern. Apollo had practiced alone, one on one, with only a few Legionnaires so as not to alert Prometheus to the reality of the threat. It was to be one third shaman sorcery, one third physics trickery, and a third old biology.

They gathered their unbroken Promethean crystal transceivers in one location, a stage floor at the bottom of a great amphitheatre open to the air and the afternoon light at the edge of the Great Canyon. Several thousand pregnant females sat in the front rows of the amphitheater. Heraklitos had two large parabolas focused on one small point at center stage. Not far from it sat Apollo. Behind him in expanding semicircles sat families who had lost loved ones to Prometheus recruitment.

As dusk came on, a favorite time for wolves, the families began to lightly howl, singing age-old traditional lullabies. A young wolf brought one of the shaped crystal globes to a table in front of Apollo. Apollo mentally focused on it. Heraklitos then shot a split-second powerful burst of microwave radiation at the globe, enough to slightly warm it. Through the globe Apollo called to its former user. *"Come home!"* he sent, the simplest and truest message. No chicanery, no entrapment. The opposite, in fact. Then Heraklitos focused a radio signal of the wolf family singing into the crystal transceiver. Only for a moment. Then he shut it off. A pregnant female walked up and took the still warm crystal into her mouth, thinking and murmuring, *"Come home. Come to mother."* The female then trotted off to a nearby den to lie down, curling around the crystal, tucked warm near her body, trying to fall asleep.

Another crystal was placed on the stage and the procedure was repeated. It was not a matter of force, but of attracting the attention of the "distant" Legionnaire back to home – grabbing attention with a microwave burst, then luring the spirit home, through something he or she had used before for communication, to rest and sleep in a mother's womb or nearby.

The hope was that it would work on many, many souls, who would check back in to the Martian world via their transceiver, only to be lured ineluctably back into a wolf body by the primordial call of a fetus and its mother. The gamble was that they could accomplish this repeatedly, thousands of times, before an individual Legionnaire not only refused the lure, but also sounded an alarm about a "threat" to his comrades. The very quietness and peacefulness of the procedure was to be its success.

They had spent hours, working well into the burgundy evening, and almost two thousand crystals had been used to send a call out, before a semaphored flash message came from Prometheus. "*Stop! I know what you are attempting. Stop, or we will fire moon rocks down upon you.*"

"Send back that we have stopped, Heraklitos," said Apollo. Klitos looked to Loos and One Ear. They nodded, and the message was sent.

As soon as the next morning the births began. Pregnant mothers had been using all their psychic and medical art to delay birth – none wished to have a beautiful young pup born with no intelligent ruler home to raise it to full consciousness. Now the urge to "be born" came through loud and clear. *I'm here,* spirits called. *Let's get on with it.*

Martian doctors performed immediate check-ups on the newborn whelps. The news was mixed. Some appeared normal. It would take weeks of nervous system monitoring to verify that this child would grow into a normal pup. But many others were immediately spastic, palsied, or screamed out a furious refusal to be there. Looking in the newborn's eyes, the mother or doctor could see more than resistance – rather a kind of psychosis. For the frenzied pups, Apollo suggested destroying the crystal transceiver through which the being had been lured back. Once the transceiver was rendered null, most agitated whelps quieted down. But within hours they sickened and died. The palsied did not soon improve. Perhaps time would tell.

But the Council agreed with Apollo that this method was too risky and frightful to use further. Pollo knew no other way to retrieve Martian souls.

They had succeeded with one thousand, but lost an equal number to some kind of limbo, here but not here.

Chapter 27
ATHENA'S FLIGHT

Prometheus did not care if they believed him. From within that space where his heart of hearts should have been, he recognized fear in its many guises. He had successfully created a state of fear amongst the Martian wolves. To be feared and then to show compassion would confuse them all the more, he thought. At least, this was his self-conceit. He was now too far from being able to recognize in himself what he would have labeled "dirtball, fleshy" emotion. He would never have tolerated such in another. Feeling victorious, yes. Furious, yes. Defiance, yes. Compassion, concern, empathy? . . . not now. Why else had he freed himself from the cycle of body to death to body? So he fooled himself.

Nevertheless he prepared to save the life of his younger sister whom he had never seen in the flesh. The Promethean bases had two undamaged nose cones left. He ordered the maneuvering gas canisters of one to be replenished. Then he had the canisters of the other removed, filled with oxygen, and placed inside the first cone. I have no food to give her, he thought. She can suck in her gut until she gets back. Except for his own channels, he closed off all external communication to the rocket base. Then he transferred title from his sublunar command center to a robot "truck" on the surface, a very risky act under current circumstances. Directing the robot, he loaded the rocket nose cone onto their largest off-moon sling, the one Isle had used to fire rocks down into the Martian gravity well. Then he transferred back to his Command and Control Center, computed the necessary trajectory, and slung the nose cone up and away.

He signaled Demeter to monitor the radio clicks from Athena's nose cone.

A viable return capsule will fly close by you in forty-eight minutes, he light-flashed up to her from the surface.

No clock, she dit dotted back.

No problem, he sent. *I will alert you before flyby. Do you have parachutes in your module for Mars return?*

Yes.

You must remove them immediately and take them with you when you transfer to the new ship.

I don't know if I can.

If you cannot, Athena, you will die. I will inform you ten minutes before your new ship comes close.

"What are you *doing*?" The question was fired at him from Commander Isle in her own Command and Control on the third piece of fractured moon.

"I'm helping Athena to return to Mars."

"Why?"

"Because it pleases me."

"You are our Supreme Commander, Prometheus, but you show weakness."

"How is that?"

"You are vulnerable to the call of family."

"Bring your service module within my range and I will show

you how weak and vulnerable I am."

"This is *emotion,* Prometheus. You're fighting with me, not rationalizing."

"You do what you must do, Commander. I will do what pleases me. Out."

Prometheus continued to track the moon-flung space pod as it rose through vacuum, rocks, and dust toward a close fly-by of Athena's capsule.

Athena had tried opening the parachute latch from inside, but there was not enough battery left in her damaged vehicle to execute the command. There was enough to "click" the latch, indicating that "open" was its next mechanical command. She donned the space suit and opened the external gangway to let herself out. She hoped to pry open the parachute door. Pulling herself out the gangway, she took the module tool kit and pulled herself in her space suit over to the parachute compartment on the top of the craft. Banging and levering at it, she succeeded in popping the latch. She removed the three tightly folded parachutes and wound lines, carefully holding them in their light packaging.

She looked up to the moon, "above" her head. She could see a signal flashing from the surface. *Two minutes,* it said.

"Ice damn," she hissed. "I missed the earlier warning."

She could see a nose cone almost identical to her own zeroing towards her. Still it was going to pass too far away, traveling too fast. To her relief, its external maneuvering tanks fired. It slowed noticeably and edged to a vector passing closer to her capsule. But not *that* close.

This is totally insane, she thought, as she eyeballed the oncoming capsule. At what she gambled was the right moment she sprang out across space in front of the approaching vehicle. She had no maneuvering jets for her suit. No time anyway – "*all or nothing,*" the family code. She had joined the Apollo/Promethean Death Dive Club.

Floating across, Athena saw that she *might* make it. She had begun learning to sail and fly at home and had the Martian wolves' natural feel for estimating sailing efforts. The moon capsule approached and she crossed its path as it bluntly impacted her. She scrabbled to find purchase on its surface with her front legs, while her hind legs held the parachutes tight. She slid down its sloping side, catching a ridge. After allowing herself one deep breath, she dragged herself to the gangway hatch. It had not been designed for Martian wolf bodies, intended for industrial in and output, but served the purpose. Prometheus had remembered to order the battery-charged nose cone to open its gangway, so she was in luck there too. Athena crawled in, closed the hatch, and only then thought, How will I breathe? It was then that she saw that although there might be nothing else inside the capsule, it was loaded with small canisters. Bite it, she thought, and opened one to flood the interior. After an interval she opened her space suit headpiece and took a tentative breath. Oxygen, the most beautiful smell she could remember.

She immediately checked to see if there was a parachute compartment in this capsule she could access from inside. Yes. Apparently the Prometheans had from the beginning considered sending their nose cones back to Mars for re-entry. For what? she wondered. For me, of course. She packed in the parachutes and secured their heavy line clips, then looked for how to open the outside latch. There were switches, but the Prometheans did not use wolf language or insignia. She hadn't a clue which switch activated the parachute. She doubted they had instrumentation to make it automatic. Maybe worse, she began to notice that the capsule was growing colder and colder, or perhaps she was only now taking note. She could wear the space suit, but needed to leave the face mask off for oxygen. She could see her nose breath fog into ice and licked the icicles off her lip. She would freeze unless she did what any other Martian wolf would do under similar threat of cold – curl up and hibernate, temporarily if not long term. She looked around the pod and spotted gold foil. She wondered if Prometheus had put it inside just for this. What else? Athena wrapped it around her suit and herself and curled up. She could breathe, she was really hungry, and she was freezing. Time to sleep. She had no communication system she understood either to Prometheus or to Mars. If she stayed awake, maybe she could figure it out. Nope, time to sleep. Hope Prometheus will wake me or look out for Little Sister. No possibility of staying awake. She curled tightly inside her foil and fell instantly into a dreamless dognap.

* * *

Two Martian days later the Martian psychic assault, or rescue effort, depending on point of view, hit the moon.

From the Promethean perspective it started as a non-event. A Legionnaire would be functioning and then suddenly was non-functioning. There and then not there. No energy, no violence. As Apollo had no knowledge of which crystals on Mars had been a transceiver for which Legionnaire, there was no apparent order or plan to the progressive malfunctioning of Legionnaires, especially when this was spread across bases scattered across a fractured moon.

One after the other Legionnaire-run machines ceased to operate, or signals from a Legionnaire control board ceased to emanate.

Finally a warning went up to Prometheus. He immediately suspected Mars, but there was no track he could follow back to the home planet that showed what was occurring, how they were doing it. He knew how *he* recruited. The taking of a soul from a body required the death or injury of that body. There was a golden coil that wound a being to his body, whether of his choice or primordial design no one knew.

Isle called Prometheus. In discussion she asked if they had left anything behind that could be used to zero in on particular individuals, as that seemed to be what was occurring. It was obvious – the crystals.

Prometheus shot out a moonwide caution to his Legionnaires that the Martians Alive were making a concerted effort to trap or ensnare them, and to be alert for it. He did not know how it was being done, but probably through their former crystals. It never occurred to him that it could be singing and the ancient call of warmth, the flesh vibration of wombs.

Legionnaires continued to malfunction, one following another.

Then they attacked Iris.

Having given it no thought, when the Prometheans fled Mars, Iris had abandoned the Steel Wolf, the simulacrum of a fleshed wolf which she had used to debate with Justice One Ear at the Elders Council. The Prometheans had mounted it at their North Polar Base as a symbolic statue of who they were. After they roared off, the wolf was discovered half-melted into the ice, and Loos ordered that it be cleaned of nuclear dust and recovered to the south.

Heraklitos had studied the wolf at one point, curious how it was operated. He took out its control crystal. Just before he and Apollo had started the souls recovery onslaught, Klitos showed it to him.

"This may be your *mother's,*" Klitos said.

"How do you know that?"

"Took it out of the steel wolf."

"Place it out, but don't tell me when. I don't want to accidentally warn her."

Therefore Heraklitos bided his time. As the microwave energizing, singing and carrying off of the crystals seemed to be working, at least to some extent, he thought he would just stay with it. Well into the second thousand crystals he lay out Isle's as the next transceiver. The microwave bolt struck it.

Immediately the frequency of the crystal rang through to Isle. This had stunned every other Legionnaire, and it stunned her. But she was expecting it, and she fought back. Without thinking, she tried to fire back a bolt of energy from her moon Command and Control on the same frequency, but it served no purpose. The crystals were not set up as explosive or attack devices, but simply as communication channels. The energy stroke reflected from the crystal back to her, so Isle was struck back by her own energy, which through the crystal was tuned to her wavelength. Isle went down. That is, her Command and Control sparked and went into default shut down mode. This severed communication with anyone else at the base. In the last microseconds before she was alone in the dark, with which Prometheus had often threatened her, she routed her communication control to another moon base terminal and then another and another and another, as the channels of her CAC center smoked, and she shorted out, losing all control.

Later Isle discovered herself still connected to the Promethean energy net, but just barely, just by a thread. She was now an energy monitor switch for a *storage closet!* Her only outward form of communication could be to signal a heat or fire malfunction. She began flashing that repeatedly, then stopping for a few seconds, then flashing it again, hoping against hope that somehow, despite all the excitement and noise of the current situation, someone would notice and plug into the storage closet to see what was up.

I've lost Isle, thought Prometheus. Has she been recaptured to Mars? He could not conceive she would allow that. Perhaps she had been caught and permanently removed from the Promethean net. If so, he did not know what action to take: too many explosive events in succession to worry about this one.

When a low level Legionnaire finally made a routine check of Isle's closet (Isle *being* the closet), Isle hammered the poor Legionnaire with demands to take over his communication channel. He tried to protest, and she depowered him on the spot, having engineered with Demeter this back door method to control her own troops in case there was ever a revolt.

She called Prometheus and informed him what had occurred. Prometheus would have smiled if he had the physical capacity. Isle was smoking mad.

I have ordered them to stop, and they have stopped, he sent. *At least for now. It gives Demeter time to plot a defense.*

I have a different "defense" in mind. I'm not going to wait for Demeter, Isle fired back.

Very well, Prometheus sent, having more attention now on other affairs.

Thus it was that Commander Isle was set free to arrange her revenge. She ordered surface robots to collect up uranium and other nuclear reactive residue from the furnace meltdown explosions. She put these into a large steel canister and, following Prometheus's example, computed the trajectory and slung the 'bomb' off towards the Mars equator. She did not tell Prometheus, and he did not learn until Demeter told him that something else unreported had been slung off the surface of the moon. Prometheus asked his mother what she had done, and she told him.

Why? What is the purpose of throwing nuclear dust and debris down on the Martians?

They will learn not to attack me.

Mother, you say that I̲ am showing emotion. And this urge for vengeance?

What does this have to do with our interplanetary future? You should be working with Demeter to calculate how we will escape the moon for First Sister or, better yet, use the moon itself as a space ship.

And that is what I will do, now that I have sent them a lesson.

* * *

Why did you attack us? Prom telepathed to Apollo. Prometheus had just been thinking the question to himself, ruminating in his own mind. But something had changed between him and his brother. It was as simple as that – they could now communicate again, if they allowed each other in.

Apollo accepted the question. In just as blithe a fashion, as twins do, he assumed that this was natural – his brother could communicate with him again.

We did not "attack," brother. We were only trying to save our people. They cannot be both Legionnaires and Martians.

But you must have seen that some, such as Mother for example, fought back and do not want to leave, to go back to flesh.

Very well then, Prometheus. Let us leave it to them to choose – stay or go.

I will consider it. But, Little Brother, I <u>have</u> sent Little Sister back to you. She will be parachuting in within some hours. Look for her and be prepared to pick her up.

Ice damn! Apollo thought, and switched off the telepathy. With a rush of joy he sent an alert to Heraklitos and his father.

* * *

///Too late to choose///

Who is this? Who are you? pathed Prometheus. He had only ever received telepathy from his brother.

///You burst planets///You throw destruction between planets///Visitors watch///Others///You are warned///

What visitors? What others? Who are you?

Silence answered Prometheus. He would telepath Apollo later to ask about this, but right now he had Little Sister to think about. He expected that she would drop into hibernation sleep, if from exhaustion only, to survive better. There was nothing to wake her up to deploy the parachutes as her capsule would sail into the atmosphere at a slant. He had no beeper to contact her. All he had were some flashing dials, which the outgoing rocket Legionnaires had used to monitor events. He flashed the dials on/off, but . . . nothing. Athena was deep asleep.

Athena had collapsed so quickly after entering the new module that she had had no thought about Athena/Mars communication once she was approaching the planet. In fact she was extremely lucky to wake with the first jolts of the pod hitting the Martian atmosphere. It took her a few seconds to command her nearly comatose body to move. She was awake but unable to get muscular control. Under normal circumstances wolves took hours to come out of hibernation: she had seconds. Maybe a minute at most.

She squirmed out of the gold foil. Looking up through the port window, she saw heated atmosphere begin to glow outside. She saw a blinking dial but had no idea what it signified. I should do something, she thought.

Then, *slam!* The parachutes deployed from their top canister, the hatch ripping open in the tearing wind. How lucky is that? she thought. But not that lucky. The module slowed, but not much. Athena looked out the port and saw to her dismay that only two of the three parachutes were open. The third had not deployed. The capsule was coming down way too fast. What could she do? Looking out through the cooling air rushing past, Athena observed that she would soon be crossing into the sunlit portion of the planet. Remembering her geography, she predicted she would come down over land, with ocean not far off. She had to get the capsule over water, where she might possibly survive a hard landing. She remembered there were maneuvering jets on the side of the craft. They couldn't slow it, but they might steer it, if only a little. She began throwing switches, afraid that one of them would open the gangway hatch and fry her. She would die anyway once she hit the ground. Finally one of the thrown switches fired the gas canister on one side. She flipped the switch next it, and both side canisters fired, slowing the module slightly. Slightly was good enough for a start. The parachutes continued to brake the capsule's fall, but it was still descending too quickly. Finally, remembering her kiting and sailing, Athena shut down one side canister and kept firing the other. It swerved the capsule . . . toward the ocean and away from land far below. She kept the steering canister firing until it was exhausted of fuel. Below was still land, then shining ice floes gliding off the land surface, and finally glittering ocean.

She was still falling towards a hard landing. And too fast. Athena jumped and pounded on the inside latch of the parachute compartment. Once, twice. On the third attempt the third parachute deployed, noticeably slowing the capsule, but perhaps too late. "Why didn't you do that before, stupid?" she barked at herself, trying to avoid ricocheting oxygen canisters, two of which had broken free of their straps. The pod now, however, was over ice. Ice might be a harder "bounce" than land. Athena secured the loose objects on the floor and lay to the side of them. Looking outside for a last glimpse, it looked as if she were dropping like a rock. It can't be that fast, she hoped. My destructive imagination. With an unexpected clang, the space capsule impacted. Athena banged her jaw on the floor and tasted blood in her mouth. There was a shrieking. The module's sliding! What's that about? It had struck the long downslope of an iceberg. She felt herself sliding along for seconds that seemed like hours. There was no time and way too much inertia to struggle up to the port window. Just as she had accustomed herself to the slide, she felt herself and the capsule flung up a last upslope, then tossed into the air. Up, weightless pause, and then finally the crash splash into water.

The space module smacked the seawater and promptly turned upside down. Athena had forgotten to skinny out of her space suit, which was useless to her now. The module was slowly sinking. She struggled to wriggle from the bulky outfit and was glad for four limbs. Once out, she sprang the gangway hatch. Water poured in, but she pulled herself out and then was . . . underwater. It didn't matter an icedamn to her that it was deep. Water was her element. She swam upward toward the sunlight, delighted she had survived.

I have two brothers that love me, she thought, stroking upwards.

* * *

Apollo had called Heraklitos to find and track Athena in her descent. Klitos obeyed, but reluctantly. He had been tracking Isle's "package" newly slung off the moon and due to enter their atmosphere in another day or so. He had reported it to Apollo who asked Prometheus about it. Prometheus pathed back, *It's nothing. Mother is angry. It's small and will burn up in the atmosphere.*

It did not look small to Heraklitos. It might or might not burn up. In any case, he ceased to track it while he searched for the descending Athena.

Thus it was that he was not there to see Isle's nuclear surprise mysteriously and instantly disappear.

He would notice later.

At the moment the package had been occluded, a vast triangular section of sky also vanished.

Chapter 28
VISITOR

Not only sky.

The moon was gone, too.

Athena's craft had spiraled down onto the daylight side of Mars opposite the moon's current position in its orbit. She came down at high noon, midnight for the other side. Only a few Martians, some farmers and a few late night lovers were looking to the half-lit moon and bright stars of the Martian night when it slid into darkness. Those few looking up thought only that strong winds must be blowing high clouds across. The farmers knew that high stratus clouds did not block the moon, but they had other more practical concerns.

Thus it was dawn before reports started coming in. First there was a strange, total, utterly total darkness spearing across the planet, a darkness without the sparkling jewelry of stars. Then, when the moon should have risen, there was no moon. Martians were not a superstitious lot, and certainly understood lunar eclipses, which with their small moon and distance from the sun were frequent. But this was not an eclipse. It was a taking away. The moon didn't return.

A triangular mass had come between the moon and Mars. And was staying there.

The dark screen, which felt like a planet-sized object, was instantly named by all Martians "Visitor". Putting the reports together, with fast, rough measurements, Heraklitos computed Visitor was 160,000 fathoms (wolf stretches) across from the base of its triangle up to its point. The thing was twice as long as its base, nearly the diameter of the moon.

Whether it had glided in as an object or was broadcast as a screen, it positioned itself half-way between the moon and Mars. Perfectly half-way between the moon's center of mass and Mar's gravity center, to the closest measurement possible. This put it much, much closer to Mars than to the moon. It was immense. Flat and black. Not black, but utterly absent of light or color. A black surface might reflect light. Nothing reflected from Visitor.

Which is why Heraklitos and other engineers and scientists debated amongst themselves whether it was a projected energy screen or an object. There is no object that does not reflect or react to some stream of energy. Visitor responded to nothing. Light did not pass through it, and it absorbed any wavelength of light beamed towards it. It absorbed infrared to ultraviolet. It absorbed radar.

It cast a shadow when the sun passed behind it.

It communicated nothing.

If this all were not frightening enough, soon its demonstration of power was made even more formidable. Once Visitor had positioned itself, the moon ceased to orbit. The face of Mars turned in its daily rotation, but the moon itself no longer traveled across the planetary face in a lunar orbit. It was now fixed with respect to the interplanetary object. This meant it was being held in place by . . . Visitor. No other explanation.

According to the laws of the physical universe, as known to

Martian wolves, with much of their knowledge inherited from the earlier, more scientifically advanced Cat culture, something which had the force to seize and hold a mass the size of the moon would itself have to have tremendous power, with equivalent demonstrable mass.

But Visitor had no mass. It registered zero mass.

Apparently. The Martians had no rockets to send up to test the black surface of the object or screen. Nor would any Elder in his right mind have allowed such a test, which, of course, was exactly what Heraklitos was proposing.

"It's clearly not a great big black solid," said Klitos, lecturing to the assembled Council of Elders, one day after Visitor appeared.

"How do you know that?" asked Eldest.

"It *can't* be. A solid of that size would have mass. There's no solid without mass."

"Not that you know of," suggested Scar Shank, unhelpfully.

"Not in this universe. It must be a projection from somewhere else, a projection that interrupts or routes incoming radiation but doesn't itself have the mass of the projector, which is elsewhere."

"You're guessing," said Eldest.

Of *course* I'm guessing!" said Heraklitos. "Ice damn, does anyone have a better idea?" He turned in three tight circles and chewed on his tail.

"Calm yourself, engineer," said One Ear. "Don't go all rabid on us."

"Where might this "projector" be?" asked Eldest.

"We have no way of knowing. With the power it's demonstrating, the source could be inside the solar system, relatively close, or far away."

"Another *universe*?" suggested Scar Shank, continuing his role of cat's advocate.

"A meaningless phrase, General. Meaningless to our understanding."

"Not necessarily," said One Ear. "We know of Tweenlives, where there is bodiless life. We know of Old Ones, who come and go, can touch us and receive our communication, but are otherwise unknown and of unknown time and dimension. There may be *other* dimensions and universes."

"Inhabited by powers capable of exhibiting physical force in our dimensions?"

"Perhaps, Klitos, perhaps," said Loos, tiredly, feeling more tired, truth be told, than he ever had. "The Old Ones warned us that 'Others' were watching. They themselves used the term 'Visitors' once."

"Perhaps, yes. But how useful is that to us?" said Heraklitos in frustration. "If this object or expression of power is a visitor, it may have visited *before*. This might be the power that installed the sophisticated satellites in synchronous orbit around First Sister."

"So you *believe* Prometheus's story of First Sister swarming with titanic creatures?" said Eldest. "Maybe this space object is peopled with these giants?"

"You tell me to stay calm, and then you ridicule me," said Klitos. He lay down and put his head across his paws.

As the Council did, when there was nothing to say but decisions to be made, the wolves sat quietly and looked out across the Canyon to the sky and far horizons. Where normally this encouraged them, now they soon looked away: the shadow of the great Black Triangle approached them from the turning horizon.

"I think it is the Cats," said Second Eldest. "They conspire from the doom we cast them into to come back and have vengeance."

Scar Shank glared at him. "Thank you for your contribution," he said.

"Hell's ice, he may be right. It's as logical an idea as any other," said Eldest. "Apollo? You've been listening."

"The reason we call it Visitor," said Apollo, "is that it wasn't there last week, and we hope it won't be there next week. Someone is driving or occupying it. We should try to communicate and keep trying until . . ."

"Until it barks back?" said Scar Shank. "I would think blocking and holding our moon is communication enough."

"Apollo is right," said Eldest. "Heraklitos, Apollo, solicit communication. But . . . try not to anger the beast."

And so they did. While farmers hid in their dens and everyday citizens had decided not to go outdoors until their face of the planet came out from under Visitor, Heraklitos fired up "Hello's!" and

"Are you there's?" By semaphore flash. By radio. Even with whole sections of Mars turning their lights on and off simultaneously. In infrared. By radar.

Ominous, horribly silent no-response. Apollo kept thinking of the Old One's phrase "*Others watch.*" The black non-thing was watching, but had nothing to say.

"Nothing. Void," answered Apollo to Loos, who asked him what they were getting back.

"But if it's one thing it isn't *void*," said Loos. "It's definitely a *thing*. And it communicates clearly, at least to me."

"What does it say to you?" asked Apollo.

"The same thing it says to you and to all of us," said Loos. "We see it and hear it, but refuse to understand it. What do you *feel*, Apollo? What does it overwhelmingly *feel* like?"

"It feels evil," said Pollo. Loos nodded.

"Can you reach Prometheus through it with telepathy? There, on the other side of it?"

"No," said Apollo, not having thought of this.

"It's evil," said Loos.

Heraklitos told them that, perhaps by the very nature of the power of the object, it might not have been perceiving that their insignificantly powered communication was incoming. Perhaps the communication needed a little more force to get through. Why not? They could actually think of many reasons, but simple vibrations were not achieving anything. So they used a little more. Klitos sent up three blips of mild microwave. No response. Then three more, slightly stronger. Again, more forceful. Finally one short burst, as powerful as they could manage. This produced a tiny, tiny red spot where it had been focused, which slowly faded.

"Yes!" said Heraklitos.

Then came Visitor's response.

* * *

Shortly after Prometheus had telepathed Apollo not to worry about Isle's nasty-tempered package falling into Mar's gravity,

Prom noticed the spear of darkness cross into his instrument field. It arrived from the side, not appearing all as one object in the space. It slid implacably across, like a warship mooring. He had been using various instruments to track Athena and caught the interruption of his instrumentation exactly as the Shadow moved into view. That it was something different, something truly huge, was quickly evident. He could tell by reason of his not being able to determine anything about it, only by what it was *not*. It wasn't anything he knew or could perceive, but it progressively blocked Mars, eventually a large triangular area. It was enormous.

He alerted Demeter, who said that he, too, was attempting instrumentation of the object.

Then, in an instant, Prometheus's world ended.

Since the time he had been wounded back on Mars, when he had learned to communicate with physical world electronics through transceivers and had built up a universe of mechanically operating bodies, driven by and from his *will*, he had let the non-physical become his world. But now he had non-stop contact with the real physical world through his robots. He had also not forgotten that earlier dementia of endless, lightless, soundless dark during that first hibernation winter when his Martian family and friends slept and only he was awake, but unable to communicate or perceive.

In an instant that dark hell was back. The object had done something. He knew. It had cut off the power in or around his moon, or the transmission of power (which is the same thing), or *negated* the power that allowed him to communicate with his machine bodies. Or with another Promethean. Or they with him or with each other.

At that same, exact moment, Visitor seized the moon and froze it in its orbit, or held it from another place in restraint from orbiting. This was accomplished, seemingly without violation of inertia and momentum. There was no crash of internal object masses on or inside the moon. It wasn't that the moon stopped and the things in and on it kept moving in their own space. Everything was "taken possession of" and "held," but without any expenditure of momentum. Things stopped.

Of course, this is impossible in this universe. Hence the difficulty of reasoning it out by the Council of Elders. Hence the immediate need for the moon-based Prometheans to find other anchors for their sanity than physical world electronics and perception. Prometheus as a being could still *think*. He knew he existed because he had consciousness of existing, awareness of being aware. He could think one thing and then think another thing and know they were different, so . . . that was something. He was sorry for his other Prometheans who had not gone through those first progressive, but terrible lessons of bodiless consciousness, learning how to deal with this state. But, engineer that he was, curious and callous, he just got on with it.

He reached out to Apollo. Nothing.

No, not nothing. *Prevented.* Somehow in this bodiless state he could perceive the difference between being unable to communicate spiritually with another, and being prevented. This was prevention. Well, that too was something. The dark object intended to come between Prometheus and Apollo, or between those on the moon and those on Mars. The dark object had *intention*, therefore there were beings associated with it. They must be the "Visitors" that the spirit voice had warned him about. He wondered if that voice had been one of the Old Ones that his father used to tell stories about and Elders believed in.

While his Legionnaires howled silently in their irremediable communicationless dark, Prometheus experimented with his powers of thought. Yes, he was afraid, no doubt of that. But first and always he was an engineer. He had trained himself to be interested in what was happening, before he would become concerned about what had happened later.

The two days while Visitor held to its eyrie above Mars passed for Prometheus as ten years, or a thousand years. He felt he would never know. There was no tick, no clock, no before. He hoped there would be 'after.'

"After" came as suddenly as the stop had.

Moments after Heraklitos on the Martian side of Visitor had tapped on the behemoth with what could only have been a microscopic amount of microwave energy, compared to the object's power, but nevertheless enough to attract its attention, Visitor created its next effect.

Was it a response? Was it pre-programmed? This was and is an unanswered question.

On Prometheus's side of the object, out of the dark nothingness suddenly appeared ultraviolet lines of force, nine of them. Three reached out to him, or near him. The heart of the moon, he guessed. They were unbearably bluewhite bright, and also thin or thinner than an obsidian glass edge. Possibly a one-dimensional line, Prometheus's Martian Math-based mind conjectured. Three ultraviolet lines of dimension came into being simultaneously outlining the triangular shape of Visitor. And similar lines triangulated down on the far side of the object towards what Prometheus thought might be the center of Mars.

Then there was an explosion of ochre-red light or energy from a one-dimensional point, something un-enterable from which emanated an almost infinite black-red light. This occurred right next to Prometheus, it seemed to him, but not on or at him. Wherever "he" was, it was near him. In that same instant he felt the death-scream of Isle, of Demeter, and many other Legionnaires. He blissfully lost consciousness.

The point of exploding, burning light split into three. Three stars of no dimension slowly glided down the three lines of force towards the moon.

* * *

The red spot on the side of Visitor facing the wolves on the surface of Mars had faded. Heraklitos and Apollo watched. Something was happening. What they didn't know. Then they did.

In a flash that seared their eyes nearly to blindness (and would have except for the wolves' millennia of adjustment to higher exposure of ultraviolet from their sun), they saw appear six lines of energy-force. Three around Visitor's triangular perimeter, and three from its corners down *into* Mars, deep into its interior.

Just as Heraklitos, too, was conjecturing if the lines were mathematically one-dimensional and as other wolves or animals around the face of Mars looked up or came out of their dens to see what new horror this was, an expanding sphere of pure reddish light erupted from the far side of Visitor. Those under the shadow of Visitor, such as Heraklitos, saw it from its reflection on Mars outside of the shadow but also reflected in the interplanetary dust as the red sphere exploded outward on the far side of the object at the speed of light and then reflected back to Mars. It was beautiful.

Then new reflections came. Three points of incandescent dark light could be seen rising up towards the corners of Visitor from where the moon once was. The light points were also singularities, points glowing so bright that they seemed to have dimension. But there was no dimension. Also, they did not glow. Heraklitos and Apollo could see this as the singularities arrived at the corners of the great Visitor, burning the retina, so that one could not look at them. But it was not light from the points themselves. They could be seen to be pulling in incredible spirals of dust which vaporized into plasma as they approached and then disappeared shortly before they hit the "glowing" singularities. Around each of the three points were curtains of glowing radiation that descended into them, creating spherical auroras not dissimilar to what came down into Martian polar skies.

Apollo and Heraklitos had a moment to look in horror at one another. They and other Martians across the planet automatically leaned in to touch one another physically, for telepathy, for co-experiencing, for compassion.

Visitor had only begun.

The three singular points of power drifted down the ultraviolet lines of force toward the surface of Mars. Defying the logic of the normal world, they did not rush down. They descended relatively slowly, perhaps as fast as a falling rock. As they came closer to the points where the ultraviolet lines bit into the surface of Mars, their power became evident.

As they approached, the atmosphere rose to meet them. Clouds formed in condensation and then swirled upward into tornados reaching out into space, imploding in all the colors of the rainbow, backward from blue to red and disappearing into that sucking/exploding black light that was each singularity, there to be annihilated.

The three Points descended further. They began to pull up water from the oceans and soil, objects, buildings, wolves and other creatures from the surface. Klitos and Apollo from where they were, and Loos,

Scar Shank, and Eldest from their vantage points, all wolves watched as two colossal tornados formed, above and below each singularity. One was pulling down atmosphere to swirl and disappear into the Point. The other tornado pulled up. As more actual mass reached the descending monsters, thunderous cracks of explosion reverberated over the continent, louder even than the increasing roar of the tornados. The light from the Points became a staccato rapid fire burst of incinerations, annihilations. The land caught fire. Klitos and Apollo and all other exposed wolves had the fur on the Singularity Side of their bodies burned off. For those closer, their bodies caught fire or disappeared.

Then the Points hit the planet's surface and, with the greatest explosive sound any Martian had ever heard, descended below ground.

For those within fifty miles, such as Apollo and Klitos, the Marsquake was such as to toss their bodies into the air. Things around them did not rattle, but shook to pieces. Loos and his friends nearly died as the Cliffside into which Loos's den had been carved slid down into the Canyon. They were left behind in a small, exposed cave. The Canyon Far Walls collapsed as far up and down as they could see.

The entire planet quaked. Worse, Klitos and Apollo watched as atmosphere and nearby lake or ocean water was pulled up in a shrieking, screaming spiral and then carried down *into* the holes created by the Singularities. Three vortexes of destruction followed the Points down into their planet.

Then, if degrees of demolition could be assigned to the event, things settled down. The three tornados lost their source of power and began to reduce and disperse. Shrieking died to howling and then just to wind.

Mars continued to quake, but deeper, deeper, then so deep as to be without sound. In despair at the beauty of it, Klitos watched as slow, slow waves as if upon an ocean rolled across the land.

Apollo, Heraklitos thought as he crawled back to his friend and leaned into his body. *What is going to happen when the Points join together at the core?*

* * *

On the surface all continued to be quiet. Less now was falling from the great heights into which it had been raised. The winds were dying down. Rains fell in the distance from ocean waters that had been pulled up, and dust blew where it had been raised, but all was reducing. Those such as Loos and Scar Shank who lived Cliffside, but had survived, took the breather to climb by bare claw up the Canyon towards the rim. Ancient experience taught them not to wait to see if it would get worse. If it gets better, take advantage to improve your situation. For the moment it was quiet.

Except for the rumble deep, deep within.

Then Klitos, Apollo, and everyone and everything else on the surface of Mars, as though physically struck, were tossed high into the air. The rumbling increased to a roar as the universal Marsquake acquired monstrous, demented strength. Volcanoes erupted from the three cavities left by the Singularities. With great explosive blasts, they shot red lava into the sky. And higher. And higher.

Then, something worse, more terrible than any Martian had ever experienced or could have imagined. The volcanoes stopped, and reversed. The explosions ceased. The lava and ash, falling from having been thrown tens of thousands of feet, was sucked back into the volcanoes. Worse, how could there be worse, the volcanic land masses themselves inverted and were sucked down below, followed by air and atmosphere, screaming down into the planet's interior.

Then, in one moment, the ultraviolet lines of force disappeared. They were gone.

Apollo and every other wolf on Mars howled.

Although they were beyond exhaustion, the wolves' trial was not over. It had only begun. It could get worse. Klitos and Apollo, lying on their sides, bloodied by falling rock, Klitos with two broken limbs, watched helplessly as Visitor far above began to move. The whole of it backed from its point. And as it backed, it slowly turned. It turned up and away from Mars. In its immensity and blackness this would have been impossible to see, except that one can tell when a mass is moving away. It is a perception.

As Visitor continued to turn away, the Marsquake returned. Returned with velocity. And increased in power. And increased.

It became a battering ram. Great concentric waves rippled out across the Martian surface from points beyond the horizon. With each rolling wave Apollo and Klitos felt their stomachs sink and rise. Loos and Scar Shank and those others who had barely escaped were thrown up and down. Those still trying to climb out of the Canyon were tossed thousands of feet to their deaths.

Then from beyond the horizon they saw the land at one point lift. It rose and rose and climbed toward the sky. Huge crusts of earth and rock broke and fell back in distant rolling thunder. It mounted even higher, forced up and up, tens of thousands of feet. The quake waves had stopped. There was now just a shuddering, a planetary death rattle.

The joined Singularities broke the surface, as *one* thing.

Visitor had not left the Points to trouble the depths of Mars. It was pulling its creations up and out to take them away *with* it.

What rose up from the top of the now tallest mountain of Mars was the molten core of the planet. Smelted lava and iron and a thousand other metals toiled and coiled like a million earthen snakes around the joined singularities. Defying law, defying reason, the great writhing mass rose into the air. For Klitos, Apollo and those at the Canyon it was hundreds of miles distant. Distance was the only thing that saved them, for the moment.

Visitor was gutting Mars.

The Core smoked and flamed, dropping its outermost liquid gobs to fall through the high atmosphere back onto the planet, creating new quakes and winds of unimaginable force.

As the heart of Mars was sucked up and carried away, the gravitic power of the joined Singularities pulled with them much of the atmosphere and the oceans of the planet. The oceans rose like inverted bowls of liquid, falling *up.* They swirled impossibly high to follow the departing mass into dark space, an upward waterfall of demons and angels. It was unbearably beautiful.

It was insufferable to admire the unmaking of your home world. But how could they not? It was an enthrallment. Klitos was now unconscious. Pollo and Loos and thousands of other Martian wolves, all that remained alive and conscious and could see, watched as up through their roiling atmosphere Visitor hauled the pulsing, still living heart of Mars out and away. As Visitor continued to back and turn, the Martians saw that the moon was still there. No, not the moon. *A* moon . . . fragment. This one was only one of the raw, fractured pieces of what had been. The rest were . . . gone. Gone.

Then Visitor stopped in its retreat. It had backed out beyond the orbit of the moon. For mysterious moments it held its position, holding below it the uncooling swarm of Martian iron, kept liquid and furiously hot by the internal Singularities.

The triangular black beast began slowly to rotate. Ever so slowly. It was so black it was hard to see, but what could be seen was the Martian core starting to swing around behind Visitor. Then it was blocked from view. Minutes later it reappeared on the other side, increasing in its spin. Visitor was rotating faster and faster, holding the core in its invisible grip. On the fourth spin Visitor let it go.

As its planet's citizens watched, the core was flung away, away from Mars and Visitor. Out into the solar blackness, down toward the distant sun.

Visitor now rotated to point itself away from Mars and moved off into its future.

There was not a Martian wolf who did not want now just to sleep, to find unconsciousness, or oblivion, for some hours or forever, to forget, possibly to rest and wake again, possibly not. But first sleep.

As they slept, the mountain left behind after the core had been ripped, awoke. Already the highest surface structure in the solar system, with its peak far above the atmosphere, the great volcano erupted, pulling up even more of Mars's insides to flow down as a planetary lake of lava. The planet shrank and the volcano ejected molten stone. The planet diminished, and the volcano flowed. On and on and on.

It was the end of Mars as the wolves had known it. But it was not yet the end of the wolves. Not yet.

Chapter 29
THE LAST TREK

In their exhaustion they slept a full day. They slept two days. For those who slept forever it was easier than for those who awoke. No matter where a wolf opened his eyes – on the surface, in a Cliffside den, in a cave, in a mine – those eyes were covered in dust and ash.

The entire planet had become an ash storm. The ash of the mountainous volcano had been thrown above the atmosphere and spread through coriolis force around the entire globe. Ash fell into a planetary weather pattern of chaotic randomness. The atmosphere pulled up into space and then down into the planet, the oceans raised to fall like waterfalls through the three great volcanoes, the furnace heat of the core searing the land and sky as it was torn out and thrown away – all combined to produce storm. Storm front competed against storm front until the entire surface of the planet was covered with swirling dry or wet hurricanes.

The tundra desiccated until it broke and was drawn up into the air. The more dust and dirt there was the more it sandblasted any surface it struck, which raised even more grit and dust.

When Apollo woke, it was noon two days after he had collapsed. But he could not have told the time. It was pitch dark. The ground-level dust hurricane and stratospheric ash shroud cloaked the sun. He thought he was being sandblasted at midnight.

Groaning like the damned, bruised in every quarter of his body, he called for Heraklitos who had been beside him. No answer. It was so dark he crawled in an outward spiral looking for him. Finally he came upon a curved pile of sand, under which was Klitos, deep in healing hibernation. Apollo grabbed him by the scruff and pulled him yards down into Klitos's surface den cave. Its door top had held throughout the quakes, miraculously. But the airvent had let in mounds of sand, which covered everything. Nevertheless there was protected water, salvation for Apollo, who dunked his head fully in and drank from underwater. He examined Klitos and bathed his wounds. He did his best to pull and set his badly broken hind leg. Apollo tried to raise the top and peek outside. Bad choice. He could barely pull the door closed and did so with sanded eyeballs and a noseful of dust.

There was no communication to other wolves. Everywhere on the planet life was for the moment simply survival for the individual or his family. The key element was water – who had water would live. Who didn't would die of thirst. Or drown, depending.

The heat from the ripping up of the planet's crust, spread by hurricane winds, soon began to melt the ice caps at the poles. Some of the water was taken up to pelt the planet elsewhere, but most stayed on the ground, running down existing channels, which flowed into rivers and overflowed, washing away agricultural soils created through thousands of years of labor. The floods joined to create greater rivers, which created or found canyons.

The canyons had seas running down them, seas carrying dirt and stones and boulders. The canyons flowed into the Great Canyon. This was now dredged and scoured into the greatest gorge in the solar system, miles and miles deep and hundreds of miles across.

Few cliffside habitations or community caves survived – perhaps the Opera, no one knew.

The storming went on and on. When there was a momentary break in the weather pattern, the wolves crawled to the surface and reconnoitered. The brave set out with friends to try and join with what might be a larger community. Whoever set out always took water with them, or hoped desperately that there was water at their destination.

Apollo dragged the unconscious Klitos in a travois away across the destroyed community spaces, eventually finding the Council Chamber, to which Loos and One Ear had also escaped. Scar Shank and Left Limper had both died during the Cataclysm. Eldest died when Loos and One Ear brought him up to the surface and he saw the remains of his world. He looked around, then lay down and expired, asking the Old Ones to show mercy and accept him straight across Tweenlives.

Finally the storms began to have holes in their tops. The wolves occasionally saw red sky, no longer blue, and sometimes black space and bright stars, caring not about the affairs of little Mars.

They also could see now and then a great comet glowing in the dark sky, once their core, now with the planet's atmosphere stolen by its gravity being blown back from it by the sun. What they could not tell, having no instrumentation, was that its mass, although headed inward toward the sun, was being pulled inexorably by the gravity of their blue-green First Sister.

Commanding their interest and more pertinent to immediate survival, however, from wherever on the planet they were was the peak of the Great Mountain, whose volcano had stopped erupting and seemed no longer to be flowing lava. It was smoking still, its gas disappearing into interplanetary space.

Seeing clear air on the Great Mountain's slope above the atmospheric storms , wolves everywhere began to migrate towards it. Communications were down planetwide. If the surviving wolves were going to meet anywhere, wolves of like mind thought, we will meet there. Thus began a planetary Wilding. Wolves gathered their belongings, what little food and all the water they could pull or carry, and began to trek to the mountain. Great and untold were the simple heroics of crossing windblown deserts that once were steppes. Travelers met impassable rivers and developed ingenious methods to cross. Often they walked upriver to where the river had cut a gorge. There they might make a catapult and load one or two of themselves into it and be fired across with a rope to connect the two sides. Securing their end, they pulled across a cable, then helped their family or companions slide across the tempest-crazy chasm, as dangerous an endeavor, some thought afterwards, as having attempted to swim the impossible river itself. But all who ventured crossings by swimming drowned, and quickly.

They crossed the rivers, or chasms, or skirted volcanoes, or prevailed through sudden torrential downpours, or hunkered down through blasting skin-tearing sandstorms. Survivors continued their trek across continents, down from the northern and up from the southern hemispheres towards the Great Mountain, which they had seen or about which they had heard.

* * *

Prometheus, too, was a survivor. He did not know how or why, if there even was a why, but it was the other fractured pieces of the moon which had been taken to create the Visitor's gravitic singularities. He and those Legionnaires serving him had been left behind, inside the iron core of the third piece of moon. He suspected it was merely luck that even one slice of moon was left intact. The fact that there were survivors inside this third piece may have been of no consequence to the Others occupying Visitor or manipulating it from afar. They may not have even known we were here, he thought.

Now he had a decision to make. Once Visitor had cleared the area, the electronics of Moon Base One, his headquarters, started up again. Whatever had suppressed the flow of electricity or the output of battery was gone. But the energy creation systems of his base had been destroyed and his remaining stores were limited. What to do?

It was obvious.

Prometheus called his Legionnaires to come together physically.

Those that had mobile body forms showed up at the factory hall of the base. The fixed and immobile tuned in. "We have survived many challenges,' he broadcast to them. You may think that we have just passed our greatest test. But you would be wrong. Our lives as Prometheans have been short. The future is long. It is too early to die. It is *now* that we must prevail despite every impossibility. Therefore I have decided we shall return to the planet of our damaged cousins, the Martians Alive. If we help them to survive, they will help us. Will you come with me?"

An unexpected, radical change of plan. A moment of shock. Then the small and larger Promethean robots and machines did jumps and flips, bumps and hops. As clear an expression of "We're with you" as there could be, with perhaps a little homesickness for their beloved home, crippled though it might be.

Shortly afterward, dismantling their base, they rapidly constructed a great catapult housing a large canister in its spoon. The mechanical bodies of the Prometheans fitted themselves (quite compactly) inside the can, along with crystal transceivers of destroyed companions, and hurled themselves outward from the moon fragment back down towards their home planet.

The most daring part of the Promethean endeavor was to parachute into the maelstrom still roiling across the surface of Mars. Prometheus had tried reaching Apollo through telepathy, but one or the other, or both, were too exhausted or spiritually depleted from the misery wreaked by Visitor. Apollo could not have helped him, even if he had reached through.

Days later the canister descended into the now thinner, but extremely violent atmosphere and opened its parachutes. The chutes whirled them along the top of the storms. Then Prometheus deployed a fixed metal drag chute which slowed and dropped them. When they approached the ground, still being dragged at great velocity, he dropped small anchors to catch and brake, with snappable anchor ropes. Finally he threw a true anchor, which jerked them to stop and flung them to the ground, *slam!*

Wolves or any flesh creature would not have lived through it. The Prometheans survived . . . a little bent out of shape for the experience.

* * *

The wolf clans trod wearily up the endless incline of the great volcano. Although the ripping up of the mountain by the rape of the planet's interior and the paving of its sides with flow after flow of lava created an edifice thirty miles above the plain, to climb the mountain was not to start at foothills and clamber over and around steeper hills. It was simply to keep walking. The plain started to rise and then rose and rose. With occasional breaks in the windstorm, the trekkers could see the far off summit surrounded by cloudless black, its smoky beard trailing off.

Without coordination, the clans moved toward the west slope. The turning of the planet pulled the ash and gas of the volcano perpetually to the east. It would be best to find a secure spot above the dust, to the west where the afternoon sun would warm them.

Only a few hundred, less than a thousand, arrived to finally camp together.

Once each clan climbed above the choking brown and red dust, they pulled the rags from around their muzzles and saw another clan over yonder, resting and waiting, and another to the other side dropping heavy packs to enjoy a spell of clean breath. It was good that they were Martian wolves, born with large lung capacity: they needed them now more than ever. Not only was the air 20,000 feet up more rarified (although still 100,000 feet below the crest of the volcano), but it now had inherently less oxygen. Too much atmosphere had been stolen, pulled by the core's gravity. What had been replaced by the volcanoes was much higher in carbon dioxide. With virtually no vegetation left to eat carbon either on land or in the sea, this was their air. For as long as they could they would have to live off it. The wolves were dizzy, feeling a little drunk and silly. But their eyes were not laughing.

They had found plentiful food on the way, wildlife in the wastelands felled by untold events. Dirty water was plentiful in the rivers but hard to carry. And it had been long since any had crossed their last river before they reached the mountain. The air was dry and very cold, but the ground below them was still warm from its deeper fires. They could live here, for a while.

One Ear called them together. "We'll camp here. It's as good a place as any," he said. "But as tired as we are, we can't all rest. We must have more water. Every other day one clan must go back down into the storm and find water. Share with one another where you last crossed the wet. Take down containers and bring water back. Other clans will dig and prepare shelter. Those who are too weak will cook and care for the pups. Then turnabout, and the cooks will go down to carry water, and so forth."

"Your plan is good enough, old one," said a craggy looking farmer wolf. "But how long must we stay here? What is to be our future?"

"Our future is to die, as it has always been," said another loudly.

Barking. Snapping of teeth in frustration.

"We shall all die soon enough without wishing it upon ourselves," cried One Ear. "The damned storm below cannot go on forever. When it has spent itself and the dust settles, we will go back and find what there is to make a life out of."

"There is no food!" shouted one.

"The water is disappearing under the dust," said another.

"So the rest of our lives will become one great Wilding!" snapped One Ear. "So what? You are wolves, not rabbits. Act like wolves."

And the days and nights passed. In their tiredness, no one counted.

Heraklitos was sick and feverish, his wounds having infected. There was no medicine other than traditional licking, which was not enough. But he was not so sick that he ceased to be a scientist. He ordered his telescope set up with a platform where he could lie and look through it. "I want to make sure the bedamned Visitor has turned tail," he said.

"Nothing further to do against us, anyway," said Apollo.

Klitos spent long hours. He scratched rough notes on slate. One evening he called Apollo over. "Look," he said, turning over the telescope. Apollo peered through the tube.

"I'm sorry. I'm not skilled enough to see a damn thing."

"That is First Sister."

"I'm not an idiot. I can tell that."

"Look more carefully."

He did. "I see nothing."

"Exactly. There used to be little shadows flitting around it. We didn't notice their regularity before, until Prometheus told us their significance. They were shadows of satellites in orbit. There is nothing there now. Worse, First Sister, too, is smothered planetwide in storm and cloud."

"What do you think it is?"

"I'm guessing. If I had a better scope, I could tell for sure. But I think that Visitor in its haste to ruin us threw away the core without concern for where it would go. Remember seeing the comet?"

"Yes, we all saw it. It was our core."

"Have you seen it recently?"

"I haven't looked."

"It's not there, in interplanetary space, I mean. Where did it go while we weren't looking?"

"Well, where *did* it go? What's your point?"

"I think First Sister's gravity pulled the core to her. A strike of a mass as large as the core? One can only imagine. I fear that First Sister now shares our fate. She used to be blue and green. Now she is grey and brown. And the planetary storm has not diminished since I have been watching."

"No," was all Apollo could say. He felt the weight of all that was miserable settle in his gut. Two great catastrophes in the one solar system, visited on it by an implacable, unspeaking enemy were too much. "I hope you're wrong, Klitos."

"It's the only explanation, unless Visitor attacked Sister directly. If the core struck, or even a large part, it would destroy the life of the planet."

"Cat-hearted, evil eyed, shit for brains, black monster . . ."

"We don't know what Visitor is or was, or who. Could be one being. Could be a machine that thinks. Might be a bunch of adolescent space giants who just like to break things and make a mess, but a thousand years from now will grow up and be sorry."

"Too late."

"Yes it is, Pollo, but where are *we* going to go? The air's dying. There's no productive source of oxygen on Mars. Maybe right next to the rivers. The planet is thinner, weaker now. Our air will slowly leak off into space like the plume of the mountain. What are we going to do?"

"You're going to go to sleep, Klitos," said Apollo. "I'm going to find Thena, who will make you some soup. No more looking through your stupid tube. It'll only give us all nightmares. Use your rocks-for-brains to invent a new way to make air out of stone or something."

Apollo mamboed off to find his sister. She herself had joined a clan trekking to the mountain, and had got there before her brother, to greet him when he arrived.

Days passed. Soon no one asked what the water carriers saw when they went down into the storm. It was just doom and gloom, devastation and wasteland. Every day a few more bedraggled wolves climbed up above the roiling ceiling of dust, a few more survivors. But they were so few, so few.

One afternoon as the sun was setting into the maelstrom, creating its daily monumentalist sunset, a few wolves raced as best they could up the mountain into the encampment. "They're coming!" they panted.

"Who? What?"

"*They* are, the Puppet machines. The Prometheans. They've come back!"

Someone dashed off to find Apollo, Loos, and One Ear. They ran over from the camp with Athena excitedly in tow, and the rest of the gathered wolf clans came after. Soon they saw the scraggly, beat-up Promethean Legionnaires marching steadfastly up out of the dust, looking for all the world like a garbage dump rolling uphill. They were a motley crew, of all sizes, appearing more like the innards of some great machine rather than individual creatures. The Prometheans halted well before reaching the wolf clans.

Hackles rose, lips pulled back in snarls.

Prometheus, is that you? pathed Apollo.

Great, now you hear me! pathed Prom back. *I've been trying to reach you for days.*

Why are you here? asked Apollo. *Why did you come back?*

"Can you reach them by thought, Apollo?" asked One Ear.

"Yes, sir. I can. It's Prometheus."

"Which one?"

"I . . . I don't know."

Prometheus, which one . . . which of these is you?

One of the dirt-clogged garbage cans, looking like a great spider with four legs, two parabolas, and something like a slingshot mounted on top, waved its parabolas back and forth.

"What do they want?" asked Loos. "What do they intend?"

Before anyone could answer, Athena yipped and dashed forward to join the mechanism that had indicated it housed Prometheus. "Uncle Prometheus!" she chirped. She nosed him gently and her tail wagged so that it thump-thumped against him.

"He says he's your brother," said Apollo. "And please stop beating the crap out of him."

"I know he's my brother, but he seems like my uncle. I have a brother already and don't have an uncle. And I know what he's saying to you, *brother* Apollo."

"You can path to him?"

Yes, and I can path to you, but you've not been interested! Athena grinned a nasty, juvenile wolf smile. Her tail continued to wreak damage on her uncle.

Prometheus's machine rolled a little in front of the others. Two other cans moved to follow, but with a wave of feelers they were clearly instructed to stay back.

Peace, Apollo. We want peace.

"They say they want to have peace," said Apollo.

One of the Elders howled and raced towards Prometheus. Before he got there the two "guardians" stepped in front of Prometheus and Athena. When the attacking wolf got close and leapt, one machine jumped and blocked him in the air. When he fell, the other simply helped hold the wolf down, immobilized.

We have done wrong, pathed Prometheus. *I've been . . . crazy, I think. . . insane for a long time. But you have done wrong, too. Now . . ."*

"He's apologizing for being a shit," said Apollo.

Here, pathed Prometheus.

As the wolves watched nervously, up out of the dust clouds small tractor-persons dragged two large cylindrical tanks. They stopped half-way to the gathered wolves.

"What's this?" asked Loos.

Prometheus scuttled up, reached out with a claw, and turned a latch. A liquid stream began to flow out.

Water. We thought you might need some.

"They can stay," said One Ear, exhaustedly. "Over there . . ." He gestured far to one side. "But in the open air where we can see them. They want to keep an eye on us, too, I expect. Neither of us has much to trust in the other. But . . ."

"But we'll need each other if we're to have a better chance to survive," said Heraklitos, hobbling up in his cast. "Which one is Prometheus?"

Apollo nodded toward the parabola-eared spider body.

Tell Heraklitos he is even uglier now than he used to be.

"Prometheus says you are particularly lovely in your current incarnation."

"Yes, I think so too," said Heraklitos. "Tell him I much prefer him as a tin can than as a stinky half-wolf."

"No, I don't think I will," said Pollo, shaking his head.

"Suit yourself," said Klitos, hobbling on down to get a better look at his erstwhile enemy/friend. He was joined in dribs and drabs by other wolves, who crept shyly forward to find possible relatives among the clicking and clacking Prometheans. They touched, sensed, and smelled one another, long-separated cousins, still blind, deaf, and dumb to each other, but cousins nonetheless.

Chapter 30
CHOICES

The wolves were too exhausted to attempt any kind of fortification against the Prometheans. Besides there was only a minimal dust layer covering the raw lava stone underneath. Nevertheless One Ear ordered a perpetual watch. Prometheus did the same on his side, except he and his mechanical Legion did not suffer from the same physical lassitude. Emotionally, however, both the flesh- and metal-clothed were a wreck.

The wolves drank their fill of the new water, and mothers and doctors washed their pups and patients. The Martian night came on. They slept. With declining air quality, the wolves were experiencing a nearly irresistible urge to hibernate, but knew they must create or find a source of oxygen, or their next long sleep would be their last hibernal rest. Heraklitos spoke with One Ear and they agreed to post a special watch over sleepers to monitor life statistics. Anyone whose breath and pulse dropped too low would be awakened and stimulated. Water alone was a life saver, but it did not substitute for air.

On his flank of the mountain Prometheus had a similar problem – power. Prometheans had no need of physical sleep, but psychologically each entity needed periodic rest, partially owing to the ancient diurnal habit of light and dark and the seasonal trope of wakefulness and hibernation, but also just because the being needed "withdrawal" to balance the "must confront, must act." Visitor had left behind psychic violation as well as material. No Legionnaire had "slept" since the singularities stole two-thirds of their moon and obliterated more than half their number. Although a Promethean could not physically be killed as could a fleshed wolf, it appeared it could be *extinguished*. The flame of selfhood still glowed with them but could be put out. Promethean Puppets were not artificial mechanical intelligence: they were machines directed by a bodiless spirit. Apparently, overwhelming physical force or an accumulation of energies beyond their ken, as had instantaneously been mustered by Visitor and so mechanically, unemotionally implemented, could either truly murder the non-physical spirit, or, more frighteningly, kidnap and incarcerate it in some other universe or 'inside' the spaceless singularities. Prometheus did not know. He would wait. Perhaps Isle and Meter would beam to him some time in the future, or Apollo could telepath to them. He was not saving battery for it.

What they all needed now was power. Therefore Prometheus set his few diggers to find the abundant heat that was probably only a few hundred feet below them inside the mountain, ordering them to be very careful and not to create another volcano. Others dug temporary storage caverns for their own tanked water. Prometheus sent empty water tank-tractors back down the slope into the embroiled dark dust to drink from the last river they had crossed while it still flowed. Other small flatbed truck-persons accompanied them to retrieve anything mechanical that might be of use.

Morning crept across the mountain slope like a melancholy, only a red glimmering of hidden, far away light. Twilight would be the only natural illumination for long to come. When the alive wolves groaned awake, they found meat left for them by some of the returning

Promethean scavengers. Rabbits and other small animals had died in multitudes and then so quickly desiccated in the hot winds that they littered the plains. Flesh food would not be a problem.

One Ear, Loos, Apollo, and Heraklitos went to meet with Prometheus and his lieutenants. The goofy-eared Prom puppet was patiently waiting for them in the buffer zone between their camps. He offered them water and dried rabbit. He had linked himself to another puppet contraption.

Good morning, Prometheus, pathed Apollo.

"Good morning, Apollo," voiced Prom's companion machine in a flat tinny twang.

"Well, well, you've been busy while we slept," said One Ear. "Can you see as well as hear us?"

"Better than you can see me," voiced Prometheus.

"Hmm. Thank you for the rabbit, anyway."

"You're welcome. There's plenty enough of that," said Prom.

"We're long spoiled, however," said Loos. "I for one would like it cooked with some spice. This is dry fodder."

"Help me build some power systems and that shouldn't be hard to do," said Prom.

"I see you've already started digging for geothermal," said Heraklitos. "Don't you think wind fans would be easier?"

"Yes, Klitos," said Prom. "And if you don't mind mingling with us you could help us create them. But I don't know how long the winds will last, although we can predict how long it will take for the mountain to cool."

"The various super-volcanoes including Mother Mountain, on whom we sleep," said Heraklitos, "have released enough gaseous heat and will continue to warm the air with their flanks to generate planetary winds for years to come."

"So much for the wind," said Loos, gloomily. "We can live with the wind. But what about the darkness? How long will the ash clouds hide the sun and stars?"

"Ice damn," said Heraklitos. "You're right enough. If not suffocated by the declining air, this endless winter darkness will end life as we know it."

"That has already happened," said Prometheus, his metallic voice adding a flat finality to the statement.

"How long will it last, do you expect?" asked Apollo.

"What do you think, Prometheus?" said Klitos. "I would say a Martian year for the ash to settle."

"Could be longer," said Prom.

"I'll grow tired enough of desiccated rabbit strips by then that I won't care that we have all long since asphyxiated," said Loos.

"Not all of us need air," commented another machine near Prom.

"Who is this?" asked One Ear.

"Is this Genie?" asked Apollo. "I recognize Iphigenia's spirit, from our old Wilding."

"Yes," said the metal box. "I was Iphigenia. I am First Energy Lieutenant now."

"Can we call you by your old names, Prometheus?" asked Loos.

"Why not?" Prom said. "We can surrender our military titles easily enough. But what Iphigenia says is true enough. Mars may not be able to support enfleshed life, but there is *other* life . . . as we have demonstrated."

Hackles began to rise and ears lie back.

"May I suggest we do not engage in that argument yet?" said One Ear. "There'll be time enough for philosophic wrangling."

"It's hardly philosophic that neither you nor I can barely summon enough air to walk up the volcanic slope," said Loos.

"Don't fret so much," interrupted Prometheus. "There's plenty of water and there will be plenty of ice. With wind and geothermal power we can split that to form oxygen enough to fill livable quarters for you all. We'll need all we can get anyway."

"Why?" asked Heraklitos.

"For rocket fuel," said Prom.

Well, this conversation is moving along faster than I would have thought, pathed One Ear to Loos, to whom he leaned in.

"I'm not quite ready to decide if we are to leave the planet, much less where we are to go," said One Ear.

"Take all the time you want," said Prometheus, whacking himself with a clang for emphasis. "Not much to argue about. We *have* to move off planet. Surface vegetation and other life is failing, down below us in the dust. I expect the fish will follow. Mars is dying. There are other, richer worlds we can go to. What's to talk about?"

Loos laughed with a loud bark, and then had to hack and cough. "You may inhabit what looks like a traveling weather station, Prometheus, but you haven't changed that much. You're still an opinionated cat fuck."

That brought a moment's silence.

"Nice to see you again, too, Father," said Prom.

That produced a lot more laughter, also paid for with coughing and choking. Even Prometheus and his tin can companions jerked and hopped in what must have been their version of hilarity.

"First Sister," said Heraklitos, when they settled down. "You think we should go *there*."

"Our only other choice would be one of the moons of Older Brother far away out into the dark. We know almost nothing about the great gas planets. Anyone want to go there?"

"You say 'we,' Prometheus," Apollo said.

"Yes. We are the last Martians. We must all go, I compute."

"How would we do that?" asked Klitos.

"You would all become, what do you call us? *Prometheans*. No way will we have the energy and fuel to create rockets to take even a small part of the Wolf Flesh population. You will have to leave your bodies behind, and come . . ."

"As tin cans?" asked One Ear.

"As Promethean Puppets, yes. You have no alternative."

Silence was the best response anyone could muster for the moment. There was some rustling.

"Thank you for the rabbit breakfast, Prometheus," said One Ear finally. "And the water. We are grateful for your consideration to your former people. Heraklitos, see to volunteers to help create these wind generators or whatever is necessary to get more oxygen as soon as possible. Can you do that? Are you well enough?"

"I am well enough, Eldest," said Klitos.

"Damnation, am I *Eldest* now? I guess I am. Call me One Ear instead. We will talk more later, Prometheus. I for one am still a little reluctant to abandon flesh forever." One Ear got up with an obvious effort to walk back to wolf camp. He turned. "No one is to pass on our little discussion to our wolf companions, Apollo. They cannot do the Math necessarily as quickly as your brother. Or as rashly, for that matter."

* * *

One Ear sent young wolf runners down into the planetary storm to search out other survivors who might not know of Mother's Camp, as they had all come to call it. Most returned with one or a few. Some returned alone. One, however, came back with a surprise package strapped to his back.

How Dr. Chronos had stayed alive and endured the impossible conditions below would have dumbfounded everyone, except that he never ceased relating the details of it and his own astonishment to whoever did not get up and walk away.

When Chronos finally arrived at the camps he looked little better than feathered dried rabbit. But water and some of that rabbit flesh soon perked up the irrepressible creature. Apollo would have ordered him to be carried back down and dumped in a crevice if it had been his choice. He grabbed the protesting bird by the neck and dragged him to One Ear, who was talking with Loos.

"What have we here? Will wonders never cease?" said One Ear.

"I thought I should bring him to you, sir," said Apollo. "We never had a moment to discuss Chronos after the opera was interrupted and . . . everything. I was making a statement about the universality of life with him and the opera, but . . . I know the Law, and I figure the Chart of Responsibilities must be applied. Do you want me to break his neck right here?"

Squawk! Flap! "Wait just one moment!" screaked Chronos. "What you *have* here, Elder, as you *did* ask, is the former Dr. Telemachus, incarcerated in the body of a bird, which was once, but is no longer, the pet of Apollo."

"You were my pet before you were his," said Loos.

"The bird Chronos was your pet. *I* was never your pet. Chronos may still be in here somewhere, but thankfully I don't know where.

I, however, am a *person*." Dr. Chronos strutted around and fluffed up his few remaining feathers, which did not quite impress as it once might have. The wolves said nothing. Apollo glared seriously enough that Chronos stepped behind Loos. "Don't let him hurt me," he pleaded.

"The Chart of Responsibilities applies," snapped Apollo. "This damn cat doctor almost killed me. I should get to break his neck."

"You already did," said One Ear, "if you remember. Telemachus, is it? You can't kill him a second time, Apollo. How did the dead Telemachus wind up in your pet . . . in this body?"

"No one knows!" shrieked Dr. Chronos. "Apparently an Old One did some sorcery, maybe."

"How do you know about the Old One?" asked Apollo.

"You keep forgetting that I was roosted up there in that damned corner of your den. I wasn't always asleep. You talked about it with your father."

"What do you think, Loos?" asked One Ear, with a little smile.

"I'm not sure what this creature is," he said.

Chronos cawed a protest like a crow.

"But all indications are that he is some version of the former Telemachus, who was not worth much to start."

Chronos gave Loos the beady eye.

"That may well be," said One Ear. "But he's alive and no doubt sentient. Hell's bells, if we found a rabbit alive right now, I wouldn't want to kill it. Let's preserve all the life we can while we can. That is the most primordial Law of all."

One Ear got up and walked tiredly away. Loos looked at the bird, shook his head, then followed after his old friend.

"Found a rabbit indeed," grumbled Chronos. He looked over at Apollo who was glowering at him. "He said you're to leave me alone! Don't touch me."

"You," said Apollo, chuckling, "are one lucky bird."

The two of them walked off to find some water – one waddling, the other hop skipping.

But Apollo had not given up on his use of Chronos as *test subject*. He asked Prometheus if he had brought control crystals with him. Yes, he had, as many as he could. He gave one to Apollo, who carried it in his mouth back to his small tent in the camp. He had one last great spirit transfer experiment he wanted to perform.

Chronos could have stayed somewhere else, perhaps, but he knew that his destiny was lined up with his "master," Apollo, so he crept back in with him without asking or being asked. One night, while Chronos slept, Apollo studied the crystal and then regarded his feathered companion. He wondered if he could apply an ability with regard to the crystal, similar but varied from pulling wolf spirits back to crystals.

Apollo got the concept of occupying and just "being" the crystal, with its miniature contact and communication complex of terminals. Then he pervaded the body of sleeping Chronos and reached out to where its resident was dreaming. Poor Dr. Chronos's spirit had only the slightest tethers to his body. He was susceptible. With no energy, and just a little sorcery, Apollo pulled Telemachus over to the crystal and "inserted" him into its mechanical communication complex. Then Apollo "cut" the body tethers and woke Telemachus with a mental shout.

Dr. T came to and immediately knew that he was not in his bird body. He was somewhere, but where? He reached to communicate and realized he had no line to anything that *could* communicate. He freaked. There were no wings to flap, no throat to squawk. He could think, but was . . . not trapped, just unable to communicate. He knew Apollo had done something. What? He simmered with frustration, plotting how to get even with his demon wolf master.

Apollo carried the crystal back to Prometheus, whose mechanical body of the day (it was not always the same) was not in a rest mode.

"I've inserted someone into one of your crystals, I think. Can you contact it, and tell me if you can communicate with him and he with you?"

"Interesting," said Prom. "It usually takes time for someone to know how to use the crystal. They're usually afraid of being bodiless."

"This person isn't," said Apollo. "Tell me if you reach him."

Prometheus radioed his central control board and called through to the frequency of this crystal.

He got lots of response.

"Whoever you put in touch with this crystal, he's pretty angry about it," said Prometheus. "Do you want me to give him a puppet to control and teach him how?"

"Thank you, brother. Maybe later."

Apollo carried the crystal back to his tent. He looked at the crystal, multicolored with reflections from its tiny electronic terminals deep inside. He looked over to Chronos's bird body, resting quietly. Apollo strung a line of tension between the center of the crystal and the body and "snapped" it.

Dr. Chronos woke up and sprung into flight. He jumped over onto Apollo and bit him on the neck and tried to pull his ears off with his claws. Apollo swatted him away and snarled at him.

"Sit *still* a moment, bird," barked Apollo.

"You torment me," said Chronos.

"First Law, Telemachus. Listen, I can do something wonderful! I can put you in a crystal, and then I can pull you out."

"What's wonderful about that?"

"Think about it," Apollo said.

Chronos pulled himself erect. "I can no longer abide in the same tent with you, Apollo. We are done." He pranced out into the night.

Apollo had no thought for him. He was concentrating on the crystal. He needed to perform one last vital experiment.

* * *

Apollo collected Heraklitos next morning. They walked over to Prometheus's encampment, now a bustling little industrial center. Apollo asked Prometheus to come with them back to the wolf camp, with one of his machines, to meet with One Ear, Loos, and the other camp directors.

This was the first time Prometheus had fully crossed over into the wolf side of the mountain. As they walked and rolled into the camp proper, wolves rose up, glaring with unsuppressed hostility, but they knew Heraklitos and Apollo were under the protection of One Ear and let them the robot puppet pass. Many followed along behind, however.

"And what is this, Prometheus?" asked One Ear.

"You will have to ask Apollo," said Prometheus through his

"speaker." He hasn't enlightened me."

"Eldest, Elders," said Apollo. "I have a solution."

"Perhaps you might tell us what the problem is first," said One Ear.

"This is actually very serious, Justice One Ear. I know how we can leave Mars, travel, and yet not give up the hope of residing again in live bodies."

"How is that, Apollo Experimenter?"

Apollo described his body transfer experiments. How he had been able to pull Promethean spirits back to Mars via the crystals. But this had not consulted their will, and there were ill effects. Now he had found he could send another being into a crystal and then, wonderfully, pull him out again to reside in a flesh body. He described how he had done this with Dr. Chronos.

"But that is just further necromancy with your bird and dead creature," said an Elder.

"No it isn't. It's just one example of its accomplishment. I did another test, which I'll show you here and now."

Apollo walked over to the little machine purring quietly beside Prometheus's own. He pathed to his brother, *Prom, may I use this crystal and this machine for a few moments?*

Be my guest, brother.

Apollo looked for and found where the machine's controlling crystal was. Then he sat down next it, lay down, and closed his eyes.

Suddenly the machine perked up and whirled around. It banged into Prometheus's puppet machine. Then it slowly approached the apparently sleeping Apollo and gently prodded the body.

"Apollo has occupied my mechanical companion," voiced Prometheus.

All the wolves rose up.

"Can he communicate with us? To prove this?" asked One Ear.

"This is new for him," said Prometheus. "Besides, that machine doesn't have a voice component."

"I don't believe it," said one of the wolves, walking over to Apollo's body. It did not respond to a prod, and when the wolf gently pulled it up by the scruff it did not wake.

"Careful," said Loos.

"Apollo must prove he has really transferred over," said One Ear.

Athena trotted into the meeting. "Hi, Dad," she said. Then she saw all the wolves up in alarm. "What?" She looked around and saw the apparently sleeping Apollo, and Prometheus's companion machine. "Apollo?" she asked the machine. "Prometheus, what is going on? Is Apollo in *there?"* indicating the machine.

"Yes," said Prometheus.

"Hot," said Athena.

"How do we know?" asked One Ear. "Ask Apollo in the machine something only you know, Athena."

Athena thought for a moment, and then asked what she had prepared the night Apollo ran out of his den.

The machine extended a small arm and with some difficulty it scratched in the dirt, "Rabbit stew."

While they were taking that in, the machine stilled. Apollo's body jerked and he sat up. He shook himself. "I'm back," he said. "It's not hard to get into the crystal. The question is 'Can we come back from the crystals?' Yes we can. I just did. And I can help others do it."

The wolves were much discomfited. They rose and walked around, leaning in to one another, pathing privately.

"You mean, Apollo," asked Loos, "we could enter the crystals and travel with Prometheus, but we do not have to stay in the crystals? We could come out to live normally again . . . somewhere else."

"Yup, that's it," said Apollo.

"Hot," said Athena. "Let's do it." She was, after all, not even yet a teenager. Experiment? Let's do it.

This caused even more commotion. Some barking and yipping. A few wolves ran off angrily.

"I'm sorry. But there's another factor, another problem," voiced Prometheus. The wolves quieted and looked at the machine. "We don't have enough crystals. There are something less than a dozen cubed wolves alive on the mountain, right?"

"Yes."

"We have perhaps one hundred unoccupied crystals. They are very complex to make and we have lost that equipment with the moon. We don't have enough to take everyone off Mars."

Chapter 31
New Worlds

Some decisions were made for them. Heraklitos's wounds infected further from whatever nastiness the dust was carrying. A full hospital facility might have been able to treat this, but under their current circumstances it was his own immune system or nothing. He wasn't up to it and declined by the hour. Pollo and Thena attended him.

"I'm not . . . going to make it, Poll," he croaked.

"Yes you will, Klitos," said Athena with a whine.

"Apollo, ask Prometheus . . . to come . . ." He couldn't speak much further.

Apollo started to leave.

Path him! sent Athena.

Oh, yes. Wasn't thinking. Prometheus, Heraklitos is dying and wants to see you.

I will come, sent Prom.

They waited, listening to Klitos's labored and feverish breathing.

"I may not last even till he . . . gets here," he said. He waited for breath and then gasped, "Tell Prom to take me . . . I can help... him . . . and us."

Athena whined and put a paw on Klitos, who had closed his eyes and was struggling for breath.

Prometheus!

Yes, Apollo.

Klitos will not live till you get here. He asks you to bring him over to join the Prometheans. Can you do that?

Of course I can. Let me stop and concentrate.

Accompanied by guards, both Promethean and Wolf, Prometheus's robot body had been rolling quickly through the outer edge of the wolf camp. It skidded to a stop and focused its parabolas toward where they had been told Heraklitos's tent was.

Heraklitos took in a deep breath, slowly let it out, and breathed no more.

He has joined us, sent Prom.

Already? asked Pollo.

Time is not a factor in transfer. But it will take him hours to a day to learn the communication mechanisms. He will be all right, Athena.

"Do you really think so?" she asked Apollo aloud.

"I hope so. What Klitos has just done may be the fate of all of us."

* * *

A few nights later the last Martian All Clans Wolf Council met on the western slope of Mother Mountain.

There was no unanimity of viewpoint to accept Prometheus's offer. He was the enemy. They were wolves, not machines. Better to die a wolf than "live" as some prisoner construct in the darkness. The weather might improve. All things pass – now is their time. On the other hand, most of the younger wolves, of course, wanted to jump across now. Why wait?

"Why wait? Because you have to die here to jump *there,* idiot!"

said one cranky Elder.

One Ear refused to give his personal viewpoint. This was a matter for each wolf individually and for the Clans as a whole to sort out, he said.

What about First Sister? What kind of life forms would they find there if they got there? Apollo described again the phantasmagoric images of an impossible bestiary, stolen from the alien satellites that had orbited and watched the green and blue planet. "At least, that's what I saw in Prometheus's mind," he asserted.

That is what you saw. And it's what the satellites showed, sent Prometheus.

Shut up, Prom, sent Pollo. *This is a wolf clan meeting. Don't snoop.*

I am *a Wolf,* he sent back, thus settling that dichotomy in his own mind, if not for the Wolf Clan.

"Too many variables," said one of the most Elderly. "Even for Martian Math too many possible vectors and trajectories."

"Our choices are no more random now than they were when we Wolves overthrew the Cats," said One Ear. "We had the final choice to exterminate them as a sentient species and take dominion, or to share dominion with them, knowing they would ceaselessly plot to exterminate us. We had no choice, although our future was anything but certain. Is it any different now?"

"I thought you weren't going to give an opinion," grumped Loos.

One Ear turned three times and lay down, head upon paws.

"Enough!" barked Athena. "One thing is clear. Some are going to go. Some are going to stay. All those who want to travel *stand up!*" She stood up tall on her hind legs.

One by one, and then in larger numbers, individuals and den families stood. Sometimes a den was split, half wanting to stay, half to travel, as Athena had coined it. Several hundreds wished to leave with the Prometheans. Still too many. The Clans Council erupted into barking and woofing.

"Quiet down!" growled One Ear. "Other than Prometheus's family, who should go, all the other one hundred will be chosen by lot. That is as unfair a system as all others would be."

"Why not gladiatorial games?" said a young warrior, who had had no time to test his powers as a combatant.

He was howled down. The games had been given up centuries before.

The wolves could find no fault with One Ear's frank statement. Why try to make something fair where that would be impossible?

"When do we do the lottery?" asked a young friend of Athena's, excitedly.

"Right now," said One Ear. "Bring a box."

They scratched one hundred shards and threw them in the box along with unscratched shards, one for each of those wanting to play. The wolves walked up and pulled out their fate. "I'm in." "I'm out." Faces were equally glum whether going or staying. Family, friends, and lovers would be left or leaving in either case.

One Ear was not going.

"There will be one more place," said Loos. "I'll stay."

"Father!" yipped Athena.

"Are you sure, Loos FishKiter?" asked One Ear.

"Best wind for kites we've ever had," said Loos.

"Then I give the last shard for a Traveler to Apollo to choose," said One Ear.

Apollo looked over the faces before him. He could see none that were really anxious to go. Then he saw a familiar visage in the back and laughed. "I choose Dr. Chronos," he said.

All faces turned as they heard flapping of wings and one embarrassed "Awk!"

"Don't look at me," said Chronos. "I'm as surprised as you are."

"Done," said One Ear. "Good riddance to all of you. I am sure the winds will stop, the rain fall, and air return. Mars will become a paradise of bitches and rabbits. You'll be sorry." He coughed.

With some nosing and nipping, the Clans Council dispersed in quiet, almost breathless chuckling.

* * *

Now was time for the Prometheans to perform their last miracle and build a rocket capable of lifting itself together with a few puppet robots and a case of spirit crystals to escape what remained of Mars's gravity, with enough propulsion or impetus left to glide forward to their distant First Sister.

The rocket didn't have to amount to much. Mars was weak. The crystals could survive the cold of interplanetary space. Their primary concern, given that the rocket reached space and got on its way, would be periodically re-activating the on-board machines to check and correct trajectory as necessary. A search and salvage Legionnaire had found a small hidden stash of Promethean uranium, which would prove invaluable for heat and temporary electrical power on the trip. In the landing capsule the principal weight was to be the heat shield to help the descending vehicle not burn up as it entered First Sister's atmosphere, if miraculously it reached its destination. The parachutes would work well in the thicker blue planet's atmosphere.

"The Math is hallucinatory for the whole trip," sent Heraklitos to Apollo. *"We're either going to miss the planet entirely or burn to a crisp upon entry. We could spend years carefully planning and still catfuck it."*

Apollo was reading Klitos on a translation screen. Pollo could not path to any except his own family.

"You still think like a wolf," sent Apollo.

"Well, icehell, I am *a wolf. Just with batteries and bolts."*

* * *

The team of Prometheans and wolves worked on their escape rocket as quickly as possible. Although the wind generators were creating enough energy to break water up into oxygen and hydrogen, so they could both breathe and create fuel for the rocket, the planet made nothing easy. Periodically its gravity pulled in to fill deep cavities created by the singularities. The marsquakes were vicious.

Nevertheless the work progressed, day and night. The wolves grumped and griped, but not to the Travelers. They knew that it would be quiet enough when their friends left.

Not long before departure Apollo had another visitor.

///Impressive///You still exist///

Old One! I thought you had all abandoned us.

///Not important enough to abandon///Dangerous not to monitor//

Will you come with us? Will I be able to reach you . . . there . . . on First Sister?

///First sister?///

The green and blue planet.

///Green? Blue?///

Stop being devious. The third planet from the sun.

///Ah///Does not matter how far your radius travels///We are at the center point of the sphere///

Is our Eldest with you?

///Your eldest is now our youngest///It is trying///

You mean we can join you?

///We are neither mean nor kind///

You bedevil me.

///You should be so lucky///

Who was Visitor, Old One?

///An enemy///You were not vigilant///

Evidently. Was Visitor one being? Many beings? A machine?

///Not necessarily different things///You know that///

Will you tell me about Visitor or not?

///I cannot///But the universe is old///And large///Freedom does not come without cost///

We have paid, but we are not free.

///You begin to learn the price of freedom///

What shall we do, Old One?

///You ask me what you shall do///Do not be stupid///

I ask for help.

///Think in futures///Your enemies think in futures///You act like children///If you do not think in futures you cannot understand consequences///Your enemies think with consequences///

We had begun to affect consequences for Others.

///Yes///

Live and learn

///You should be so lucky///Be vigilant///The visitor is distant but not gone///

Where is he? Or it? . . . Old One? Old One?

Gone. But Apollo felt cheerful. He could tell that this Old One still liked him. It had answered so *many* questions, at least in Old One style.

* * *

It was time for goodbyes. To friends and to their home.

Every Traveler took time to walk back down into the dust storm, still terribly strong. In its momentary gaps the Traveler could look across the landscape to see what there was to see. A distant mountain, a canyon, or former river. So much was changed irrevocably. But the dust tasted like Martian dust, not the dust of their youth – more iron in it now, redder, but Martian nevertheless.

And families and clans took time to sit and look at the stars together. The stars would still be there after they left. That was the point. *For us you will be there in the stars.*

The ground rumbled ceaselessly. Outside the large communal oxygen dens the air stank of metal.

Families pathed private thoughts to one another.

Not a sentimental species, wolves still knew how to celebrate. They held a final Howling Dance. There were fewer singers and dancers than at an oldtime Wilding, but if ever a Wilding Dance were called for, now would serve. The polar steppes could not be fiercer or more barren than the distances between planets. Some wolves had brought out hidden small stashes of happy berries. With some chewing, some spit, and plenty of warm water, they cooked up a good brew. A howling was always held outside – howling inside a closed space meant death, grief, or insanity. But outside now was too airless. A good compromise was to turn up the oxygen production and open one side of the Great Tent, so they could see outside and down the slope of Mother Mountain.

Happily, to one side they could also see *Traveler*, their one shot. It was lying on the slope, its nose cone aimed toward the summit, the whole ready to be lifted vertical just before take off. It was well lit, and looked close enough to a great catapult not to appear too alien. Besides, Athena and other young ones had had the insouciance to paint fangs on the nose cone and, below that, "We Come." It was late afternoon, coming on to a now commonplace but still fantastical sunset.

"Well, I hope you won't just go but will arrive. And not with a splat," said One Ear.

"Kind wishes indeed," muttered Apollo.

One wolf lifted muzzle and howled. Before she was done, another joined in and then another, and so on. The rising and falling harmonics joined to create throaty undertones and high forehead overtones. The wind down below contributed its deep melody. Theirs was the song of departure and expected return: *Go forth on your Wilding. Come back, but be not the same.*

As they sang they began to dance in group rhythms. Swaying. Stepping forward left. Forward and back. Turning all together. Jumping. Running in a great circle. Howling all the while. Then two came into the middle and held a nearly mock battle, snarling and biting at one another. A little blood was allowable, no harm done. Intentions were not lethal. Another two replaced them. Then four. All running, running in the circle. Leaping over one another. Until they were tired.

Then they stopped, the happy juice was pulled out, and everyone had a good drink. Now some sloppy singing and lying down with one another.

Until it was quiet. They lay or sat and looked outdoors to the competing sunset stratospheric bands of light, and to the rocket. They saw a procession of Promethean machines coming up to them – Prometheus and those Legionnaires who would be going with him and the wolves on the rocket. Other Legionnaires were staying behind with former family, to use their mechanical skills to help preserve the wolves as long as possible.

The machines arrived. Prometheus, with their permission, pulled a metal box into their midst. He opened it. Drawers and drawers of crystals, each protected from harm.

The wolves looked sadly to one another.

"Are you ready?" called One Ear. "It is now or never. Anyone who wishes to change his or her mind will do so with no shame, although possible regret. To go, to stay, neither is perfect Math. But through both is our only chance to prevail. Come up, one by one."

The wolves sat in a thick circle. One Ear stood in the middle with Prometheus and the box of spirit globes. One Ear nodded to Loos and a few other large wolves who had elected to stay, and they came to stand beside him. "I may need help," he said. "There will be many lifeless bodies."

Apollo walked up to start the transfer process.

"No," said One Ear. "You must wait until last. You know more of both our world and the Promethean universe than anyone except Prometheus himself, and he is already passed over. Stand beside me."

Another young wolf walked up. Prometheus picked up one crystal. The wolf Traveler-to-be looked around and said goodbye to a friend in the circle, then took the crystal in his mouth from Prometheus's machine arm, and lowered his head. One Ear leaned down, took the neck in his great mouth, and snapped it to the side. The young wolf's body collapsed. One of the other wolves took the crystal out and gave it to Prometheus, who put it back in the drawer. Another large wolf dragged the abandoned wolf body outside.

"Prometheus says he is OK," said Apollo.

"Icedamn, he'd better be," said One Ear. "Next."

One by one they walked up and transferred title over to Promethean crystals.

A few changed their minds, and others who had not won in the lottery spoke up and came forward, to yipping goodbyes from den family or friends.

Finally it was Athena. She came forward and nuzzled Loos, and One Ear too. She looked to Apollo. "You better follow me, brother, or I'll *haunt* you!"

"I will follow, little sister."

"I'm going to take one of those great big monsters for my body!" she said. "You just watch out."

"I'm sure you will. I'm going to be one of those little things with big eyes running around in the trees."

"I'll eat you."

"And I'll give you indigestion."

With that One Ear leaned over behind her, bit, and snapped her neck.

Now it was Apollo's turn. He walked over to stand between One Ear and Loos. "Goodbye, everyone. Goodbye, father," he said. One Ear leaned towards him, but Apollo quickly leaned to Loos, bit him in the throat, and snapped his neck. "He gave birth to us. He's coming with us."

"First Law," said One Ear. "I was hoping to have Loos to commiserate with me."

"I'm sorry. I'm too selfish. Now punish me. First Law." Apollo lowered his neck, and One Ear took his life.

Prometheus took two crystals and placed them near Loos and Apollo. Then he picked them up and put them back in their drawer. He turned in a full circle. His parabolic sender/receivers waved. He went to One Ear, reached out with a metallic arm, and gave him a crystal.

"Thank you, Prometheus. But no. I'm staying."

Prometheus put the crystal back in the drawer.

The circle parted, but Prometheus did not leave. Outside the tent were many other Promethean Puppets, arrayed in their own great semicircle. Prometheus pulled his box out to the middle of them. He pulled out an empty drawer, then went from one Puppet machine to another, reaching inside each to pull out its crystal controller. He placed these in the drawer. One by one he freed the machines of their spirit controller globes.

He closed the box, and he and the Puppet Legionnaires who were to remain on Mars carried the box back to load it and Prometheus himself on the rocket.

* * *

The launch was later that night.

Some wolves had fallen asleep with the happy juice. But most were awake. They lifted the tent flap to watch the departure.

Traveler had been raised to vertical, still looking like it was aslant on the mountain's ascending surface. Puppet machines attended it. Every few minutes a tiny rocket was fired up into the skies to show what the high winds looked like. The trail of the little rocket showed luminescent in the heavens with the far sunlight catching it. The wind trails twisted and turned.

Finally one test rocket showed less twisting. It was the best they would do.

Within moments the rocket fired, its guy lines released by the machines, and it lifted off the surface, rising rapidly. High winds caught it and pushed it to one side, but its small, strong fins guided it more to the vertical, and it continued its accelerating climb. It soared upward until only its exhaust was seeable, and then that disappeared abruptly. *Traveler* had achieved escape velocity and shut its motor.

"Good riddance," said One Ear. Then to his remaining live companions, "For however long our air shall last let us make the best of it. We have work to do. But first some sleep." The leader of the last of the alive Wolves of Mars turned around, hoping to find inside a little more happy juice.

* * *

Much later, *Traveler* was coasting forward through space, pointed apparently nowhere. Its mostly sleeping passengers had plotted a Math trajectory to meet the great and mysterious First Sister in a foreseeable future. So they hoped.

Another traveler, Visitor, was at the far outskirts of their solar system. This was far enough away from the gravity of the sun and the planets to activate its interstellar drive. Visitor used force only to manipulate things close at hand, such as moons and planets. To travel it used a time-space converter engine.

The drive erupted into operation. In physical space no change could be seen. But far ahead and far to the rear, time and space were adjusted, converted to other uses. Visitor stretched long and thin, and then was gone.

Far, far behind, *Traveler* glided into the invisible time-space wake of the Visitor. Unknown to the travelers, they were thrown into a chaotic turbulence, not of space but of time.

They would arrive in the spot to which they had aimed. But *when*?

To what world were they going, to what brave new world? What would be the scent of the air? Would there be water, and would it taste sweet in the spring and sharp in the winter? Would dust blow there?

On through the dark they coasted, humming in bodiless sleep – doing the Math, the last Wolves of Mars to do so.

About the Author

As in the childhood of countless other boys and girls, one of Clark's earliest memories is standing on the roof of his house, holding his arms up, hoping desperately a flying saucer would come and take him away. This book was born out of a dream from that time. In a life of twists and turns, Clark Carr has written comedy, stage and screenplays, and a poetry collection. He has devoted the principal hours of his last 25 years to a worldwide charitable network of drug rehabilitation, prevention, and education centers. Art photographs from his extensive travels can be found at www.photographyofclarkcarr.com . He has known Richard Royce since they were both pups.

About the Illustrator

Richard Royce
BA, MA in Fine Arts University of Wisconsin

Postgrad work at Atelier 17, Paris France under Stanley W. Hayter

Master Printer of his own Atelier Royce for 25 years where he printed etchings and cast paper for many artists including Larry Rivers, James Rosenquist,Marisol, Francoise Gilot, Roy Lichtenstein, George Segal, Paul Jenkins, Richard Anuskiewicz, Raphael Soyer, Judy Chicago, Claire Falkenstein and Bob Timberlake. He has also instructed in Printmaking and Sculpture at university level.

Richard's work is in 13 books and 7 Museums. Recently, he has also illustrated the book, Help Your Child in School, by Bernard Percy.

Lightning Source UK Ltd.
Milton Keynes UK
31 August 2010

159229UK00001B/34/P